Rabl
in
Switzerland

Ethan Crane has had short stories published in *Aesthetica* magazine, 3AM magazine, Dogmatika and in an anthology for Earlyworks Press. If you'd like to read more of his short stories, or download a free copy of *The Tyranny of Careers*, his non-fiction book on the ambiguous rewards of work, these can be found at ethancrane.com.

Talia Ripley works as a midwife at an unnamed NHS hospital trust. If you're interested in the real-life stories that inspired the midwifery scenes in the novel, see Talia's blog posts at The Secret Midwife: www.thesecretmidwife.co.uk.

Contact the authors at
rabbitsinswitzerland@ethancrane.com.

This story, whilst entirely fictional, is based in no small part on the authors experiences as a couple with two small children during Talia's training as a midwife.

Also by Ethan Crane

NON-FICTION
The Tyranny of Careers

Rabbits in Switzerland

ETHAN CRANE
& TALIA RIPLEY

Silver Robot

for our lovely children

contents / rota

THURSDAY NIGHT: ON DUTY

'It hurts *so much*.' The naked woman on all fours opens her eyes and pleads with Luisa through the tunnel of her thighs. 'Am I doing okay? Is everything okay? Are you going to kill my baby?'

Maybe she didn't say kill, thinks Luisa. Maybe harm my baby? Check my baby. Probably check my baby.

And even if she did say kill – that means she thinks I haven't already killed her baby. She thinks I'm doing okay here, taking care of this birth. No, no – Vicky is taking care of this birth. Though as far as the Nursing Midwifery Council and their strike-off committee are concerned, I am taking care of this birth. Making sure this is one of those easy, normal births, the kind seen in educational documentaries with the swearing cranked down.

'Everything is just fine,' coos Luisa.

By which I mean, at this particular moment in time everything is just fine. But if everything suddenly becomes not fine, if your baby decides that it does not want to be born in an easy, normal manner, maybe you could try to understand – Luisa hears the plea ending in a sob, the political prisoner to her kindly but resolute kidnapper – maybe you could try to understand why I don't have the definitive answer to whether or not your baby is okay?

And this may be a surprise, coming from a woman in one of the caring professions, but right now I'm not sure how much care I'm capable of mustering. Florence Nightingale may not have cared so much, had she had to set down her lamp and return home each night to a family who had forgotten there was a war on. Maybe she only appeared to care, even whilst she did lots of caring. Maybe appearing to care *is* caring. Maybe the overriding reason for the lamp was to blind soldiers to the sight of her face so they could not see she was half dead and wanted desperately to be somewhere else, in bed, asleep, with no prospect of screaming demands for the relief of pain.

'You just keep breathing through, Matilda,' says Vicky, the student midwife. 'Everything is going just to plan.'

Matilda sucks in air and blows out noisily through her next contraction.

All to plan, yes this *is* all to plan, isn't it? Vicky's here, that's twice the requisite number of midwives. And Vicky is one of the capable students – I've only seen her cry once. She has this birth completely under control. Though only of course, until something goes wrong. Because I am the midwife in charge here, and when something goes wrong, then I am in control.

'Now, Matilda,' says Vicky. 'Luisa is just going to check the baby's heart again whilst I make up a warm perineum pad.'

'I am. Yes, I am,' Luisa grips the foetal heart doppler, glad for something to hang on to, a solid object located in reality. She reaches between Matilda's thighs to ensure she has the doppler's flattened end pressed just above the pubic hair-line, had one been in evidence. This forces her to angle her face slightly, to avoid pushing it into Matilda's inhumanly splayed anus.

'You're in transition now,' Vicky sing-songs.

Vicky has learnt to speak sing-song, thinks Luisa, as she hears the wet-train chug from the doppler handset. There is the heart of the baby. I can, at least, monitor the baby's heart.

'James,' croaks Matilda, her face pushed into the floor mat. 'James.' She scrabbles her hand around on the floor beside her head, and James pounces on it, clinging to the life raft.

'You're doing so well,' says Vicky. 'Won't be long now.'

I could stand up, thinks Luisa, I could stand from my little hidey-hole under Matilda's thighs, stand and punch my fists in the air and do some screaming. Why don't you, Matilda, do some screaming, and then I'll scream along with you? If we're both screaming Vicky will almost certainly join in, and then maybe James, and then people will come running, midwives, co-ordinators, doctors will come to help, to take over, and that will be it. It for me, it for my career, it for everything. And you have a perfectly good reason to be screaming, because from where I'm scrunched on the floor, down the business end of this birth, your anus has puckered to a size you would not believe, with the beginnings of a dark stool poking out.

The heartbeat, that's low. Luisa looks at the doppler handset. 87. Fine for my heart, in fact much lower than my heart right now. But not good for a baby if it stays that low. Maybe this is not the baby's heart. Maybe this is Matilda's heart. Luisa peers under the stretched pink of Matilda's vulva to reposition the doppler.

'So, Luisa is just finding the baby's heartbeat again,' says Vicky.

Luisa glances up and meets Vicky's eyes for just a moment. I may feel deranged, she thinks, but those are signifiers I can still read: the immediate descent of Vicky's smile, the higher octave of her voice. Vicky is scared. Luisa shifts the doppler across Matilda's belly. The slow heartbeat becomes fainter, then drops out altogether.

'Is everything okay?' asks James.

Luisa adjusts the doppler, but only for it to read 87 again. What if that's the baby? If that's the baby that's an emergency baby.

'Sometimes it's difficult to find,' sings Vicky. She has the perineum pad gripped tightly in her hand. She stares at Luisa, her eyes wide.

Luisa peers over Matilda's buttocks, towards the door, towards the emergency buzzer to the left of the door. The buzzer, that's the correct course of action, the formal way to summon other midwives. Better than screaming. Midwives will come running, and another midwife will take over. But what if it's nothing? How long is that without a decent heartbeat?

Luisa shifts the doppler again. Any moment now I'll hear a soft heart thud and this will all be normal. Maybe I could press the buzzer anyway, just to be safe. But if I press the buzzer all the lights will come on, everyone will run in, run in to see the incapable midwife. Matilda will want to know why I have ruined what, up to now, has been a lovely normal birth, will get all frenzied with adrenalin and that'll be the contractions fucked. There she is, Jenny will say, Luisa, the buzzer-happy, stupid midwife.

Maybe I am stupid. I feel stupid. Maybe I cannot coordinate my hands with this little sleep, maybe that's why I cannot move this doppler into the right position.

How long now without a decent heartbeat?

No, this baby is in distress. And they'll ask, in court, as Matilda and James stare at me from the gallery, stare at the baby-killer, as the tabloids dig back through my life, and delight in the drug-addled nineties, the lawyers will ask: what was going through your head, Ms Keane? Why did you do nothing when you hadn't heard a decent heartbeat in over a minute? Did you not know the baby was in distress? Surely your training told you that you needed to deliver this baby quickly?

'What should we do?' says Vicky quietly.

Mucus drips from Matilda's vulva onto Luisa's arm.

How long now? How long can you ask how long until it is too long?

THE PREVIOUS MONDAY NIGHT: OFF DUTY

Her phone rings as Luisa stands by the bedroom mirror in her underwear, sideways to the glass, only glancing at her reflection. The river of nausea seeps into her stomach, but the call is not from the hospital. On the phone screen is Justin in the cowboy hat.

She sees the time: 21:13. The comedy night has already begun. Perhaps he is calling to say *let's give the night a miss, let's go another time.* Then that's him cancelling on her, and she's in the clear.

'Our rail system has reached its baroque period,' says Justin, 'an era of its history from which it appears unable to emerge.' He is trying to set the mood dial on light, but his voice has the tight anguish of the Zen Buddhist who knows his life of measured calm has all been for naught. 'But if I catch a cab from the station, maybe we can make it for the second half, at least?' he says. 'I'm really up for catching the second half. Isn't the second half funnier, anyway?'

'We'd be heckled. Getting to our seats,' says Luisa. 'No one goes in just for the second half.' She hates comedy nights. Open mic comedy nights are the worst. The pain, the anguish of watching someone else's pain and anguish. How can this be entertainment, the spectacle of a young person's artistic dreams shattered in real time?

'Let's give it a miss then,' she says, and the alternative plan takes form in her head in the time it takes to say the words.

Half an hour later she stands outside their tiny blue Peugeot in the station car park, and her plan feels less realistic. She slouches against the car door, head back, one foot across the other, trying to ignore the cold northerly wind that whips up her skirt and onto her buttocks.

Some commuters glance at her as they stream from the darkened arch of the station's exit, and she sees them thinking, *look at how relaxed she is, leaning against her car*. Though they could just as easily be thinking, *she must be freezing, in a skirt that short, her thighs cold against the metal*. She wants to stand up straight, but is committed to her character.

Her phone rings in her bag. She reaches into the car and looks at the screen: an unlisted number. Only the hospital calls from an unlisted number.

'Hello, Luisa Keane?' she answers.

'Oh, Luisa. Is that you?'

'Hi, Fran.'

'This isn't Debbie?'

'This is Luisa. You called me.'

'I was after Debbie.' says Fran, as though accusing Luisa of screening Debbie's calls.

'Is this about the rota again? Why are you still at the hospital? It's almost ten o'clock.'

'I thought I was calling Debbie. There's been a bit of a mix up.'

'But I'm still on tomorrow night? And Thursday and Friday?'

'Well, I can check if you want me to. But it's Debbie I needed to talk to.' Luisa hears papers turning over, turning back again. 'I'll call you back,' says Fran.

Her phone goes dead. Luisa squints to look for Justin again. What if he went out the other entrance? Then she spots him, the silhouette slowly transforming into his hairy Latin features. She raises a hand and Justin starts, wary of her as of a high street charity collector. He lifts a limp arm in reply.

'Why are you here?' He looks surprised by his own bluntness. 'What I mean is – I thought you weren't coming to get me. I mean thanks, that you did.'

'Maybe I didn't just come and get you,' she says, but she forgets to add a sultry tone.

'You didn't?' He looks at the car.

'I mean to drive you home. We were going to the open mic night, weren't we?'

'I'll go,' he says. 'I'll go if you want to.'

'Don't want to go,' says Luisa. 'But I came anyway.'

Luisa steps around the Peugeot, leaving him to ponder her meaning. As she opens the driver's door she looks across the roof of the car to fix her eyes on him. Justin is already in the car.

'What can I say?' he says when Luisa climbs in. The tiny car means they sit close to each other, but in a way that is less intimate, and more invasion of personal space. Justin lands a kiss on her lips more suitable for a cheek. 'When I called I thought I'd be here at least by – .' Justin looks at his watch. 'Oh, shit. I have to make a call. Sorry. The Bishop.' He looks at his watch again.

'Now?'

'Not right now.'

'Do it in the morning.'

'In – one minute and fifteen seconds. At nine fifty-seven. It has to be nine fifty-seven. He had us synchronise watches. After The Apprentice, before the news starts. I'll only be five minutes. I've only got five minutes.'

Luisa steers the car down the ramp of the multi-storey, wrenches the wheel as they hit ground level and swings the car out onto the road.

'Your Grace. I'm so glad we've got the chance to speak again.' Justin turns away from her, looks out the window. Luisa accelerates towards the orange lights, scares herself by over-revving the engine and has to brake sharply to stop before the red cycle zone. Justin keeps his voice level even as the momentum throws him towards the windscreen.

'The missionaries' WiFi speed, that's all in hand now. We've engineered fixes,' says Justin. 'And Marion assured me that this time they changed the password on Reverend Jonathan's iPad to something he would remember.'

Luisa watches him speak, sees the smile that accompanies his chirpy tone, and the effort required to produce it.

'Absolutely,' says Justin. 'I'd be happy to. It'll give us a chance to finalise the last documents.' He checks his watch. 'And thanks for your time. Of course. I'll see you Thursday. Yes, at ten exactly. Thank you, Your Grace. Goodbye.'

Justin lays the phone in his lap, stares down at it.

'You're good with Archbishops,' says Luisa.

'Bishops. That arsehole's not even the fucking Archbishop yet. For a man of the church he can be a hard-nosed bastard.' Justin stares down. 'I have to go meet with him again.'

'What does he want now?' She totals up points for and against, and calculates it favourable to go along with Justin's game, this game of The Bishop's an Arsehole.

'I think he's got it in his head that by helping us instigate a fucking micro-finance project for the poor it will increase his chances of sainthood. He won't stop going on about St Joseph of Leonessa. Does the Church of England even do saints?'

'Fuck the Bishop,' says Luisa violently.

Justin smiles at her. 'Yeah. What a loser.'

'He's just annoyed that no one goes to church any more. Forget him. Him and his – cassocks.'

'His stupid Latin.'

'His praying.' Praying doesn't trump Latin and signals the end of the exchange. Though in a way this is Justin's fault, because the Church of England doesn't use Latin.

'Although,' says Justin.

'What?'

'I've still got to go to Canterbury again on Thursday. Means I need to leave early.'

Luisa casts this rock of information and its implications aside, out the window and onto the roadside. She races through town, taking the quietness of the Monday night streets as a provocation, a reason to break the speed limit.

'There's still time to do something else. Tonight,' says Luisa.

'We're not going to the comedy night?'

'I didn't think you were that worried.'

'I wanted to go,' he mumbles. 'If you chose it I wanted to go.'

'It was all I could find on a Monday. But we can still make the most of the night. We've got a babysitter til eleven.'

'Claudette?' says Justin.

'Your mum,' says Luisa.

'Mum?'

'She said she'd love to help out.'

'That's what she said. But you said if it ever actually happened Elsie and Ellie would end up looking after her.'

To her relief she sees Justin is smiling, that he doesn't really mind what she says about his mother.

'I *like* your mum,' says Luisa. And she does like Bea, but is not sure this is the same as to like to be around Bea. She cannot explain these anxieties to Justin – partly because Bea is his mother, but also because Luisa is not sure of the exact nature of these anxieties herself. Bea had never even met her granddaughters until six weeks ago, when she returned from India directly to their doorstep, unannounced, enfolded Elsie and Eleanor in her screen-printed dress, piled them high with presents, and disappeared back into her idling taxi, excusing herself from the cab window with the claim she needed to get to the estate agents before it closed, as she had to sign the exchange papers on a house only a few roads away.

'Oh. Well that's good,' says Justin. 'It's good for Mum to be with the girls.' He switches on the radio, punching the arrow until he finds a station with music. 'So – where are we going?' he says.

Luisa turns from the roundabout onto the main road that leads to their estate, forsaking the protection of the town centre's warm sodium glow. She already knows what Justin wants to add: *I'm tired, I've been on a train for the past three hours*. She waits to see if he will say these things, but he just stares ahead. The car breaks the silence with one of its mysterious engine rattles, then it too falls quiet.

'I have food,' announces Luisa.

'I am a bit hungry, actually.' He shifts in his seat. 'Train gin doesn't really cover any of the major food groups.'

'It's a snack. A car snack.' Luisa nods behind at the back seat.

Justin reaches over and lifts a chocolate mousse pack onto his lap.

'Yum,' he says. 'Chocolate mousse, part of a man's balanced diet.' He rips the cardboard, grabs one pot, pulls off the foil. 'Not that right now I give a shit about a balanced diet,' he adds. 'Um, don't suppose – a spoon?'

'Glove box.'

She watches him pull the handle and rotate the glove box open. In the top lies a silver spoon, nestling in Luisa's black knickers.

Justin glances at her, and away again. Luisa stares out at the street lamps that line the road. He gingerly takes out the spoon, closes the glove box, and sits with the dessert pot in his lap.

'I was wearing those when I first got to the station,' says Luisa.

Justin tears away the foil lid and digs out a big spoonful of mousse.

'But I'm not wearing them now.'

She watches him ladle mousse into his mouth, more than is sensible to balance on a teaspoon.

'I thought we could – a surprise. I could surprise you, as a surprise.'

'Okay,' Justin does not look surprised.

'You know, now we can't go out?' She wants to take back the *you know*. 'We have a babysitter for once, we can – take advantage? I'm going to drive us home. Then *I'm* going to eat the other chocolate mousse.' She replays her words. Are they – erotic? Sexy? 'Without a spoon,' she adds. 'Then you can fuck me in the cul-de-sac.'

'I didn't think you were into that any more,' says Justin.

'I meant – at the end of our road. We'll have sex in the car at the end of our road.'

Justin has another large spoonful of mousse in his mouth. Luisa takes a roundabout at speed.

'Not in our road,' says Justin. 'Too bite.'

'Too what?' The mousse makes it difficult to hear him.

'Bright. Too bright.'

'It is, you're right, it is,' says Luisa. Too bright is not an outright refusal. 'We'll go to the car park. The car park by the playing field.'

'You don't want me to eat this, then?' Justin holds up the other dessert pot. Now he has accepted his fate he appears happier – enjoying himself even.

'That one's for me,' smiles Luisa.

They are quiet as she diverts from the usual route home and turns left down the gravel track that leads to the sports club car park. She wants to break the silence, but is afraid that words might invite reasons to abort the enterprise if she doesn't hit the right erotic tone.

Ahead of them someone has parked a car on the track's verge, and Luisa wonders if perhaps they are not the only people here for this purpose. She peers inside as they pass, but the seats are dark, empty. They pass through the height barrier into the car park and Luisa drives to the far end, as far from the sports pavilion and street light as possible.

'Into the back seat.' She strains at her seat belt to lean over and kiss him. He tastes of gin and chocolate, a disgusting combination. 'Come on, get over there with you.'

Justin pushes the chocolate mousse containers onto the dashboard, twists round and steps between the seats. He lies down on the back seat, arms behind him, his head on the palms of his hands. Luisa climbs over and sits astride him.

'Someone still might see us.' Justin raises his head to look out the window.

'Would you like that? Do you want someone to see us?' Luisa pulls aside his jacket, picks at the buttons of his shirt, then changes her mind and buries her face on top of his. She waits for the feel of his hands on her back, on her buttocks, somewhere, but they stay where they are, tucked next to his ears. Don't leave this all to me, she pleads in her head. Let's be a team, work at this together. She reaches to unhook her bra, and then down for his belt.

Justin pulls his face away. 'Condoms,' he says. 'We haven't got condoms.' He arches against the side of the car, his head pushed into the child's sun visor suckered to the window.

'Doesn't matter,' Luisa's words are indistinct, her face pushed into his neck.

'But I have some.' Justin strains to push himself up, but she has him pinned. 'I have some, in my bag, I think.' He reaches around the front seat for his bag, pulls it into the rear foot well.

'It's safe at the moment,' she says.

'Is it?'

'I should know, shouldn't I?'

'Maybe.' Under Luisa's weight he cannot move to see into his bag, but nevertheless plunges a hand inside. With a grin he holds up a condom pack to show her.

'Justin, I'm forty-three, for god's sake!' she laughs, and pulls the condom from his fingers. She follows the turn of his face with her own in order to kiss him again, pushing her tongue into his mouth. His tongue moves back against hers, but only just.

'I really am quite hungry,' Justin pulls away to speak. 'I might – I think I need to eat first. Properly. I think I might need a full meal.'

'Later. When we get home.'

Justin lies there, silent and inert. Luisa presses on with a half-hearted performance of freestyle massage for a full minute, until she can no longer ignore the lack of response.

'I thought this was – fun.' She sits up on his stomach. 'Something different.'

'It is different. And fun. But I haven't eaten. That train, it took – three hours.'

'Take the stress off. Forget about all that.'

'Maybe just – not right now?'

'You have to want to some time! It's been, what, eleven days?'

'Are we counting now?' says Justin. 'I've been tired. I'm tired, with work. I'm tired of work.'

'But isn't it more exciting like this?' She sounds curious, like a documentary presenter. 'In the car, out of the house?'

'It is exciting. It is.'

'We wanted to do something exciting. More exciting than open mic comedy.'

'I just didn't know it was going to be tonight,' says Justin.

She looks down at his open work shirt, a disapproving frame for his naked chest. She waits for him to explain, to give a reason she can easily dismiss. Justin says nothing.

'You have to say yes sometime,' says Luisa.

'I don't think that's how consent works.'

'We don't need consent! We're grown-ups! Consent's for young people.'

'I don't think you really mean that.'

Luisa sits up. She is unsure what to do with her hands, and so she holds her own breasts, for comfort rather than modesty.

'Maybe, maybe it's this kind of approach?' says Justin. 'Maybe it isn't so – appealing?'

'Oh. So you don't find me appealing?' Appealing is a terrible word. A fifties' word. Her parents' word.

'No, no.' He reaches up a hand, holds her arm. 'I still – fancy you. Still want to have sex with you. It's just when.'

'What?'

'When you're – when there's this – desperation? It's not – I'm not – so much turned on?'

Luisa sits more heavily on top of him. 'The fact I want sex more than you makes it desperation? Did I ever call *you* desperate, back before?'

'No, but – '

'How can that be fair! One of us has to be more keen! That's just simple probability!'

'It's not a competition.'

'Maybe we can make it a competition.'

'It's only recently. It's just – not such a turn on.'

'You're not turned on because I'm enthusiastic? What kind of fucked up logic is that?'

'I'm just thinking – '

'Why not not think, and just have sex with me instead?'

'But when – '

Luisa opens the door, clambers out and stands on the tarmac. The moon is bright enough that her unfastened bra throws a shadow across her naked breasts, and she pulls the halves of her shirt across them. She wants to march off across the car park, but still holds out for the possibility that Justin will apologise, will apologise and invite her back in the car, ask her to finish what they have started.

'Let's take this home,' calls Justin. 'We can talk about this at home.'

Luisa hears nothing more. She is marching, striding off over the white lines, filled once more with this curious new energy that demands she keeps moving. She breaks into a slow jog. You need to pay attention to this one, her motion is saying. This isn't any old walking off. Am I going to stop at some point, she wonders, stop and wait in the dark? Or stop and turn around, go back and – do what? She strides on, buttoning up her shirt against the cold, heading towards the gravel track. Beyond the woodland that lines the track she sees streetlights marking the main road to their estate. It is not far, she can walk home. She can do anything she likes.

Luisa hears the car engine start up behind her and quickens her pace. The headlights illuminate the poles of the height barrier as she passes between them. As she steps onto the gravel road, Justin pulls alongside.

'Get in, Lu, please,' he says through the open passenger window.

Luisa keeps her eyes fixed on the dark track ahead. 'I thought you'd been drinking.'

'Why don't you drive? I'm happy for you to drive.'

'I'm happy for me to walk.'

'We should – '

There is a crunch of metal, which in her electrified state she does not instantly register. Luisa continues walking, until she realises the car is no longer alongside. She turns back but cannot see, cannot see Justin through the windscreen, due to the glare of the one remaining left headlight. What she can see is the driver's-side front wheel raised off the ground, the bonnet-front resting atop the parked car on the verge.

Luisa analyses whether she is in any way responsible and concludes she is not. She stays where she is, waits for Justin to emerge, for his apology. He might be hurt. But he has attained a victory of sorts – sex seems unlikely now. He might be unconscious. He wouldn't rather have a head injury than sex with me, would he?

'Justin?' she calls. She runs to the car, past the glare of the headlight, peers through the windscreen. The driver's seat is empty.

A silhouette rounds the rear of the car and raises an object in the air. Luisa feels a stab of fear, even whilst knowing it must be Justin. He swings the object in a circle, and it bounces off the passenger window.

'What are you doing?' Luisa steps around the front of the car. Justin holds a child's scooter by the hand grips, turns the steering column in his hands in order to raise it above his head again.

'What happened?' says Luisa.

He swings the scooter against the window again, and as it flies past, Luisa sees Elsie's Frozen sticker on the scooter's underside. She steps back, for fear of flying glass, but the window remains whole.

'Justin.'

'This time.'

'Why are you breaking the window?'

'Piece of shit.'

Luisa flinches.

'Not you. The car.' He ineffectually thumps the scooter against the window again. 'We weren't here,' he says. 'We didn't do this. I didn't do this. This was joyriders.'

'But it's insured.' She has not seen him this physical in weeks – she steps back to watch. 'We can just report an accident.'

'Can't. Too drunk.' Justin winds the scooter around his head, and this time his swing is wider, has more momentum. But he has misjudged the centrifugal force in the scooter's motion. He staggers and connects weakly with the wing mirror.

'That's not really working,' says Luisa. She reaches out a hand, wants to take the scooter from him.

'It never worked! This fucking car only works when it *feels* like working. Is that how I work? No.' Justin's laugh is falsetto. 'But insurance works. Insurance works when something's really, really broken.' This time he aims the scooter against the side panel of the car. His unbuttoned shirt tails swing out to the side. 'It's okay,' he says, calmer now. 'This is what you do. Mum taught me. When I was twelve, she set fire to our car for the insurance, and that was in our driveway. They paid out no problem.'

Luisa has heard the car fire story before, but the way Justin tells it you would think it was a staple of everyone's family lore. That Justin thinks to use Bea as a source of legal precedent is not a great comfort. She watches him pound the panel, and is curious at how little the dents in the car door mean to her.

'But you need the car, sweetie.' Luisa gently touches his arm. 'You need to get to Canterbury to go see the Bishop, remember?'

'Courtesy car. All that lovely insurance gets me a shiny fucking courtesy car. A courtesy car won't break down on the way to Canterbury. Ooh, you bad joyriders.' He brings the scooter down with a chop and this time takes off the wing mirror.

'Want a turn?' He holds the scooter out to her.

Luisa makes no move to take it. Instead she strides past him, round to the back of the car, and reaches into the boot.

A car slows at the entrance to the lane.

Luisa swings the hammer around her in an arc, and even though its trajectory is to the side of him and towards the rear windscreen, Justin throws up a protective arm. He catches Luisa's wrist, catches and grips tight. She stands in momentary awe at the strength of his grip, and makes no move to twist out. In the red glow of the rear lights, they hold their hammer and scooter weapons aloft: the most desperate Marvel comic cover in history.

Desperate, she thinks, but also quite sexy.

'What are you doing?' says Justin.

'Helping. Doing the back windscreen.'

'Good tool. The hammer,' he nods. 'But too noisy right now. I saw headlights.'

'Where?'

They look past the car, down the lane. Headlights whizz past the lane entrance, but no car has turned in.

'We need to be quieter,' he says, and lets go of her wrist. She nods. Now they are a team, a team with a mission.

'Is that the paint for the girls' bedroom in the boot?' says Luisa.

'I ~ don't remember?' Justin says.

Luisa moves back round to the boot, pulls the paint tin to the front, and with a tight arc plunges the claw of the hammer into the lip of the tin. It misses the lip but penetrates the lid. Luisa levers the handle forward to crack it off, and in one fluid motion grabs the tin handle and empties paint all over the car roof.

Justin cackles with laughter, scrunches into himself. He scrabbles on the ground, picks up leaves and smears them in the paint. Luisa smashes a rear light with the hammer, giggling.

'Shhh,' says Justin, but he is still grinning.

Luisa smashes the other light, quieter this time, then hands Justin the hammer so he can break open the steering column and pull out the ignition barrel.

They lean on an unpainted section of car to catch their breath.

'Joyriders would use spray paint,' says Luisa, and Justin laughs some more.

A dog barks, and they snap upright. Justin grabs Luisa's hand, drags her around the rear of the car towards the woods, pushes her down the shallow incline into the ditch. He lets go, and she plunges into the thick leaf pile, falling as she hits solid ground. She turns to see him scrambling back up the slope, wrenching open the passenger door, pulling out his work satchel and her bag from the foot well.

'Get out of here Steve, it's the law!' cries Justin, not in his own voice, but in a patchy attempt at an Eastenders' accent. He bounds down the slope and grabs Luisa's hand again, pulls her through the trees. She follows his dodging to left and right, her unfastened bra threading its way down her arms as she does so, and they run until they are fifty or so metres into the woodland, near the tree line which opens out onto a playing field. He throws himself to the ground behind a pile of logs and pulls her down with him.

Justin hides his face on his arm, giggling. He peers up through a gap in the logs, and Luisa kneels so she can view from his level. Back on the road, illuminated by the single headlight they see a man standing in front of the car, peering into the woods.

'Joyriders, hee,' exhales Justin right into her ear. 'He knows it's joyriders.' He slides back into the leaves, and pulls Luisa on top of him, her breasts pressing into his chest. Justin kisses her, chews at her, and they roll to one side, and snap a branch beneath them. They clutch each other tight and hold still, but there is nothing to hear.

'He's never coming down here,' whispers Justin.

'My knickers are in the glove box,' says Luisa, and they press their faces into each other to muffle their giggles, Justin's cheek sandpapering her own with his stubble. Luisa rubs her cheek back across his.

'Maybe this is more us,' she whispers. 'Maybe this is more our kind of night out. Outside. Crazy nights out.' She pulls her hand back to look at his face. 'Nights like we used to. You remember?'

'Just about,' says Justin.

'We can do that again. At some point we'll do that again.'

Justin nods, but by moving his head upwards rather than down, a less convincing agreement.

'I made a new friend the other day,' says Luisa. 'She goes – she's into clubbing.'

'When do we have time to go to a club?' says Justin.

'I'll make time.'

Justin jerks his hand downwards, an end to this conversation. He grips the inside of her thigh, perhaps for support. Luisa rolls onto her back, moves her leg apart.

'Police, please.' The voice of the dog-walker carries down to them. Justin takes his hand from her leg.

'I'm quite cold,' she whispers to Justin.

'I think he's calling the police.' Justin remains motionless, listening.

'Only reporting the joyriders.'

He pushes his mouth onto her neck, and she reaches down for his belt.

'And I left the condoms in the car.' Justin raises his head up again.

'Doesn't matter.' Luisa pulls at his clothes, tries to haul him back down.

'We have to put the cover story in place first. First, I have to smooth it over with the police. They're going to call me, the car, it's in my name. I need to be ready to answer.' He pulls his phone from his pocket. 'Then it's all sorted.'

'Please,' says Luisa. 'They won't call yet. And you can just switch it off.' She pulls the strap of his belt from its buckle.

The phone rings. But the sound is quieter: it is not Justin's phone, but hers.

'Maybe they're calling you,' says Justin. 'You're on the policy as well. They're calling you.'

She rails against the word, policy. Policy, police-y, whatever it is, these words are her enemy. Luisa rips the phone from her bag.

'It's not the police. Don't worry, it's not the police. Only Bea. Your mum.' She looks at the time on the phone: 23:05. 'She's just wondering where we are. We won't be – ' She doesn't want to say long. The phone continues to ring.

What if something is wrong with the girls? With Eleanor? The girls will be okay. There are other important issues in the world besides looking after children, there are vandalised cars, and joyriders, and relationships, relationships between children's parents, and right now she is dealing with those other issues. She can be a better mother, later, and to be a better mother she first needs to be a better woman. A woman feeling better.

Justin is still looking at her.

'Hi Bea,' Luisa answers the phone. 'Sorry, we got delayed. I meant to ring you. We'll be home soon. The comedy night ran over a bit.'

'Oh, there's no problem,' says Bea. 'We're having a fine time.'

'You are? Still?' At Luisa's surprise Justin looks over. 'Are the girls not – ? I mean, that's good. Great.'

'We've been whittling. Eleanor seems to have a knack for pointillist art.'

'Yes. Right.'

'Shall I talk to her?' says Justin.

'Well, it is – late,' Luisa shakes her head at him. 'We'll be – we won't be too long. I'm glad everything's okay. The girls are probably tired.'

'Thanks for calling!' says Bea.

'What did she say?' says Justin, as Luisa puts the phone back in her bag. 'Why's she calling?'

'Something about whittling. Nothing important.'

There is another noise up on the road, and Justin's head snaps towards it.

'I said we'd be a bit longer. A little while,' says Luisa. She stays seated on the ground, pushes her chest forward to expose more naked breast. She is cold.

'We should get back. Make sure the girls get to bed,' says Justin.

'Ju-stin,' keens Luisa.

'Let's just get home. Can't we carry this on at home? Then I can eat something. I do need to eat something.'

'But you'll be *tired* then,' says Luisa. 'You'll be full of food and tired. And then we won't get to have sex all week.'

'And why is that?' Justin snaps. He stands up, straightens his clothes.

Luisa senses the night's energy draining away, and forges ahead in desperation. 'You know I'm working tomorrow night. And just for this week I'm on Thursday and Friday nights as well.'

'That's almost all the nights.' Justin picks up his bag. He glances at Luisa just for a moment, then looks away.

'Babies are born at night as well, aren't they?' says Luisa. 'That's why I thought we could do something tonight.'

'Maybe I don't always feel like sex on a Monday,' says Justin. 'Maybe I'm more of a Tuesday kind of guy.' He steps away from Luisa, looks up to the road and then in the other direction across the playing field. 'We should get back. Check on the girls.' He picks up his bag and walks towards the edge of the woodland, leaving her on the ground. Beyond him, across the other side of the field, are the rectangles of light on the houses in their road.

Luisa strides after him, trying to keep up, her chest still exposed to the night air.

'I'm cold,' she says.

'You're not really dressed properly,' says Justin.

'I just wanted to do something,' says Luisa, and takes his hand. 'Something sexy. Maybe I'm not very good at it. But please don't blame me for trying.' Her voice wobbles, and she goes with the wobbling. If sympathy sex is the only offer left on the table that's what she'll settle for. 'We can do this again. Can't we?'

They are in the middle of the playing field, heading towards the line of houses.

'It's probably not sustainable as far as cars go in the long term.' He has opted for sarcasm over sympathy, and Luisa has never heard of sarcasm sex.

They cross the rest of the field in silence, and as they reach the darkened alleyway that cuts through to their cul-de-sac, Justin slips his hand from hers.

Luisa looks up, up at a circular moon, in an irregular black frame of the wide sky. Then it is gone, obliterated by a whoosh of cloud.

TUESDAY DAY: OFF DUTY

For years, decades, I wanted to be a thing, thinks Luisa. Wanted people to say, *Luisa? She's a midwife.* And they, people, now say this. Because I am that thing, am a midwife. A proper adult. I chose this profession, an ancient, revered profession, almost the oldest profession. In some ways connected to the oldest profession. I underwent training, I qualified, they handed me a certificate to show I was qualified. I *wanted* this.

Luisa stares at three half-eaten bowls of pasta on the kitchen table. They taunt her, asking her to do something with them.

But did I really choose? They were on a remote Australian beach, her and Justin, drunk on cheap wine, when she said it. *When we get home I'll find a worthwhile job. Something rewarding.* Quite the mood killer at the time, the implication that here, right now was a bit shit, this expansive moonlit stretch of magical Australian coastline. Back home Luisa wrote a list of possible rewarding jobs, a list so short writing it was not strictly necessary: teacher, nurse, midwife. She didn't want to be a teacher, she knew too many depressed teachers. Sick people made her feel a bit sick. But midwife: because she once met a lovely German midwife in Thailand, who spoke about the feminist importance that it was women, female midwives rather than male doctors, who helped other women through the greatest female rite of passage. A calm, relaxed, inspiring woman. A woman on holiday, lying in a hammock.

What if I chose midwifery because it was the only uncrossed-out job on the list? What if I should have scratched midwife from the list as well?

Luisa turns away from the pasta bowls and calls the hospital for the third time.

'I'm calling for Fran,' she says.

'Fran's not here,' says a male voice.

'But I've been trying to reach her all day. She was meant to call me back about the rota.'

'Maybe she's gone home.'

'It's not even five yet.'

'If she hasn't rung you, then I'm sure it's not urgent. Maybe call back tomorrow.'

'But sometimes it is. Urgent,' says Luisa. 'I just want to be sure.'

'Fran's not here.'

Luisa's phone beeps to indicate another call coming through. 'Sorry,' she says. 'I need to get this.'

'Not a problem for me.' The man rings off before Luisa can switch calls.

'Tina?' says Luisa.

'It's me,' says Justin. 'Who's Tina?'

'A mother. The mother. Isobel's mother,' says Luisa. 'Tina's coming to pick up Isobel. Isobel is a friend of Ellie and Elsie's.' Except Tina isn't coming to pick up Isobel. Hasn't come to pick up Isobel. 'What are you – what's up?'

'Nothing,' says Justin. He's high-pitched, over-cheery, which he appears to realise immediately. 'Don't worry, I'm not going to be late,' he adds in a much deeper voice. 'Who's Isobel?'

'The girls must have mentioned Isobel.'

She does not tell Justin that Isobel is only at their house because the previous week she overheard Tina say the word *clubbing* in the playground at school pickup and decided, on the strength of that word, to follow or maybe stalk her to a nearby cafe. This was the first mention of dancing, of clubbing, Luisa had heard since the twins were born – a beacon to a previous incarnation of herself. She had parked herself at Tina's table and informed her that Elsie and Eleanor were desperate for Isobel to come round for tea.

'I just wanted to check,' says Justin. 'About the insurance. For the car. You said you'd do it?'

'And I have. It's done. All done,' she says. As though she hadn't thought at all about insurance fraud for the forty-five minutes she was on hold to the insurance company. Casually defrauding insurance companies might be second nature to Justin, learnt from Bea along with knife-throwing and chicken-plucking and charming the police. But when the mechanical hold voice warned Luisa of the perils of a false claim declaration, she had to calm herself with confessions to other, non-insurance transgressions: *my children were planned*; *midwifery has lived up to all my career expectations*; *I have no fear of dementia in old age*.

'They said they might need to inspect the car,' says Luisa.

'Standard procedure,' said Justin.

'My knickers are in the glove box.'

'I'm sure that won't invalidate the claim.'

She wants to capitalise on his joke to remind him of the car-smashing and woodland-groping of the night before, but she cannot be certain he is joking. Perhaps the only subsequent reminders will be via bureaucratic reference to insurance. And besides, what she really wants to tell him is that Tina still hasn't arrived to pick up Isobel, that there is only one hundred and five minutes until she needs to leave the house to get to the hospital, but she can't, because that relates to time, to punctuality, a subject which Luisa has declared off-limits between them, as if she and Justin are OCD Cistercian monks undergoing aversion therapy.

'So I can pick up the courtesy car today?' says Justin.

'You have to call the garage to pick it up,' she says. 'I have some code number.'

'I have to?'

He's only clarifying. 'You're the main driver,' she says.

Elsie marches into the kitchen. 'Isobel won't let me play on her iPad,' says Elsie.

'I have to go,' says Luisa. 'Where is Isobel? I think she's tired and wants to go home.'

'She won't let me have a go. I hate her.'

'But she's your friend.'

'She's not my friend. Can't you tell her to let me have a go?'

'You have the tablet you can use, don't you?'

'It doesn't work.'

'Maybe I can make it work.'

'I don't think so. Daddy tried to fix it.' Elsie slides the tablet onto the kitchen table, knocking against a pasta bowl. The entire screen is shattered into tiny spider-web cracks.

'It wasn't me,' says Elsie. 'Daddy tried to fix it.'

'Daddy did this?'

'Daddy tried to fix it last week when you were at work. He took it into the garage and tried to fix it with a hammer. But he didn't.'

Justin has given the screen meticulous attention, has not spared a single square inch, the cracks all a similar hairline variety. It is almost beautiful.

Her phone rings. The screen displays Tina's name, and her stomach clenches, anticipating further delay. 'I have to go,' she tells Justin. 'Isobel's mum is calling.'

'Hey, babe,' says Tina.

'Hi!' says Luisa.

'I'm here.'

'Here where?'

'On your doorstep, where did you think?'

Luisa pulls open the front door and there is Tina with her phone to her ear. Tina doesn't do doorbells, she thinks, okay.

'So sorry, babe.' Tina steps into the hallway. 'It's my bloody car. I can't find it. I had to get a taxi here in the end.'

'Someone stole it?' They move through to the kitchen, Tina leading Luisa.

'I doubt it. It's most likely in the multi-storey somewhere.' Tina takes up position at the table, taking off and dumping her leather jacket amongst the bowls of pasta.

'So how are you going to get it back?' Does this mean she will need a lift? thinks Luisa. There's no time for a lift. Then she remembers the car: the paint, the hammer, the wet leaves on breasts.

'I would give you a lift,' says Luisa. 'But our car was done over by joyriders.'

'Oh, don't worry. I'll take a taxi around to look again tomorrow,' says Tina. 'Or else the police will find it. That's what happened last time.'

'Well I've fed Issy, anyway. They made a den, then were all playing upstairs last time I looked.'

'You gave Issy dinner? God, I'm surprised she ate anything. She normally eats with us about eight. Can I? I'm guessing this was Issy's.' Tina drags an almost-full bowl of spaghetti and tomato sauce towards her, spoons it into her mouth. 'I'm ravenous.'

'Can heat it up if you want.'

Tina waves a hand to imply that won't be necessary, her mouth full of food.

'They've all been having a nice time together. I think, anyway. I haven't really seen them. Isobel should come round again.' She whispers, in case Elsie hears.

'You have her whenever you want her,' says Tina. 'Bonus chance for a lunchtime drink, you asking her round. What is it with these half-term holidays? Is that a new thing? I never remember them,' she laughs..

'I'd be up for one of those sometime,' says Luisa. 'A drink. An evening one?'

'Don't mind if I do,' says Tina. 'I'll go white if you've got it.'

'But not now. I mean I can't now. I have to work, to go to work. Quite soon.'

'God, really? Tonight?'

'I should get ready soon, actually,' says Luisa as though this has only just occurred to her.

'How horrible. You have to work at night? Is it one of those Japanese things?'

'No. Not really. I'm a midwife.'

'You know, it's always been a mystery to me, what midwives do. What midwives are.'

Luisa looks to see if Tina is joking, though she cannot imagine what the joke might be. 'We help women give birth,' she says.

'When I had Isobel in Hong Kong, the doctors said they wouldn't let any midwives in unless I paid extra. So what did I miss out on?'

'Midwives are there to support women as they give birth.'

'God. It makes me sick just to think about it.'

'Midwives?'

'Not that. You know.' Tina puts a hand over her mouth. 'God, I think I'm going to vom.'

'You don't like – blood?'

'Just the whole, ugh. Can we just stop talking about it? And Christ, why did you ask to have Issy in half-term when you've got to go to work? You mean *all night*?' laughs Tina. 'You're mental.'

'I am a bit mental,' laughs Luisa. 'Though I'm fine, as well. I don't need much sleep. I never did.'

'I hate it when Boris works at night.'

'I like it, actually,' says Luisa. Tina thumbs down her phone screen. 'I mean, when I worked in offices, doing shit jobs, it was nothing like this. On labour ward – there's an edge to it. It's just a group of women – and there's a lot of gay women for some reason – there's this camaraderie. A kind of feminist thing. It's hard to explain.'

She waits for Tina to ask her to explain more. But Tina doesn't need more detail, because Tina isn't listening.

'I can't imagine doing a normal job,' continues Luisa. 'I mean on any given week I've stuck my fingers in more women's vaginas than Justin has in his whole life.'

'I getcha,' says Tina, and now she stops to look at her. 'I mean, who doesn't want a bit of feminism?'

'Exactly.' There, thinks Luisa. Perhaps we are similar. We just need to get to know each other better. We'll probably be great friends in six months time. 'And it's a really rewarding job in many ways.'

'Gives me all manner of urinary tract infections,' says Tina. 'If I go out for a big one and don't get enough sleep.'

'So you go out?' says Luisa.

'Well, yeah. Of course,' laughs Tina. 'I've got a stash of Co-amoxiclav in the cupboard. That usually sorts me out.'

'I really want to go out. For a, you know, big one.' The words sound ridiculous. 'Where do you go? Around here I mean. We only moved here recently.' Like, five years ago.

'Mummy, the WiFi here is rubbish,' says Isobel, coming into the kitchen.

Go away, thinks Luisa. You sit upstairs all afternoon and you choose now as the time to come talk to us?

'Maybe you could show me?' she says to Tina.

Tina looks at Luisa, unsure to what this refers. 'So. You've been making dens?' she says to Isobel.

'I didn't make the den.'

'That's cool.' Tina smooths her daughter's blonde bob back over her head.

'We all took a turn in building,' says Luisa. She watches mother and daughter exchange a glance that suggests dens are a bit puritan, a bit National Trust.

'We'd better let you get to work,' says Tina, and throws her jacket back on.

'Okay, sure. Wait.' Luisa moves to the kitchen doorway, obstructing their exit. 'Ellie! Elsie! Come say goodbye!' Luisa smiles back at Isobel, who squeezes past into the hallway, followed by Tina. 'Issy must come over again,' says Luisa. 'And we should – '

Elsie and Eleanor slide out of the lounge and along the hallway wall.

'Well, look at you two! Proper Mediterranean beauties!' says Tina, as though the decision not to describe them as hot only just failed to make the cut. Elsie fixes Tina with her gaze, unembarrassed.

'Their dad, Justin – he's half-Cuban,' says Luisa. 'And we should, you know, go out sometime. Let's go out out.'

'Absolutely.' Tina thumbs her phone.

'I mean how about Saturday, this Saturday? If you're free.'

'I don't do Saturdays. Saturdays are generally a bit shit.'

'Bye, then,' says Elsie, and turns back into the lounge. Eleanor follows her.

'Well, we'll be seeing you,' Tina opens the front door.

'Let's stay in touch.' Luisa grabs the side of the door.

'Sure.' Tina nudges Isobel out ahead of her.

'Something soon.'

Tina pauses, as though considering whether to speak. 'How about a drink on Friday?'

'Great! No, wait. I can't do Friday, I'm working Friday, Friday night. What about a week on Friday?'

'Sure you're not working?'

'I'll make sure.'

'I couldn't do what you do,' says Tina. 'I really couldn't.'

Luisa likes the acknowledgement of her talent, her special skill, until she sees that this could mean its opposite, not that Tina cannot do this, but that she really does not want to.

'Well it can be, you know. Pretty rewarding, sometimes.'

Tina steps down to the path.

'Some other time, then,' says Luisa, too quiet to hear. She closes the door, and turns around to find Elsie standing behind her.

'Well, that was nice,' says Luisa.

'No it wasn't,' says Elsie. 'Isobel is an annoying cow.'

'Don't say that, sweetie. You shouldn't call someone that.'

'I don't want her over to play ever again,' says Elsie.

'You don't have to.'

'Do you promise?'

Luisa does not promise.

*

At 18.30 Luisa deconstructs the encampment, the structure she intended to leave for Justin as a symbol of her half-term day with the girls. Now she tidies in place of a breathing mantra, as a distraction. She can feel the block of the silent phone in her jeans pocket, goading her to call him.

'Noo!' cries Eleanor in front of the monitor. She thumps the computer keyboard with her fist, and the browser window showing the iPlayer closes.

'Yeah, good one, well done,' says Elsie.

'You can decide between you, can't you?' says Luisa, and clicks the icon to reopen the browser. 'Talk to each other.' Rather than sulking in silence like me.

At 18.40 she types a text.

Everything okay?

You've remembered I'm working tonight?

She deletes the second sentence, swipes to rewrite it with the same words and presses send.

The front door opens. Luisa steps out into the hall to see Justin, phone in hand.

'I remembered you're working,' he says. 'You remembered it takes me longer to get home? Without the car?'

Luisa has not remembered, but Justin's mention of the car recalls the excitement of the night before. She searches his expression in vain for some residue of that feeling. Justin hangs up his coat, then looks to her as if questioning why she is standing there, why she feels the need to watch.

'The girls have eaten, they're just watching something. All you need do is just get them ready for bed,' says Luisa, but this sounds pointed, too harsh. 'And I'm afraid I've eaten without you. They made a complete mess. But it's tidy now. And we made sunflowers. They're shit but at least we made them.'

Justin looks past Luisa into the lounge. 'Hey lovely girls,' he says. Elsie and Eleanor make no reply, their eyes fixed on the screen. 'Okay,' he says to Luisa, and moves off into the kitchen.

'But the insurance is all sorted.'

'Whose keys are these?' says Justin.

Justin twirls around, pulls the stack of bowls into the sink and vigorously scrubs them in cold water. 'Okay, great. Thanks for sorting that.'

'Eat your dinner first. Just start the microwave.'

'It's fine. I'll just get this done.' Now he takes the bowls from the sink, tips out the cold water and refills with hot. 'Then I don't need to do it after.'

'Or just do it in the morning.'

'I have to work in the morning.'

'Not tomorrow. You have the girls tomorrow, don't you?' Luisa lowers her voice to even out the winning point.

Justin swings round and presses two fingers against the calendar that hangs over the cupboard door. Almost all the calendar's boxes are full of words in two distinct writing styles.

A low noise emits from Justin, a wordless vocal fry.

'I thought. But I have to go to London tomorrow.'

Luisa shakes her head. 'No, no you don't. We arranged this before. You have the girls tomorrow, for half-term. On Wednesday. That's what the calendar says, isn't it?' She knows it is.

'I thought I was just taking them to school, to breakfast club. But they're not at school. Because it's half-term,' Justin explains to some other accuser. He moves around the kitchen, tidying pencils into a drawer. He grabs a jay cloth and scrubs at the extractor fan above the oven.

'You'll just have to tell Al and Marian you're working from home. You said you can work at home sometimes, didn't you?' She holds her anger in check, aided by the knowledge that this is his fuck-up, and he knows it.

'I can't,' says Justin. 'Not tomorrow.' He is pleading, but, Luisa notes happily, it is to himself. 'The meeting with the Bishop, on Thursday. Things have changed. We've got to redo the whole presentation, I have to be there tomorrow,' he says.

'It's on the calendar,' repeats Luisa.

'We never had calendars when I was young.'

'The calendar was your idea.'

'Mum wouldn't have them in the house.' Justin does not look at her, and instead flails around the kitchen, until he ends up back at the sink. 'If she found one she used it for lighting fires. And then complained they were too glossy.'

'I can't have the girls tomorrow,' says Luisa. 'I'm working a night tonight.'

'You really can't?'

'I'm working a night!' Her anger seeps out for an instant, and she clamps it back down before the end of the sentence.

'I'll sort it,' says Justin. He goes back to the washing up.

'I'm leaving for work in ten minutes,' she says. 'So what's going to happen tomorrow?'

'I'm thinking.'

Luisa waits for a moment, whilst Justin engages in a sombre meditation with the soaping of a bread knife. She grabs her backpack from the kitchen table and checks through: scrubs, hospital swipe card, watch, name badge, pens. There are no pens in her bag. Where are her pens? Justin dumps lumpen spaghetti from a saucepan into the bin. Luisa wrenches open the fridge door and a milk carton falls from the door to the floor on its side, leaking a small puddle. She puts the carton back and ignores the puddle, and stares at her tupperware container of carrot sticks. She closes the fridge, takes a six-pack of crisps from the cupboard and stuffs it in her backpack.

'Is there any chance you could take annual leave?' says Justin.

'For my shift that begins in an hour?'

'You said when this all started that you'd be able to use your annual leave in the school holidays?'

'Everyone wants annual leave in half-term. I've only been back at work for eight weeks. I'm not exactly first in line.'

'Mum!' cries Elsie from the lounge. 'Why would you want to bury someone in a Y-shaped coffin?'

'What are they watching?' says Justin.

'I don't know.' She sounds as though she doesn't care. She does care, she wants to go see, but there isn't time. 'What are we doing about tomorrow?' she says, going nowhere and seeing nothing.

'Of course. Well it's obvious, isn't it?' says Justin. 'Mum. Mum can look after them. She's already done it once, she knows what to do now.'

'Bea? For a whole day?' Luisa unzips her backpack again, looks inside without knowing why. 'I'm not sure she does know what to do. Why did she think it would be okay for them to watch *Don't Look Now*?'

'That's how she taught me about the dangers of shallow ponds.' Justin takes his phone from his pocket.

'She has her life-coaching clients during the week. We can't ask her.'

'Not even ask?'

Luisa sees a momentary flash of anger in him, some deep blood loyalty.

'We can't ask your parents,' he says.

'No. I know we can't.' She zips the backpack up again. From the day Luisa told her parents she was pregnant, they began a highly financed, aggressive marketing campaign to re-brand themselves as 'foresightedly self-sufficient': their plan, laid out in document form, maintained that as soon as the health of one of them was failing, they would book themselves onto back-to-back international cruises, on a schedule which meant they never had to leave the ship. An option, as Luisa's father never failed to mention, that was 'considerably cheaper than residential housing or a care home, and with superior medical attention'. For years her mother had nagged Luisa about when she would make something of her life, and once Luisa thought she had, her mother wanted nothing more to do with her. Her parents had met the girls only twice, in Le Havre and Reykjavik.

'Mum. It's me,' Justin says into the phone. 'Can you talk? Not in the middle of something?'

Bea will be okay, thinks Luisa. Justin is still alive after all. Isn't keeping the girls alive all that is required?

'I didn't know goats could even digest chestnuts,' says Justin. 'Actually, I need to ask a favour.'

Luisa goes to the hall, takes down her coat. She looks into the lounge. Piped flute music plays over rolling credits on the screen.

'So, Grandma India might look after you tomorrow,' she tells Elsie and Eleanor.

'Right,' they say together without looking up.

'Is that okay?'

'Is that grandma with the knives?' says Elsie.

'What knives?'

'Are we going to her house? Can we go to her house?'

'I don't know,' says Luisa. 'It's not definite. Ellie, do you mind? You remember Grandma India, from last night?'

Eleanor pokes the keyboard of the computer. 'Does she know I don't like baked beans?'

'You'd better tell Dad. Mum has to go and work. I have to work,' she corrects herself. Because I'm not the Queen, I don't talk about myself in the third person.

'Can I stick the sunflowers on the wall?' says Elsie.

'Ask Dad.' Luisa kisses both of them on top of the head.

'All sorted,' Justin says from the doorway, waggling his phone. 'She seems really excited by the idea.'

'Remember we don't have a car to drive them over,' says Luisa.

'Where *is* our car?' says Elsie.

'The car went wrong.'

'Did Daddy crash it? He said he was going to crash it.'

'Did he?'

'That's not exactly what I said, lovely girl,' says Justin.

'Promise you won't say that to anyone,' says Luisa. 'I have to go.'

'I just said it to you.' Elsie looks worried.

'Anyone apart from me. Daddy only meant he'd *like* to crash it. In a game. But not a fun game. And thinking about it is not the same as actually crashing it.'

'I can't say it to anyone,' says Elsie, 'because you haven't crashed it. You just said so.'

'Why would you want to crash our car?' says Eleanor.

'A new car is coming tomorrow,' says Justin. 'A brand new car.'

'I thought you couldn't afford a new car,' says Elsie.

'No, we definitely can't. You can say that to anyone. Mum's driving over,' Justin tells Luisa. 'She'll be here before you go to sleep in the morning and will take the girls to hers. Plus – she said they can stay the night at hers as well.' He is too animated, the solid victory on the Bea-childcare issue flooding him with bravado.

'Really?' By which Luisa wants to mean: are you insane? Have you lost all concept of parental care? 'She's never had them overnight before.' But then if she has them overnight I can stay in bed on Thursday morning – I can get some rest for Thursday's night shift.

'I have to go,' says Luisa. 'You decide, make sure the girls are happy with it. That Ellie doesn't mind. And you'll need to get things ready for staying the night.' I can *lie in*.

'Yep. Going to do all that.'

'I have to go.'

'So all sorted then,' says Justin, following her to the door. 'And by the time we get to the Christmas holidays my work will have calmed down and you'll have more time to arrange annual leave.'

Luisa forces the last coat button through its hole, encasing the volcano of words in her chest.

'Dad?' says Elsie around the frame of the doorway. 'When you and Mum were boyfriend and girlfriend did Mum ever threaten to leave you? By putting pokers in your eyes?'

'Why would she do that?'

'No reason.'

'Mum and I have always been together.' Justin keeps his eyes on Luisa. 'We've never split up.' This was true. They had met at a party at his shared London house in the year after university, and she had stayed, forever, because it was a freezing February and some gatecrasher had stolen her coat.

Justin follows her out of the front door, pulls it to behind him.

'I have a plan,' he says. 'We need to be more relaxed. Calm things down.'

'I am relaxed.' And this is true, she thinks, our life is relaxed, in that nothing much of interest happens in it. 'I have to go,' she says, which is not relaxed at all.

'But sometimes I worry.' Justin sits on the doorstep, playing the old-timer chewing the fat, discussing other people's distant lives. Philosophising, and so not arguing. 'When you get – when you're like you are. Like after a night shift, sometimes. In the mornings.'

'When I'm like what?'

'It's only because it's early. You've been up and I'm just awake.'

'I don't even tell you most of it.' The words blast from her mouth, fuelled by the memory of mornings on their doorstep, when she is socked full of fear and adrenaline because one of her women has come within minutes of having a brain-damaged baby, a baby that made the genetic mistake of owning shoulders wider than its head. A morning when he gives her a sideways glance and disappears down the driveway. 'Sometimes I don't say anything.'

'I'm not complaining. Just worried. It's like – a mania. A kind of madness? Is that good? Madness?'

'I haven't gone mad, Justin.'

'But when you do. When it makes you cry,' he says. 'When you cry at afternoon films that aren't even sad.'

'Why can't I cry at films?'

'But when the postman gets involved.'

'He wasn't a proper postman, only temporary. He was studying film part-time. I have to go.'

'Anyway. I called Dr Zed this afternoon.'

'Jamie?'

'He only goes by Dr Zed now.'

'I thought he was – you know, locked away.'

'He's back. Apparently he got time taken off for starting up a very successful prison gardening club. Reduced re-offending by sixty percent, so he said. And he's going to get us some weed. Grass.'

'Do we still do that?'

'I didn't know we stopped,' says Justin. 'Why did we stop?'

'I don't know.' She does know. During midwifery training one lecturer declared it was her job to sign off each qualified midwife as being 'of good character', had asked if there was anything which would mean Luisa and her fellow trainees were not of good character. I can be a good character, Luisa insisted at the time. I might not always have been – but there's no way you can find out and from now on I can be.

'I thought it would relax us more,' says Justin.

'Good. Yes.' He is making an effort. She does need to relax more. Relax with Justin.

She moves back to the doorstep, kisses him goodbye. 'Right. See you in the morning.'

He smiles at her. Luisa looks away and heads down the driveway.

The neighbourhood is silent, the darkness damping down sound. Luisa sets off at a pace, down the road and round the corner, past the bus stop.

'Evening,' says a voice. It is Colin, who lives on his own two houses down, standing motionless under the shelter's plastic roof, a dog sat at his side.

'Hi,' calls Luisa. She is travelling too fast to be polite. I'm in a hurry, I'm late, she thinks, then slows down and stops. 'Hi,' she says again.

'Hullo there,' says Colin.

'Hi.' Luisa looks down at Colin's black Labrador, who looks as confused about the direction of the conversation as she is. 'Well, I'm off to work.'

'Good. That's good.'

'Running a bit late, actually.'

'Where is it you work?'

'The hospital. I'm a midwife.'

'Oh. Wow,' says Colin. 'Delivering babies. That must be really rewarding.'

'It is. Yes it is. I'm actually going to be a bit late for my shift already,' she laughs. 'I'd better be going.'

'You definitely better.' Colin raises a hand in salute.

*

As she passes the phone mast at the crest of Blackdown Hill and the view over the city appears, her phone rings.

'I'm extending our time together,' says Justin.

'That's nice.' She picks up speed as though he is delaying her somehow.

'You know what we can do? If Mum's having the girls overnight tomorrow? We can do something Wednesday night. Something exciting. We won't have to get up for the girls.'

'Sure.' Except Wednesday night is my one night off in a week of night shifts. Last night was going out night. 'Well why don't we go properly out then?' she says. 'I mean I'm going to be pretty nocturnal this week. Let's go out. Let's go out out.' That's how to do this, suggest the impossible and appear gracious by settling for the mundane.

'On a Wednesday?' he says, to her relief.

'Why not a Wednesday?' says Luisa. 'We can go dancing like we said. Find a club.'

'A club? What club?'

'I know one,' says Luisa.

'I have to see the Bishop Thursday morning,' says Justin.

'If you don't want to,' she says, as though disappointed. 'Perhaps we should just go to a restaurant then.'

'But you hate restaurants,' says Justin. 'After we went to that diner place in town you said you never wanted to go to a restaurant ever again.'

'I don't think I did.'

'You told the waiter. When he asked how your meal was. You said you never know when you're going to get your food, and it makes you tense. And that you never want to order a starter, because it ruins your appetite, but then you order one, and then you end up eating some of mine because having food in front of you makes you hungry. And that that makes me cross. And that you couldn't enjoy yourself because we're sitting there as a couple and not talking, and it felt like people were looking at us like we're one of those couples who shouldn't be together. And because that made you panic and start talking complete crap. And then because at the end of it all we actually had to pay for the whole experience.'

'Are you angry with me?' says Luisa. He messed up looking after the girls. He's not allowed to be angry.

'No. Of course not.'

'Maybe angry at my job?'

'Why would I be angry at your job?'

'You might be.'

'I'm angry at *my* job. I shouldn't have to go to London tomorrow. Or to see the fucking Bishop again on Thursday.'

'I think the work you do is great.' Has he ever said that he thinks her work is great? 'Poor people get money because of you.'

'Not yet.'

'But they will.'

'Let's just have a nice night in together. You're sure about cooking?'

'I can cook us a dinner. I have to go.'

TUESDAY NIGHT: ON DUTY

'Limbering time,' says Gina, as Luisa enters the delivery suite changing room. Gina squats on her haunches, arms raised above her head, a hand holding each opposite elbow. 'Make sure you limber, Luisa. If you don't keep the body fit, you'll never fight off your illness.' She rolls her body forward into a push-up position, her head almost inside the nearest locker.

'I'm not ill,' says Luisa.

'And that's what I like, a positive attitude. Illness is very much in the mind.' Gina taps her temple, balancing her weight on one hand. 'But you are ill. We're all ill. It comes with the territory.'

Gina was right – illness in the midwifery unit was rife. Sick bugs shot through the delivery suite, aided by the midwives who dragged themselves to work regardless of their fevers and violent coughs, spreading infection so as not to let down their colleagues and to be there for the birthing women. The one consistently healthy person was Debbie, and she took more sick leave than anyone.

'I don't think I'm ill right now.' Luisa takes the scrubs from her bag. 'In fact I'm feeling good tonight.'

'That's good. Work your way through it.' Gina lowers her body to the floor. 'Carla Jones. Nineteenth of the seventh ninety-nine. APGARS 2 at one minute.' She pushes herself back upright. 'You want to say your own with me? Sandra Emmentine. Fourth of the third two thousand and six. Shoulder dystocia, eleven minutes.'

'I – did some before I left.'

'The mantras?'

'Exercises. Stretching.'

'I thought as your mentor I recommended mantras. Keep the near misses screaming at the front of your mind.'

'I did try,' says Luisa. 'But I didn't find it that helpful.'

Gina jumps forward into a squat and crouches in front of Luisa. 'Don't hold back,' says Gina. 'Tell me what's terrifying you.'

'I'm not sure there's much that terrifies me,' says Luisa. Apart from the very tall consultant who demands random birth observations I can't recall. Or Dora, the midwife who no longer works on delivery suite, who only speaks in grunts. Or that when I ask Diane why Dora can no longer work, Diane laughs and says she shouldn't say, and then doesn't say. Or the equipment supplies cupboard where, when I am almost confident I can locate a cord clamp in under thirty seconds, discover someone has reorganised the cupboard, and the search has to begin again. Or the rota – more specifically the rota changing with just a few days notice, and the effect this has on Justin's ability to speak to me. Or the thudding noise the lift makes when it reaches the ground floor. 'I mean I'm learning where things are all the time. And everyone is really helpful and nice.'

'Bollocks,' said Gina. 'Back after extended leave in a new unit? You must be terrified. And how can you think Jenny is nice? Come on, what keeps you awake at night? What are your danger points? It's my job to know.'

What kept her awake were lovingly detailed scenes of emergency caesareans and shoulder dystocias, that returned to her in vivid clarity at three o'clock in the morning. Images of babies born white and limp imprinted on her retina as she woke, frozen in terror, unable to pull the emergency buzzer. Luisa had not always dreamt of being a midwife, but now she dreams of being a midwife all the time.

'Well – I'm a bit worried about being out of practice, I suppose,' said Luisa.

'So, terrified of making a mistake during a birth? Good. And?'

'Not terrified. Just – a bit anxious.'

'Let's move from anxious back to terrified,' said Gina. 'I want you terrified. No midwife should be anything other than terrified. If you're not terrified, you're not paying attention.'

'But I'm getting better,' said Luisa. 'I can sense it getting better.'

'Nor do I want you getting better,' said Gina. 'I haven't had a solid preshift bowel movement in the ten years I've been here. I wouldn't have it any other way.'

'But I am getting better,' insisted Luisa. 'I'm keeping focussed on having some really good births.'

'Forget births.' Gina stretches her leg up in an arc behind her. 'It's not like women spend much time actually pushing the baby out, is it? Your priority is the welfare of women. And what a great privilege. A sacred reward at the first stirrings of life. You're with woman.'

'I am?' Luisa pulls on the cotton trousers at speed, her foot catching in the green material.

'With Woman. Midwife, With Woman. The Old German. Didn't they teach you that in training?'

'No – '

'We had to chant it to a drum beat on the university playing fields. Caring for women, that's always our primary role. Whatever the circumstances. And as your mentor I don't want you pushed around and told what to do by Jenny or any other co-ordinator.'

'But isn't it the co-ordinator's job to tell you what to do?'

'You can't be a good midwife if you don't trust your own instincts. Who says you should even listen to me? I don't want you taking any notice of me, either. Not if it's your decision. Don't listen to me. What do I know?'

*

Luisa first wanted to be a midwife before the birth of the twins. Midwifery fitted her idea of a life's work. At least it was the life's work she wanted before actually doing the job. Now she was actually doing the job, this was only one activity amongst many she wanted to do: sleep, spend time with Justin and the girls, read a book without falling asleep, talk about something other than midwifery.

Even when she not working as a midwife she was forced to talk about working as a midwife. No one asked insurance people, or bankers, or greengrocers how their work was going. Not, at least, at the beginning of every conversation. And what *How is midwifery going?* meant, was *Are you enjoying yourself? Are you enjoying yourself more than I do in my job?* A need to confirm that their hierarchy of job satisfaction was intact, that catching babies as they are born, helping women bring new life into the world was as beatific as it sounded. 'Oh, it must be so rewarding,' said everyone.

The triangular maternity office is empty when Luisa walks in. She hurries to the white board, scans the two columns of boxes.

'Checking out the competition?' Nikki comes up behind her, puts her hands on Luisa's hips and wiggles them, in a way that if a man did the same would be a solid case for sexual harassment.

'Um. No?'

'I think of it like a casino,' says Nikki. 'Who will I get tonight? The red or the black?'

'You mean blood or meconium?' says Luisa.

Nikki does not reply, and instead dances back and forth on the spot, shaking one foot after the other. She doesn't mean anything.

'I'd just like to get a good birth in tonight,' says Luisa. 'I haven't had a nice easy birth for a couple of weeks.'

'I went for three whole months once,' laughs Nikki. 'Nothing but caesareans and forceps. It was terrifying. I tried to get my therapist to agree that I was cursed. I didn't see what else it could be.'

'And did she? Agree?'

'My therapist never says anything. Waste of money if you ask me, I always have to do the talking. She's worse than Martyn. I think I'm going to dump her,' says Nikki.

'Are you always terrified?' Luisa whispers, though there is no one else in the office. 'Gina says I need to stay terrified.'

'Oh no. I'm past that.'

'And where are you now?'

'To be honest I kind of miss those loose bowels before every shift. Kept me slim. I used to vomit up my lunch most days.'

'You were actually sick?'

'Only for the first couple of years. But don't let on to Jenny. If she thinks I've stopped being sick, she might start asking me to act up as co-ordinator.' Nikki sees Luisa's expression. 'But I love it now, of course. And hey. You've only been here a month or so, haven't you? Of course you're still being sick.'

'Eight weeks. I've been here eight weeks.'

'And no one's died,' laughed Nikki.

'I worked in another unit. A while ago.'

'Well, there you go.'

'But birth is amazing, isn't it?' Luisa nods her head at Nikki. 'Such a privilege to be with woman when they're giving birth.'

'So beautiful,' says Nikki. 'There's nothing quite like a nice birth.'

'Exactly.' Luisa grabs Nikki's wrist. 'A really beautiful birth.'

Nikki slides her hand down to Luisa's, links fingers and slow dances her around in a circle.

Other midwives file into the office, and Luisa releases herself from Nikki. She turns back to the board and scans down the names in the boxes. Eloise. Eloise, P2 both SVDs. Eloise is mine.

'So if we're all here,' says Jenny, when midwives have filled the office, lined along the desk and wedged amongst the two computers. 'We've got Philippa in Mary Cronk, who is epileptic. She's been quiet so far. Two prostins and was ARM'd at 17.15. Should have started synto already.' Jenny taps the white board with a green marker pen.

Luisa stands motionless to avoid a bid, the penniless auction gawper, angling her eyes past Jenny at the poster on the wall. SAFETY TIP OF THE WEEK: *Do Your Counts. A swab left in a vagina is a never event.* The text runs in a circle, its colours moving through a rainbow gradient.

A doctor appears in the doorway that opens onto the corridor. Gina spins to the doorway, blocking his way. She wears a hi-vis tabard – across its back are the words: HANDOVER IN PROGRESS. DO NOT ENTER.

'I wondered – ' says the doctor.

'It's handover,' says Gina, a hand on either side of the door frame. 'Can't you read?'

'Read what?'

Gina spins around to show him the tabard. 'Come back in ten minutes.'

The doctor leaves without a word.

'If we aren't allowed doors, someone has to stand guard,' says Gina to Jenny.

'Why aren't there doors any more?' says Nikki.

'Infection control,' says Jenny.

'How does that help infection control? says Nikki.

'How the hell should I know?' says Jenny.

'I'll take the epileptic.' Diane sits in the one office swivel chair, a half-stitched blanket over her knees and a large embroidery needle in one hand. 'I haven't seen a good grand mal in a while.'

'Not you,' says Jenny. 'We keep you back in reserve, don't we Diane?'

'Right-ho, captain.' Diane salutes, almost stabbing her eye with the needle.

'I don't want her flapping all over my ward. Nikki, I'm giving Philippa to you.'

Jenny moves down the board, assigning women, until she gets to Eloise.

'I'll take Eloise,' says Luisa. 'We have a bit of a connection. I mean I know her slightly.'

'Really?' Jenny peers round at Luisa, a hawk sizing up her territory. 'I wouldn't normally dump her on one of the newly qualifieds.'

'I'm not newly qualified.' says Luisa.

'Well, whatever. If you want her,' says Jenny, and scratches LISA next to the box for Eloise. 'I was going to give someone like her to Gina. Given her history.'

'Hit me,' says Gina.

'I don't know her that well,' says Luisa.

'That was her boyfriend who assaulted one of the MCAs last week,' says Jenny. 'When they were kept waiting in triage. Apparently he's on the sex offenders register, and there's a pile of child protection issues. The baby's being removed at birth.'

'I don't want to mess up your system,' says Luisa. 'Maybe it's a different Eloise that I know.'

'Shall I take her, then?' says Gina. 'So we can stop playing musical chairs with labouring women? I mean she sounds like the sort of woman who needs the best midwifery care, don't you think?'

'If you want her, Gina.' Luisa looks down, hands clasped, the penitent nun.

'Not a question of wanting. Never a question of wanting,' says Gina.

To Luisa's relief Jenny scrubs out her name and replaces it with Gina's.

Jenny assigns the other women and the midwives file off out of the office.

'So, Lisa, I'm going to give you – ' says Jenny when only the two of them remain in the office.

'Luisa,' says Luisa.

'What?' says Jenny.

'Sorry. I'm Luisa, my name's Luisa. Not Lisa.'

'So *Luisa*, I'm going to give you Cheryl in Shelia Kitzinger,' says Jenny. 'Do you think you can handle her? Primip, bit needy. Should pop quite soon.'

'Of course. And I'm not newly qualified,' says Luisa. 'I'm just new at this hospital.'

'That's newly qualified in my book.' says Jenny. 'I'll keep an eye on you, don't you worry.'

She could mean anything, thinks Luisa. Perhaps that's being kind. Or maybe an outright threat – with Jenny it is impossible to tell.

'And Luisa,' says Jenny. 'Tonight's watchword is?'

Luisa opens her mouth but says nothing.

'No need to look so carved up about it!' laughs Jenny. 'I don't do tests. I'm telling everyone. Bladder care. Tonight's focus.'

'Bladder care. Right. Thanks, Jenny.'

Jenny does not hear.

*

Luisa knocks on the door of Sheila Kitzinger and goes straight in.

'And who are you?' A bearded man whips inside the privacy curtain that encloses the doorway, pulls the two halves together behind him.

'I'm Luisa,' says Luisa. 'Your midwife?'

'Oh, er. Hi.' The man releases a hand from the curtain and holds it out to Luisa. 'I'm Eric. I'm the groundsman.' Eric runs one hand and then the other through his waxed hair. 'Come in, come in. We'll need to, need to go over a few things.'

The strip lights in the room are unlit. Instead three standard lamps circle the bed.

'Oh look,' says Annie, the day-shift midwife. She sounds surprised, excited even, at Luisa's entrance. 'This is Luisa. She is going to be your night time baby catcher.'

The woman on the bed exhales a noisy breath. The bed inclines her at forty-five degrees – a sheet covers the ball of her abdomen and up to her chest, where a lilac paisley shirt takes over. Her hands grasp tight to her belly.

'Hello, Cheryl,' sing-songs Luisa.

Eric steps between Luisa and the bed, blocking her view of Cheryl.

'So you're going?' Cheryl says to Annie. *Don't leave me, I think I'm going to die, who is this woman?*, the tenor of her voice implies. She blows out another long stream of air.

'I'm off to bye-byes now. You'll be fine with Luisa.' Annie says to Eric. 'Luisa's a brilliant midwife. You're going to have a lovely birth with her instead.'

'We are.' Luisa cranes her head to the side in order to see Cheryl, but Eric moves with her. 'We're going to have a lovely birth,' she says to Eric's denim shirt.

Annie pushes Cheryl's notes booklet into Luisa's hand. Her eyebrows dart up and to the side in a chaotic pattern, an attempt to communicate with a woefully small vocabulary.

'So, when Cheryl came in, there was a little bit of the red stuff, just a couple of thimbles,' says Annie. 'We had a bit of a tizzy over that, so we thought we'd have a little extra check on baby with the, the.' Annie lays a hand on the foetal heart monitor.

'Have you seen Cheryl's birth plan?' Eric's flitting eyebrows are bushier than Annie's, darker and thus more informative, and manage to both criticise Annie and direct Luisa towards the ring-binder he thrusts into her hands at the same time. He flips over the title page – Luisa cannot be certain, but thinks she saw a calligraphic quote.

Luisa skips the birth plan's introductory paragraph and looks at the first item on the bulleted list.

Keep discussion to an absolute minimum to allow Cheryl to focus.

Eric jabs a finger to a line lower down the list, in bold:

No direct conversation with Cheryl, all conversation to go through Eric to aid maximum concentration.

'Our antenatal midwife, Josie, said we should do everything we can to relax and be comfortable,' says Eric. 'To make Cheryl relaxed and comfortable.'

'Of course. That's what we all want,' says Luisa.

Cheryl would like no overhead lighting (we will provide our own lamps*). *Does the hospital have a service lift?, the footnote reads.

Cheryl wishes to be free to have an active labour, with a variety of mats, beanbags and slings at her disposal.

No medical interventions, drugs or pain relief unless absolutely necessary.

We would like hospital staff to acknowledge that although for yourselves this is one birth amongst many, for us this a unique and sacred event.

Cheryl will have a vaginal birth.

Annie is doing her own finger-jabbing, trying to turn the page. On the next sheet it says:

CHERYL HAS A PHOBIA OF MEDICAL LANGUAGE. PLEASE KEEP TO AN ABSOLUTE MINIMUM.

'Well, that seems fine,' Luisa says to Cheryl, then swings her gaze over to Eric. Cheryl is oblivious – she emits a moan from deep in her diaphragm and drags the gas and air mouthpiece towards her to take another nitrous oxide hit.

'Baby had a bit of a funny turn, and the beeps went slow for a minute or two,' says Annie, nodding furiously. 'That's why we're keeping Cheryl in bed, still on the machine-y thing. And the – baby door was four centimetres at 19:45 – a quarter to eight. So next look at a quarter to midnight.'

Eric frowns, processing each word, in fear of missing the ones that mean *this woman and baby are both going to die.*

'The next – ?' says Luisa.

'Her whoopsie,' says Annie. 'You need to check Cheryl's whoopsie at a quarter to midnight.'

VE 23:45, Luisa scribbles on the notes.

'Well that's me done.' Annie makes a point of speaking directly to Cheryl. 'You two have a lovely baby with Luisa,' she says, and disappears behind through the curtain and out the door.

'I'm so *uncomfortable*.' Cheryl accuses Luisa. 'It just *hurts*.'

'Well how about changing position?' says Luisa. 'Perhaps some moving around? For active labour?' Luisa remembers the birth plan phrase.

'Annie said Cheryl needed to stay on the bed.' Eric's frown is still in place. *Have they have given us the stupid midwife?* it says. 'For the machine.'

'Well let's just check the machine.' Luisa extends the concertinaed paper from the foetal heart monitor. The monitor has drawn a regular mountain range except for two deeper V's an hour earlier, a sign of momentary foetal distress. Safe to ignore if not repeated, thinks Luisa. That's Annie fussing, saying she needs to stay on the machine. Or is that Annie being sensibly cautious?

'Well, my advice is that we get Cheryl off the bed and moving around,' Luisa says to Eric.

'You want me to move around?' says Cheryl.

'Only if you, if Cheryl wants to,' she smiles towards a standard lamp. 'It'll get things moving. Towards a lovely natural birth.'

'I want to move around!' cries Cheryl, and bursts into tears. 'Can I just get off this bed!'

'But what about the monitor?' says Eric. 'Annie said we need to keep monitoring.'

'We can still monitor the baby and let you move around,' says Luisa. In theory, anyway.

'Annie didn't want to let me move around,' sobs Cheryl. 'I want to do what feels natural. I mean our ancestors never gave birth in hospitals, did they? And tribal women get by okay without caesareans, don't they?' She laughs, the teacher mocking the pupil's stupidity.

'They do,' says Luisa. Apart from the ones that died in childbirth, of course.

'We did want to birth at home, really,' says Eric.

Cheryl gets her feet off the bed and onto the floor, and Eric unrolls a yoga mat before her, a very short red carpet. Cheryl sinks to her knees and forward onto her hands, and with the monitor cable tight against her skin her shirt rides up so she is almost naked.

'Well when there's been a little bleed it's good that we can look after you here,' says Luisa.

'Oh god. That's so much better!' Cheryl bursts into tears again.

Eric bursts into tears as well. 'Oh, thank you!' he says to Luisa.

'Annie was so unbending,' sobs Cheryl. 'I can't work with unbending people.' She screws up her eyes and grabs Eric's hand.

'Well, all of us midwives have different ways of working,' Luisa says to Eric. Luisa rests an arm over Cheryl's shoulder as she breathes through the next contraction. 'Tell Cheryl she's doing well,' says Luisa to Eric.

'You can talk to me,' says Cheryl, snorting out through her nose. She leans her head on Luisa's shoulder. 'You understand. I want you to talk to me.'

'I'm here for you,' says Luisa. 'We're all here for your lovely birth.'

'Don't leave me,' says Cheryl.

*

'And how's it going in here?' An hour later Jenny bursts through the delivery room door, sweeps back the privacy curtain. Eric squat jumps to his feet, but Luisa intercepts first.

'We're fine,' says Luisa. She looks around the room for anything she might be doing wrong. 'We're in a quiet phase.'

Jenny grabs the notes booklet, still in motion. Jenny is always in motion – during her orientation tour Jenny told Luisa to think of the co-ordinator's role like the space probe Voyager, orbiting through the rooms and using their energy as a gravity slingshot to the next.

'So when did we last have a wee? Have we been regularly voiding?' Jenny circles the room and peers down at Cheryl. Eric tries to insert himself in front of Cheryl.

'We've had a big wee, haven't we Cheryl?' says Luisa. She cannot be sure of the size of the wee, as Cheryl refused to use a bowl.

'And you've done a recent pulse? Up-to-date with obs?' says Jenny.

'Perhaps I could have a quick word outside?' Now Luisa docks with Jenny's pace and steers her in the direction of the door.

'It's just that Cheryl has a bit of a phobia. A fear of medical language,' says Luisa outside the room.

'Really? That's brilliant.' Jenny sounds genuinely delighted. 'Never had one of those myself. What are you using, sign language?'

'I'm trying to keep her as quiet as possible. She's very keen on a natural birth. Her birth plan says she doesn't want a caesarean unless absolutely necessary.'

'What was that?' The Registrar appears next to Jenny.

'Apparently Luisa's woman doesn't want a caesarean unless absolutely necessary,' laughs Jenny. 'I heard you were really into unnecessary caesareans. It's one of your specialities, isn't it?'

'Love them,' The Registrar turns to Luisa. 'I'm not in the habit of performing caesareans unless absolutely necessary.'

'It's – what Cheryl says in her birth plan,' says Luisa. 'It's what Cheryl wants.' She tries to find another reason to use Cheryl in a sentence, but nothing comes to mind.

'Cheryl's the one with the bleed, isn't she?' the Registrar says, more kindly. 'What's the trace look like now?'

'It's definitely normal,' says Luisa. 'Just one decel. Or two. That's why I thought it was fine to take her off constant monitoring,' she says to Jenny.

'One or two decels is fine,' says the Registrar. 'So long as there's no more bleeding. Shall I come have a check?' says the Registrar.

'I'd like you to check,' says Jenny.

'The decels are for less than half of contractions.' Luisa says to Jenny's back. 'So still normal by the new NICE guidelines.'

Luisa knocks and re-enters Shelia Kitzinger. Eric sees the Registrar and jumps to his feet.

'Er, hello,' says Eric. 'And who are you?'

'I'm the doctor,' says the Registrar.

'Cheryl, honey?' Eric calls over to the bed. 'Are you okay with the doctor coming in?'

'I'd like the doctor in please,' says Luisa. 'If that's okay.'

'Is that okay, Cheryl?' calls back Eric.

'If Luisa thinks it's okay, it's okay.' Cheryl takes a gasping hit from the gas mouthpiece.

'I'm the groundsman,' Eric says to the Registrar. 'Cheryl wants me to keep an eye on who comes in and out of the room,' he says, as though explaining why he's brought his football sticker album to show her.

'Gatekeeper!' Cheryl shouts through the gas and air mouthpiece. 'You're the gatekeeper!'

'The doctor has come to have a check on – to check on baby,' says Luisa. 'To check the machine for the baby's heart.'

'What's wrong with the baby's heart?' says Eric.

The Registrar examines the concertinaed readout of the foetal heart monitor.

'There's nothing wrong with the baby's heart. We just want to be sure there are no dips like before,' says the Registrar. 'There's some big gaps here,' she says to Luisa. 'What's with the gaps?'

'We were mobilising – to promote normal birth,' says Luisa. 'But the traces in between are fine, yes?' Luisa points at the print out.

'Well, I don't know what's been happening in the gaps,' says the Registrar.

'We've been trying to have an active labour,' Luisa looks to Cheryl for some acknowledgement. Cheryl eyes the doctor suspiciously.

'It says it here in the birth plan.' Eric proffers the booklet to the Registrar.

'Well the trace looks pretty normal up to here. I'd recommend leaving it on until we have a solid stretch of normal,' says the Registrar, smiling at Eric. 'Also, I can't see anything in the notes about bladder care. Bladder care is a concern. May I?' the Registrar asks Cheryl, her splayed hands almost touching Cheryl's belly.

Cheryl looks as though she wants to kill her, and nods.

The Registrar finger-squeezes Cheryl's lower belly. 'When did we last go to the toilet?' she says.

'It was just over an hour ago,' Luisa inserts herself between the Registrar and Cheryl.

'And you voided properly?'

'I did. Cheryl did,' says Luisa. 'Didn't you Cheryl? You said it was a big wee?'

'I don't know it was that big,' says Cheryl. 'Is that why it hurts so much? I haven't been able to wee properly the last couple of times.'

You traitor, thinks Luisa. You never said anything before.

'You need to make sure to keep the bladder emptied. I can feel that it's a bit full,' the Registrar says, and it stings Luisa all the more coming from the nice teacher.

'Maybe catheterise to empty the bladder,' says the Registrar as she leaves. 'I'll come check in again a bit later.'

'I can't have one of those tubes in me,' says Cheryl when the Registrar has gone. 'I can't deal with tubes. I'll just go for another wee.' Cheryl pushes herself up to her elbows.

'We did say in the birth plan,' Eric reminds Luisa. 'About keeping medical intervention to a minimum.'

'The thing is, you might not be able to wee now.' Luisa says this to the trolley as she finds the in-out catheter. 'Because of the baby pushing down. But we don't have to use a tube that stays in.' Luisa matches her deep inhalation to Cheryl's own. 'We can empty your – all your wee with an in-out one. One that doesn't stay in.'

Cheryl and Eric are silent as Luisa holds the thin plastic catheter tube over Cheryl's parted labia, a bowl in her other hand. Vagina, urethra, clitoris, Luisa reminds herself. Not too high. Don't try and catheterise a clitoris again. She slides the tube into the urethra and urine jets from the end of the tube.

'Is that much normal?' says Eric, peering over.

'It's a little more than normal.' Luisa levels the almost-filled bowl and tries to press her thumb over the mini-funnel at the end of the catheter.

'It looks like too much,' says Eric.

'What's too much?' calls Cheryl.

'Would you mind helping me a moment, please Eric?' says Luisa.

The bowl overflows, Cheryl's urine seeping over the side and down Luisa's arm.

'What can I do?' Eric watches as Luisa's sleeves darken.

'If you could fetch another bowl from the trolley.' Luisa feels the warm liquid exit the end of her sleeve, dribbling down her stomach and into her knickers.

'This one?' Eric skips over with the bowl, and Luisa swaps full for empty, tipping in some excess and spilling only a little more over her hands. She has never seen so much urine.

'Now I'm going to need to pop out for just a minute,' Luisa says as she removes the catheter.

'You're leaving?' says Cheryl, and screws her face in preparation for another contraction.

'If you remember from the birth plan,' says Eric, 'we did say that we didn't want to be left unattended at any point.'

'I need to pop out for a second. To change.'

Cheryl looks at Eric, pleading. Eric looks down at his bowl of piss.

'I just got a little of – that on me.' Luisa points at the bowl.

Cheryl starts to cry, though Luisa is not sure whether in apology or pain.

'And how are we getting on in here?' Jenny enters the room without knocking, moves directly to the foetal heart monitor.

'We're fine, we're good,' says Luisa. 'I was just about to write up the notes. We were just having a wee. Bladder care,' she nods at Jenny.

'Message of the week!' sings Jenny. 'And what time do we have scheduled for our next vaginal examination?'

Jenny looks only at Luisa, a landowner excluding the peasants from the conversation. Only Jenny could take *No direct conversation with Cheryl* and convert it into a sick rudeness for her own amusement, thinks Luisa.

'23:45,' says Luisa. 'I'm about to write it all in the notes. I just need to get changed.'

'I've put a foetal heart CTG review and sticker in the notes. Left a space for your notes,' says Jenny. 'If I were you I'd be keeping a monitor on at all times. And I've used your last sticker. You'll need to get more CTG stickers.' Jenny waves a hand behind her as she leaves the room.

'I thought we didn't need the monitor on all the time,' says Eric.

'Let's put it back on for now.' Luisa waddles back over to Cheryl, clips the monitor back on. She can feel Eric and Cheryl watching her.

'I have to leave for just a moment,' says Luisa.

'Is the baby's heart okay?'

'It's fine at the moment. And I'll have another check when I'm back.'

'If you do have to go out,' says Eric, 'would you mind getting Cheryl some more water?'

Luisa feels Cheryl's urine cool in her sleeves, on her belly, down in her underwear. She walks to the door with a wider stance, to separate her legs from the sodden trouser material. 'I'll fetch some more water when I get the stickers.'

*

'Just getting CTG stickers,' says Luisa to Jenny in the crowded office. She puts down the empty water jug and rifles through the stationery drawer. The drawer is crammed with paper and blood test envelopes and patient information leaflets on DVTs, but no stickers. 'Aren't the CTG stickers kept in this drawer?'

'In that box,' says Erin, the maternity care assistant. She points to a nondescript cardboard box under the desk. 'But there aren't any more,' she says, in a way that suggests this is symbolic of not only the organisational principles of the hospital, but the entire fabric of human society.

'Need to get you more familiar with where everything is, Luisa,' says Jenny. 'I should give you one of my little tours. Seeing as you're new.'

'The stickers are normally in the drawer, I think,' says Luisa. 'And I know where the stickers are kept now.' Luisa checks her watch fob: she has been away from Cheryl for almost ten minutes, and though she is in clean clothes has neither water nor stickers.

'I can't do you one of my tours now,' says Jenny.

'I don't think I need another tour,' says Luisa. 'Where do I find more stickers?'

'Shall I fetch some?,' says Erin. 'Is that what you're asking me to do? You can say.'

'Oh please. Thank you, thank you so much, Erin.' She wants to ask Erin where she is fetching them from, but Erin has marched out.

'I'll give you one of my tours when you're back on tomorrow night,' says Jenny.

'Thank you. Thanks, Jenny. I think I've already had a tour though,' says Luisa. 'And I don't think I'm on tomorrow night. I'm Thursday night and Friday night.'

'You don't think you're on? Or you're not on?'

'I'm not on. Not tomorrow night.'

'Vertex visible in Joy Gardner,' calls Rebecca through the open doorway.

'I think someone hasn't been checking the off-duty,' says Jenny. 'Wednesday and Thursday nights, Luisa, that's what the off-duty says. I was only just now checking tonight's numbers. I'll be right there,' she calls through the doorway to Rebecca.

'No. No. I checked last week. The off-duty said Thursday and Friday.' Luisa's voice shifts up an octave. 'I can't be on tomorrow night. I've got something on tomorrow night.'

Luisa grabs the black off-duty folder from the shelf, pulls it open onto the desk and threads sheets around the rings.

'Well, that's Fran for you,' laughs Jenny. 'Why they allow someone who's a numerical imbecile to look after the rota I'll never know.'

In the column for Wednesday night Luisa sees LUISA KEANE written on a sticker that covers the name underneath, and a line scrubbed through her name for Friday.

'But I can't work. I've got something arranged. With Justin. My – boyfriend.'

'Not any more you haven't,' says Jenny. 'They did the same to me last week. I actively thought about killing Fran.' Jenny laughs, in a way that offers no reassurance that she would not actually go through with Fran's murder.

The office telephone rings. 'Hello, maternity?' Jenny grabs the receiver.

Luisa stands facing her, wanting to be part of the telephone conversation.

'Don't we need rings for that, darling?' says Jenny softly. 'No, I don't think they'll let you do it without rings.' Jenny frowns at Luisa, and Luisa steps away. 'Well, I don't know if Ratners even exists any more. No, of course, of course. Thursday is fine. Of course I want to. I want everything the way you do. I'm just thinking that for a special day like this everything should be good and ready.'

Luisa picks up Cheryl's water jug, which is still empty. She needs to get back to Cheryl.

'Love you, darling,' says Jenny, and puts down the phone. She stands with her hand on the receiver.

'What's that about a special day?' Diane looks up from the swivel chair and her embroidery, her head torch casting a lighthouse beam around the room.

'So guess who's getting married!' Jenny turns around, shields her eyes, and to Luisa's surprise, and horror, cries big tears that drop from her cheeks to the ground.

Diane squeezes Jenny's arm in a way that looks painful. Luisa wonders if she ought to hug Jenny.

'Is that to Karl?' says Gina from the computer.

'Oh yes. Always Karl. Karl's my rock,' says Jenny.

'I'm so glad you two worked things out,' says Diane. 'I thought you said Karl was always quite against marriage.'

'He become a lot more keen when I pointed out that without us married it might be difficult for him to get half my pension,' says Jenny. 'He hasn't got anything of his own, poor lamb, what with him taking care of the children all these years.'

'So romantic. So when's the big day?' asks Diane.

'To-morrow,' sings Jenny.

'Well that's lovely. I'm so happy for the two of you.' says Gina, exhibiting none of the familiar traits of happiness.

'And Karl's booked it for the afternoon,' says Jenny, 'so I'll even be able to get some sleep in beforehand. I want you all there, of course. If you're not on shift.'

'Was it – a surprise, then?' Luisa says, desperate for an entry back into conversation with Jenny.

'You could say,' laughs Jenny. 'Bit of an impulsive romantic is my Karl.'

'He threw that on you, for tomorrow?' says Diane. 'He's lovely, your Karl.'

'He's thrown a lot worse at me before. Though only lightweight stuff. Soft toys, mostly. It's understandable. It's been hard for him with the Richard thing.'

'Mm,' says Diane. 'I liked Richard, he was nice. Still is nice, I imagine.'

'You've never met Richard,' says Jenny. 'Or Karl.'

'Even so,' says Diane.

'About tomorrow night, Jenny,' says Luisa.

'But it had to end,' says Jenny. 'It did have to end. Even though I loved Richard. Love him.' She starts to cry again.

'So Karl never found out that Richard was actually Phoebe's dad?'

says Diane.

'He wasn't though, was he?' says Jenny. 'The DNA test was conclusive.' Jenny pulls herself off the desk and stands up. 'Well. It's worked out for the best, hasn't it?'

'Here you go,' says Erin, and dumps a plastic-wrapped block of sheets into the cardboard box under the desk.

'About tomorrow tonight, Jenny,' says Luisa.

The phone rings again. Jenny picks up. 'Hello, maternity?'

'So you and Justin having a night together?' Diane looks up, her head torch blinding Luisa.

'Oh. Yes.' Luisa cannot remember ever telling Diane Justin's name. 'Trying to. It's difficult when shifts change at the last minute.' Can Diane help? Diane can't help. She turns to the computer, but Gina has gone. Only Jenny can help. 'Diane, the light. You've still. On your head.'

Diane reaches up and clicks off the head torch, but leaves it on her head.

'Not a problem for me any more,' giggles Diane. 'Robbie left me more than twenty years ago now. Well I suppose I left him.'

'Because of midwifery?'

'Oh no. Because we never saw each other.'

'That's why I need a night with Justin. Tomorrow night.' Why tell Diane? Diane is crazy. Because Diane is there, is listening. 'And Fran has put me down for tomorrow without telling me.'

'Poor Luisa.' Diane goes back to her patchwork squares.

'It's difficult. When our shifts change at the last minute.' She speaks loudly, in the direction of Jenny. Jenny turns to to shield the phone receiver from the noise.

'Does he demand sex in the garden in the mornings yet?' says Diane.

'Robbie did that?'

'Not as such.'

'We haven't had sex in two weeks,' says Luisa.

'I haven't had sex for two weeks either,' says Diane. Luisa is not sure what type of who Diane hasn't had sex with. 'To be honest with all these vaginas around I'm not bothered about my own,' says Diane.

Luisa wishes this conversation was happening with someone other than

Diane. Anyone other than Diane.

'Jenny.' Luisa sees Jenny replace the phone receiver. 'About my shift tonight. It's just I've had something arranged with Justin for ages.'

'Are we still talking about that?' says Jenny, heading for the doorway.

'I have some hours owing.' Luisa moves to block her exit. 'I could use those. Take some of them for tomorrow night?'

'Highly irregular. I have to go check on Rebecca's woman, Luisa.'

'I didn't know I was working until now,' says Luisa.

'Well.' Jenny narrows her eyes. 'If you want, I'll have a look at the numbers again. No promises.'

'Please. Thank you. Thank you, Jenny.'

Erin sighs, crouches to retrieve the block of stickers, rips them open and hands a sheet to Luisa.

'And thank you, Erin,' says Luisa. 'Thank you so much.'

'It's a good while you've been away from that iffy trace in Sheila Kitzinger now, isn't it Luisa?' Jenny disappears out the doorway.

*

I can tell Justin he got the dates wrong again, thinks Luisa. *I was always working Wednesday night. You didn't check the calendar again. Your mother didn't believe in calendars, and you don't understand them.* She pictures her indignation, but her imaginary self turns away from Justin, embarrassed.

Luisa opens the door to Sheila Kitzinger. She looks at the time on her watch fob: 22:37. Too late to call Justin. Actually not too late. But don't want to talk to Justin, anyway, don't want to ask Justin. Don't want to have to ask.

She stands, motionless, inside the chamber enclosed by the curtain around the inside of the door, and realises she did not knock. She turns and raps on the inside of the door.

'It's just me, Luisa,' she calls.

'But you're already inside.' Eric stares at her through the gap in the curtain.

'Yes I am.'

'Oh. Weren't you going to fill that up?' Eric nods at the empty water jug in Luisa's hands.

'I was. I am.'

A buzzer sounds, this one whooping up and down, treble to bass: the emergency buzzer.

'I'm sorry, I have to go again,' says Luisa.

'To fetch the water?'

'For the buzzer. An emergency. The emergency buzzer?'

'But what about the monitor?'

Luisa runs into the room, glances at the monitor trace. The print out looks normal and healthy, the regular bouncing mountain skyline. The emergency buzzer whoops. Luisa runs back towards the door.

'Is it okay?' says Cheryl.

'It looks absolutely fine. I'm sorry, I'll be back very soon. There's an emergency,' she says again. 'With another woman. And,' she adds as she grabs the door handle, 'when I come back I'll bring some water. Lots of water.'

*

The red emergency light flashes above Joy Horner room, the first entrance to Luisa's left. She pushes open the door and runs in.

'We've got shoulders!' calls Sue, as if this is the next meal up in this busy cafe.

Luisa stops in the middle of the room. The blonde woman on the bed looks at her anxiously, a baby's grey head protruding from her vagina.

'Someone put out a four twos,' Gina swerves into the room, moves past on the right of Luisa and over to the bed.

Four twos. Are eight. Fast bleep call out. Should I do that? thinks Luisa.

'I'm on it.' Nikki appears on Luisa's left, then swings around and heads back out the door. 'Obstetric and neonatal, yes?'

'We need legs back,' Gina swings the bed out from the wall and squeezes herself into the gap, at the same time sliding her hands under the blonde woman's left thigh. Sue is already lifting the right leg.

'So who is it we have here? Excuse-y me.' Diane lays a hand on Luisa's shoulder, easing her aside.

'This is Julia,' says Sue, imitating Diane's sing-song tone. 'Can someone flatten the bed?'

Luisa has missed Erin entering the room, but there is Erin, flattening the bed. Luisa waves jazz hands at either side of her head.

'Someone take from me,' says Gina.

'So, Julia,' Diane takes Julia's right leg from Gina, and pushes down against the knee, forcing Julia's thigh into her chest. 'Your baby's just got a little bit stuck. Sorry luvvie, I know it can seem really scary. And sorry about all the moving and poking you around, but it's important that we do everything really fast. Gina here will get your lovely baby out before you know it.'

'Somebody get the resuscitaire,' calls Gina.

The resuscitaire. I can do that. That's me. Luisa turns and runs out of the room, has to stop running almost as soon as she's started. The resuscitaire stands against the wall to her left. She grabs the long handle on the front, pulls at the white unit in the direction of Joy Horner. The resuscitaire remains fixed against the wall.

'It's too heavy,' says Luisa.

Jenny grips the resuscitaire handle, forces Luisa to relinquish to her, and hooks her foot under the lever at the unit's base, flicking it upwards with her toes.

'Brakes, Luisa.' Jenny pulls the resuscitaire away from the wall, pushes it against the door of Joy Horner, opening it ahead of her. Luisa follows her in.

'Can we have some super-pubic pressure?' says Gina. 'Oh – don't worry. We're good. Here we go.'

From the back of the room Luisa sees the baby's purple shoulder emerge underneath Julia's raised leg. The entire body slithers out into Gina's waiting hands. Gina lifts the baby up and onto Julia's stomach.

'My god. She's so chubby, isn't she?' cries Julia.

'Towels, towels, towels,' says Gina. 'Who's got towels?'

Where are the towels? Luisa crouches and looks on the bottom of the trolley. No towels.

'Here's towels.' Erin unfurls and hands a towel to Gina over the baby girl lying on Julia.

Gina rubs vigorously at the towel-covered baby.

'Excuse me.' The paediatrician comes in and stands next to Luisa. 'So where are we at?'

'Um. The shoulder was a bit stuck,' says Luisa.

The baby's cry fills the room.

'Shoulder dystocia, called at 22:38, baby delivered 22:40,' says Gina. 'Good APGARS. You may stand down,' she tells the paediatrician.

Midwives file past Luisa, out of the room, and she follows on from Gina at the end of the line, the last duckling.

'That was good,' Luisa says to Gina. 'How you did that. That was – good.' Unlike me who did nothing.

'What was?' Gina continues down the corridor.

'The emergency. I didn't know – '

'Didn't know what?'

'Everything was done. There was nothing else to do.'

Gina halts, swings round, almost into Luisa. 'How is your woman, Luisa? Are you supporting her?'

'Fran swapped my shifts. I have to work tomorrow night.'

'And?'

'Diane told me you said they can't do that so soon before. That they won't do that to you.'

'Don't listen to Diane.'

'So they can do that?'

'I mean don't listen to Diane about anything. What's the problem with working tomorrow night?'

'I have a thing. A thing I have to do. With Justin.'

'Well, tell him you can't do it.'

'But we had it – arranged. Diane said they never change your shifts.'

Gina stops and faces Luisa. 'Is it him? Justin? Jealousy again?'

'Again?'

'I mean is he another one of those who can't handle that you're a woman with an empowering job?'

'Yes. No – '

'Always complaining that you're out of the house?'

'Not all the time.' Why is she defending Justin? Because he is not the kind of man Gina thinks he is. No man is the kind of man Gina thinks he is.

'If he doesn't understand what you do, that's his look out,' says Gina. 'If I had it my way we would have mandatory public workshops for midwifery orientation. But if he won't understand, that's up to him.' Gina puts a hand on each of Luisa's shoulders. 'You do realise that men kick up and feel threatened when a woman has an empowering job? After centuries women are slowly gaining a foothold in career parity and men cannot stand it. You want to nip it in the bud. We've all had to do it.'

Luisa nods weakly. 'Does your partner complain?'

'Not any more. I saw it coming a mile off, and gave him the red flag treatment.'

'And that worked? The red flag treatment?'

'Never heard from him again.'

Luisa wipes her eyes with the back of her hand.

'You're a protector, Luisa.' Luisa worries for a moment that Gina will take hold of her hand. Gina takes hold of her hand. 'You look after women through one of life's great experiences. Don't you know that? Go back and support your woman. How is your woman?'

'She wants everything,' says Luisa.

'Support your woman and everything else follows.' Gina releases Luisa's hand and casts her off, a figure skater pushing their partner away across the ice.

But I'm not like you, thinks Luisa.

*

Luisa knocks and enters Sheila Kitzinger, pushing through the curtain with two jugs of water.

'We – ' starts Eric.

'It's me,' Luisa says. 'I'm back now.' The words leap out of her, belligerent. Not belligerent. Firm.

'Where were you?' moans Cheryl from the floor.

'There was an emergency but now I'm back.' She stares at Eric, holds her whole body still, defiant. I was helping save a baby's life. Not really helping, but I was there. 'When that siren goes we all have to drop everything and go help.'

Eric's mouth opens, closes again, and he looks away. 'Is – everything okay now?' he says.

'Oh yes. All okay now. Emergencies actually happen quite often.' Luisa kneels and lays a hand on Cheryl's shoulder. 'They're only small emergencies. It's not like anybody's going to die. Well, it's an emergency so of course there's a small possibility. That's why we have to run. But it never happens. Hardly ever, anyway.'

'Sometimes babies die?' says Cheryl.

'What we need is to focus on the energy of this room,' says Luisa.

Luisa checks the foetal heart monitor: the trace now has regular downward U's at each contraction, the line recovering slowly back to the baseline with each one. Luisa's own heart dips in solidarity with the baby.

She unfolds the monitor print out, holds it so Cheryl can see. 'Here,' she says. 'See these dips?'

'Oh god,' says Eric.

'These are irregularities,' says Luisa. 'But we're going to see if we can deal with them right away. And we're going to hopefully make them better. Let's put you on your left side.'

'Is my baby in danger?' says Cheryl.

'If you're on your side, it means the heavy weight of your womb isn't pressing down on your vena cava.'

'The what?' says Eric.

'Vena cava. Not a medical term,' she adds. 'It's Latin.'

'But aren't a lot of medical terms in Latin?'

'More Greek these days,' says Luisa. 'Interestingly that's why no one knows how to spell diarrhoea.' That makes no sense, she thinks, but Eric appears to accept the explanation.

Cheryl lies on her side for the next contraction – as it ends the monitor beat slows from techno to waltz. Luisa shows her and Eric the new trace: the V is shallower, the heartbeat recovered more quickly.

'Is that better?' says Eric.

'Oh yes,' says Luisa. But will they revert to normal? 'Those dips are definitely shallower than before.'

'But it's not good?' cries Cheryl.

'It's better,' says Luisa. 'But we'll see if we can do even better still.' Once I've called the Reg. Though if I call the Reg they'll really get worried. Should I call the Reg?

'The good old vena cava,' says Eric, with tears in his eyes. 'Thank god you're here.'

'So. Any progress?' The Registrar is back in the room. 'What dilation are we at now?'

'We were about to do an examination.' Luisa looks over the Registrar's shoulder at the trace. The U's are the same size, no deeper, but no shallower either. 'We were just changing position. To help with the decels.'

'Mmm.' The Registrar continues to stare at the trace. 'Well, you carry on. I'll wait.'

'So, Cheryl,' says Luisa, 'as you probably know, we offer checks, you know, downstairs checks, every four hours.' She stares straight at Cheryl to avoid seeing the Registrar's expression. 'And we think it's probably a good idea, to check just about now.'

'Okay,' says Cheryl. 'Can you tell me the leg thing again?'

'Feet together, flop open your knees,' smiles Luisa over her shoulder as she washes her hands in the basin.

Luisa kneels on the floor next to Cheryl. Her gloved fingers round the curve of Cheryl's vagina and she feels along the upper wall of the vagina to find the cervix. 'Well, baby seems to have lots of hair!' she says, as always. She parts her fingers into a V, pushing against the edge of the cervix. Is that five centimetres? Please let it be five. Six? It feels like five. How can I be sure when I can't see my fingers?

'Well there's definitely some progress there,' she says. 'You were four centimetres, and now we're five. Maybe up to six.'

'Which is it?' says the Registrar. 'Five or six?'

'Five.' Luisa nods at Cheryl.

The Registrar looks again at the trace, then lets the graph paper fall against the stand. 'I think I'd like a check myself. Sorry to do it twice. But when it's an important decision, I think we need a second opinion.'

'When what's an important decision?' says Eric.

Luisa can see Eric bursting with supplementary questions but he waits whilst the Registrar performs a second vaginal exam: teacher marking her homework in front of the whole class.

'That's closer to four,' says the Registrar. Luisa looks to see if Cheryl has heard, but her face is screwed in pain as the next contraction begins. 'Not that far on, to be honest.'

Midwife and doctor stare into the distance as Cheryl's contraction finishes, Eric alternating between squeezing her hand and glancing up at Luisa's painful mannequin smile.

'We would normally recommend a hormone drip called syntocinon,' says the Registrar. 'When your contractions aren't moving things on to achieve a vaginal birth. But I'm a bit worried that your baby might not cope.'

'My baby can't cope with what?' wails Cheryl.

'We're keen on is a vaginal delivery,' says Luisa to the Registrar. 'Aren't we?'

'But didn't you get the examination wrong?' says Eric to Luisa. 'What does that mean?'

The Registrar looks down at the notes. Luisa has to answer. 'Well – '

'And now you're saying we should use this synthetic drug?' says Eric. 'We didn't want any drugs. Don't you remember in the birth plan we said we didn't want any drugs?'

'We don't have to use synto,' says Luisa. 'It's just that things haven't progressed as well as we might want. I mean you've made great progress. But not quite as much as we – but of course everyone is different. Each labour progresses at its own pace. But your pace is just a little bit slow. But I'm asking so we can get your perspective and your feelings on the idea of using synto.' You can't use that many buts in a sentence.

'Is it safe?' says Cheryl. 'Will my baby not be safe?'

'Of course there are risks. There's always some risk.' The Registrar's voice is low and even – no amount of bad behaviour is going to get to her.

It's alright for you, thinks Luisa, you're going to waltz off in a minute. They're my children – I have to live with them.

'That makes it not safe!' cries Eric.

'In any procedure there are always risks,' says the Registrar.

'My baby is not having any risks!' sobs Cheryl.

'Well if you feel strongly,' The Registrar looks to Luisa. 'If you decline synto, then we'd need to go ahead with a caesarean, anyway. There are of course also risks with a caesarean.'

'I want a caesarean!' cries Cheryl. 'I want this baby out now!'

Now you want a caesarean? What about your fucking ancestors and the tribal women? cries Luisa in her head.

'Then I'll set it in motion.' The Registrar heads for the door.

'Okay. Thank you. Okay.' Cheryl looks sad, but holds her composure as the Registrar leaves.

'I'm not sure I understand,' says Eric. 'I don't get it.' He is animated, moving around the room on Cheryl's behalf.

'Well we have known about baby's little dips, haven't we?' says Luisa. 'We've known for some time.'

'But why?' Cheryl snorts in, then floods out tears. 'I thought if we did everything you said I wouldn't need a caesarean?'

'Well I didn't say for sure. This was always a possibility. Because of the little dips.' And also because you wouldn't let me say the word caesarean.

Jenny knocks and comes straight in. 'Luisa,' she says. 'If we're going for caesarean, you need to get started with the theatre pathway.' She pushes a booklet into Luisa's hands and leaves without looking at Cheryl or Eric. A proscribed schedule for the next few minutes shunts into Luisa's brain: gown, theatre pathway questions, check when theatre ready.

'The doctor is always looking to the whole, holistic picture.' Luisa looks down at the theatre pathway booklet, at all the little boxes to be filled out. She crouches next to Cheryl. 'Now Cheryl, I just need you to answer a few questions.'

'Can't we do this later?' cries Eric. 'We need a bit of a minute to regroup. I mean, who tears open the chrysalis and allows the butterflies to escape?'

'It has to be done now, I'm afraid. When did you last eat and drink?' Luisa focuses in on Cheryl, on her crumpled face.

'It's not like I'm *hungry*,' wails Cheryl, and looks to Eric, as if at least he might say something sensible.

'There's a few checks we must do. We just need to know if your stomach is full.' Luisa wants to hug her, a human hug, but there is no time. Instead she flicks through the notes booklet to find labels printed with Cheryl's name, peels off and attaches one to the theatre pathway booklet. In the booklet's boxes she writes Cheryl's name, her own name, the Registrar's name. The name of the consultant-in-charge. Who is that?

'It would have been useful if we had understood what those things on the trace meant.' Eric flaps his outstretched palms up and down, his camera almost swinging into Luisa's face. 'As we were going along.'

Luisa cannot remember the name of the consultant-in-charge. But she does know that it makes no difference. She writes Mr Stone, in a scrawl, in a way that could easily be confused for someone else.

'Well we did know about the little dips,' says Luisa softly, back to air hostess. She hears her tone of authoritative finality, suggesting further questions and alternative choices are now pointless. 'I'm sorry.' She waits for three, four, five seconds. 'What about eating and drinking, then?' Luisa scribbles in more boxes to avoid looking at Cheryl.

She works through the questions: caps and crowns? any loose jewellery? any prosthetics? Cheryl answers in a monotone, and Luisa cannot look up as she answers, since she needs to flick through the notes to find Cheryl's stats: due date; gestation; risk factors. To her relief Cheryl becomes occupied by her next contraction, and Luisa leaves her with Eric whilst she frantically scribbles.

'But weren't we doing really well before?' Eric stands with Luisa as the contraction finishes. 'I thought we were doing really well?'

'You were doing really well. Emotionally you were, you were both doing great.'

'And now we're not even doing that,' says Eric, and looks so sad that Luisa wants to hug him as well.

'Luisa.' Jenny appears behind her again. 'About tonight. I've checked, and it does seem that you have a few hours owing.'

Luisa turns to face her. 'I don't have to work tonight?' She looks back at Eric, then back to Jenny.

'Steady there,' says Jenny. 'You have four hours owing and our numbers aren't completely decimated for once. Which means if you want you can start at midnight.'

'Midnight? That's, umm.'

'It's up to you. You can do the whole shift if you like.'

'Midnight sounds great. Thank you. Thank you, Jenny.'

'So – if you don't mind,' says Eric behind her. 'Can you tell us what happens now?'

Erin knocks and comes straight into the room, and hands Eric a square of blue cotton scrubs. 'If you can just put those on,' says Luisa. 'For theatre.' She almost makes the traditional reference to looking like George Clooney, but Eric's face warns against it.

The Operation Department Practitioner, already in scrubs, knocks and comes straight in. 'Hello, Cheryl,' he sings, and takes the checklist from Luisa. 'When did you last eat and drink? Do you have any caps or crowns?'

'Didn't I answer all this?' wails Cheryl.

'They have to check,' says Luisa. 'It's important to check, to check what I did. If you can just answer the ODP's questions, Cheryl.'

'No, then,' sobs Cheryl. 'I've failed. Failed. What did we do wrong?'

'Nothing. You did nothing wrong,' says Luisa. 'Sometimes this is just how it happens.' God might know, thinks Luisa, but there is no god. Even the tall consultant, even he doesn't know.

Eric emerges from the bathroom, kneels to hug Cheryl. The scrub trousers end halfway down his calves, the cotton so thin that the words Calvin Klein are visible at his waist.

'Are *you* okay?' Cheryl grabs Eric's hand.

'I'll be fine so long as I don't have to sit down,' says Eric.

'Are you good to walk to theatre, Cheryl?' says the ODP, as to his deaf grandmother. He hooks a hand inside her elbow and helps her to her feet. Cheryl steps obediently to the door, Eric falling in behind.

'Caesareans are very common nowadays,' says Luisa. But Cheryl and Eric are gone.

It is past three o'clock by the time Luisa has assisted at Cheryl's caesarean and processed her upstairs to the postnatal ward. That's what I did, she thinks, processed her, shunted her through and spat her out the other end.

For the next few hours Jenny has Luisa cover breaks, and she drags her body around the ward, until the faint morning light in the large corridor window breathes new energy into her: a new dawn. It's a new day. It's the same life and I'm not feeling good.

At 07:15 she pulls out her phone and switches it on. It beeps immediately with a text from Justin.

Checking in for switch over time.

Luisa powers down the corridor as the long blast of a call buzzer sounds, and slips into the changing room. Didn't hear the buzzer, she thinks, as she taps Justin's picture on her phone. From the changing room toilet comes the sound of someone straining.

'It's me,' she says. 'What are you checking?'

'Only when you'll be back. Me, the girls, we're up.'

'I'll be back when I'm always back.'

'Though you remembered about the car? I can't drive, so I'm walking to the station?'

'Sure, the car.' She has forgotten about the car. She knows he's not trying to make her feel guilty, but mentioning the car has done so anyway, and resentment balloons in her again.

From the toilet comes the sound of more straining. 'Sorry! Sorry, whoever that is out there,' calls Diane. 'I'm always like this on nights. It's all those bloody cakes lying around.'

'Poor you,' calls Luisa, to demonstrate her lack of embarrassment.

'Thanks,' says Justin. 'Thanks, sweetie.'

'Not you. There's a woman here, in the toilet.'

'You're with a woman in the toilet?'

'Not in the toilet. There's a woman, in the cubicle.'

'So as I'm needing to walk to the station.' Justin chirps, like a relative cracking jokes at a funeral. 'I just wanted to check you're going to be home a bit earlier. On time.'

'I'm going to try. I have to go. So that I can leave on time.'

'I need to leave dead on eight twenty-five.'

Luisa listens to the new noises from the toilet cubicle, like Diane is tapping out morse with her feet.

'You finish at eight, yes?' says Justin.

'I can't guarantee it, Justin.'

'You know, my train. I can't be any later because I'm leaving early to be back for tonight. For date night?'

'Is that what we're calling it? Date night?'

'Isn't date night that Fifty Shades of Grey thing?' calls Diane.

'You remembered?' says Justin.

'I remember,' says Luisa. 'I'm looking forward to it. I have to go.' Home, sleep, food, sex, make sure Justin is asleep, back to the hospital: she pictures the timeline of the day ahead. It looks almost manageable, on paper. 'I'll text you if I'm going to be late.'

Luisa steps out of the changing room, eyes on the dark screen of her phone.

'Can you get to triage, Luisa.' Jenny is moving so fast she only just pulls up without a collision. Luisa smells a mintiness on her breath. 'Right now please. There's a multip in there. Seven centimetres and she's getting a bit grunty. You can put her in Joy Gardner.'

Luisa looks at her watch: 07.35. I can't do a handover baby, she pleads, but only silently, to herself.

'Sorry for the handover baby,' says Jenny, and Luisa has never heard anyone make the word sound so empty of apology.

'I do have to leave on time today,' says Luisa.

'Don't we all? Your baby, your paperwork, Luisa. You know that.' Jenny walks away, a hand in the air. 'Everyone loves a handover baby!'

'Hulloo, Kayleigh,' says Luisa as she enters triage. 'I'm Luisa. I'll be looking after you now.'

On the bed a young woman on all fours gives no sign she has heard, and instead focuses an intense gaze at the wall.

'So I'm going to feel your stomach.' Luisa puts a hand on Kayleigh's belly: the uterus muscle is rock solid.

'It's her third,' says a middle-aged woman in the chair who looks so similar to Kayleigh, even down to the same highlights in her hair, that she cannot be anyone except her mother. 'Her second was very fast. Can you get her to a room, please? The other nurse said she was seven centimetres, and it's going to be quite soon.'

'Well, sometimes a third baby can surprise you.' Air-hostess tone, but firm, in a way that invites no comeback. Luisa glances at Kayleigh's mother, trying to assess how pliable she might be. 'And babies born slower do of course stretch your perineum more slowly.'

'Well, I think this one has been quite fast,' says Kayleigh's mother.

'Well, you never know with babies.' You never know anything. Babies, boyfriends, careers – everything's unknown. 'We've got a room ready for you. Shall I find a wheelchair to get you there?' she asks Kayleigh. 'Then you can have a sit down.' And it'll take me a few minutes to find one.

'Don't need one.' Kayleigh climbs off the bed with remarkable agility and grabs Luisa's arm. 'Walk me.'

Luisa guides Kayleigh along the corridor, pausing for each of her contractions, which Kayleigh conducts in a businesslike manner, so calm that her mother offers no words of encouragement or sympathy. Luisa can see the day-shift midwives arriving and pulls up her watch fob: 7.42. Less than twenty minutes to go. This birth does not have to happen in the next twenty minutes. You never really know with births.

Outside Joy Gardner room Kayleigh stops again, and emits a cry, the last gasp of a dying soldier in a pointless war.

'I think I need to push,' says Kayleigh, and pulls herself into the room.

'Well, you were only seven centimetres before.' Luisa steers her inside the curtain to the bed, her voice light and carefree. 'I would hold off pushing until we know for sure that you're fully dilated.' A wash of shame brings her out in goose-pimples.

'She could be fully dilated,' says the mother, dropping two bags by the bed. 'Can't you check?'

'Well we generally only do vaginal examinations every four hours,' says Luisa. The mother's expression demonstrates that she has already lost any respect she might have had for Luisa. Which as she took over Kayleigh's care less than five minutes ago must be some kind of record. And which is fair enough, because right now I am a pretty shit midwife.

Kayleigh lies on her side on the bed. 'I'm going to push now,' she cries.

'You push when you need to, love,' her mother grabs Kayleigh's hand.

'Okay. Maybe we should get to pushing,' says Luisa.

There is a knock at the door. 'Excuse me one moment,' says Luisa and retreats out of the curtain. 'You just do what you feel you need to, Kayleigh.'

Annie is at the door, and Luisa feels slightly faint at the idea that in the intervening hours Annie has been home and enjoyed a whole night's sleep. Hidden behind Annie is a nervous student midwife.

'Nadine here needs to get her birth numbers up,' says Annie.

'Oh. Great. Lovely. Yes, we're almost there!' Luisa grabs Nadine by the arm, pulls her into the room and hands her some surgical gloves. 'Here we go. This is Kayleigh. Low risk. Para two. Two SVDs. Rhesus pos. Spontaneous onset. Seven centimetres at 7.15.'

'It's coming!' cries Kayleigh from the other side of the curtain.

'Is anyone going to actually deliver this baby?' says the mother.

'Yes, me!' says Nadine. Annie and Nadine disappear behind the curtain.

That was my best handover ever, thinks Luisa. Brief, no extraneous information. Perhaps I work well under pressure.

She checks the time again: 07.55. I can go. I can leave!

Luisa runs to the changing room, pulls off her scrubs top as she goes. For once her clothes are on the hook where she left them. She dumps the scrubs in the laundry basket. Can I leave before eight o'clock? I've done everything, haven't I? There's nothing Jenny can say.

She peers out the changing room door, and with no one in sight, runs to the delivery room double doors, swipes her card and there's the lift, the lift door is open, waiting. And she's in, going down. Safe.

Luisa exits the lift and strides out into the multi-storey car park, moves towards daylight, and the sun rejuvenates her, her body light, nothing weighing on her. Her bag is not weighing on her. She isn't carrying her bag. My bag is in the locker. My purse, phone. My keys.

Five minutes, it'll take me five minutes, she thinks as she runs back to the lifts. She looks up at the illuminated numbers above the left hand lift, and then above the right, as they slowly descend. The left hand lift stops on 6. Stops and waits. The right hand stops on 9.

This isn't fair, thinks Luisa. Not fair.

WEDNESDAY DAY: OFF DUTY

At 08.32 Luisa approaches the junction of Arcadia Close and the main road at a run. She can see a figure standing on the corner and slows her pace to a walk.

'I got here as soon as I could,' she calls when within shouting distance.

Justin has a plastic bag in one hand and binoculars in the other.

'It's okay. I'll still just about make it,' says Justin.

'What about the girls?'

Justin points back down the close. He hands Luisa the binoculars. 'See? In the front garden. They're happy. I have a clear line of sight.'

She puts the binoculars to her eyes, and sees Elsie and Eleanor seated cross-legged, eating from bowls, Elsie with her fingers. Luisa waves to them, to assure them that everything is fine. And it is all fine: they're safe, they're eating. The girls wave back.

'I need to go.' He kisses her, avoiding contact with any part of her body. 'Mum should be here any minute. She rang to say she was dropping off some scaffold boards. I'll get some wine for later, yes?'

'Wine?' The idea of wine makes her nauseous.

'For our night in?'

'Oh yes. Yes, get some wine.' But I can't drink wine, not if I have to work. 'Not too much, for me. Don't get too much.'

'Think the minimum is one bottle,' says Justin.

'Sure. A small bottle.' A few sips. A few sips will be okay.

Justin pushes the plastic bag into her arms. 'Can you take this back? My jogging bottoms.' He starts up the main road. 'I didn't know if I might need them. I wasn't sure.'

'I was only going to text if I was late,' Luisa calls after him, but he does not hear.

'Have you been out?' asks Elsie as Luisa ushers the girls off the front lawn, towards the side door of the house. 'Have you been to the pub?'

'I don't go to the pub in the mornings,' says Luisa. I never go to the pub. 'I've been at work, remember?' Luisa picks up a small child's bike with stabilizers, lying on its side in the drive.

'Can I take my bike to grandma's?' says Elsie in the doorway as Luisa wheels it past.

'It's not your bike any more, lovely girl. It's way too small.'

'Still my bike. And I've been riding it, anyway.'

'I mean grandma won't be able to take too many of your things with her.'

'I'll leave my clothes here. I don't need any clothes.'

Elsie takes the bike from her, and pedals it in a continuous circle around the driveway, singing to herself, her knees hitting her arms.

'Come inside, Elsie.'

'If I can't take it to grandma's I want to ride it now.'

Luisa leans against the front door frame, then goes inside. Her body is heavy, getting ready for shutdown, a cold, tingly sensation, like the onset of flu.

'How long are we staying with Grandma India?' says Eleanor from the hall. She takes a pyjama top from the bag.

'Just one night.' Luisa sees that alongside two overnight bags Justin has also stacked a box of toys and games and two pillows.

'I don't like these pyjamas.'

'Change them if you like.'

Eleanor drops the top on the bag and races upstairs. Since Justin has everything ready, there is nothing for her to do but stay awake and wait for Bea.

'Daddy wouldn't let me choose,' says Eleanor, coming back down with an armful of clothes.

They sit on the floor, mother and daughter, empty Eleanor's bag and arrange two piles of clothes, Eleanor's yes and no pile. It is almost enjoyable. Luisa leans back against the hallway wall.

'Melody won't let me be friends with her,' says Eleanor, picking up a toy dog.

'You give Melody a nice squeeze and a cuddle and I'm sure she'll be your friend.'

'She punches me when I cuddle her.' Eleanor is on the verge of tears.

'Melody punches you?' says Luisa, realising that Melody is a girl and not the toy dog.

'Not all day. She's nice sometimes. She has a phone.'

'You don't want to be friends with someone who punches you, do you?'

'I do!' cries Eleanor.

'You don't need to cuddle people to be friends.' An image of Justin, his back receding as he runs to the station, pops into her head. She strokes Eleanor's hair.

'What then?'

She remembers casting smiles at Tina in the playground. Tina was one of the cool kids, Luisa knew about wanting to hang out with the cool kids. She wondered if Tina would punch her.

'You just play nearby, Ellie. Play with some other people, and maybe your games will mix together. If you and Melody start playing together, then you'll become friends.'

'But how do we start playing together?'

'I think we've almost sorted everything. Haven't we done well?' says Luisa.

'I'm changing my toys as well,' says Elsie. Luisa has not noticed her coming back into the house. Did she fall asleep? Both girls race up the stairs, Elsie pushing Eleanor into the wall to get in front. Luisa wants to say something, but instead goes to sit at the kitchen table. She closes her eyes, holding the weight of her head on her hand, stands and goes to the fridge where she finds the bowl of fruit and muesli Justin has prepared for her.

Luisa wakes lying on the kitchen table next to an empty bowl, woken by the sound of a cry. She licks a smear of strawberry from the back of her hand.

'Elsie?' she calls.

'Helloo-oo,' comes the cry again, 'may I cross the threshold?' Luisa lifts herself from the table to see Justin's mother in the open kitchen door. Bea wears a white shawl imprinted with a gold Aztec pattern and has a large plastic sunflower fixed in her pinned-back hair.

'Lovely to see you.' Luisa jumps to her feet, kisses Bea on the cheek. 'I was just – '

'You carry on, dear. Rest your head again if you need to. I'll scoop them up and get out of your hair. Eleanor! Elsie! Grandma's here again.'

'Thanks so much for this. It's with it being half-term, you know,' says Luisa. 'Working shifts. Sometimes it gets a bit complicated.'

'You mustn't apologise, dear. You're a midwife.'

'Yes. I am.'

'That must be so rewarding.'

'It is.'

'I'm lucky I can do my own work from home, I suppose.' Bea picks up a saucepan from the drying rack and puts it in a cupboard.

'You have to work whilst the girls are with you?'

'Oh don't worry. I still be able to keep an eye on them. I won't let them run out all over town if that's what you're thinking. My clients will help if anything. Children can be very therapeutic.'

'Well – ' says Luisa.

'Hello, lovelies!' Bea spots Elsie and Eleanor coming down the stairs, struggling with a heavy object between them.

'Can you help, grandma?' says Elsie.

Bea makes her way up the stairs and Luisa sees that the floor of the hallway is now almost invisible, covered with duvets, a doll's house, a pool of Lego pieces and an additional pile of clothes, some of which Luisa recognises as her own. With Bea's help the twins bump the vacuum cleaner down the last few stairs, one at a time.

'It's lucky I brought my big new car, eh,' laughs Bea to the girls.

'I'm sure grandma has her own hoover,' says Luisa.

'I don't as a matter of fact,' puffs Bea, supporting the hoover's weight.

'It was Ellie's idea,' says Elsie.

'That's a massive lie,' says Eleanor, and lets go of the handle. The hoover tumbles down into Bea's arms.

'Woah!' Bea throws her hands wide. The hoover crashes past her and over onto a duvet.

'You don't really need a hoover, do you?' Luisa struggles to lift the hoover back to an upright position.

'Not today,' says Bea. 'Besides you might need it yourself. To clear up after your night in.'

Eleanor looks up. 'What are you and daddy doing?'

'You have yourselves a lovely night.' Bea steps in close to Luisa, opens her eyes so far Luisa can see all around her pupils.

'We will,' says Luisa, though she has no idea what kind of mess Bea might mean, the kind that might require a hoover.

'I have throws on my sofas,' says Bea. 'That way I can just throw them in the wash. Hence the name.'

Luisa cannot continue with this conversation, but no one seems to mind as she breaks off to repack the girls' bags. She discards most of the toys, and once they are lighter carries them through the kitchen to the back door.

'Mum, have you seen grandma's car?' Eleanor crashes back through the doorway and pulls at Luisa's hand.

A red people-carrier is parked in the driveway, backed in so it almost touches Elsie's old bike.

'You bought it – to take the girls?' asks Luisa.

'No! That would be a bit wasteful, wouldn't it? I can't abide waste. The bank gave me the money when I told them it was for work.' Bea's gleeful tone suggests she does not realise the bank will want this money back at some point.

'For life-coaching?' says Luisa.

'For day-trips out.'

'I didn't realise that was part of life-coaching.'

'I do all sorts. I believe in a holistic approach.'

They load the luggage into the spacious boot, next to two fishing rods. Elsie watches from inside the car, bouncing up and down on the back seat.

'Elsie,' says Luisa.

'I won't let her travel like that,' says Bea.

'Are you taking them fishing?'

'No!' Bea laughs. 'Who in their right mind would take two six-year-olds fishing?'

Luisa straps the girls into their booster seats and kisses them goodbye.

'What if I throw up?' whispers Eleanor.

Then they are gone, onto the road and out of the cul-de-sac. The driveway is empty, the bike gone with them.

Luisa's heart sinks, because she has never found that one person who will truly love her, because she is alone and the time for birthing children has passed, has slipped by without notice in the intervening years. Then she remembers: no, she lives with Justin, she has a boyfriend, a boyfriend of many years. She never thought she'd have a boyfriend! A boyfriend with whom she shares this bed. A boyfriend she may one day live with, people will look at her and her boyfriend together and say, they knew how to do it, they figured it out. She pictures the twins as babies, possibly conceived in this same bed, the bed she is lying in now, maybe in these sheets wrapped around her legs. That's why she can't move them. And why she can't breathe. She remembers, she is a midwife. She has a boyfriend, but one she needs to deceive somehow so she can be a midwife again at midnight. She looks over at the clock: she has been asleep for seventeen minutes.

The room is bright, too light because she has not drawn the blackout blinds. She refuses to use them because they were Justin's suggestion, because he installed them even though she said she didn't need them, installed them at speed and in a rage because, he said, she obviously didn't have the time. Plus the cord catches every time someone pulls the blind. And anyway, she works night shifts, she can sleep at any time of the day.

She turns in the bed sheet, which is covered in what she thinks of as grease, though not grease, not as in cooking. More the many days build up of body sweat, caught in the sheet folds, grease that somehow causes the material to wrap itself tighter than if this was a clean, white sheet.

These are not helpful thoughts – there are no mindfulness techniques devoted to contemplation of the cleanliness of laundry. She needs more sleep to get through her night with Justin – not get through, to enjoy. Tonight is for enjoyment, not endurance. But she has to get through the evening to get to work, she needs a plan, needs a plan that she can lock down in her head so that she can stop thinking about the plan, can stop thinking about the plan and go back to sleep. Justin must be asleep by eleven. Don't plan now. First step in the plan, more sleep.

A few more hours sleep is possible because the girls are not here. Where are the girls? The girls are at Bea's. Sleep, go out to buy food to eat with Justin.

Food, wine, sex. Is she even cooking? She cannot remember what they agreed on the phone. Why does she have to cook? We need to be naked by nine.

Luisa sits up in bed and turns the clock face down on the bedside table. She picks up her book from the floor, and reads, but after three pages realises she's read this page before and puts the book down. Better off with music for sleeping, I can lie down. Or the best soporific of all: Melvyn Bragg and In Our Time. This book is too heavy. Heavy boring is good, good for sleep, but heavy weight means she has to balance the book on upright knees. Who goes to sleep with their knees up? Only prisoners in Guantanamo Bay. Are there prisoners in Guantanamo any more? Don't want to think about Guantanamo. She ought to think more about Guantanamo, sometimes.

She throws the book to the floor, pulls her phone from the bedside table, and in clicking it out of sleep the screen presents her with a clear declaration of the time: 11.37. She taps the YouTube icon. She'll watch Sergei. Sergei counts as music.

Luisa props the phone against a pillow on the far side of the bed, lies on her side with the duvet tucked to her neck. She'll drift off to Sergei. Sergei kneels on the floor of a wood-frame building, sunlight pouring in through windows open to the trees outside, lies on his arched back, tattooed and dressed only in ripped skin-coloured tights. And hairless, she notices for the first time. Sergei is writhing, twisting, flying. How can bodies do these things? Bulge in such a way. What young man who looks like that does ballet? Is it only gay men?

In her mind's eye it is not her and Sergei – not her as Luisa. When she imagines the thighs, his thighs standing above, it is never her. It isn't real, because the picture never quite forms a solid image, an image close enough to a real human form. Thighs then bum then chest: more a sequence of stills than moving film. What about his face? Sergei's face? She feels bad for not listing his face. Though he'll never know. Even if she meets him, one day, she doesn't have to say. She watches the video again from the beginning, pauses on a mid-air leap. Her imagination is defective, perhaps. Or she is prudish, too loyal: her mind does not allow the full-colour, properly edited pornographic version. Not edited, jump cuts. One long, smooth shot. She closes her eyes. Sergei's hands are pulling himself across the floor. Luisa's hands are pulling against her own body.

Luisa throws off the duvet to feel the breeze of the morning on her, knocking the phone to the floor. The clunk of a household item brings her to full daytime mode: she is a mother to two girls, not a horny teenager slavering over eastern European ballet videos. What if she is a forty-three-old-woman slavering over the beauty of the male body, what the hell's wrong with that? What's wrong is that she's doing this at eleven in the morning when she has been working all night and needs to sleep.

*

She wakes, her back and legs warm from where she has wrapped herself in a woollen jumper whilst asleep. Her buttocks are cold. She pulls the duvet back on top of her and lies for an indeterminate time staring at the sheet with one eye, the other pressed into a pillow. She reaches for her phone from the floor: 15.19. There are eight answerphone messages from Bea.

Luisa stands at the window and pulls back the curtains, but with too much force. The plastic curtain rail clicks and bends away from the wall – she catches the end to prevent the weight from pulling the whole rail down. It's okay, nothing is broken – she can see the connector has come unclipped. She pulls a nearby chair towards her, on which the cat is sleeping. The cat raises her head and settles back into her curl. Luisa pushes up onto the edge of the seat not occupied by the cat, her foot slips to the floor and she hangs on to the rail to steady herself, pulling another of the connectors away from the wall. The cat is awake and angry. Is my nakedness visible through the blinds from the street? It is immaterial, the day cannot continue until I let go of this curtain rail. The cat jumps off the chair to the bed. There. Now I can stand on the chair. She climbs up and pushes the rail connectors into position on the wall. Do you turn the clips through ninety degrees or one hundred and eighty? She peers underneath to identify the position of other clips, but in doing so twists the rail forwards, now all the connectors on one side have come free and it requires one whole arm to hold the weight of an unsupported curtain. She pushes the rail back against the wall. The last connector comes loose, the rail tears out of Luisa's hands and crashes to the floor. The cat runs from the room.

Downstairs in her dressing gown Luisa presses Bea's number on her phone.

'Hello, dear. I hope I didn't wake you,' says Bea.

'No, no. I was already awake. Anyway I called you.'

'But I called earlier – it kept going to answerphone.'

'I turn it off when I'm sleeping. After I've done a night shift.'

'I thought there was something wrong – that you were dead or something. Though I didn't say as much to the girls.'

'How are they? Are you having fun?' Luisa's tiredness makes Bea's voice muffled and clear again in waves.

'The girls just wanted to say hello.'

'Are they okay?'

'Oh yes. Elsie! Ellie! Mummy's on the phone.'

'They don't – '

'Hi Mum.' Eleanor is there too quickly.

'Have you been okay?'

'We've been playing football.'

'I didn't know grandma liked football.'

'With Ian. Not really football, we're not kicking. Throwing a football. You catch and say Daisy Wilson.'

'Daisy Wilson?'

'Something you don't like. Each time you catch.'

'Who's Ian?'

'Elsie!' calls Eleanor. The phone clatters on a surface.

'Elsie?'

'Mum. I don't like pasta.'

'You do like pasta.'

'Not now I don't. I said pasta in the game. I can't eat pasta. All the rest of my life.'

'It's a game, sweetie. You like pasta. Who's Ian?'

'Ian doesn't like his dad. And anchovies. What are anchovies? Helen doesn't like sex.'

'Can I talk to grandma?'

There is no reply. Luisa wonders if she should hang up.

'You go back to sleep now, dear,' says Bea, as though she has been listening on another line all along, like the Stasi. 'I won't ring this number again. I know that now. How are you feeling? You must get awfully tired.'

'You can always ring. If you need to ring, ring,' says Luisa. 'The girls said they've been playing football with your friends?'

'My morning clients. I don't call them friends, though of course we're better friends than most friends. But friends damages the therapist relationship. Not that I'm allowed to use the word therapist. *Life coach*.' Luisa can see the pronounced tongue movements. 'I'm learning all sorts from the girls in Face Your Demons.'

'Maybe they're a bit young for coaching?'

'Just talking, really. You go back to sleep. Don't you worry about them. I've made beds in the attic already.'

Luisa runs through the list of reminders for the girls in her head. But Bea has gone. What is that buzzing noise?

The buzzing must be in the kitchen, but in the kitchen there is no buzzing, only the cat, asleep on the bread maker.

'How come you can sleep, you bastard?' she says.

The cat lifts its head, the movement shifting her body weight enough that she slides off the bread maker into a row of empty wine bottles lined on the window ledge, flailing her legs to get some purchase as the bottles twist and roll around her with a clatter that hurts Luisa's ears.

She picks up the cat and cuddles her to her chest. The cat jumps from her arms and disappears upstairs.

Luisa follows, for now it is clear the buzzing is coming from upstairs, and in the bedroom she discovers the source, slaps the buzzing alarm clock. She picks it up, trying to understand, and sees the time: 15.30. An alarm to wake her from her morning sleep.

She climbs into bed with the clock cuddled against her, crushes the alarm button, eyes tight, and faces away from the sunlight streaming through the bare windows. The knowledge that the day has now moved into the afternoon seeps through her thoughts, a spreading flow of post-placenta blood. Afternoon is time to get up.

The doorbell rings.

'Hey babe. Sorry to bother you, I'm not going to be long, really,' says Tina, when Luisa opens the door. 'Think I left my keys, my car keys, here last night. Have you seen them?'

'Of course!' Luisa expunges any tiredness from her voice. 'Come in.'

'No, no. Not going to bother you.'

'It's not a bother. I'll just get them. Come in!' Luisa heads inside to the kitchen, but Tina stays on the doorstep.

Luisa looks around the kitchen surfaces for keys but they are clear, tidy.

'Found the bloody car,' calls Tina from the door. 'Then found I couldn't get into it. Idiot that I am.' Luisa opens the drawer that contains the square silver box, the key box, and there she sees an unfamiliar set of keys. Justin put them there.

'I'll leave you to get on, then,' says Tina, taking the keys from her at the front door. 'Imagine it's pretty full on, yeah, half-term. What with twins and everything?' Tina moves back off the doorstep.

'Oh the girls aren't here,' says Luisa. 'They're away with Justin's mum.'

'Oh. Great!' Tina is past her, and through into the kitchen. 'In that case I will come in.'

'Not with Isobel today?' Luisa catches up with her in the kitchen. Tina sits at the table – she fills the house, as though she lives there rather than Luisa.

'Oh no. Holiday club. She loves it. Loves the structure.' Tina makes a face. 'I like this.' She strokes the sleeve of Luisa's dressing gown. 'Kids away and being all naked round the house in the afternoon.'

'Maybe I'm not naked.' Luisa's attempt to cover her embarrassment makes *naked* sound sarcastic, and thus somewhat flirty.

'Well what are you wearing under there?' Tina reaches for the join of the dressing gown at Luisa's cleavage and pulls it to one side, exposing a half-breast. There is no reaction that occurs to Luisa.

'Cup of tea?' she says.

'Sure,' says Tina, and folds the dressing gown back in place. The whole exchange leaves Luisa strangely satisfied, pleased that Tina has mistaken confusion and exhaustion for detached loucheness.

'But haven't you just worked all night?' says Tina. 'Is that why you're in this?'

'Finished at eight,' says Luisa. 'I've had a sleep.' Haven't I?

'Must be nice sometimes, isn't it? To have the excuse? Wandering round, not getting dressed, watching crap TV. Eating jelly.'

'I kind of like it. Not being nine to five. You know.' Luisa fills the kettle.

'So, are you still up for it?' says Tina.

'For?'

'Going out. Could have sworn you mentioned going out yesterday? I thought we could do a drink tonight. Not a school night, after all.' Tina swipes her phone.

'Oh. Oh I'd love to. But – '

'You're working.' Tina looks up.

'No. Not really. But I've promised that Justin and I, that we'd hang out together. Tonight. Going to make a night of it.'

'Where to?'

'Just a home one. At home.'

'Oh. Sex and drugs night?'

'Something like that.' Luisa twists her shoulders. Wouldn't you like to know? her shoulders say to Tina. But Tina already knows, doesn't she?

'Boris likes to work at night,' says Tina. 'Drives me crazy. Then wants sex all time in the day. I'm not having it. Don't you think?'

'Is that what happens?' Why can't Justin want sex in the day? Maybe he does. Maybe it's our geography that's wrong. 'When men get older they want sex in the day?'

'Not if I can help it,' says Tina.

'I've sort of been wanting sex in the day,' says Luisa.

'Bully for you.'

'Is that weird?'

'Hardly. The forties thing? We've all been there.'

Tina is the person she can talk to. Tina is her friend, her new friend.

'I mean I seem to be thinking about it all the time,' says Luisa. 'Don't you find? And it makes it so I can't really sleep. I haven't really slept today to be honest. I've got a bit obsessed by ballet. Something about ballet really moves me. Have you seen how high they can jump?'

'Not really a ballet person,' says Tina.

'Nor am I. Not ballet.'

'You're got to consider all your options,' says Tina. 'Sign yourself up on Tinder if that's the way you want to go. Watch the twenty-nine-year-olds roll in.'

'Twenty-nine?'

'According to my friend Julia.'

'I have a nephew who's twenty-nine.'

'Well, then.'

But I'm forty-three, thinks Luisa. 'Let's go out some other time,' she says. 'I do really want to go out some other time.'

'They've got you working Friday, haven't they?' Tina sounds annoyed.

'Nope. I changed it. I'm not working Friday now.'

'Then let's do drinks. On Friday.'

The idea of going out reminds her how tired she is. The doorbell rings.

'Somebody's popular,' says Tina.

'Oh. Oh, I'm so sorry,' says Helena on the doorstep. Her twins stare up at Luisa. 'I should go. I didn't realise you were working. I've woken you, I've woken you.'

'It's alright,' says Luisa. 'I've been up for a while.' She can hear Tina making a noise with keys in the kitchen.

'So how many lovely babies did you have last night?'

'Oh. None. None last night.' She could say more but she doesn't want to give Helena a reason to stay. Tina and Helena shouldn't exist in the same room. 'I'm just having a lazy day.'

'Well can I take Elsie and Eleanor out for you? I could take them to the park.' Helena looks down at her own children. William has her hand in Helena's pocket. 'For a while. An hour.'

'It's okay. Thanks. They're at Bea's. Justin's mother's.'

'Oh I see! I see. Well that's nice. That they get some grandmother time.'

Luisa sees that Helena is waiting to be invited in. She does not want to invite her in.

'Hi-i,' says Tina.

'Hello. I'm Helena.' Helena holds out a hand. Tina frowns, but shakes.

'This is Tina,' says Luisa, when she sees that Tina will not tell Helena her name.

'Hi Tina,' says Helena. 'Say hello to Tina, loves. This is Rowan. And William.' She rests a hand on the back of each of her children.

'I was going, anyway,' says Tina. 'Just need to grab my bag.'

'Don't go,' says Luisa.

Tina disappears back to the kitchen. 'I should go,' whispers Helena. 'I'll come back. I didn't realise you'd have people round.'

'Let me know about Friday, eh?' Tina steps out past Helena. She gives a little wiggle of her hips, her arms in the air, turns back to hug Luisa and kiss her on the cheek. 'Nice to meet you,' she waves at Helena, travelling too fast down the drive to possibly mean it.

'See you Friday!' calls Luisa.

Helena has a restraining hand on each child, unsure whether to move forward or back.

'Tina's an old friend,' says Luisa. 'We haven't seen each other for ages.'

'It's a bad time,' says Helena. 'I'm so sorry. I'll call you later.' She ushers the children away.

*

When she wakes again, on the sofa, it is to the sound of someone hammering their fist on the front door and calling her name: 'Elaine! Elaine!' But her name is not Elaine. Luisa opens her eyes and sees that the man shouting is Dustin Hoffman, hammering on the glass partition in the church as he tries to persuade Elaine not to marry her fiancé. Dustin Hoffman has some nerve, because only a few minutes earlier he was sleeping with Elaine's mother, was sleeping with Luisa in the role of Elaine's mother. She looks at the clock, but the clock is not where she thought it was. The lounge is in darkness. Daytime is over for her, sunlight finished for another day.

Luisa hears a key in the front door – she is still in her dressing gown. Maybe a dressing gown is appropriate for date night, makes for a speedy date night? She digs through her bag for her phone: 18:30. Four hours to get Justin drunk enough to sleep so she can leave for work. She opens the front of her gown to confirm that she has forgotten to dress in the corset and suspenders as intended, and this is how Justin finds her, staring at her naked body, as he comes into the lounge.

'Hey,' says Justin. Luisa snaps the gown shut, and he looks away. She wishes she had left it open.

'What time is it?' she says. She wants to tell him she has just woken up, but she does not want to remind him of her need to sleep in the day, or remind him of anything connected to midwifery. Whenever she does his eyes look all sad, and she hates him – only a little, but more than she imagined she'd ever be capable of hating the person with whom she shares this one, her only life. Tonight she wants to love him, or at least to love him enough.

'I've just had a shower,' she tells him.

'All ready then?' He waggles a bottle of red wine.

Drinking wine before work is a sin – a sin against midwifery. The religion of midwifery. How has she ended up in a job so antagonistic towards the drinking of wine?

As she follows Justin through into the kitchen Luisa realises he means ready for dinner, remembers her promise to cook. She isn't hungry at all. Her mouth is full of glue.

She circles around and hugs him, and her dressing gown falls open. The buckle of his belt is cold against her stomach.

'I think I don't really want wine,' says Luisa.

'I thought wine was what you wanted,' he says.

'Maybe I'm starting to find wine a bit same-y. But don't let me stop you.'

'Well as it so happens,' grins Justin, 'I met with Jamie at lunchtime today. Went to his penthouse suite, right in the centre of town, the whole top floor. Crazy place.'

Justin pulls a DVD-sized freezer bag of grass from his satchel. 'Though he's only really wholesale now. Got this for mates' rates, really cheap. So as a wine alternative.' He flips the bag of grass from one hand to the other.

'Not right now.'

'Perhaps I'll roll one for later.'

'Why don't we eat something?' says Luisa. 'I'm starving.'

'Whatever. Whatever you want.' Justin dumps the grass on an armchair and marches through into the kitchen where he pulls open the cutlery drawer and scrabbles for a corkscrew. Luisa follows behind as monitor.

'Maybe I will have some wine now. A little bit of wine.' Luisa takes down two wine glasses from the cupboard – she needs to control the glasses.

'Fuck!' Justin fishes a finger inside the neck of the wine bottle. 'I've pushed the fucking cork inside!' He grabs a glass from Luisa, pours into it from the bottle, but the cork floats into the neck and only a few red drops slide into the glass. He rights the bottle then tips it again, with the same result.

'It doesn't matter,' says Luisa. 'I'm not that – '

Justin brings the bottle down hard on the edge of the counter, a pistol-shot crack takes the neck clean off, and splashes only a little wine onto the floor.

'There we go,' he says. 'Wine problem solved.'

The silence after such brutal noise is more extreme, more panicky. The neck of the bottle lies by Luisa's foot, a razor edge pointing at her toes. 'What about splinters?' she says, not looking at him.

Justin grabs a coffee filter from the packet by the coffee machine, stands it in the wine glass and pours through the jagged opening.

Luisa looks from Justin to the wine dripping from the filter.

'Splinters are not a fucking problem,' says Justin. He pulls the filter from the glass, throws it on the counter and downs the wine. He takes a new coffee filter and pours the other glass, holds it out to Luisa.

Potential glass-shard drinking followed by a sensible filtering solution – this is Justin all over.

'Yeah. Fuck the splinters.' Luisa upends her wine glass against her face, squeezing her lips tight so that neither wine nor glass fragments might get through. Drinking ground-up glass would at least resolve a whole host of other problems, she thinks. Some wine goes into her nostrils.

'Hah!' Justin pulls Luisa against him again. He plants his lips on hers. She grabs hold of his arms. Does he mean sex right now? She looks over his shoulder for the clock: 19.15. Justin pulls away.

'We should eat first,' he says.

'Should we? Yes, we should,' she agrees. If they have sex now he might stop drinking, might not drink himself to sleep. 'I'm cooking.'

Luisa looks at the onion and two carrots she placed on the work surface earlier in the afternoon. 'I found some vegetables. Though perhaps not enough.'

'Let's get takeaway. Get Thai,' says Justin. He pours himself a second glass through Luisa's filter – the process has become normalised already.

'I love Thai.' Luisa grabs her full glass and carries it through to the lounge. 'You order. I'll put some clothes on.'

In the bathroom Luisa scrubs at the tell-tale red stain that colours her upper lip and the underside of her nose. She pours half her wine down the sink, washes away any traces of evidence, and hurries to the bedroom where she puts on a corset and suspenders. She wonders whether to go down for dinner dressed like this. Too cold for eating. She adds a skirt, and a thick jumper over the corset.

Back in the kitchen she shadows Justin as he tidies, sloshing wine into his glass when he isn't looking from another open bottle.

'Jamie gave me these,' says Justin, when the takeaway has arrived and they are sat at the kitchen table. He leans down to open his satchel, and Luisa swaps his almost empty wine glass for her own full one. 'For the girls. He always remembers the girls.' Justin throws two iPads onto the table.

'He's only met them that once.'

'He never meant to puncture the bouncy castle. He just doesn't know his own strength sometimes. And this, it's nothing to him. He had a whole stack of them.'

They finish eating. In the silence both of them take time to arrange their cutlery on their plates.

'Need the loo,' says Justin.

Whilst he is out of the room Luisa fetches the two single-serve pots of Thai ice cream from the freezer, but instead of sitting back at the table takes them into the lounge.

'Bring the wine, honey,' she calls. She pats the sofa cushion next to her.

They sit side-by-side, nibbling at mini-spoonfuls, and the moment Justin puts his empty pot on the coffee table Luisa grabs his hand and puts it on her breast, Mrs Robinson taking charge of Dustin Hoffman.

He pulls her face to his and kisses her, which turns her head towards the clock on the mantelpiece: 21.10.

'I'm going to have a shower.' Justin pulls away from her.

'Now?'

'I want to take off this work stuff. I'm all sweaty from the train.'

'Don't be long.' She is unsure how this sounds.

Luisa waits on the sofa. She hears the shower start upstairs – after a couple of minutes the gentle thrum of the water lulls her, and she leans her head back against the top of the sofa. Her eyes close.

She jumps to her feet and climbs the stairs to the bathroom. An extension lead snakes under the bathroom door from the landing plug socket. Luisa pushes open the bathroom door. In amongst the steam Justin rotates his seat on the edge of the bath so that the laptop on his knees creates a shield between them. His pants hang loose around his feet.

'I'm not working,' says Justin. His eyes are heavy, his pupils unable to focus on her. 'This isn't email.'

'I don't mind.'

'If I'm working?'

'If you're – whatever you're doing that's not work. What're you watching?' She wants him to tell her, to tell her without embarrassment.

Luisa steps over to look at the screen, but with a one-handed key combination Justin closes the browser window.

'The only thing is, honey, you can't hide that.' She nods towards his lap. 'Put it back on. I want to see.'

'I was a bit tired. I needed a bit of geeing up.' He brings the browser window back up. He has paused the video on a naked man crouched behind two partially clothed girls lying atop each other, in a room with almost entirely white furnishings. Through an open window a turquoise sea is visible. Justin looks at the screen then back at Luisa. The cat jumps onto the keyboard and stands in front of the screen. Luisa pulls the cat away, pushes her out the bathroom door.

'Aren't you going to play it?' says Luisa.

'I don't always do this.' Justin presses a key.

'Maybe I sometimes do this.' Can ballet be porn? Some kinds of ballet are porn.

'You do?'

'I want to see.'

'You like – this one?' He nods at the screen.

'I like it if you like it. That's what you want to do?'

'But – who would we ask to join in?'

'I mean that way round. Him doing – that.'

They watch the screen together in silence. Every thirty seconds or so the configuration changes: one girl, the other girl, the two girls together, back to the first girl, onto her back, start round again. It is somewhat erotic, but boring, and with little sign of an ending.

Luisa checks Justin has his eyes fixed on the screen. She crosses her arms in front of her and pulls the jumper up and over her head. A thread catches on the wire ribbing of the corset – she tugs harder and breaks it, but the neck won't move any further. She latches her fingers under the material, tugs at the neck of the jumper.

'Are you okay?' The jumper muffles Justin's words.

'I think it's the buttons.'

Luisa moves her hands away and feels his fingers on her neck as he reaches inside the jumper and flicks one button clear of its hole. He tugs again at the main bulk of the material, so hard that he pulls her onto her knees on the bath mat.

'Sorry,' she hears, and pictures herself, on all fours, in her underwear but muzzled like a rabid dog.

'I'm rather helpless,' she calls. There is a moment's silence, then she is surprised by a violent slap on her arse.

'Do it again,' she says, and feels another sharp slap on her other buttock. She turns round, reaches for where she thinks his balls should be, and locates them on the second attempt.

'You could tie me up.' Luisa says through the jumper. 'Tie me to the radiator.'

'Isn't that a bit – kidnappy?' says Justin.

'In a good way.'

He wraps a towel around her arm, and moves it to her wrist. Justin slips, clangs some part of his body hard against the radiator.

'The towel's a bit thick,' he says. His hands are clumsy, not capable of operating heavy machinery.

'I'm going to tie you up.' It'll be quicker if I do it, Luisa thinks, and she stands, forces the jumper over her head.

Justin lies on the bathroom mat. 'I think the wine is making me do crappy towel knots,' he says. He could have used that as a joke, she thinks, but it is clear he is not joking.

'Come on.' She pulls him up by the hand, ushers him into the bedroom.

Tying Justin's wrists to the headboard uprights seems to take forever. The silence is panicking her – each extra second of quiet skewers the mood, drags it back to normality. In this kind of calm they could be reading books, or reattaching the curtain rail. Luisa focuses on her scarf knots to avoid looking at Justin.

'Why are the curtains on the floor?' he says.

'Not important,' says Luisa. 'Not now.' Though it will be in the morning when I'm trying to sleep.

'The condoms are – '

'Shhh. Shut it.' She puts her hand on his mouth. 'You're not getting out of *that*.' She plants a soggy kiss on his neck, looks down at his untied feet.

'Don't worry about legs,' says Justin. 'I just won't move them.'

'Why are you talking? Did I say you could talk?' Luisa points a finger in his face. Justin opens his mouth, smiles and shakes his head. Is this okay? At the start of the scarf-tying there was a penis flicking at her leg – now it has stopped. He's looking sleepy. She gulps down the anxiety of drama class improvisation. 'The only talking you're allowed,' she whispers in his ear, 'is answers to my questions.'

She pulls her knickers off over the suspenders and climbs back onto him, moves her mouth to his ear. 'I want you to tell me something really dirty,' she says. 'Tell me something really wrong.'

Justin edges his head away from her – she has shouted in his ear.

'Tell me other women you think about fucking,' she says.

Justin stares. 'I don't.'

'I don't mind,' says Luisa. 'I sometimes think about fucking Ukrainian ballet dancers. What about you?'

'The woman at the Foundry Arms,' he says.

'Do you?'

'Not all the time.'

'The tall one?'

'Tallish. With black hair.'

'Like quite long hair?'

'The tall one,' he repeats.

'And what do you want her to do?'

'I – imagine her locking me in after hours.'

'And what do you do to her? I want you to do that to me.'

'I – she sucks me off whilst I sit on a bar stool.'

'We don't have a bar stool. What else?'

'Then I – fuck her, as she's leaning over the bar. There's beer everywhere. It's all sticky. She sticks to the bar, her tits. Naked.'

'We can – '

'And there's that woman at the girls' school, I'm having sex with you and her – ' Justin talks more quickly, his voice raised up a pitch.

'Tina?'

'Who's Tina?'

'Which woman from school?'

'The teacher, the one in – '

'Don't tell me which one.' She grabs hold of his now-erect penis.

'And I might make a million pounds out of Christian Aid!' he cries.

'Ooh, you dirty capitalist!' She smothers his chest in kisses, licks down towards his navel. 'Might you?'

'We could be rolling in it! I could actually make that kind of money.' His face is red. 'And if I do, we can both give up work. You can give up being a midwife! You wouldn't have to be a fucking midwife any more!' he cries.

Luisa sits up with a start. She looks out through the uncurtained window, at the ceiling light in the bedroom over the road.

'Give up being a midwife?' She looks back at him.

'Well I'm certainly not going to work like this if we make a load of money.' Justin's smile stretches painfully across his face. 'And you wouldn't have to either. We can stay naked in bed all day. Hire a nanny. For a few days, anyway.'

Luisa looks out the window again.

'It's only a fantasy,' Justin's eyes are wide, darting.

'You agreed it was a good idea to do midwifery training. You said you'd support me.' She can no longer feel his penis against her leg, his erection a barometer for the mood of the room. Luisa crosses her arms across the corset – a cold front of low pressure.

'I did support you.'

'I'd want to be a midwife even if you did make a load of money. That's not why I do it. I do it for – you liked that I was a midwife!'

'And I do,' he says. 'But – '

'It's an important job! Don't you understand that?'

'I thought you wanted me to say something wrong,' mumbles Justin.

'Not that kind of wrong! Because now I have this job where I can use my brain, use it to, to help people! Help women.'

'I'm glad. I really *am* glad. But don't you see how it also makes you –' he trails off.

'What?'

'A bit – miserable.'

'I'm not miserable! I'm tired! I work night shifts. At night!'

'But you're not only tired after night shifts.'

'How can you say to me that you hate midwifery?'

'I didn't say I hated it.'

'You might as well have done.'

'Okay!' cries Justin. 'I hate midwifery! I do!'

'I cannot believe you said that. I truly do not believe you could have said that.' Each extra word she packs into the sentence gives it additional force, greater momentum. 'I *help* people.'

'But what has it done to us?'

They both look to Justin's wrists, tied to the headboard.

'I mean what about our insane calendar system?' cries Justin. 'We've just got over having twins for god's sake, we were getting things into some kind of order. And now your job ploughs through all the rules. The hospital wins out every time. Wins out over our life.'

'I thought you hated sticking to the rules.' Luisa rolls across the duvet and sits upright on the side of the bed.

'I *do*! I hate it!' Justin tries to pull himself up from the bed, but the scarves restrain him. He flails from side-to-side like an angry toddler, rolling his head back and forth across the pillow. 'So why a job that's so high maintenance?'

'How can you call me high maintenance?' cries Luisa. 'I'm so low maintenance! I'm the one who was happy to shit in a carrier bag and take it to a bin so that we didn't have to call a plumber in Greece!'

'Can you get these off me, please?'

Luisa does not move. 'Your job makes *you* miserable. What's so good about your job?' She feels the tears welling in her eyes and faces away from him.

'Nothing.'

'Well then.'

'I want us to be happy. Happier,' he mumbles.

'Well I'm not happy.' She wants to clarify that she means not happy right now, not happy with the turn this conversation has taken, not happy with the fact that she is almost naked but has still not had sex. But the bedside clock has rolled into view, it is four minutes to eleven, and this whole situation, though it may be electric, though it may be the very kind of situation that culminates in make-up sex, is swept aside by the knowledge that she needs to be at work in an hour. 'Well maybe keep stuff like this to yourself!' she hollers, and storms out to the bathroom. She wrenches the bathroom door behind her, which swings shut until it hits the extension lead, then bounces wide open again.

'I'm leaving,' she shouts, and is surprised by a stab of euphoria. This solves one problem – the problem of how to get to work without Justin knowing. Storming out is the solution to her problem.

'That's not what I want,' calls Justin. 'How have we got to leaving?'

'I mean I'm going out.'

'Where?'

'Out!'

'It's eleven o'clock.'

'Some people go out at eleven o'clock, Justin. Tonight it's me.'

She storms back into the bedroom, grabs the first clothes to hand, pulls on a pair of jogging trousers before she realises she is still wearing suspenders.

She is afraid to slow down, afraid that in the time it would take to remove her corset Justin will bring this around, will remove her right to storm out. To storm out and go to work.

'Can't we talk?' He pulls at the scarves holding his wrists, moves his head to grab at the material with his teeth.

'We just did. Don't get up. I might not be back tonight.'

'What do you mean?'

'I'm going to stay somewhere else.'

'Who with? Helena?'

'I know more people than Helena!'

She runs downstairs, thrusts her feet into her trainers, grabs her backpack from the hall and is out the front door. She sets off at a jog, but it is too fast, too fast because she has not jogged anywhere for more than five years. Also because she does not like jogging.

She slows her pace, skipping a few steps, running a little, then simply walking quickly.

Now she is on her way to work her mind is strangely free of the problems behind her, as though they are all boxed within the confines of the house. She remembers her few sips of wine. How many was it? Five, maybe six? Is that a glass? Over a couple of hours that's less than a glass, down to less than a unit, surely?

She moves to the edge of the pavement, walks both feet along the kerb. There, that's a straight line. Isn't it? She waggles her head from side-to-side. I'm fine. I'm fine until something happens later this evening, then I won't be fine, then I'll be a midwife who was drinking before work. An ex-midwife who drinks before the work she no longer has. She is so busy watching her feet on the kerb she hits her head on the upright of the bus stop.

'Hi there,' says a voice as she steps back onto the usual course of the pavement.

Colin sits in the bus stop, his dog at his side.

'Oh. Hi, Colin. I'm off to work. Again.' Why does he catch buses at eleven at night? Are dogs allowed on buses? Of course they allow dogs on buses. But why take a dog on a bus when it needs exercise? She wishes she had a dog, and is immediately glad she does not. How could she have a dog if she and Justin split up? Luisa comes to a halt at the thought, so abruptly she almost falls over. Is that what this has come to, her and Justin splitting up? She does not want to split up. That's even more trouble, with the girls, with money, especially with sex. Maybe not so much trouble with sex? But who would have the dog? She shouldn't get a dog.

'Actually,' she turns and calls, 'I'm not going to work. I'm going to stay with a friend.'

'Right you are,' waves Colin.

She is out of the estate, out onto grassland, heading for the hill behind the hospital, where she takes up jogging again.

Justin has not called her. Why hasn't he called her? He is good at apologising, much better than her. He enjoys apologising. But he has not called. He is still tied up, maybe he can't get free. Maybe he'll stay tied up all night, will be there in the morning. She tries to remember how tight she tied the scarves.

She stops at the start of the chalk path that leads to the phone tower on top of the hill, pulls her phone from her backpack. If he's tied up he won't be able to answer, if he doesn't answer she should go back, go back to untie him. She can't go back, she'll be late for work. He won't answer, anyway.

The screen bursts into life with the image of Justin's smiling face, Justin wearing that stupid cowboy hat, looking to the side at a crowd. What festival was that?

'You got free,' says Luisa.

'You don't have to stay somewhere else,' says Justin. 'Come back, Lu. Come back and talk about this.'

'Go to bed. So you can get up in the morning.'

'I'll stay up.'

'No, I'm going to stay at Tina's.' Luisa sets off walking again, up the hill.

'Come back and talk. Look, this is kind of – childish? Why can't we talk about it?'

'Well I'm having a bit of trouble dealing with the fact you hate me being a midwife. I need a bit of time. To think about it.'

'That came out wrong. I don't – hate it,' he says. 'I – quite dislike it. Dislike what it's done to us. I thought you knew that.'

'You never said before.'

'How would I not hate it compared to what we had before?'

'This is the work I want to do. Work I like. Worthwhile work.'

'Maybe,' says Justin, 'Mrs Martin Luther King would have liked it if Martin had stayed at home a bit more. If he hadn't gone and got himself shot.'

'Perhaps Mrs Martin Luther King was a bit more supportive.'

'Perhaps she both admired and hated, disliked what he did. Like me.'

'So you're comparing yourself to Martin Luther King?'

'No, to Mrs Martin Luther King.'

'Who had a name, you know. So now you hate me being a midwife *and* you're racist?' I mean sexist. Luisa is about to correct herself, and realises this probably isn't sexist, either.

'Can you come home?' says Justin. 'So we can talk about this sensibly?'

Turn round, jog back home. Go to bed. Have make-up sex. Phone in sick. Phone in drunk. I'm not drunk.

'You're telling me I should give up being a midwife. Is that what you want?'

'No.'

'You just said you did.'

'I said I hated it. Disliked it. You can't give it up.'

'I can. I could tell them tonight.'

'Don't do that. I don't want you to do that.'

'What, then?'

'I don't know. But I don't want you to give it up.'

'You hate it but you don't want me to give it up?'

There is silence on the other end of the phone. She looks at the screen to check the call has not ended.

'Justin?'

'You'd be angry at me forever. Every time you wondered what you were doing with your life you'd blame me.'

'You don't want me to give up because of how you would look?'

'Everyone would think I was some kind of chauvinist who ordered you around, said what kind of work you could and couldn't do.'

'Isn't that what you're doing?'

'I can't tell you what to do.'

'So I'll give it up.'

'I don't want you to.'

'You're ordering me around again.'

'I don't want you to give up because you don't want to give up. We have to live with it. We're stuck like this.'

'Maybe it's not us.'

'What, then?'

'I don't know.'

'Where are you?'

The hospital comes into view over the crest of the hill.

'I'm going to Tina's.'

There is no answer. She looks at the phone to see if he has hung up.

'It's Coretta,' says Justin.

'What?'

'Mrs Martin Luther King. She was called Coretta.'

'Are you googling?'

Luisa thumbs the phone to end the call.

WEDNESDAY NIGHT: ON DUTY

As she enters the lobby for the lifts, Diane is there, waiting. Luisa smiles. She is not sure she can cope with Diane.

'I wouldn't do your running through the wards if I were you,' says Diane. 'Too many trip hazards.' Diane is struggling with the zip of a silver bumbag around her waist.

'I'm not doing any running.' Now that Luisa is no longer in motion, fatigue takes over, and she leans against the wall of the lift.

'That's good. Running's over.'

'I didn't know you think you were working tonight.'

'Not tonight, Josephine,' says Diane. 'Picked up a little gizmo from the post room. Taking it for a test drive.'

As they ascend in the lift Diane fiddles with the zip on the silver bumbag, and from amongst pens and flash cards takes out a GoPro camera. As she struggles to get the strap around her head, two small glass bottles fall out of the bag and onto the floor.

Luisa picks up and hands back the empty bottles.

'Thanks, dear. Don't want to lose my bottles. That one's my favourite.'

Luisa smiles again.

'You look a bit peaky, if you don't mind me saying.'

Luisa does mind her saying. Diane's face is very close to hers. She peers over Diane's head and tries to judge how her eyes look, reflected in the lift door.

'Here.' Diane hands her her a bottle. 'Maybe you need this.'

'I don't think there's anything in it,' says Luisa, and hands it back.

'Oh, not that one!' Diane grabs the bottle back and swaps it for the other which is half-filled with a liquid. 'That one's my London Underground!'

'What does that do?'

'Do? It doesn't do anything. Air from the underground isn't going to help your maladies now, is it? If anything it'll be a bit stuffy. I like the smell. The memories.'

'I don't really – use therapies. Thank you, though. I'm just tired.'

'Well thank goodness for that. I don't use them either. They all smell the same, for one thing. Some women here seem to like them though, I thought you might be one of them.' She shoves the bottles into the bumbag. 'If you're tired, you'll want to be checking your iron levels. Have you checked your Hb?'

'No. No? Does lack of iron stop you sleeping? Can you test me?'

'On what?' Diane puts the bottles back into the bumbag.

'Iron. Can you test my iron for me?' Luisa checks her phone: 23:30.

'Let's go, daddio,' says Diane. 'To the clinical room.'

In the clinical room Luisa lies back on the bench seat. The room is lit by a single table lamp, and she is careful not to close her eyes. 'What else do you need iron for? Can low iron affect your sex drive?'

'Never been a problem for me.' Diane is invisible in the darkness beyond the lamp glare. She withdraws the lancet.

'Maybe it makes it – stronger?' says Luisa.

'Oh look. You're only ninety-six.'

'Ninety-six! That's properly low, isn't it?' Leukaemia low? Not leukaemia. Run-ragged low.

'Depends what you like,' says Diane. 'Not good if you're having a baby. Aside from that, who knows?'

'Do you ever think – sometimes I wonder if I'm making mistakes? Here, at work. If I can't sleep and I'm making mistakes because my iron is too low.'

Diane leans in close to Luisa's face, and Luisa sees she still has the camera strapped to her head.

'Are you filming this?' says Luisa.

'I'm filming everything from now on,' says Diane. 'As evidence. Then no one can get rid of me.'

'Who wants to get rid of you?'

'Jenny does, I'm almost sure. But she has her reasons.'

'What reasons?'

Diane doesn't answer, and packs away the equipment, humming to herself. The room is quiet, aside from the thrum of the pipes in the wall, a gentle throb. Luisa's eyes close. She rolls herself off the bench, lands on her feet and hands like a cat, then springs back upright.

'Don't tell Jenny about your iron,' warns Diane.

*

Luisa opens the changing room door and is relieved to find the room empty. On the wall by the lockers is a new poster:

MEDICINE MANAGEMENT TRAINING.

Any nurse or midwife who wants additional support or learning opportunities on the safe and efficient usage of medicines is invited to attend this training session. This is a learning tool and is not compulsory.

Scrawled across the top of the poster in black marker are the words, 'EVERYONE MUST DO THIS.

Gina bursts into the room.

'Need a quick shower,' says Gina. 'Waters burst, all over me.' She crab-walks over to the shower cubicle, her blue cotton trousers cleaving to her legs.

'I'm on late,' says Luisa, needing to explain. 'Starting at midnight. I made Jenny let me come in late.' She pulls down the zip of her jogging top to see she is still wearing her corset underneath and zips it up again.

Gina strips off her blue trousers and her knickers. She wrenches open the door to the shower, to find the shower head piled high with coats.

'It doesn't work,' says Luisa, wanting to be helpful. 'I don't think it's worked for ages.'

Gina pulls the pile of coats from the shower head, dumps them on the changing room floor. She twists the shower handle, but no water appears, and she kneels on the floor to examine the pipes, hitting them with the side of her hand. Luisa unzips her top again, pulls at the top corset hook and eye.

Gina steps back out of the shower, stands in the room, naked from the waist down, her legs glistening. Luisa turns her back, pulling the jogging top across her chest.

'I'll get on to maintenance again,' says Gina. 'And if they don't do it this time, I'll bring in the tools myself.' Gina goes into the toilet cubicle, from where Luisa hears the splashing of water. She peels off the jogging top and pulls her midwifery tunic straight over the corset.

Gina exits the cubicle, naked from the waist down, and wipes her legs and hips with a handful of paper towels. It is impossible for Luisa not to stare at the chaos of Gina's pubic hair, though Gina does not appear to mind, and from the way she stands appears to be offering encouragement.

'I meant to say, Luisa. You forgot to sign the theatre book yesterday. For your caesarean?'

'Did I?'

'You did.'

'Did Jenny tell you to tell me?'

'I don't need instructions from Jenny. I saw it was blank. But you need to make sure it's always signed. It's on the protocol list.'

Luisa's eyes fill with tears, tears she wants to blame on the tightness of the corset, on the pain from the wires poking into her sternum. How is she supposed to remember if she signed the book or not? But Gina is only trying to be helpful, isn't she, only trying to be helpful in that bitchy way of hers? She's not bitchy. Forthright. This is information, if Gina says she didn't sign the book then she didn't. What else has she forgotten? How much is it reasonable to remember? A tear slips down her cheek.

Gina stops wiping her leg. 'What, I've upset you? It's not important.'

'No, no.'

'So what's up?'

'I have low iron,' says Luisa. 'My iron is only nine point six.'

'Are you taking ferrous sulphate?'

'Not at the moment.'

'Well don't start. You shouldn't take ferrous sulphate. Ferrous fumerate is preferable. You've done iron studies?'

Luisa shakes her head.

'Don't assume it's anaemia. You need studies. Who told you it was iron? A doctor?'

'Diane. She tested me.'

'You're taking medical advice from Diane?'

'Maybe it's not the iron.' Luisa wipes the tear from her cheek with a finger. 'Justin told me he hates midwifery.'

'He said he hates midwifery?' Gina spits.

'I sort of – forced it out of him.'

'That's worse. That's even worse,' says Gina. 'That passive aggressive crap. People need to say what they mean. Get it out in the open.'

'I think he was – trying to be polite.'

'Don't take that. You can't take that. He's jealous that your work gives you dominion over life and death. Life and death! I mean what does he do whilst you help women bring new life into the world?'

'Normally he just looks sad.'

'I mean what work does he do?'

'Programmer. Computer coder. He's built an app to give small loans to poor people in Africa. I don't really know.'

'There you go.'

'He did support me becoming a midwife. He's a good guy, really.' Luisa notes she is again defending Justin.

'Well you're the one who can tell,' says Gina, but it is clear that Gina is the one who can tell. 'And you're the one who has to decide. Just know I'm here for you. You can always sofa surf at mine. Whatever time of night.'

'Thanks,' says Luisa. 'I think I'm overtired. Maybe it is my iron.'

'Get yourself a better plan. A life LTR. Like your LTR for midwifery.'

'I don't think I – have an LTR.' Luisa has no idea what an LTR might be.

'I don't mean one of those crappy ones you can buy online. You haven't made your own?'

Gina karate chops her left arm downwards, as though shaking off water droplets. A rectangular wedge of plastic shoots into her palm.

'David made it for me,' says Gina. She pulls back the sleeve of her tunic to reveal a metal rod fixed to her forearm. 'Back when I started, before I threw him out. He was in special effects. Still is, I imagine.' Gina flips over the pages of the laminated book. Luisa sees a bulleted list, colour-coded from red to green: raised maternal temperature; commence ceph & met; arterial bloods; HVS; MSU; Blood for FBC & CRP; 4-hrly paracetamol.

'I'll get one,' says Luisa. 'I'll make one myself.'

'This is my one for midwifery. I have six or seven others, for all kinds of things. Kitchen, bathroom, holidays, cat. You have to make your own. Lots-To-Remembers need to be personal.'

Luisa imagines making flip cards, sitting at her kitchen table. She pictures the scene at night, then in the day, with and without the girls running around. She leans against her locker – her body is increasing in weight, requiring more effort just to stay on her feet. More tears run down her cheeks.

'Last night I thought my woman was going to make a complaint about her emergency caesarean,' says Luisa, seeing Gina watching her.

'Don't get stressed about complaints.' Gina pulls Luisa into an embrace, crushing the ribbing of the corset between them. 'Civilians come in here with their huge, exacting birth plans thinking they can order nature around, and when their bodies don't live up to their expectations, we get the blame. Suck it up and push on through.'

'And sometimes I'm just terrified,' sobs Luisa. 'Properly terrified. I haven't slept. I'm terrified I might make a mistake through lack of sleep. A fatal mistake.'

'You can't worry about that.'

'I can't?' Gina will advocate for her. Maybe Gina will talk to Jenny, tell Jenny she has to go home.

'So long as you're terrified there's no way you'll fall asleep,' says Gina.

Jenny enters the changing room. She looks at Luisa cradled against Gina's chest.

'I had waters in the lap,' says Gina. 'I'll have to work commando.' She unwraps her arms from Luisa and instead takes her by the hand. 'What are you wearing?' she asks Luisa.

Luisa puts her hand to her chest, as if surprised by the corset herself.

'I – didn't have time to change. To get here for midnight,' she says, directing this at Jenny.

'Well good,' says Jenny. 'Can you go straight into Sheila Kitzinger? I need you to cover Clarissa's break. She's got a primip with PET – just started mag sulph.'

'Make sure it doesn't impede your work.' Gina looks at Luisa's chest. 'Maximum flexibility.' Gina drops into a crouch, her arms outstretched.

'Need to keep it nimble. Swivel round.'

Luisa pulls the scrubs tunic over her head and turns her back to Gina. Gina sets about unhooking the corset. 'Big breath in.'

'I'll be right there,' Luisa says to Jenny.

Each tug on the corset causes a violent wrench of her head. Jenny watches as Luisa's eyes fill with tears again.

'I'm wondering whether to say anything to you about your work attire, Luisa,' says Jenny.

'Luisa is having life partner problems,' says Gina. 'We're discussing options.'

'It's not that bad,' says Luisa.

'I've offered my sofa bed,' says Gina. 'I think perhaps senior management could show some kind of help in kind this time.'

'You never said,' says Jenny, as though this is breaking work protocol, for not informing her manager.

'We had a bit of an argument.' Luisa's head moves from side-to-side as Gina roughly removes the corset laces. 'I'm not leaving Justin.'

'Leaving begins with thinking about leaving,' says Gina.

'So. You're feeling a bit shaky?' says Jenny. 'Is that what you're saying?'

The corset falls loose at her front, and Jenny watches as Gina reaches round to pull it away, brushing the material across Luisa's nipples.

'Don't flake out on me, now.' Gina hands the corset to Luisa and rummages through a locker.

'I tell you what I'll do,' says Jenny. 'Clarissa's woman might be a bit tricksy. I'll put you on the multip birth in Michel Odent.'

'You don't have to do that,' says Luisa. 'I can do a primip with PET. It's fine.'

'It wasn't a request.' Jenny has lost interest now. 'Take over the multip, please Luisa. Low risk early epidural, won't be giving birth any time soon.'

'I'm capable of all the things I can do.' The words fall from Luisa's mouth, the sentence all lumpy.

'It's my job as coordinator, Luisa.' Jenny tears a poster from the wall and crumples it into a ball. 'To keep everyone safe.'

'I am safe.'

'I mean the women.'

*

Michel Odent room is lit only by two small desk lamps, both plugged into an extension lead snaking from a wall socket. Low music is playing, some kind of album of natural sounds, perhaps dolphins or rhinos or owls. The room is calm, womb-like – just right for the birth of a baby, and also a den of temptation, a sleep torment.

The lamp leads trailed on the floor mark out the territory of a man lying on a yoga mat. He is covered in a blanket, the encampment of a homeless man with his worldly possessions. Rather than plastic bags or old rucksacks, the items that surround him are brand new: carry cot, car baby set, and a holdall from which folded clothes and nappies spill onto the floor.

A high-pitched foghorn sounds, startling Luisa. In the bed, bathed in the soft light, sits an Asian woman, asleep, her head lolled against the metal frame of the headboard.

'We're all quiet here.' Nikki says from a chair by the wall of the delivery room. Only the lower half of her face is visible, but Luisa knows it is Nikki from the way she sits. 'Apart from the whale noises. They make me feel like dropping off myself.'

'Sorry,' says Luisa. 'I didn't mean to disturb you.'

'No, no. Anyway, I wasn't *asleep*.' Nikki sits upright in the chair.

'Alarm you, then.'

'Maybe I was asleep. I thought you might be Jenny.' Nikki steps over to the monitor, checks the readout and writes in the red notes booklet. 'I have to sleep sometime, anyway.' Nikki is back, moving at daytime speed. Her bleached bob hangs symmetrically over her face, her scrubs hug her figure as though she has spent time dressing herself.

'I can't sleep,' says Luisa. 'I don't think I slept all day.'

'I can never sleep in the day. I grab it whenever I can.'

'You always seem so chirpy. So awake.'

'But inside I'm dying.' Nikki giggles. She picks up the notes booklet. 'So this is Seema. And Donal.' She nods towards the figure on the floor. 'She's para 3, rhesus positive, low-risk pregnancy, placenta clear of os, came in at 4cm, wanted an epidural straight away. No synto running.'

'Para 3, rhesus positive, low-risk, placenta clear, 4cm, wanted epidural. No synto yet,' repeats Luisa.

'I can never sleep when Martyn's home. And makes it harder when the other person in bed is always awake.'

'Why is Martyn in bed?'

'He's not working right now. So he's at home quite a lot.'

'In bed?'

'I like something to cuddle. I'm just thankful he's happy to fit around me. So to speak,' she giggles again. 'My boyfriend before, Ryan, he was often too depressed for sex.'

Luisa scribbles on the notes: half hourly CTG review, 15 minute FH check. VE at 03.00 or earlier if indicated. Nothing until three. 'Men get too depressed for sex?' she whispers.

'Oh yes. It was his work, I think.'

'What did he do?'

'Credit card fraud. It seemed to stress him out a lot. He made me promise never to tell anyone when we were together. It's quite a relief to tell everyone now.'

Luisa repeats the foetal heart check and notes it in the book.

'Well, I'm off for my break,' says Nikki. 'Don't have a baby without me!'

A whale signals across the room again. She could pretend the album was finished, couldn't she? A phone glows on the white sheet by Seema's arm, a wire trailing down to somewhere unseen under the bed. Luisa stands over the bed, removes a dark hair caught alongside the epidural tube taped to Seema's shoulder, rising with each of Seema's snores. The IV pump ribbets as it pumps fluids into her arm. Snore, ribbet, whale cry. Luisa leaves the phone alone and sets her own breathing in time to the pattern, paces around the bed, her feet in rhythm. This is how prisoners stay awake in their cells, to confound their jailers. But prisoners don't try to stay awake, do they? Prisoners want to sleep. This is how jailers keep their prisoners awake.

Luisa knocks into the side of the bed, snaps her eyes open. The blood pressure cuff around Seema's arm beeps. Nikki has gone. These are her safety checks, that is why they beep. Everything beeps. Even if she is asleep, she'll wake up from the beeps. Luisa checks the foetal heart rate again, and in the book writes, 00.30, foetal heart 142bpm, PLAN AS ABOVE.

Her legs ache but she does not dare sit. She leans her hands against the wall, angles her body at forty-five degrees, stretches one calf muscle and the other, each stretch corresponding to a whale call. This is far too slow a rhythm. She picks up Seema's phone and skips forward to the next track. The whales change to monks.

'How many centimetres is it now?'

Luisa starts at the red-haired man peering up over the side of the bed, a blanket around his shoulders. Adrenalin courses through her, the drug she requires.

'She's fine,' says Luisa. 'No change there.'

'How can you tell?'

Before Luisa can answer the man is back on the floor, asleep again.

'Foetal heart the same, Seema sleeping, everything normal,' Luisa whispers to no one. She wanders the room again, avoiding the chair by the monitor.

Diane slips in through the door, the GoPro atop her head. She slips to the floor on her knees and crawls forward under the bed. From her standing position Luisa sees the light of the camera's LED sweep across the floor. Then Diane is up and out the door.

Luisa takes the birthing ball from the collection of items around the sleeping husband and sits on the top, bounces a little, her feet just touching the floor. To rest her legs is delicious. She lifts both feet an inch off the floor to see if she can balance and she can, she can. She can sit on the ball, she can't fall asleep on the ball, if she did she would fall, fall to the side and she'd wake, wake from the falling. You can't drown by sleeping in a bath, she's read that. It makes sense you can't sleep sitting on a ball. She has this under control, she is handling the situation. Look Justin, she says, I'm handling things. I'm doing my job, to the best of my ability, and I have a pretty fucking good ability.

I want us to be happy, says Justin. Happier.

I want us to be happy too.

The IV line throbs again, and her wrist hurts. Why does her wrist hurt? The drip is in Seema's wrist. Is this one of those things where you take on the patient's symptoms, in sympathy, is this Stockholm Syndrome? Or is that kidnap victims?

We'll get a new mattress, says Justin. We've needed a new mattress for a while.

I'm sorry I ran away. Luisa threads an arm around Justin's waist.

Have you seen. I can do a jeté now. Justin stands effortlessly on his toes, his feet vertical.

That's nice. But it doesn't make up for what you said.

Luisa tries to remember the word for Justin's pose: a plié? Underneath the ballet tights are the contours of his muscles, defined and shadowed.

'Are you wearing a – jock strap?' asks Luisa. 'I didn't know you had a jock strap.'

'I don't.'

'But that's not – '

The monitor beeps, three insistent stabs. It is quiet, then repeats. Luisa opens her eyes and sees hair, red hair – she is lying on the yoga mat. She is lying behind Donal. She snatches her arm back from around his waist.

The alarm is still beeping. She stands, frozen in a musical statue pose, waiting to catch out Seema or Donal, for them to move, to be out. The monks have stopped. She moves to the monitor, taps the screen to stop the beeping. This is fine. Her plan is still as above. Luisa grabs the book, writes in the time in the column below, 01.15.

The numbers written above her own are not in her handwriting. The numbers above say 00.53, but they are not her numbers. G1 P0 40+4 spontaneous onset. Last VE 6cms. She didn't write that.

She checks the signature in the right-hand column. L something C. A doctor's scrawl. Fuck. Not her handwriting. And she's not C.

Luisa runs out into the corridor, looks both ways. If that was the Senior House Officer she won't still be around, will she? It was twenty minutes ago. She wants to explain. To explain what? That she was having a bit of a cuddle with the husband? Can she explain?

Luisa runs to the office, puts her head around the door. Annie sits inside at the computer, her face far too close to the screen.

'Have you seen the SHO?' says Luisa. 'The SHO or the Reg? Who are the doctors tonight?'

'No one ever tells me,' says Annie.

'You don't know their names?' Luisa moves to the notice board, flips up random A4 sheets.

Luisa finds the list of doctors. There's only three whose surnames begin with R: one Lilitha and two Peters. It's Lilitha. She wants to fist punch. But how does it help to know her name?

When Luisa re-enters Michel Odent the husband is awake, on his feet. He is a ghost haunting the bed – when he hears the door he turns with a start, as though caught suffocating his pregnant wife. The monk chants are back again – they end a cycle and rise a tone.

'Well hello,' says Luisa. 'You're all come round now, I see.' She smiles, keeps the smile as she crosses the room. The woman in bed is also awake, watching her husband, eyes heavy.

'Hi. Hello.' The husband strides around the bed and extends his hand. 'Donal. And Seema.'

'I'm Luisa,' she sing-songs. She is back in midwife mode, auto-piloting. If she keeps to the script, she can stay on track. Questions and answers, standard answers. What's the standard answer to 'why were you spooning me on the floor?' That doesn't appear to be one of his questions. Luisa looks to Donal's sleeping nest, and brushes at the creases in her tunic. 'You were sleeping.' Luisa moves to the head of the bed. 'Hi there, Seema. I'm Luisa. Nikki's on her break.'

'We were wondering where you were,' smiles Seema.

'Just popped to the office,' says Luisa. 'You were all sleeping sound when I left. The doctor came to check on you.' She glances at Donal. He is tidying his nest, moving bags, rolling the mat.

'I think I was out from the epidural,' says Seema.

'Good, that's good. Now, we'll need to examine you soon, Seema.' Now she is moving, now that there are tasks to fulfil, the room calms Luisa. This is her, this is her work. She reels of instructions to Seema: knees, together, up, flop. A performer, playing her role. Playing it well. There will be mistakes, simple mistakes, because it is night time, because we are all tired. Everyone makes mistakes.

Luisa performs the vaginal examination, keeping her expression frozen

– otherwise her face suggests she has lost something in there. She slides her fingers all around the baby's head, brushing against hair. She can't feel the bald smoothness of the cervix – Seema is fully dilated.

'So we shouldn't be too long now,' says Luisa. A birth, this is what I need. This is what I trained for. She removes her gloves, washes her hands and checks: towels on the radiator, Syntocinon plus needle on the tray, ready to be drawn up. She pulls open the top drawer of the trolley. Delivery pack all ready. She moves her eyes to the notes.

'Now?' says Donal. 'It's coming?'

'*She*'s coming,' says Seema.

'Number *four*,' says Luisa, adding the note of surprise. 'How ex-*cit*-ing.'

'We're really excited,' says Seema. 'Aren't we Donal?'

'Really excited,' says Donal. He looks at Luisa, his eyes wide.

'Well now,' says Luisa. 'As we're going to be there soon why don't you have a go at emptying your bladder? Before we get going?'

Seema eases herself off the bed.

'Maybe you can help, Donal. Give her some help to the loo.'

'I'm fine,' says Seema. She grabs the drip stand and pulls herself to her feet. Donal takes a step back to move out of her way.

'It's only a precaution,' says Luisa. 'After the epidural. In case you're a bit wobbly in the legs.'

'No need.' Seema experiments with a crouch. 'Leg's feel normal. I know this. I'm used to it by now.'

Donal's hands are up, palms out. Seema wheels the drip stand into the toilet cubicle and closes the door.

'I just want to say,' whispers Donal. He stands very close to Luisa, and the trolley prevents her from moving away.

'I'm sorry,' says Luisa. 'But – '

'Don't be sorry,' Donal whispers. 'But can I ask, quickly? I was wondering, perhaps – you'd like to meet up?'

'Meet up?'

'I don't know if you – we could catch a film? Or just a drink.' Donal looks down, and his hair falls over his face. 'Maybe you don't drink.'

'I – ' Luisa looks up at him, back at the trolley then up at Donal again. 'I don't think it's appropriate.' She picks up the lead from the CTG machine and curls it into her hand.

'I don't mean now. Later. Another day.'

'Your wife is giving birth.'

'She is now. But then it'll be nappies, shit and vomit. I'm going – backwards.'

'It doesn't last long. The early years,' says Luisa quickly.

'And then she'll have another one! Another *baby*...' Donal sounds as though he has only just realised it is a baby that Seema will give birth to – not a kitten, or puppy. 'I thought, you might – '

'You're the father.' Luisa risks a glance at him. Now she can see him in the lamp's glow he is surprisingly attractive. 'It's quite normal. For parents, for fathers to get nervous before the birth.' That's the way, back to sing-song, back to professional.

'I know,' says Donal mournfully. 'I'm desperately nervous. Or just desperate. I'm sorry.'

'You'll be back to normal in a while.' Elsie and Eleanor are six – is six years a while? Her and Justin, are they back to normal? What is that?

'She keeps having them,' says Donal. 'I'm not even sure where this one came from.'

'We have leaflets.' Neither of them laugh, but she is glad to say it, glad to fill the silence.

'I thought you might like to meet up,' says Donal.

'I don't,' says Luisa.

'But what about – on the floor? What was that?'

Without warning Luisa begins to cry.

'Oh,' says Donal. 'Oh.'

The toilet flushes, and the rattling and knocking of the drip stand against the door frame signal Seema's exit from the cubicle. Luisa steps behind the trolley, uses the low lighting to cover the wiping of her face.

'I'm all empty now,' says Seema. 'I'm ready. Ready for the final push.'

'You put yourself back in bed,' sings Luisa, 'and I'll let the coordinator know your progress.' She doesn't ask Donal to help, doesn't want to mention him at all. As Luisa moves to the door, she sees him help his wife back on to the bed.

In the corridor Diane is reading a noticeboard.

'Do you know where Jenny is?' asks Luisa. 'I need to find Jenny.'

'They do music recitals at lunch hours,' says Diane. 'At the church around the corner. Did you know that?'

'I didn't. Have you seen Jenny?'

'No. They're every Thursday.'

'You should go.' Luisa looks up and down the corridor.

'Oh, I can't. There's never time.'

The poster makes Luisa angry. She never has a lunch hour, certainly not an hour, not really a lunch, and never at the time people eat lunch. 'Who put that up?' Luisa takes hold of the bottom edge of the poster, ready to tear it down.

'I did,' says Diane. 'I like the colours.'

'Luisa, I was looking for you.'

Luisa lets go of the poster and turns to see Jenny behind her. 'What's going on in your room?' says Jenny.

'I was coming to find you,' says Luisa. 'I was looking for you.'

'Mmm,' says Jenny.

'I've just examined her, Seema. She's fully.'

'Ahh.' Jenny makes a face, a bad smell face. 'Well I'm going to change you round, put Rebecca and Vicky on for your birth. I want you down in post-natal.'

'I'm okay,' says Luisa. 'This can be my birth. I'm okay.'

'No, I'm giving it to Rebecca and Vicky.'

'I mean – I can do this.' Luisa widens her eyes at Jenny.

'Vicky needs to get her student birth numbers up.' Jenny stares Luisa down. 'She's way off forty. I don't want the bloody university on at me again.'

'Oh. Okay. So Vicky can get her numbers up.' Luisa glances back to the small wired window in the right-hand door of Michel Odent and sees Donal's eye and cheek flattened against the glass. 'Sure. I can go to postnatal.' She hates postnatal at nights: full of exhausted hormonal women paranoid something is wrong with their baby. For any one of whom perhaps there is something wrong with their baby.

'Can you?' Jenny peers at her.

'If that's where I'm needed. Or I can stay on labour ward. Wherever I'm most needed. Don't worry.'

'Do I need to worry?'

'No.'

'Handover to Rebecca and Vicky, then off you go. And make sure you tell them up in postnatal that you're on a piece of string.'

*

'I'm on a piece of string,' says Luisa to Debbie, in the post-natal office. 'Jenny said she might have to call me back downstairs.' I am a piece of string. Frayed at both ends. A frayed knot, she giggles. Then stops, too suddenly.

'Well I can't help with anything much up here at the moment,' says Debbie. 'The woman in 4, her blood pressure's completely fucking around. She needs me most of the time.' Debbie sips at a cup of tea, lies back in her chair. This is obviously not one of the times when the woman in 4 needs her. 'I've got the SHO with me,' Debbie says, though Luisa cannot see how this improves her excuse.

'Lilitha Choudrouy?' says Luisa. 'Is she the SHO?'

'Could be.' Debbie sounds unsure, and clear she will not go to the effort of finding out.

'So which rooms should I do?' Luisa hears the hum of the heavy industrial fridges, a drone that rises and falls with her breathing, is controlled by breathing.

'Is that the fridges?' Luisa stops breathing, and the noise is gone.

'What fridges?' says Debbie.

Perhaps this is the sound of her own blood, blood pumping around her body. 'Who shall I look after?' she says.

'Why don't you do 8 and 10? And look in on 9. And the woman in 10-3 needs antibiotics. At some point anyway. I was about to do it.'

'So I should do her antibiotics?'

'I'm not in charge,' laughs Debbie. 'Ask Diane if she is doing it. She's got the rest of the odd number rooms.'

Luisa looks down the ward list: in Room 8 she sees Cheryl Costello. 'I'll do 9 and 10,' she says Luisa. 'That's two four beds. You could look after 8.'

'I can't do 8,' says Debbie.

'You can't?'

'Like I said, the woman in 4 is talking all my attention.' Debbie pours herself another cup of tea.' Plus I've got Sarah Marchant in antenatal in 2. She's the medical claims lawyer Jenny keeps harping on about.'

'Medical claims?'

'Sarah Marchant. She's a lawyer, works in Medical Claims. Jenny said she's to get whatever she wants. So I'm sticking with her. Can't really let her out of my sight.'

Luisa says nothing.

'Check with Jenny if you like.'

'I'll do the IV woman in 10-3,' says Luisa. She heads down the corridor towards Room 10, then turns back to 8. Get it over with.

'Hi!' Luisa puts her head around the door. 'Good to see you all again!'

Cheryl looks up from her bed, first to Luisa's right, framed by the turquoise curtains pulled back on their curved rail. Eric's face turns from behind the screen of an enormous camera, the extended lens poked into the V formed by Cheryl's breasts and a feeding baby.

'Oh, Luisa!' says Cheryl. 'Oh, I'm so glad you came to see us.'

'Look at him,' says Eric, moving to the side. 'Have you seen him?'

Luisa steps between the curtains. 'He's beautiful.' Eric's camera obscures her view, and she can only see the back of the suckling baby's head. 'So you're all doing okay?' She stops herself from adding 'now'. Don't forget the IV drugs, she thinks.

'We wanted to say thank you,' says Cheryl. Luisa searches Cheryl's face for a smile, even the hint of one, but what she finds instead is that under the strip lights Cheryl's face is a smooth, pale orange colour.

'Well it was my pleasure to look after you,' she smiles.

'We have a card.' Eric rests his camera on Cheryl's legs and rummages through the holdall beside the bed. 'We have a card somewhere. To say thank you. I don't know what I've done with it.'

'That's very kind of you. So, you're all happy with – how it went?

In the end?'

'We have a lovely baby!' laughs Eric. 'All a bit scary at the time, I suppose. The caesarean and whatever.'

'I can go through your notes with you if you like, talk over why we made the decisions,' says Luisa. 'So it's all clear.' The IV drugs. The IV drugs, the drug chart, get Metronidazole, find Diane to be checker.

'We'd like that,' says Cheryl. 'I'd really like that. Though I am so *tired*.'

'Well, now you can get some sleep,' says Luisa.

'It must take it out of *you*, working nights. Here, have a seat.' Eric sweeps his camera satchel off the chair. 'Please.'

Luisa looks at the padded chair. The chair is dangerous – the chair can exploit her weakness. 'I've got used to it, really.'

'Now I've managed a bit of sleep,' says Cheryl. 'I'd really like to go through all the details.' Cheryl shuffles over in bed, making space for Luisa to sit down.

'I do need to do some checks.' Luisa takes a step back towards the door. 'On all the women I'm looking after,' she says. 'I'll come back, soon. To go through the notes.'

'Of course,' Cheryl and Eric chorus.

'Whenever you've got a moment,' says Eric. 'And I'll find that card.'

The IVs, Luisa thinks. But she wants to pay one more unit of attention and steps back to the bed. 'So the feeding looks like it's going well,' she says. Elijah opens his mouth wide and slips off of Cheryl's breast. His lips burble for another purchase. 'He's latching on the, the.'

Cheryl guides his head back into position and Elijah feeds again.

'You've got him nicely latched onto the, the,' says Luisa. She stares at Cheryl's chest, trying to remember the name for the round purple thing in the middle of the breast, the part with the speckled bump. There's another one on the other breast. Hillock? Pupil? Luisa sees that Cheryl is wearing mascara, her face is fully made up, that the orange is some kind of foundation. 'He's latching okay?'

'He does this thing, sometimes,' she says. 'I don't know if it's anything. But perhaps you can see. He's not doing it now,' says Cheryl. 'He might in a minute.'

'You're a good colour anyway,' says Luisa. 'Considering you lost quite a lot of blood.'

'It's Total Coverage.'

Eric clicks four or five pictures of the three of them: Cheryl, Luisa, and Elijah. 'Sorry,' he says. 'Do you mind?'

'Please,' says Luisa, trying to work out what total coverage might mean. 'I love seeing photos.'

'I've been documenting the whole thing. The whole pregnancy.' Eric pulls a tablet from the camera bag, taps and dabs a finger back and forth across it.

'If it's settled down,' Luisa says to Cheryl, 'I'm sure there's not a problem.'

'He'll do it again if you keep watching.'

Eric steps around the bed so they can all view the screen. He stops swiping on a stark black-and-white image of a cornfield – to one side stands a naked Cheryl, side view on, staring into the distance with her hand on her distended belly.

'You take great photos,' says Luisa. The IV woman, in 10-3. Is it 10-3?

Eric continues to hold the cornfield picture. At last he swipes across to the next, identical except Cheryl wears a hat.

'Well I'll be back a bit later,' says Luisa. 'To go over the birth.'

'There's quite a few more you haven't seen,' says Eric.

'They're beautiful pictures,' says Luisa, and heads to the door.

'Can I ask?' says Cheryl. 'Would it be okay to have another blanket? I'm a little cold.'

'Of course. I won't be a moment.'

'Thank you,' says Eric. 'Thank you so much.'

Luisa turns left out of Room 6, back to the post-natal office at the end of the central corridor, and takes the drugs chart from its folder.

'Nipple,' says Luisa. 'Nipples.'

'And the same to you,' laughs Debbie, sat in the same chair where Luisa left her.

'I need someone to do a drugs check,' says Luisa, looking at the chart. 'For the IV woman.'

'Can you ask Diane?' Debbie holds the keys to the drugs cupboard up to

Luisa, pinched between two fingers. 'I need to get back to this woman with the blood pressure. The SHO's in with her now.'

Luisa marches down the corridor and puts her head into the darkness of Room 1.

'Diane?', whispers Luisa. 'Diane?' She repeats the call in Rooms 3 and 5, and is about to leave when she hears, 'Here. I'm here.'

'Why are you there in the dark?' whispers Luisa back into the room.

Diane stands and emerges from the darkness. 'Julie here couldn't sleep,' says Diane. 'I held her hand, and sang to her a little. Now she's gone down.'

'I need a drugs check,' says Luisa. As Diane follows her to the supplies room Luisa sees she is wearing blue eye shadow, so much eye shadow it is almost a war paint streak across the bridge of her nose.

Luisa unlocks the drugs cupboard, takes down a bag of Metronidazole, mixes it with the powdered Cefuroxime.

'Look, no fish,' says Diane, and holds up the bag for Luisa to see.

'Sure,' says Luisa. 'I can't see any fish.'

'I mean there are no particles in the bag.'

'No. Right. I already checked.' Luisa shakes her head, trying to clear. 'Right patient, right drug, right dose, right route, right time,' she mantras. I need to write out a sticker for the IV bag. But Diane has already done so, hands the sticker to her. Luisa looks on the drugs chart: Diane has recorded everything.

'Do you use a Lots-To-Remember?' asks Luisa.

'I have nothing to remember. Nothing,' says Diane, as though a final declaration before exiting, a suicide cry, but she continues: 'She loves begonias, the woman in 5. She says thinking about begonias got her through her contractions.' Luisa hands the IV bag to Diane. Diane hands it back to her. 'That one's yours, I think,' says Diane.

'It is,' says Luisa. 'I need to get it to 10-3.'

'It's a long time since I've seen a begonia,' says Diane.

Room 10 is also dark, and quiet. All the bed curtains are drawn, and Luisa stands for a moment in the centre of the room. She closes her eyes, squeezes them shut, squeezes the IV bag and opens her eyes. She repeats the circuit: squeeze, shut, squeeze, open. Cheryl's blanket. Bed 10-3.

Luisa steps around the curtain of bed 3. The woman is snoring.

'Hello, Tara.' Luisa reads the name from the band on Tara's wrist, and rests a hand on Tara's shoulder. Tara's eyes bolt open. 'I'm about to give you your antibiotics,' Luisa lilts to her.

'Now?' says Tara, staring.

'It's time. So I'm just going to give you your antibiotics. These are intravenous antibiotics.' Didn't she say that already? She's explaining, it's fine. 'If you can remind me, your name and date of birth.'

'You just said my name, didn't you?' says Tara.

'It's so we know they're going to the right person.'

'Tara, Fisher,' says Tara.

'And date of birth?'

'Fifth of March. Nineteen eighty-four.'

'Thank you, thank you for that,' says Luisa. She lifts the IV bag to hook it onto the drip stand, but there is no drip stand, and therefore no pump. 'But to give you your intravenous antibiotics I'll need an electric pump, and I don't have the pump with me right now.' She puts the IV bag in its tray on the window sill, as though that is the next stage in the procedure.

Tara continues to stare.

'So now I'll go and get the pump,' says Luisa.

In the equipment storeroom at the end of the hall there are no drip stands with pumps. Luisa hears the hum of the industrial fridges again, and this time it does not stop. Erin passes the cupboard doorway.

'Erin,' calls Luisa. 'Do you know where the Baxter pumps are?' Further down the corridor she sees Eric move out from the doorway of Room 8, and look left and right. Luisa steps back into the shadow of the equipment storeroom.

'They took them all to labour ward,' says Erin.

'Could you go get me one, do you think?' Luisa peers out to see Eric go back inside Room 8, and she steps out from the cupboard again.

'Are you in or out?' says Erin.

Luisa stares at her, until she realises Erin is referring to the cupboard.

'I'm out,' says Luisa. 'I'm out now.'

'I can go in ten minutes,' says Erin. 'I'm helping a woman breastfeed right now.'

'I actually need it quite soon.'

'I can go in ten minutes.'

'Don't worry. I can do it.'

Luisa calls the labour ward from the office. The phone rings and rings. Luisa looks down the corridor, towards the lifts, and back the other way, straight into the eyes of Eric.

'I'm going to get you that blanket,' Luisa calls to him in hushed tones, her hand over the receiver.

Eric turns his ear towards her and frowns.

'I don't want to wake other people.' Luisa keeps the same volume but opens her mouth wider as she speaks. Labour ward not answering, she thinks. I could fetch the blanket and call again in a minute. But I have to fetch a pump. 'I'm going to get a blanket,' she mouths to Eric again.

'Hello, maternity,' says Jenny down the phone.

'It's Luisa, in postnatal.'

'Hello Luisa in postnatal. I'm going to pull your string and bring you back down here in not too long. I've got a couple of women on their way in who are sounding pushy.'

'I think you've got all the Baxter pumps. Can someone bring one down?'

'Just send the MCA up for one.'

'She's a bit busy right now. If you could send one down when – '

'Well we're a bit busy here, too. What are you doing up there now? I need you back down here soon.'

'An IV, that's why I need it,' says Luisa. 'The pump.' Eric watches her from the doorway, waiting for her to finish the call. Luisa holds up a finger to him.

'When you've done with the IV come straight back up here,' says Jenny.

'I need to fetch the pump first.'

'I'll put one in the lift. I'm doing it now.'

'Right. Okay, yes. Thanks.'

'And Luisa. Wait.'

Luisa hears a muffled sound that suggests Jenny is covering the receiver. She hears voices but cannot make out the words. She does not want to look up, does not want to look at Eric again.

'Mmm-hmm,' she nods into the phone. 'Mm-hmm. Okay.' She nods some more.

'Luisa,' says Jenny.

'Yes, okay.'

'Rebecca needs a bed up there. Needs you to book a bed in postnatal. Seema O'Reilly. Can you do that?'

'Of course.' Book bed, IV, get straight back downstairs before Donal gets up here. She presses the space bar of the office computer to bring up the Word document showing the ward list. There is only one bed available, in Room 8. One of hers. Luisa brings her watch fob into her palm: 03.45. Donal and Seema shouldn't be here until at least four-thirty. Finish the IV and I'll be back on labour ward long before then.

'The bed's booked,' says Luisa quietly. The phone is dead.

The Senior House Officer steps into the office. Luisa has a flash vision of her standing over Luisa on the floor of Michel Odent, cuddled up to Donal.

'Hi,' says Luisa.

'You were downstairs earlier, weren't you?' says the Senior House Officer.

'I'm not sure. I don't think so.' The Senior House Officer looks up, confused. She is just being friendly, thinks Luisa. 'I was downstairs, but now I'm up here.'

'Right,' says the Senior House Officer. 'Okay.'

'Worst time of the night, isn't it?' says Luisa. 'I don't mind shifts but I can never nap. Not on my breaks, or anytime. Sorry,' she trips off, out of the office. 'I've got a pump coming. In the lift.'

'Okay,' says the Senior House Officer.

Luisa sprints to the double doors out to the corridor, wondering if Jenny's lift will have returned downstairs, slaps her swipe card to the reader, shoulders open the door. The corridor strip lights blind her, she holds up an arm to cover her eyes. Both lifts are at floor 2, ground level. She presses both call buttons, watches the numbers ascend.

The lift displays remain in sync, or almost. They display the same ascending number but Luisa is unsure which lift the creature is in. The pump is in. Luisa leans against the wall of the corridor, the lifts chime in unison, the doors open. It is in the left one.

'Come on,' says Luisa, as to a puppy. She jams her foot against the lift door to prevent it closing, grips the drip stand by the neck and wheels back into the ward.

Eric stands at the linen cupboard next to the office, peering up to the top shelf, one hand inside.

'Sorry,' says Eric. 'Cheryl was getting – she's a bit cold. I know you're busy.'

'There's no blankets in there,' says Luisa, and she is past the cupboard, has to turn around and come back. 'Not in there. I'll start off these antibiotics and I'll be with you.' I could grab a blanket now, couldn't I? Wouldn't it be easier to grab one now?

'If you let me know where,' says Eric. 'Or should I ask the other lady?'

Luisa sets the drip stand in motion again. 'Yes, yes. Ask Erin. She's the one to ask.' She cannot see Erin, but this feels like a solution.

'Hello again, Tara,' coos Luisa back in Room 10. 'Here we are with the pump.' Tara's eyes snap open. Now I have a complete IV system, thinks Luisa, now I am ready. She pierces the IV bag with the end of the IV line, hangs the bag on the stand, closes the wheel on the line, squeezes the chamber to move the fluid in. She has done this a hundred times. Tara watches, Luisa sees Tara watching. Watching her helping. Luisa crouches to push the plug of the Baxter pump into the wall socket, and the green light flicks on, and the machine emits two piercing beeps. Tara turns her head away.

Did you hear the sound test? asks the screen on the pump.

Yes, I did, thinks Luisa. She stabs the Yes button and unwinds the line until the end rests next to Tara's hand on the bed.

'Now I just need to check that your cannula is okay.' She places her fingers under Tara's palm, lifts her hand, there is no resistance. Tara peers up at her. Luisa inserts a syringe into the tube taped to the back of Tara's hand, injects saline. Tara's face contorts, but she makes no noise.

'Did that hurt?' says Luisa.

'It hurt,' whispers Tara. 'Not *too* much.'

'Was it cold?'

'I don't know. Compared to what?'

Diane puts her head around the doorway. Luisa looks up, and Diane says nothing, does not smile or frown or anything, hangs there like an ornament for the door frame.

'Okay, Diane?' says Luisa.

'Jenny called for you,' says Diane.

'When?'

'Tonight.'

'But what did she say?'

Diane's head disappears. Luisa looks down at Tara, who stares back. She depresses the syringe again, but with too much pressure.

'It's fine, I think,' says Tara. Her eyes are wet.

Diane's head appears again.

'Is Luisa there?' says Diane.

'I'm here, Diane,' says Luisa.

'I'm just telling you what Jenny said.'

Diane disappears again. Luisa knows she cannot use the cannula – it is no longer inserted into the vein. She doesn't want to replace a cannula, she hates doing cannulas. The potential for pain infliction, the apologies. She doesn't have time to replace a cannula, she needs to get back downstairs. Back down to Jenny.

'Are you finished?' whispers Tara.

'Almost done. I won't be a minute.'

As she crosses the corridor, she scans for Eric. Her way is clear. She glances into Room 8. Seema and Donal not here yet.

In Room 4 Debbie sits in a chair by the bed.

'And have you been having any bad headaches?' says Dr Choudruoy to the woman in the bed.

'I won't be able to get over there for a while.' Debbie says to the woman in the bed, slotting her conversation between the doctor's questions. 'A few months at least.'

'You contact my mother and father when you go. You tell them how you looked after me.' The woman in bed squeezes Debbie's hand. 'No headaches,' she says to Dr Choudruoy.

'Tara in 10-3,' says Luisa. 'Her cannula has blown, and she needs a new one. I have to get back downstairs, Jenny keeps calling.'

'Selentia here is still a bit iffy,' says Debbie. 'I can't really leave her on her own right now.'

'You're so good to me,' says Selentia.

'You can do cannulas, can't you Luisa?' says Debbie. 'Or ask Diane?'

'I have to get back downstairs.'

'Have you given it a go?' says Dr Choudruoy.

'I have.' Luisa blushes. 'I don't really have the time now. 'Things keep coming up. I need to find a blanket.'

'Will you be there, for when I have the baby?' says Selentia to Debbie. 'I want it be you.'

'Selentia's from Slovenia. It sounds like a beautiful place,' Debbie smiles at Luisa. 'I'm thinking of going myself.'

'It's – I need to get back downstairs.' Luisa hears her voice wobble. 'Jenny needs me,' she says fiercely, at Debbie.

'Well, whatever Jenny wants,' says Debbie.

'It's okay. I can do it,' says Dr Choudruoy, and puts down Selentia's notes booklet.

'Thank you,' says Luisa. 'Thanks for that. I've done the rest, the pump and IV line, it just needs the cannula.'

I can go, thinks Luisa when back in the corridor. I can go downstairs. She passes the linen cupboard: blanket. She tucks a blanket under her arm.

A woman in a hospital gown stumbles from Room 6. Her gown has fallen undone to reveal a narrow naked strip all the way from her feet to her neck. A taught IV line tethers her to an unknown source back in the room, and slackens as the drip stand crashes out of the doorway and to the floor.

'I'm sorry,' sobs the Room 6 woman. Vomit covers the front of her gown, as well as her arm where the IV connects to the cannula. 'It came on me all of a sudden. I'm sorry.'

'It's okay. It's okay.' Luisa picks up the drip stand with her free hand. 'Here, let me.'

'I'm fine. I'm fine now. I need to – do you have another gown? I'm sorry.'

'Let's get you all cleaned up.' Luisa collects vomit from the woman's arm into paper towels whilst the woman sobs.

'Hi, Luisa.' In the corridor behind her comes Seema, in a wheelchair pushed by Erin. 'So you're down here now. Sorry,' says Seema to the Room 6 woman, looking at the vomit.

Luisa looks for Donal, but he is nowhere to be seen. Damn Rebecca and her heartless efficiency at shunting women out of labour ward. Dr Choudruoy walks past, and Luisa watches her examine their huddle: Luisa, the wronged wife, vomit woman.

'I'm about to come see you and your baby,' Luisa says to Seema. She balls together the vomit-filled paper towels and guides the woman back into Room 6 by her clean arm. Inside she puts the blanket on the bed, and helps undo the ties at the back of the Room 6's gown.

'I'm so sorry,' repeats Room 6. 'I can do this myself, I can.'

The gown is off but the IV line still runs through the sleeve, and the woman cannot see that the gown's complete removal is impossible. Luisa uncouples the IV line from her cannula, removes and wraps the gown into a ball. Together they wipe her arms and thighs with paper towels.

'Thank you,' says Room 6, as Luisa helps her into her own clothes. The woman looks on the verge of tears again, this time with gratitude, 'I'm so sorry. Thank you.'

'It wasn't a problem,' says Luisa, as the woman climbs back into bed. Of course she is happy to help – helping is what she does. This is her skillset. 'I have to be going now, I'm afraid.' She takes the gown and blanket from the bed, and as she exits the room sees that a small trickle of translucent vomit has run from the gown and onto the blanket. She angles the blanket to one side, and the vomit slips to the floor.

'Oh, thank you!' Eric stands just outside the room. 'Erin told me where they were but I didn't know where she meant.' He reaches for the blanket. Luisa increases her grip, preventing him from taking it.

'Not this one,' says Luisa.

'No?' Eric looks devastated.

'This one's not clean.'

'It looks fine to me.'

'It's got – a little bit of sick on it.'

'Really?' Eric leans in closer. 'I can't really see – it's fine. It'll be fine.'

Erin passes them. 'Jenny's after you,' she says. 'She called down. Did you say you wanted me to fetch a Baxter pump?'

'I'll get you another one,' says Luisa.

'I don't need a pump. But do *you* still need one?' says Erin.

'Another blanket,' Luisa says to Eric.

'I'll just work it out myself, shall I?' Erin walks away.

'This one is fine,' says Eric, and he pulls it from Luisa. 'I know you're busy, I do.' His pained expression reminds her of Justin, of his attempt at nonchalance when she listed her shifts for the Christmas holidays. Now Eric has the blanket in his hands and she cannot retrieve it without a certain level of physical force, and physical force is against the NMC Code of Conduct. Eric disappears back into Room 8.

Why can't we speak like normal people, have a normal conversation? In the real world, outside, her and Eric might be friends – here a professional wall exists between them. Whose fault is that? Jenny's? The babies'? Justin's? The government's? No one's? She's too tired to take a side, and too tired to blame no one.

Luisa follows into Room 8.

'I can't let you take a soiled blanket,' she says quietly to Eric.

Cheryl looks up and smiles at her. 'Luisa,' she says, as to an old friend.

'I'll get another one,' says Luisa, but no one is listening – Eric and Cheryl are distracted by the voices from behind the curtain of the neighbouring bed.

'You're getting it on the sheet,' she hears Seema say.

'She keeps – I'm trying to get it off,' says Donal.

Luisa turns back to the blanket.

'There's poo on my sheet as well,' says Seema.

'I could do with some help. Press the buzzer for some help,' says Donal.

'Do you want to deal with that?' Eric asks Luisa quietly.

'I think they're okay,' says Luisa, even more quietly.

'The buzzer's on the floor,' says Seema. 'I can't reach. My legs don't move, remember?'

'I can't hold her and press the buzzer.'

'Don't touch me!'

'I should help, yes,' says Luisa. 'And I haven't forgotten about you. About going through your notes.' Cheryl watches as Eric pulls a tissue from his pocket and scrubs at the corner of the blanket.

Luisa steps around Seema's curtain, pulls it shut behind her.

'Oh, Luisa. Thank goodness,' says Seema.

'You're here. Up here.' Donal holds their baby girl by the head and feet, dangling her meconium-covered buttocks and legs in between.

'I work here,' says Luisa. Why should she be embarrassed? She sets the balled robe of vomit on the floor, takes the baby from Donal, and sets about cleaning up. Donal steps back until he touches the curtain.

'Thank you. I think we've forgotten what it's all like,' laughs Seema. She lies back, and says nothing more.

In the silence Luisa changes the sheets on the cot and sets about cleaning the baby. She wills the baby to cry, to make some noise, but she appears to be asleep. 'Early poo is really tricky,' says Luisa. '*Really* difficult. Oh, it gets everywhere. So thick, like tar.' She works quickly, scrubbing hard at the black tar. 'Interestingly enough it's completely sterile, meconium. Doesn't even smell.'

'Sorry,' says Donal, but it is not clear what he is apologising for.

'It gets all over the place. It's so thick,' says Luisa. 'Remember you don't want to go poking around too much. In her vagina,' she says to Seema.

Seema is asleep.

'But if,' she turns to frown at Donal, 'but if you've got poo in her vagina, you have to get that out.'

'Sorry,' says Donal. 'In who's vagina?'

'The baby's. Your daughter's.' Luisa snaps together poppers on the babygro. 'Are you good to take over now?'

'Yes, yes. Please go,' says Donal. 'I mean, please get back to whatever else you have to do. And thank you,' he adds.

Luisa picks up the balled robe of vomit and slides out the room. Cheryl and Eric's curtains are closed.

In the sluice room Luisa puts the gown ball in the red plastic sack and stands at the sink, letting the warm water run over and over her hands. She leaves them there for longer than necessary, and the the unfamiliar lack of movement leaves her dizzy. She grips the side of the wash basin. Does she need a fresh blanket now? A fresh blanket will take no time at all, but swapping the vomit blanket for the fresh one will only draw attention. Fresh blanket or no fresh blanket? Get back to labour ward, to Jenny.

Luisa emits a high-pitched squee from her tight-pressed lips. Why does it matter, to whom does it matter, who will know, who will remember? She will remember. Why will she remember this, when she forgets so much else? No fresh blanket, no time. No time to debrief Cheryl and Eric.

Exiting the sluice room she almost bumps into the Dr Choudruoy.

'That was weird,' says Dr Choudruoy. She is calm, jolly sounding even. 'I don't think I've ever managed to cannulate a woman whilst she's asleep before.'

'It's amazing what you can do in your sleep,' says Luisa. 'What I mean is, people can do anything to me when I'm asleep. If I want them to. When I'm asleep.' I keep saying sleep. Stop saying sleep.

'Right,' says Dr Choudruoy. Her expression could mean anything, from *you're weird* to *I'm not listening* to *I want to have as little to do with midwives who cuddle sleeping husbands as possible*. 'So, she's all ready for you. For the antibiotics.'

'Still need to do antibiotics,' says Luisa.

Dr Choudruoy's bleep goes off and she turns away.

'I'll do them now,' says Luisa.

Tara is still asleep, the room silent. Her hand lies on top of the blanket, the insertion point of the cannula ready and waiting. Luisa takes the screw thread at the end of the IV line, crouches down and attempts to insert the screw into the cannula. Her hand is shaking. The screw thread bumps the edge of the cannula hole.

'Fifth of March, nineteen-eighty four,' murmurs Tara, and opens her eyes.

'Hello, Tara,' sings Luisa from her crouching position. 'Is is okay if I start the antibiotics?' Their faces are very close.

'No allergies,' says Tara. Her eyes close again.

Luisa lifts Tara's hand with her fingers, presents the cannula to her sleeping face. I have consent, she thinks. She consented earlier. I don't need to ask again. She screws the line into the cannula. Tara makes no movement.

'Luisa! Luisa!' A poltergeist hisses her name, from somewhere under the beds. Diane appears from the shadows. 'Phone call.'

'Tell Jenny I'm coming.' Luisa touches the IV line – it is screwed tight.

'Jenny says to bring a wheelchair down. There's a woman just come in she wants you to look after.'

'Almost done.' And she is, she is done. She rolls forward the wheel on the IV line, checks the dosage rate on the pump. Everything is done. Outside the room Diane has left a wheelchair parked by the doorway. Luisa does not allow the wheelchair to break her forward motion, simply grabs the handles and pushes it ahead of her. Blanket, fresh blanket. She passes the linen cupboard, the door is open, she pulls down a blanket without stopping, throws it into the seat of the wheelchair, pushes on to Room 8.

'I've got you a new blanket,' says Luisa into the room.

Eric is asleep in the chair, Cheryl asleep with the sick blanket tucked around her, their baby on the sheet next to her. Luisa tugs at the sick blanket, but Cheryl's grip is too tight.

The baby opens its eyes to look at Luisa – deep blue, huge, almost too big for his face. She wants to put her finger inside his wrinkled palm.

'I brought it,' whispers Luisa, and lays the blanket over Eric. 'But now I have to go.'

Luisa waits with the wheelchair by the lift. She is free, free of the postnatal ward, she has succeeded. Has succeeded in making it back. Back to labour ward. She wonders what time it is, how close it is to the end, the end of the shift. Of her life. Of her working life, anyway. Could it be tonight? Maybe Dr Choudruoy is talking to Jenny right now, telling Jenny that she was asleep whilst on duty, that she was asleep whilst spooning a man whose wife was about to give birth. That sounds awful – written down, written down on an appraisal sheet, typed up as an official warning. She pushes the wheelchair footpad against the lift doors, angry. She doesn't have to take that – she can resign, tonight, can go to Jenny right now and say she is leaving. But she will have to work another month, a month's notice. The idea of a month's more work, that enormity of that block of work time brings tears to her eyes. And that is only if she hands in her notice right now. Otherwise it is not a month, it is – forever. But she can just leave, leave without saying a word. Go down in the lift to the hospital entrance, dump the wheelchair, walk out and never come back. What will they do without her wages, her and Justin? Something. Something, something else.

The lift doors open, and inside is Dr Choudruoy. Luisa wheels the chair in.

Dr Choudruoy smiles but says nothing. Why is she saying nothing? Luisa is saying nothing, and perhaps this is why Dr Choudruoy is saying nothing. Why am I saying nothing?

'I was downstairs earlier. With Seema,' says Luisa.

'Who?' says Dr Choudruoy.

'The woman in Michel Odent, the multip. The Indian woman I spoke to back there.' Better not to deny, to come clean. 'I looked after her, earlier, when I was down in labour ward.'

The lift descends.

'Oh yes. I reviewed her earlier. She had an epidural, yes.' Dr Choudruoy looks at the panel of buttons. 'Are you – ? You've missed labour ward. I'm going down to A and E.'

'Oh. I'll come back. I'll come back up.'

'I've been wondering about that all night,' says Dr Choudruoy. 'About her. What is her name?'

'I don't know,' says Luisa. 'I don't know her very well. I only spoke, spoke to her.'

'When I went in, to do the review.' Dr Choudruoy smiles, puts a hand to her mouth. 'I kept trying to work out who was with who. There was a couple on the floor, sleeping. But cuddled up to each other. Was that her husband? But who was the other woman? It was all dark, I couldn't really see.'

'The husband, yes,' says Luisa. 'I don't know though, not really.'

'So was that the woman's sister?'

'Her sister?'

'The one on the floor. Cuddled up to the husband? That was the sister?'

The lift dings and the doors open on floor 2. Dr Choudruoy steps out and Luisa puts an arm across the door to prevent it from closing.

'I – was a bit confused myself,' says Luisa. 'When I saw them.'

'So who *was* she then?' Dr Choudruoy turns and grins, a lewd grin.

'I didn't really want to ask.' Luisa allows herself a smile.

'It's really interesting, isn't it? You think you know all about your culture. Well that's if I can call it my culture, even if I've always lived here. But I thought I understood Pakistanis, their customs. I get it shoved down my throat enough. Perhaps I have no idea,' she laughs.

'Kashmiri,' says Luisa. 'I think it's a Kashmiri thing.'

'Ah,' says Dr Choudruoy, and turns away.

Luisa moves back into the lift, exhales without a sound. She presses button 12 for labour ward. The lift descends again, and she punches button 12 repeatedly, thumps it with the side of her fist. The bell dings and the doors open.

She is in the basement, assaulted by the low thrum of poorly maintained industrial appliances. She presses button 12 again, presses and presses, but nothing happens.

Lift functionality cannot be her responsibility. Jenny cannot expect her to fix the lift – there was no training module for lift engineering. This is an emergency – she presses the emergency alarm. She expects a klaxon, something shrill, but there is no sound at all.

'I'm stuck,' she says into the tiny holes of the intercom. 'I'm stuck in the lift. In the basement. Tell the labour ward. Can you tell the labour ward Luisa Keane is stuck in the basement?'

All she can hear is static, then silence.

At last a voice says: 'Please wait – someone – there. With – soon.'

'Please can you tell the labour ward? Luisa Keane is stuck in the lift.'

The voice does not answer. There is nothing more to do. For once there is nothing to do. Luisa sits in the wheelchair. She has to wait – all she can do is wait. And if she is waiting, she can sit down.

When Luisa opens her eyes, it is because of a sharp pain in her finger. Her eyes are very close to a section of green canvas. An eco-coffin, thinks Luisa. Perhaps I've died from exhaustion and Justin decided that an eco-coffin was what I wanted. She brings her head back upright and sees that the green canvas is a hospital screen, enclosing her on three sides, and that squashed in with her is the Registrar, holding Luisa's fingers in her hand.

The Registrar takes the blood sugar monitor from Luisa's lap.

'Your glucose levels are only 3.1,' says the Registrar. 'That's pretty low.'

Luisa pulls at the canvas and the panel rolls to one side on wheels. She sees Jenny standing at Reception.

'Ah. There you are,' says Jenny. 'You were looking a little untidy, Ms

Keane. Hence the screens.'

Luisa peers over the reception desk to see Debbie with a telephone cradled on her shoulder.

'Yes, taxi please. From the Royal Victoria hospital. I've got to go home,' Debbie tells Luisa. 'It's not fair to spread germs to all these women. I shouldn't be here when I'm ill.' This last line she directs with some venom at Jenny.

'No one said you should work when you're ill,' says Jenny.

'I was in the lift,' whispers Luisa to the Registrar. 'Why aren't I in the lift?'

'They wanted to take you to A and E,' says the Registrar. 'Your glucose levels are almost diabetic. You shouldn't have glucose that low.'

'Of course her glucose is low,' says Jenny. 'And she's not diabetic. She's a midwife at the end of her shift. She's probably not eaten for twelve hours.'

'What time is it?' says Luisa.

The doctor looks at his watch. 'Almost seven.'

'Have you not been having any snacks?' says Jenny. 'Where are the biscuits?'

'I might as well go wait downstairs,' says Debbie. 'They said the taxi won't be long.'

'You need to do some kind of handover,' says Jenny.

'It's all on the board,' says Debbie. 'I have to go or the taxi will charge me extra for waiting.'

'It might not be my glucose,' says Luisa to the Registrar. She watches Jenny move off down the corridor, wants her to come back, wants Jenny to hear all that is wrong with her.

'Make sure you eat properly,' says the Registrar.

'Is that all?' says Luisa, but the Registrar has gone.

'Got to go,' says Debbie. 'I tell you, this place. You know what I was thinking the other night?' Debbie leans over the desk. 'I'm thinking I'll have a baby. You get a whole year off with a baby. I mean right now, I don't sleep properly between shifts, I get into arguments with Stan. And when I do come in we have to deal with this kind of madness. I need a bit of a break from it all.'

Then Debbie is gone, off through the double doors.

Jenny writes on a form, leaning on the Reception desk.

'I'm sorry,' says Luisa.

'I want you to promise me you'll eat more on shift,' says Jenny. 'I'm not having any of my staff with low glucose levels again.'

'Jenny, the primip has clawed her way to 9 centimetres,' says Rebecca, striding past them without slowing down.

'I'll be just there,' says Jenny.

'The lift was stuck,' says Luisa. 'Was everything okay here?'

'I took over your woman. It's her I'm going to now.' Jenny is still writing.

'The lift was broken.'

'Well it seems to be working now.'

'I must have fallen asleep whilst I was waiting for the lift to be fixed.'

'She delivered fine, anyway.'

'So everything is – okay?'

'Nobody died, if that's what you mean.'

She'll report me, thinks Luisa. She's going to DATIX me. I won't let her. I'll say I'm leaving. If I leave she can't put me on a disciplinary.

But then I won't be a midwife.

Jenny walks away. 'Can you sort her out please, Luisa? She's in Carol Decker. Delivered at 06:20, make sure she's got tea and toast, and get that baby fed. It's a scrawny little thing.'

'I was stuck in a lift,' says Luisa, too quietly for Jenny to hear. She climbs out of the wheelchair, heads toward Carol Decker.

'Thank you for your service.' Jenny raises a hand and is gone.

THURSDAY DAY: OFF DUTY

'Couldn't face it this morning?' says the taxi driver.

'Mmm,' Luisa watches the bushes and trees flash past the taxi window, the wheels whisking through the rain of the main road. The wheels are loud. The trees are louder. How do trees produce sound?

'I used to train,' the taxi driver continues. 'Used to go about three miles and think, why am I doing this? Then I'd have to walk home. Complete waste of my time.' He looks over his shoulder at Luisa.

'I don't get the train,' says Luisa.

'That's what I like to hear.'

Luisa replays their words, and then again, but they still make no sense. Perhaps she has forgotten some of the words. She is losing her grip on other people, sinking into her world where conversation is no longer possible, where people are entirely content to say sentences that have no bearing on the words that came before. She looks down and realises the taxi driver is referring to her clothes, to her jogging clothes.

'Oh, I hate jogging,' she says.

'Me too. That's why I always go by car.' The taxi driver laughs, satisfied by this conclusion.

They turn into the estate, past the turning that leads to the sports club, to the sports club car park. Luisa peers down the track – there are no cars visible. Maybe their vandalising of the car never happened. It did happen. It happened, and it was fun.

'Up early, then, if it's not jogging,' says the taxi driver.

'Work,' says Luisa. 'Midwife.' She can get by on nouns.

'Wow,' says the taxi driver. 'Must be a really rewarding job, that.'

'I can't work nights. I'm not sure I can do nights any more.' She listens to herself say the words.

'Oh god, tell me about nights. Used to do them. I got so ill, the doctor says I was this close to complete liver failure.' The taxi driver holds up a finger and thumb pressed together. 'It's not natural, working nights. They've done research that shows each time you do a night shift it takes one point two hours off your life. I had to stop. I start early now.'

'One point two?'

'Must be really rewarding though, midwifery.'

'Mm.' Maybe I'm not going to be a midwife any more – maybe Jenny is reporting me for falling asleep, right now? Can't quit. Can't actually give it up – there's too many people I've told, told *I'm a midwife*. What kind of example would it be to the girls if I gave up my career? Why can't Justin give up his career? Because we need the money. Maybe it's Justin. Maybe it's us I should give up. But then I'll need to move out, need to organise somewhere else to live. I'll need some money. I should keep my job so that I have some money. If Jenny reports me I won't *have* a job.

Her thoughts trail off, overwhelmed by the multitude of possibilities fighting for space in her mind. She looks at her phone again, at the 23 missed calls from Justin. Perhaps I'll take some time off, take a holiday, take a holiday in order to split up with Justin. But I'll have to book the time, I need to give notice, what, a month? Don't do or say anything to Justin. I have to let him know I'm okay.

They pass quietly down the road leading to Arcadia Close. A car in a driveway pumps exhaust smoke, waiting for them to go by. A schoolgirl plods forlornly down the pavement. The phrases in her head sound with long echoes, stretching away from her into a distance that somehow still fits inside her mind. Why is she in a taxi? She never takes taxis. She can't afford to take taxis if she doesn't have a job.

'This is me,' she says, before the taxi reaches her road. 'I'm good here.'

She pays the driver, but when he has gone continues on across the entrance to Arcadia Close, up onto the pavement on the other side. She has to talk to Justin before he leaves for work, but she has forgotten her plan of what to say – cannot remember if there was a plan. She looks down at her lycra leggings, swooshed with orange, and starts to jog, very slowly, barely more than walking. The rhythm calms her. The taxi passes her in the other direction. The driver stares at her in confusion.

She turns on the spot, still jogging, heads into their cul-de-sac, passes the five houses to number 16, jogs onto their driveway, where there are now two cars: the shiny silver courtesy car and behind it, partially blocking the pavement, their paint-splattered Peugeot.

Through the window she can see Justin standing in the kitchen, sipping from a mug. Luisa dives sideways, and crouches down below the hedge that borders the front of the garden. She doesn't want to talk to him, not now. She's too tired, she won't make any sense. How long until he leaves? She does not want to take her phone from her bag, movement might draw attention.

Why is the Peugeot in the driveway?

Colin walks past her with his dog, and raises a hand in greeting. Luisa smiles and raises a hand in return, careful to keep it below the height of the bush, and he passes on by.

She hears the click of the front door and opens her eyes. Not asleep, just closed eyes. She clasps her knees into her chest, holds her breath. She hears the central locking of a car clunk open, and a door open and thud close. The engine starts. And stops. The car door opens again.

'Jesus fuck,' she hears Justin say.

The car door thuds shut again, the engine revs, there is a scrunching noise on the driveway, the sequence repeats over and over. Luisa wants to look up, to see what is happening, but just as she moves upwards in a half crouch the hedge tips towards her. She dives to the side, just as the hedge is flattened against the pavement, the silver car pushing the branches ahead until it pops forward over and onto the road. Luisa scrabbles forward to hide behind the Peugeot, watches as Justin wrenches the steering wheel, turning the car and powering up the road.

Luisa pulls out her phone, taps Justin's name but her finger is shaking, shaking so much she hits send without writing anything. Tell him, she thinks, tell him he almost killed her. But I don't want him to know I was hiding. Why am I hiding? She swipes: Stayed at Helena's, deletes Helena, replaces it with Tina. He didn't know I was behind the hedge, how could he? He was taking control, sorting the situation. I was really upset, she taps, deletes upset, shaken by your admission, admission predicts itself as *armsl?*. She hears the car brake to a halt at the end of the street. Her phone rings.

'Lu. Are you okay?' says Justin.

'I'm fine,' she whispers.

'Where are you? I was worried, I tried calling. You shouldn't have done that. Run out like that. Are you okay?'

'I'm fine.'

'You're very quiet.'

'I have to talk really quietly.'

'Why? Are you being held hostage?'

Is he making a joke? He doesn't sound like he is joking. 'I don't want to wake the children.'

'You're at mum's?'

'Helena's children. Not Helena, Tina. Tina's children. Child.'

'We need to talk about last night.'

Tell him. Tell him you might be sacked, you might have to find another job. That you want to find another job? She remembers Justin, naked, telling her he hated midwifery. This is my job.

'But not now.' She grits her teeth to hold back the anger. 'Keep going now, you'll be late. Don't stop.'

'Where are you?'

Luisa slowly raises herself into a crouch that allows her to waddle to the end of the driveway. She kneels and eyes up the road from under the Peugeot's bumper, from where she can see the rear of the silver courtesy car.

'I know you've stopped because I can hear panting,' she says. 'Now you're not panting. Breathing. You're always breathing. When you run to the station.'

'I'm not running. I have the new car, remember.'

'Maybe run,' says Luisa. 'Maybe you need exercise.'

'I want to talk,' says Justin. 'I'm confused. About everything.'

'Tonight.' Her vocabulary is diminishing, moment to moment. 'Face-to-face.'

'You'll be at work. Almost gone to work. By the time I'm back from Canterbury it'll be almost time for you to go. I'll ring you at lunch.'

I have to work tonight, Luisa remembers with horror. 'Not lunch. I'll be sleeping.' Too snappy. She inhales deeply for a last effort at speaking. 'Tonight, face-to-face. I'll have everything sorted, the girls, tea, everything ready so that we can sit down and talk. I have to go.'

She ends the call, and shortly after hears the car start up again.

'Have you lost something, Luisa? Can I help?'

She looks up to see her neighbour Claudette, in her own driveway, peering over the Peugeot at her.

'Oh, er. Hi.' Luisa stands up too quickly, and has to lean on the car for support.

'Keeping up your fitness.' Claudette nods at Luisa's jogging trousers. 'You're so good. I keep meaning to do more, more exercise myself.'

'No, I'm not – I don't do jogging. I've been working. Just finished. A night shift.'

'Oh yes. Because you are a midwife! In Quebec we do not really have them, I'm so interested in midwives! You must tell me sometime. André, he works in medicine, I know he would like to hear as well.'

Claudette's appearance reminds Luisa that mocking their neighbours is one of her and Justin's few remaining bonding topics, ever since Claudette invited them to a fantastically tedious dinner, the first week she and André moved next door. On the days when they are easy in each other's company, Luisa formally presents oven chips to the dinner table as Claudette, announcing their crispness and origins in prime Kent mud, and Justin plays André, with a discussion of the merits of their cheap supermarket wine.

The obvious response is, *oh well you must come back for dinner at ours sometime*, but Luisa just stares at the Peugeot.

'But what happened to your car?' says Claudette. 'You had – an accident? Who did this?'

'We did this,' says Luisa. 'Justin and I did this.'

'I understand,' says Claudette, scrunching her eyes in confusion.

'An art project. It's a bit of a work in progress.'

'Okay.' Claudette looks away from the car, away from Luisa. Now she is looking at the hedge, flattened onto the pavement. 'There are many things I must learn about England,' says Claudette. 'The things that you must know.

When you've lived somewhere all of your life.'

'We haven't lived here all our lives,' says Luisa. 'We lived in London until the girls were born. Justin and me.'

'People do this to hedges in London?'

'I don't like hedges,' says Luisa. 'We're taking it out.'

'Oh!' Claudette smiles, and goes to the examine the hedge removal. 'But I thought all English people liked hedges?'

'Not me,' says Luisa. 'I'm sorry. I have to go to sleep now.'

'Of course. It must be so hard, working at night. Oh look.' Claudette points down at the roots of the hedge, where there sit two bowls with spoons, cereal crusted around their edges. She picks them up. 'Is this what you were looking for?'

'Yes. Thanks,' Luisa takes the bowls from Claudette, and makes her way inside.

*

Luisa wakes because her pelvis is bouncing up and down on the mattress. The duvet is over her eyes, and she pulls back the material to see a hobbit jumping on her bed. But the hobbit is the Queen, is dressed down to its dirty feet in the kind of red velvet cloak that Luisa remembers from ceremonies on television. The Queen's expression is stony – upset with her.

'Hi Mum!' says the Queen, and pulls up the mask to reveal herself as Elsie. 'We're back! Did you miss us?'

Eleanor climbs up from the side of the bed and in beside Luisa, cuddles up around her neck.

'Hello, lovelies.' Luisa pulls her body weight up onto her elbows. 'Where's – grandma?'

'Downstairs,' says Elsie. 'We've been on a train.'

'You came home by train?'

'Yesterday we went on a train. We went somewhere called Exceleter – '

'Exeter,' says Eleanor.

'We went to EXCELETER,' Elsie shouts, 'and then we ate all the marmalades for breakfast and I took two to bring back for you.'

'I brought some back for Ian,' says Eleanor. 'Grandma says Ian needs female attention. I'm afraid I don't have any spare for you.'

'Girls!' calls a voice from downstairs. 'Leave Mummy alone! Come on down here, darlings.'

'She's awake,' the girls cry in unison, and scramble off the bed and out of the door.

Luisa looks at the clock. The numbers change from 9:30 to 9:31, and she is grateful for the extra minute. 'I'll be down in a bit,' says Luisa, but there is no one there to hear.

She climbs from the bed, pulls a shirt from the wardrobe, then sees she is already dressed, is still wearing her jogging clothes from the day before. She goes downstairs, but the cat blocks her way on the stairs. Where's my fucking breakfast? asks the cat. Justin will have fed her. She grabs her and pushes her out the door into the garden. The cat immediately wants to come in again, mewling at the door.

'I'm sorry if they woke you,' says Bea. 'We made a compact, in the car, about holding a meditative atmosphere once inside the house. But maybe they lack the experience.'

Bea drags another bag through the kitchen into the hallway, a large blue holdall that Luisa does not recognise. Bea shoves it alongside the girls' overnight bags and Elsie's bike on the floor of the hallway. The bags are open, are empty – their contents cover most of the floor. Bea is bringing everything in, thinks Luisa. Then Bea will go, and we'll put on a film, and I'll sleep on the sofa. Many films.

'It's okay,' says Luisa, sitting on the stairs. 'Perhaps it was time for me to be up, anyway.' She leans her had against the wall and closes her eyes. 'Though I didn't sleep that well.'

'So a good night in?' Bea makes quote marks with her fingers. 'You and Justin?'

Luisa sits up straight, pulls herself upright.

'Nice. Really nice. Thanks so much for having the girls.'

'We had a lovely time.'

'Did you go somewhere on a train?'

'Oh yes. The girls loved the train.'

'To Exeter?'

Elsie piles back into the hallway from the lounge. She pulls items from the holdall: a plastic T-Rex, an oversized pencil, a cube of what appears to be mud with neatly-cut turf on top.

'Where have you been?' says Luisa.

'Where haven't we been!' says Bea. She picks up the mud cube, moves around the hallway as though looking for somewhere to place it as an ornament, then finding nowhere suitable puts it back on the floor.

'So you had a nice time then?' Luisa tries to pull Eleanor into a cuddle, but she races past into the kitchen, her cloak trailing behind her.

'I thought they'd be a bit bored being at my old house the whole time. So we went on an adventure. I've fed them, you know,' she nods at Luisa.

'I've had pasta, and jelly, and banoffee pie,' lists Elsie on her fingers. 'And pancakes this morning. In a stack! With syrup dripping down the sides. I ate six. And I didn't feel sick on the train,' she says to Bea.

'That's a different breakfast from usual,' says Luisa.

'It's good to mix things up a bit,' says Bea. 'That's what I tell my clients. Keeps the mind fresh. Receptive.'

Elsie runs off into the lounge soundtracked by a war cry.

'I do sometimes find though,' says Luisa, as cheerily as she can manage, 'that Elsie is bit more controllable when she has a few boundaries.'

'Oh, they were no problem,' says Bea. 'I find adapting to what they want to do much easier.'

'You don't find it helps,' says Luisa, 'to have boundaries?'

'Oh I have boundaries,' says Bea. 'The edge of town, out by the ring road.'

'They've been out to the ring road?'

'Oh no. They're far too young for that.'

'But you said the ring road?'

'That's my absolute boundary. Don't you worry, I'd never allow children to go further than that. It's too difficult for them to find their way home. Those roads all look the same.'

Bea has promised the girls are not allowed out on their own. At least for now. She can deal with later later. Next year later. Who knows about next year. Bea might be dead by next year – then there'll be a whole different kind of problem. She doesn't want Bea to die.

'Ellie said she bought marmalade for someone called Ian,' says Luisa.

'Ian's a very clever man,' says Bea. 'One of my best.'

'Ian has been looking after the girls?'

'He comes as a client to me, but at the same time he's starting his own business.'

'Does he come to you when you have the girls?'

'For now. But he's becoming more independent. He's got plans to train dogs. That's just one of his ideas. Train them to drive cars.'

'A dog can't drive a car.'

'Not yet. But it's a wonder what they can do these days. When he's worked out how to train dogs to drive, he's going to start a business where they drive you home from the pub if you've had too much to drink. He's calling it Rovers Return.'

Bea holds out Christmas streamers and Luisa takes them from her.

'Thank you so much for everything,' says Luisa. 'But I don't want to take any more of your time. I'm sure they must have tired you out.'

'Oh, I can take it,' says Bea. 'I've really enjoyed myself. But you, dear, you look a bit overtired.'

'No, no. Just work. From the other night. Maybe night shifts mess a bit with my sleeping.'

'It must be so rewarding, being a midwife,' says Bea.

'It is. Yes it is.'

'That's what everyone needs, isn't it?' says Bea. 'Work that they really want to do. Ian and his driving dogs, my life coaching, you and midwifery. I wonder about Justin sometimes. Do you think he's fulfilled in his work?'

'I don't really know,' answers Luisa. But Bea does not require an answer. She takes the streamers back from Luisa and hands them to Elsie as she runs past, as if in a relay.

'Are you sure you want to look after the girls right now?' says Bea. 'I mean it's no problem for me to take them off your hands again. I'm making up for all the silent years in India.'

Luisa stares at her blankly.

'I think maybe – ' says Luisa.

'Girls!' Bea shouts upstairs. 'We're off with Nanny B again. Let's go!'

'Are you sure?' says Luisa. 'Don't you have work today?'

'They're good for my work. They add a new ingredient, their honesty, their innocence. Girls! Let's get to work!'

Luisa leans back against the wall, watches as Bea packs the dinosaur, the mud cube back into the holdall. 'Maybe they'd rather just be at home,' she says, but Bea is collecting up, sweeping through the house.

When Luisa wakes, her body folded into the zigzag of the stairs, the house is silent, ghostly. She takes her phone from her pocket – it is only twenty minutes later. She taps Bea's number.

'You're like Rip Van Winkle, Mummy,' says Elsie, who answers the phone. 'Are you going to grow a beard?'

'Women don't grow beards, sweetie. Can I talk to grandma?'

'Grandma's driving.'

'What's the name of the road, Eleanor?' says Bea in the background.

'B-R-O... Brufton, it says Brufton,' Luisa hears Eleanor say.

'I need to know before we reach the junction. Nanny B can't do turns like the last one every time.'

'Where are you going?' asks Luisa.

'Brufton somewhere,' says Elsie. 'We'd be there by now if I'd been map reading.'

'Can you ask grandma when you're coming back?'

'Grandma's busy driving,' says Elsie. 'We're coming back at three.'

'That's what grandma said?'

'That's what I'm saying.'

The phone goes dead. Luisa wants to call again, but to what effect? The house is empty, she can sleep. She can sleep. Luisa goes upstairs repeating the word sleep to herself, stripping off her jogging trousers and vest top to the beat of the syllable. She pulls earplugs from the bedside drawer, rolls them into her ears and falls on the bed.

*

The music begins as a heartbeat, a rhythmic pattern, not unpleasant.

The unpleasantness begins when Luisa realises she is awake, she is awake and someone is playing Madonna's *Like a Virgin*, somewhere close by.

As her hearing begins to focus she realises that the song is coming from downstairs, that it is not Madonna singing but someone else, someone with less experience of playing to a crowd.

Luisa descends the stairs in a t-shirt and knickers to find, in the lounge, a circle of two women and a man cross-legged on the floor. One of the women is Bea, though it takes a moment for Luisa to recognise her under the white Amish-style headscarf. Bea grips the hands of the man and the other women, holding them at shoulder level. Inside their circle stands a young woman with a microphone, next to plate of broccoli.

'– for the very first time!' she sings, deliberately missing off the line's first word.

'What's going on?' says Luisa.

The woman breaks off singing.

'Mum!' cries Elsie angrily from behind the door.

'It's Belinda's turn, Mummy,' says Eleanor. 'Don't stop her singing.'

'I'm not stopping her singing, darling. I'm just wondering what everyone is doing here.'

'Belinda is using the power of song to overcome crippling shyness,' says Bea.

'Isn't that stammering?' says Luisa.

'I was trying to sing,' says Belinda. 'I'm just not very good at it.'

'Of course you are, darling,' says Bea. 'Anyone can be good at anything.' Bea gives Luisa a quick smile, as if to say, what the hell are you doing, you insensitive cow, except it is just a smile, and the the accusation is Luisa's own. The instrumental *Like a Virgin* continues in the background, oblivious.

'I meant singing helps with stammering,' says Luisa.

'Luisa – I'd like to introduce my clients,' says Bea. 'Belinda, Ian, Martha and Antoinette. Bima for short.' Luisa starts slightly at the word clients, reinforcing her recurring notion that Bea was once a high class prostitute, flying around the world servicing rich men as a sixties' air hostess.

'Carry on, Belinda,' says Bea. 'The circle isn't broken just because we have another body in the room. Just carry on.'

Belinda brings the microphone up to her mouth but no sound comes out, because she has noticed that no one is watching her. Everyone is looking at Luisa, all except for the man in the circle, who keeps his eyes fixed on his feet. Luisa looks down at her naked legs.

'And the funny thing,' says Elsie, 'is that Belinda isn't a virgin at all. Do you want to join in? Nanny can Mummy join in or will that mean doing the ceremony again?'

'I'm not sure I'm up for singing right now,' says Luisa.

'You don't have to sing. I won't choose singing for you,' says Eleanor.

'I might,' says Elsie. 'You don't get to choose all the time.'

'Did you tell Mum to come down in no clothes?' Eleanor accuses Elsie.

'I'm wearing clothes,' says Luisa. 'But why are you all here? What I mean is – how come you're working here?' she says to Bea.

'Oh, the girls decided,' says Bea. 'It was out of my hands. Out of all of our hands.'

'No speak!' Elsie points at Bea. Bea goes quiet, then raises a hand.

'Permission granted,' says Elsie.

'Permission overruled,' says Eleanor.

'Permission *regranted*,' says Elsie.

Bea widens her eyes at Eleanor to check, and Eleanor gives a small nod.

'Today is Wisdom of the Child day,' Bea explains to Luisa. 'It's like The Dice Man, but more innocent.'

'Everyone tells us what's wrong,' says Eleanor, 'and then we say how to fix them.'

'Everything the group do today is decided by Elsie and Eleanor,' says Bea proudly. 'We are under their instruction.'

'It's so liberating,' says Antoinette, a tall woman in a business suit.

'It was my idea that no one can use the bathroom upstairs,' says Elsie. She grabs Luisa's hand. 'So that we wouldn't wake you.'

'That's kind,' says Luisa, 'but what if people need the toilet?'

'They use the shed.'

'Everyone has to wee in the shed?'

'In a bucket,' says Bea. 'We've put a bucket in there. And no one's needed a poo yet. One problem at a time,' she smiles.

'Let them use the toilet, Elsie,' says Luisa. 'Now that I'm awake.'

Belinda looks hopeful.

'Don't tell me what to do,' says Elsie fiercely. 'You can't tell me what to do.'

'It's fine,' says Ian. 'We don't mind.'

'I'm your mother, Elsie.'

'Grandma says you're too cluttered with adult ideas to think properly,' says Elsie.

Elsie is right – she cannot think properly. For a moment Luisa considers sitting down and joining the circle.

'I'm not sure I really want to play the game,' says Luisa.

'It's not a game,' says Bea to the circle. 'More of an exercise.'

'Eat more broccoli!,' cries Elsie.

Ian takes a broccoli spear from the plate, pops it in his mouth and chews with evident distaste.

'Antoinette's becoming a beekeeper!' says Eleanor, and Antoinette smiles. 'What's wrong with you?' she asks Luisa.

'I'm really tired,' says Luisa, but as a reason to stop the conversation rather than an answer. 'What time is it?' She looks at the clock: 12:07.

'Go back to bed,' says Eleanor.

'I want to spend time with the two of you. Your grandma has looked after you for long enough already.'

'Please don't take them away,' says Antoinette. 'Why don't you tell them your problems?'

'I don't have any problems.' But you do. Why don't you just ask them? Ask Elsie and Ellie if I should carry on being a midwife. Let them decide.

'You spend a lot of time going to sleep,' says Elsie.

'And you don't play with us like you used to,' says Eleanor. 'That's a problem.'

'We spent all day playing on Tuesday,' says Luisa.

'You kept lying down on the sofa.'

'I was just resting before work, Ellie. I have to rest when I work nights. Look, I don't want to interrupt your class any further,' Luisa says to Bea. 'Really, it's fine for you all to go now, you've done above and beyond anyway. We're going to have a Studio Ghibli marathon this afternoon.'

'I hate Studio Ghibli,' says Elsie. 'I want Frozen again.'

'Remember about projecting positively, darling,' says Bea.

It should be me saying these things, thinks Luisa. But her brain is not supplying the reactions at a fast enough speed.

'If you're still tired,' says Bea, 'have you considered that it might be hormonal?'

'I have low iron,' says Luisa. 'I need to eat more iron.'

'Broccoli?' says Ian, and offers up the plate.

'Maybe you need red meat,' says Antoinette.

'Yes, go and buy some red meat,' says Elsie.

'I'm vegetarian, sweetie.' Luisa thinks about the meaty taste, the metallic sensation of liver. She wants liver.

'It's Wisdom of the Child day,' says Elsie, and shoves a carrier bag into Luisa's hands.

'You shouldn't eat meat,' says the last girl in the circle, who must be Martha. 'You don't need iron from meat. Meat is killing the earth.'

'If Elsie says Luisa needs red meat, Martha, then we are duty bound to listen,' says Bea.

I need food. I can go buy food and buy some liver, thinks Luisa.

'It's Wisdom of the Child day,' says Luisa, and Elsie and Eleanor both wrap themselves around an arm either side of her. 'I want to eat liver,' Luisa looks at Martha. She wants to eat liver, and this is her house.

'Thank you. Thank you, Eleanor,' says Belinda. Eleanor steps into the circle and gives Belinda a hug. The circle watch in silence – every time Luisa thinks the hug must end, it continues, Eleanor's head pressed tight against Belinda's chest. Standing in her knickers and t-shirt Luisa acts as decoration for the circle, a skanky Venus de Milo. She has never enjoyed an embrace of this length with Eleanor.

'Okay, Ellie,' says Luisa. All eyes turn to her in confusion – Eleanor and Belinda make no move to break apart. 'Well done, lovely girl,' says Luisa, and this appears to satisfy, at least in as much as first Ian, and then everyone, looks away from her, back to Belinda and Eleanor.

'I'm going to go,' says Luisa, and this time no one reacts. 'I'm going to the organic butcher in Caroline Crescent.'

Luisa goes upstairs, pulls on some clothes, grabs her bag and a coat and leaves the house, pulling the front door behind her. The Peugeot stands there, waiting, ready to go. You can't drive the Peugeot. You can't drive at all. Why is the Peugeot back in their driveway? She stands on the doorstep for a few moments, then heads off down the road on foot.

She is on the number 7 bus, in the front-most seats, the seats reserved for the pregnant and disabled, because she is disabled, she is disabled with tiredness. This is insulting to disabled people, she thinks, but right now she does not care about insulting the disabled. Luisa closes her eyes and instantly the world surrounding her is heavy and brassy, she opens her eyes and it might be thirty seconds, five minutes later. It might be Friday. They are only at the end of estate, turning onto the main road to town. She jumps up and walks back to the driver's cab.

'Can you let me know when we're at Caroline Crescent, please?' she asks.

'Comes up on the display,' says the driver.

'Can you call down to me as well, please?' The driver looks at her, not annoyed, but not friendly either. 'I don't have my glasses.' She points to her eyes, as though the driver does not know where glasses are worn. He is not a glasses-wearer, he might need reminding. He squints at her – maybe he needs glasses. If he needs glasses he shouldn't be driving a bus. 'Have you thought that you might need glasses?' says Luisa, and returns to her seat.

She opens her eyes to see an old lady's face pushed very close to hers, only inches away. The old lady is speaking to her in a foreign language that she doesn't understand, until Luisa realises it is English.

'See.' The old lady turns to speak to a young woman with a blue bob in the seat behind. 'I told you she wasn't dead.'

The throb of the engine has stopped – the bus is parked. Luisa is slumped in her seat, her head below the metal bar of the back rest. She twists to look out of the window and sees shops, centre of town shops.

'Have we passed the butchers?'

'You didn't answer,' says the driver, leaning against the luggage shelf. 'I called but you didn't answer. They thought you might be dead. This lady here said she'd check you over.'

'I'm a medical student,' says the blue bob woman. She is no more than a girl, a schoolgirl.

'I'm a midwife,' says Luisa, then sees that this is rude, that she is suggesting she doesn't need the girl's medical intervention. 'You checked me over? Thanks for checking me over.'

'She's a midwife,' says the old lady to a man dressed in a boater and sailing pumps, with a small Pekinese dog on his lap, seated on the other side of the bus.

'Oh, midwives, they're *wonderful*,' says the boater man, and leans forward to nod at Luisa, to pay her the compliment directly.

'I'm fine,' says Luisa, and sits up in the seat.

'She said you were dead,' says the driver. 'I didn't realise you were a midwife.'

'Why did you think I was dead?'

'They should have those jumpy heart things on buses,' says the old lady. 'As standard. If there'd actually been some I'd've used them myself.'

'You need training,' says the medical student. 'You can't go around bopping people with those whenever you like.'

'I'd like some all the same,' says the old lady firmly. 'Imagine if we'd let a midwife die on a bus.'

'You can fill out a suggestion form if you like,' says the driver to the old lady, and stands up from his slouch. 'I'm glad you're okay, madam. If it's okay with you we'll be on our way.' Luisa cannot be sure but it looks as though he touches the front of his hair. Tugs his forelock? He's just moving his hand. The driver heads back to the cab.

'You do a remarkable job,' says the old lady, laying a hand on Luisa's arm. 'It must be so rewarding.'

Luisa stands and walks down to the cab. 'On our way where?' she says to the driver.

'I'm afraid we've passed Caroline Crescent,' says the driver. 'I tried to wake you. I didn't realise you were a midwife. I'm sorry.'

They are parked in a lay-by in the town centre, outside Bartholomew Square. Across the square she sees the town hall.

'You bring life into the world,' says the driver.

'Luisa!' Outside the bus someone is shouting her name. 'Luisa! I'm so glad you're here.' Jenny steps onto the bus, grabs Luisa's arm and drags her out of the door.

'I have to go,' Luisa tells the driver, as though he has been forcing her to stay on the bus all along.

Jenny wears a sea-green satin dress, and a matching hat ringed with lace. As she moves Luisa across the square, a hand in the crook of her arm, Jenny leans against her, and the hat pokes Luisa in the eye. To speak to Luisa's face Jenny has to lean back on her heels.

'Can I get you to be a witness?' says Jenny.

Luisa instinctively sets the words to the Marvin Gaye tune in her head. 'What's happened?' she asks. 'Has there been an accident?'

Perhaps Jenny is about to pass out. Perhaps she has just been run over. Maybe she's just pretending she's been run over for the insurance money. Luisa turns to look at her. Jenny is just the kind of person to be an insurance swindler. No one would suspect her – she's probably been doing it for years. Luisa remembers that she herself is an insurance swindler.

'You saw the invite poster then?' says Jenny. 'It was a bit of a last-minute rush job. I couldn't get the hospital photocopier to work.'

'It's your wedding,' says Luisa. As they near the double doors of the town hall she sees Diane standing in the entrance way. 'Is Diane a witness?'

'I'm not having Diane as a witness,' says Jenny. Luisa cannot be certain that Diane has not heard. 'So you'll do it then?'

'Hello, Luisa.' Diane is wearing freshly-pressed midwifery scrubs, and brandishing a bouquet. 'Isn't this all so lovely?'

'I have to get home.' Luisa says to Jenny. 'My – mother-in-law has the children. I have to get back to her.' This is the first time she has ever referred to Bea as her mother-in-law. Bea is not her mother-in-law. Bea could never be anyone's mother-in-law without a complete overhaul of the public understanding of the phrase.

'This won't take long,' says Jenny. 'I thought there'd be others here. They must have got stuck at work.'

'But I have to work tonight,' says Luisa.

'Oh, that's not for hours,' says Jenny. 'I'd be ever so grateful.'

Luisa suddenly remembers her last sighting of Jenny, from the wheelchair in reception. Peering down at her. Scowling. 'So I'm on tonight, then?' she says.

'Are you rota-ed for tonight?'

'Yes,' says Luisa quietly.

'Well then that'll mean you're working tonight, won't it?'

'I can be witness,' says Diane. 'No bother to me. I'm not rota-ed on tonight.'

'Let's just all go in.' Jenny takes advantage of Luisa's hesitation, grabs her arm, pulls her through the double doors. Diane follows behind.

'Last night – ' says Luisa.

'Oh, let's not worry about that now,' says Jenny. She turns to stare at Luisa for longer than is polite, longer than is human. 'I'm sure no one wrote anything official, anyway.'

'Someone wrote it down?'

'I said no one wrote it down. So, you don't mind?' Jenny indicates with a wave that Luisa should go through the door before her.

'How long will it take?' asks Luisa.

'Oh thank you. Thank you. It'll be so nice. You and Freddie.'

A smiling grey-haired woman holds open an ornate glass-panelled door and ushers them inside.

'How are you? I'm Ursula, the registrar.' Ursula smiles at Luisa.

'How long do these last?' says Luisa. 'How long will this go on?'

'Doesn't look like a big one,' says Ursula. 'Half an hour or so, tops.'

In the front row of the audience seating a young man rolls his jacket into a ball and puts it on the chair next to him, on top of which he places a sandwich bag. Diane, further along the row, pats the chair next to her. Luisa cannot see a way to refuse.

'I thought I'd get out,' says Diane. 'For such a special occasion.'

'See, I told you I could find someone,' Jenny faces the front of the room, standing with an enraged-looking man, whom Luisa assumes must be Karl. Ursula faces them, a book open in front of her.

'Well let's make a start, shall we?' says Ursula. 'Are we all here?'

'This is as good as it gets,' says Karl.

Ursula works her way through the lines of the marriage ceremony, her inflections all over the place.

'And are we to have any readings?' says Ursula.

'Oh, no! We didn't get to thinking about readings, did we Karl?' says Jenny. 'Did you bring any readings?'

'Did *you* bring any readings?' says Karl.

'But it doesn't matter if we have readings or not, does it?'

'Like I really give a shit.'

'Remember, Karl.' Jenny touches his hand, 'No blame culture.'

'I have some poems,' calls Diane. 'I'm the woman for readings. Shall I do them now?'

'We don't need readings,' says Jenny.

'Later, then,' says Diane.

'Let's just get it done, shall we?' Karl swings round to glower at Diane. 'Are we doing this fucking wedding or what?' he says to Jenny.

Jenny squeezes Karl's arm and beams at him.

Ursula continues, until her tone rises and Luisa recognises with relief that they are coming to the vows.

'Do I actually need to say it?' says Karl.

'Legally, yes,' says Ursula.

'Oh, Karl,' says Jenny. 'You always were a bit of a shy one.'

Piped music plays from hidden speakers as Ursula beckons Luisa and Freddie to sign the register.

'How do you know Jenny?' Luisa asks Freddie. The registrar points at a line on the bottom of the page, and Freddie scrawls a signature.

'Jenny's the bride, right?' says Freddie.

Luisa nods and adds her own signature.

'My girlfriend used to babysit for her, for her and – Karl.' Freddie reads the name from the marriage certificate.

'It's good of you to come be a witness for her.'

'I was actually in Subway, on lunch. She saw me in the window.'

'Well even so. Very nice of you.'

'She's paying me a tenner. But I need to get back. Can I go now?' he asks Ursula.

'One more signature here,' says Ursula, 'and here.'

'I really need to get back too,' says Luisa. Freddie is the one person here with whom she has affinity, she thinks: we both have to get back somewhere.

They file out of the Regency Room and along the hall towards the exit, Jenny and Karl at the front, a quiet funeral procession.

'Is it okay if I take the money now?' says Freddie. 'I really need to get be getting back.' He looks apologetically to Karl.

'Of course.' Jenny opens up her small green clutch bag. 'Oh, Karl. I don't have any change. Do you have any money on you?'

Karl stuffs his hand into his suit pocket, and from his wallet takes a ten pound note. He throws it into the air and marches away across the square. Jenny tries to catch the note as it floats to the ground, giggling as she misses.

'Much obliged.' Freddie picks up the note, makes to go then turns back and kisses Jenny on the cheek. 'And congratulations. Glad to be here.'

'Say hello to Lisa for me,' Jenny calls after him.

'Bye,' calls Luisa.

The town hall clock sounds a heavy chime on the hour. Luisa wills it to stop after three, but it carries on regardless with a fourth.

'I have to go too, Jenny,' says Luisa. 'I'm on tonight and I need to sort out the children.'

' "I wonder, by my troth, what thou and I. Did, til we loved." ' Diane's voice carries across the square.

'Not now,' Jenny turns sharply to Diane. 'How many times do I have to tell you?'

'Maybe after the photographs,' says Diane.

'Photographs!' cries Jenny. 'We forgot to do photos! Wait – Karl!' She looks across the square, but Karl is nowhere to be seen. 'Let me get him back. Can you wait just a minute?'

'I do really need to go,' says Luisa.

'I really think it should be you to do the photos, Luisa. You are such a capable person. I'm always saying so.'

'My mother-in-law has the children. I have to get back.'

'So you keep saying. Wait right there,' says Jenny. 'Don't move. And you must come for a drink afterwards – I'm not taking no for an answer. Drinks on us, of course. After everything you've done.' Jenny is away across the square, in the direction of Karl's escape.

'I'll cover for you,' says Diane. 'If you have to go. I'll tell her you've got an emergency C-section in Carol Decker. Anyway I can be the photographer. I used to work in sonography, after all.'

Luisa walks quickly across the square, crosses the road and steps inside Cafe Nero. Through the window she sees Jenny with her arm linked through Karl's, leading him back across the cobbles. Jenny's eyes search the far side of the square, see Diane waving at her. Luisa feels sick.

She pulls out her phone and pushes Bea's name.

'Hall-ooo,' coos Bea.

'I got on a bus and now I'm at a wedding,' says Luisa.

'Pagan or church?'

'Church. But I'm at a registry office.'

'Oh, I do love a good wedding,' says Bea. 'Well there's no need to worry. The three of us drove my clients home, and now we're back at yours again. The girls have been really great. Belinda told me she doesn't think she can carry on without Eleanor.'

'Carry on living?'

'Carry on with life-coaching. She doesn't mean it. She said the same about Barabas last week. I'd like to have the children help again. Perhaps take them on as employees. Fair rates, of course.'

'They're still at school. They have to go back to school next week. Who's Barabas?'

'They open everything up. I want them to show me everything.'

'I meant to be back ages ago.'

'It's no problem. Did you get the liver? Not the cocoa, darling,' says Bea. 'Think about the taste.'

'I'll be home as soon as I can.'

'Whatevs,' says Bea.

Luisa emerges from the cafe and Jenny beckons her over. Following Jenny and Karl is Diane and an enormous crowd of pigeons.

'I've really got to get back,' says Luisa. 'If I'm working tonight.'

'Well, likewise,' says Jenny. 'You're not the only one on duty. You've got time for a few photos, haven't you?'

They look down at a pigeon that nips at Diane's court shoes. 'They love my breadcrumb confetti,' says Diane. 'It's all the crusts from breakfast – I got that lovely Endre on Floor 3 to collect them for me. But don't worry, I'm saving some for the photos.'

'I've left the girls for too long already,' says Luisa. 'It was a lovely wedding.' She kisses Karl on the cheek, who just stares at her.

'Of course I haven't actually done the DATIX yet, Luisa,' says Jenny. 'From last night. To report that an on-duty midwife was found asleep in a wheelchair. I mean these DATIX-es do all end up in front of the managers. I might not have time to write it up tonight. And then I might just forget.' Jenny takes a large-lensed camera from Karl's shoulder and holds it out by the strap to Luisa.

Is this blackmail, thinks Luisa? I never expected blackmail to be part of midwifery. Or weddings. But then there's lots of things I didn't expect to be part of midwifery.

'Where shall we do this, then?' says Luisa. 'In front of the town hall?'

*

Sitting on the bus causes the heaviness in her limbs to return. Every few moments Luisa lolls to one side, leaning in towards a woman with shopping bags on her lap, then jerking awake. Eventually she goes to stand in the buggy and wheelchair area, holds on to a strap handle above her head. She is a medieval prisoner, trussed up by the hands in a tower, into her third day without sleep, prodded and tortured by cruel guards. She lets out a small moan, not a prisoner's moan, but a real one, a midwife's moan. She cannot work like this. It is dangerous to work like this. Babies may die. Mothers may die. She herself might die. People talk about dying of exhaustion. Why would such a phrase exist if this had never happened in reality? She cannot go to work.

Luisa sits down again and takes her phone from her bag. There is a text from Justin.

Coming home early. You okay?

I'm feeling a bit sick, she replies. You are sick, sick with fatigue. Call in sick. You cannot work, you're dangerous.

She calls the hospital.

'Can I speak to the midwife in charge, please?' Luisa asks when the phone is finally answered.

'Katie's busy right now. Can I take a message?' Luisa recognises the desire to end the call quickly, to eliminate this annoying interruption.

'I need to speak to her. It's Luisa. Who's that – ?' She hears the receiver dropped onto a hard surface.

'Sorry,' says the midwife when she returns. 'It's a bit mental here at the moment. A couple of people phoned in sick for tonight. You're not available now, are you? Can you come in and do a bank shift tonight?'

'But I'm already working tonight,' says Luisa quietly. 'Sorry, who is this again?'

'Did you want Katie to call you back then? She's in with a forceps delivery right now. I don't know how long she'll be.'

'Maybe I can't come in,' says Luisa. 'Maybe Jenny has put me on a disciplinary.' But the midwife has gone.

As she approaches the house Luisa sees the front door is open and picks up her pace. Sofa cushions prevent her from fully opening the door, and the rest of the hallway floor is invisible from the sea of coats and toys and plants. She tries to imagine what kind of game this was. Houses? Restaurants? Post-apocalyptic camping?

'Hello Luisa! Mummy's home, girls,' Bea calls around the kitchen doorway. 'We have a surprise for you.'

'Don't come in!' shouts Elsie from the kitchen.

'We've cooked dinner!' shouts Eleanor.

Luisa puts a sofa cushion under one arm and shuts the door behind her.

'Don't you concern yourself with any of that.' Bea disappears back into the kitchen.

The key turns in the lock and Justin enters the hallway.

'Are you okay?' Justin looks at Luisa and the hallway.

'Everything's a mess.' Luisa speaks quietly so Bea cannot hear. 'Bea kindly had the children for the rest of the day. So it's a bit of a state.'

As Justin reaches up his arms to take off his coat a sleeve brushes against something suspended from the lampshade, an action man, hung from a woollen noose around his throat.

'I had to go to a wedding,' says Luisa. 'I got stuck at a wedding. I only got back just now.'

'Whose wedding? Was I supposed to go?'

'It was a midwifery thing.'

Justin nods, requiring no further explanation.

Luisa avoids his gaze, and through the doorway sees the courtesy car in the road, and the Peugeot in the driveway. 'Why is the Peugeot here?' she says, the simplest of all their questions.

'I went and fetched it,' says Justin. 'Last night. After you left.'

'From the sports field?'

'I was walking round that way. I went walking after you left.' Justin stares at her, emotionless, wanting her to respond. 'And there it was and I brought it home.'

Luisa wants to mention how drunk he was, but what is the point? He is not drunk now, he is not driving the car now. They have a stolen car, vandalised and then stolen, by them, in their driveway.

'I had to drive over the hedge to get to Canterbury,' says Justin. 'I forgot the Peugeot was in the driveway. And so the hedge.'

'I never liked the hedge.' She pictures her commando roll across the grass. Was that her, just this morning? That couldn't be her. 'But you went to Canterbury.'

'Shouldn't have even bothered. Fuck the deserving poor and their micro-finance. So you've called in sick.' Justin says this as though it explains everything: the state of the hallway, his drunk-driving, the undefinable smell coming from the direction of the kitchen.

'I called the hospital on the bus.'

'Good. That's good. I think it's just taken it's toll on you.'

'What has?'

'You know. Work.'

Luisa looks up to the hanging action man. His eyes are blank, cold, dirty grey. If I looked at Justin now, his eyes would look the same, she thinks. But she cannot see Justin's eyes because he is down on the floor, picking up cushions.

'Katie is going to call me back,' says Luisa. 'The co-ordinator.'

'What for?'

'To see if I'm sick.'

'Hello, darling.' Bea steps into the hall. Luisa wonders if she has been listening, choosing her moment to make an fortuitous entrance. Some kind of life-coaching skill for maintaining equilibrium.

'Hi Mum.' Justin steps over the coats to hug his mother.

'Come and see what we're cooking!' calls Elsie.

'The girls and Bea have made dinner for us all,' says Luisa, as though it was her idea.

The kitchen is hot, incredibly hot, the type of heat emitted by an open furnace that is bearable for a few moments but then you need to step away. In the corner is a den, an igloo house the girls have constructed from duvets.

'I need oven gloves.' Elsie stands before the oven, holds her arms out straight in front of her.

'You want me to get you oven gloves.' Eleanor picks the padded mittens off the floor and slides them onto Elsie's hands.

'Excellent closed-loop communication, girls,' says Bea.

Luisa watches as Elsie pulls a huge tray of irregular-shaped pasties from the oven, not daring to intervene. She slides it expertly onto a wooden board on the table. Luisa's phone rings. The call is unlisted.

'Katie?' answers Luisa.

'Um, this is Lauren,' says a woman's voice.

'I needed to speak to Katie.'

'Maybe you spoke to Katie before? I can deal with this now, madam. I have all the details of your car onscreen.'

Luisa steps up from her chair, ranges around the kitchen.

'My car. My car is, is.'

A sudden movement from Justin catches her attention – he moves his hands up to his chest and back down again, exhales deeply. Luisa recognises this mime. She fills her lungs, breathes out all the way.

'I'm just calling about the current location of the car,' says Lauren. 'Registration X152GBP?'

'Breathe,' says Luisa. 'You need to breathe.'

'Do I?' says Lauren.

Justin makes a thumbs up motion at her. 'You're doing really well,' says Luisa.

'Well thank you!' says Lauren brightly. 'Maybe you could mention that in the survey at the end of the call? So I just need, to process your claim, the current location of the car. For our inspectors. The police report says the car has been located.'

Our car is in our driveway, thinks Luisa. I'm going to be arrested and then the NMC will strike me off the midwifery register. They'll strike me off and I won't be able to be a midwife any more. 'No,' says Luisa. What does she need to say in order to be arrested? She looks at the girls. Justin is scribbling in crayon on the white edge of a newspaper. He holds it up to Luisa.

'Someone is at the door,' Luisa tells Lauren.

'No there isn't,' says Elsie.

Bea slips one hand over Elsie's mouth, and the other over Eleanor's.

'Can you call me back?' says Luisa. 'There's someone at the door.' She ends the call.

'I don't want to be arrested,' says Luisa.

'You did really well,' says Justin.

'I don't think I can do this any more.' Luisa exhales deeply again.

'I'm sorry, darlings,' Bea releases her hold on Elsie and Eleanor. 'We had to have complete radio silence.'

Luisa sees Justin and Bea exchange a complicated eyebrow semaphore.

'Eleanor tells me you've been visiting the Archbishop of Canterbury today,' Bea says to Justin. 'How is he?'

'A bishop *in* Canterbury,' says Justin. 'He's a dick, as it happens.'

'But they're going to call back,' says Luisa. 'And the car is in the driveway.'

'Just pass the phone to me,' says Justin.

'Well I think we all need to sit,' says Bea. Justin takes a seat, and Luisa follows, instinctively. Arrested, not arrested, struck off, not struck off: they're all good, she thinks. And bad. Which are which?

'It's a shame you didn't come back earlier,' Bea says to Luisa. 'We could have put your liver in the pasties. Maybe that would have helped.'

'Helped with what? Are you eating liver?' asks Justin.

'I've got low iron,' says Luisa. 'I had my iron tested and it's really low. So I went to buy liver.'

'I thought you went to a wedding?'

'When I set off it was for liver.'

'Shall we make a plate for the baby?' says Eleanor. 'I think the baby might be hungry.'

'That's a nice idea, darling. Have you thought about your menstrual cycle?' Bea turns to Luisa. 'Of course it's when you're ovulating that you have your most feminine energy.'

'Is that the same for chickens?' asks Elsie.

'We're all just animals at heart,' says Bea.

'So you're saying that you're ovulating?' says Justin to Luisa.

'It's the best time for harnessing your creative spirit,' says Bea. 'When you're at your most fertile. It makes sense, really. All life poised at it's greatest potential.'

'Belinda was ovulating today, says Elsie. 'That's why she was singing. Belinda was, but not Ian.'

'Who is Belinda?' says Justin. 'And Ian?'

'Ellie is in love with Ian,' says Elsie.

'I am not. Anyway Ian is gay so he wouldn't love me.'

'Now that's not true, is it darling?' says Bea. 'Remember the discussion we all had about the different types of love. I'm sure Ian loves you very much.'

'Maybe Ian doesn't love Eleanor,' says Luisa. She looks at the clock: 18:17. I'll have to call. She pulls her head down to her shoulders, cringing at the idea of calling in sick this soon before a shift. I have twenty minutes, twenty minutes before I'd normally leave. Time for a meal even, time to sit down for a meal. Before I get ready for work. But tonight I will never be ready for work. Tonight I am dangerous, I am a danger to people.

'This looks great!' says Luisa, as Eleanor digs a pasty from the baking tray with a spatula and puts it on a plate in front of her.

'Ian doesn't love his dad,' says Elsie. 'We're lucky because we love our dad. And our dad loved his dad so much he still gets sad – and he wasn't even his real dad!'

'Girls,' says Bea. 'I think we might be getting into rather dangerous territory here, don't you think? Let's not forget client confidentiality? Remember those forms you signed?' Bea draws a finger across her lips to zip.

The girls nod.

'You told them about Dad?' says Justin to Bea. 'I thought – I might do that. I hadn't told them yet.'

'Oh goodness.' Bea holds her hands to her face. 'I never thought it a secret. I didn't know.'

'It doesn't matter.'

'I thought it could hardly be a secret when Martin had freckles and blistered in Totnes.'

'So grandma told you about your real grandad?' says Justin.

'I can't say, Daddy,' says Eleanor, putting a finger on her lips. 'I signed a form.'

'It's okay to say here, darling,' says Bea. 'Since the client is present.'

'Grandma says it's too far to go and see him,' says Elsie.

'To see who? Are you still in contact then?' Luisa asks Justin, curiosity momentarily overriding all thoughts of work and babies and death.

'Martin was my dad, even if he wasn't my real dad. He would have loved to be your grandad, too,' Justin tells the girls. 'But he died just when you were born.'

'Of course he would,' says Bea to the girls. 'And your daddy always said he didn't want to know about his real father, and that's completely fine.'

'Well I want to know,' says Elsie. 'I want to know about Cuba. I want to go to Cuba.'

'A very interesting country,' says Bea. 'So much dancing. So many men with guns.'

'Is Grandad Cuba dead?' says Eleanor. 'Like Grandad Martin? And Grandad Jimmy?'

Eleanor carries a pasty-filled plate high up in front of her face, and slides it onto the table in front of Luisa.

'Grandad Jimmy isn't dead,' says Luisa. 'He was just really tired when you last saw him.'

'Did Grandad Cuba have a gun? Mum, why did everyone have guns?' Elsie looks up at Luisa.

'Well,' says Luisa, 'it was very interesting. Cuba had what's called a revolution, some people thought the country was being run the wrong way.' Luisa realises she knows almost nothing about Cuban history. She takes a bite from the pasty and goes straight through, pastry to pastry, which sticks to both the top and bottom of her mouth, making it difficult to speak. 'A man called Che Guevara took over the country – '

'That was Fidel,' says Bea.

'Fidel Castro, Elsie' says Justin. 'Castro took over Cuba.'

'Definitely Fidel,' says Bea. 'And strangely he was always very jumpy around loud noises. Which is surprising when you consider the life.'

'You mean you met Castro?' says Luisa.

'Well, yes. Yes I did.' Bea glances at Justin, stands and quickly clears the baking tray to the sink. 'He came to meet all the air hostesses. All around the country he was. Always seemed to be there. Always reaching out to the people. Making connections.'

A unexpected silence descends on the room as everyone works through their dry pasties.

'I have something to tell everyone,' says Justin.

That he's Fidel Castro's son? thinks Luisa.

'It's about work. I'm making some changes.'

He's moving out, he's going to say he's moving out, and he's going to say it in front of the girls so there's no going back. He probably learnt that from Bea, a revolutionary tactic.

'There's pudding,' says Elsie. 'You can have pudding before you go to work, can't you?' she asks Luisa.

'Mum's not going to work,' says Justin.

'Aren't I?' says Luisa.

'You're sick. You said you were sick. I thought you called in sick.'

'I never said I called in sick. I said they're calling me back.'

'Well do it now.' Justin takes Luisa's phone from the table and holds it out to her.

'I can't call in sick. Not this soon before the start of a shift.' Luisa stares at Justin. 'It's unprofessional.'

'I thought you were sick.'

'The unit is down three midwives.' It was only two. Why has she made it three?

'Well in that case I'm going to drive you.' Justin stands up too quickly from the table. Plates jump and clatter back down. 'So we can talk.'

'I'm fine walking.' Luisa pictures the route, the hill. She cannot possibly walk that far.

'I'm going to drive you,' says Justin.

'But what about pudding?' says Elsie.

'I'm coming back,' says Justin.

'Can baby have some pudding?' A young woman crawls on hands and knees from the den. Luisa recognises her: she is Belinda, the reluctant Madonna.

'Baby doesn't get pudding unless baby has finished all her dinner,' says Elsie.

Bea nods at Elsie approvingly. Belinda backs up into the den and pulls what Luisa recognises as the lounge curtain across the entrance.

*

Justin drives, past the bingo hall where there is no bingo. The courtesy car is so soundproof it is like a padded cell, all soft thunks, no treble. Neither of them have spoken since they got into the car. Now an ending of the silence feels too weighty, too explosive.

'So things are going to be better now,' says Justin suddenly.

'Which things?' Luisa pulls her head upright, from where it has fallen against the door, lulled by the car interior. Whatever things he is talking about, she thinks, they almost certainly don't include the fact that in less than half an hour I will be making decisions, multiple decisions, affecting the health of unborn babies and their mothers. Those things will not be better. Just before they left the house she heard Justin tell the insurance company that the police were currently unsure as to the location of their stolen car. That didn't seem like a situation that will get better, either.

'Everything.' Justin grips the steering wheel. 'You're getting ill, you not sleeping. I've been thinking a lot about it. I mean you've worked really hard to get where you are. It shouldn't have to be you who changes your work. The woman.' He pronounces the word strangely, Roger Moore-ish, and wrinkles his nose. 'This is the twenty-first century. My work can change. I've decided.'

'Decided?'

Now this conversation is started Justin is relaxed, more relaxed than Luisa has heard him in ages, and this adds to her anxiety. 'Why should it just be down you?' says Justin. 'I can change my work and spend more time with the girls. Maybe it's time to give up this stupid app idea.'

'No. You can't just say that.'

'I just did,' he smiles.

'But what if I was thinking about giving up my job?'

'I should never have said what I did. That was wrong of me. I know you don't want to. You love your job.'

She can see the roof of the hospital now, rising above the houses, a looming icon of sickness and death. Birth, also.

'You can't just give up your job without us discussing it,' says Luisa quietly. 'What will we do for money? We can't survive on just what I earn.'

'I have ideas. I've been looking into it.'

'Like what?'

'And we can spend less money. I'll save money not going to work.'

'That's hardly going to cover it! And ideas take time.'

'But more importantly you won't be going so crazy.'

'I'm not crazy!' She is crazy. Crazy is exactly what she is.

'Running out on me last night. Isn't that a bit crazy?'

Luisa notices she is crying, but since she has only just noticed and it has been going on for some time she makes no attempt to dry her face. Crying does not appear to alter the emotional tenor of the situation. 'I think the work you're doing is amazing,' she says. 'Enabling small loans to help the African poor climb of poverty? You're making a difference, to thousands of people's lives!'

'Not at the moment I'm not. Maybe not ever.'

'But you're a philanthropist.'

'A philanthropist gives their own money. And there's people saying micro-finance doesn't even work, anyway.'

'What do they know?' cries Luisa.

'What do I know?' Justin's taps his fingers to the song on the radio. 'Plus Innovata have caught up. Overtaken us probably. We're pretty sure they're going to get to market with their own app before us.'

'You said they were a bunch of cunts with the moral integrity of termites.'

'They're termites who know how to lick a Bishop's arse. Maybe that's the kind of talent required for this project. And anyway, poor people are still going to get their fucking micro-finance, whoever provides it. That's the point of it all, isn't it?'

'But what about Al and Marian?'

'They're fine with it. I told them this afternoon. To be honest I think they were quite relieved. It was just which of said it first.' Justin grins, but the grin disappears when he sees Luisa's face.

'Then you've already decided.'

The force of her voice causes Justin to brake too hard, and they lurch forward in their seats.

'I can't believe you decided to quit without discussing it with me,' cries Luisa.

'What about when you decided to start midwifery? We didn't exactly discuss what that was going to be like either, did we?' snaps Justin.

Justin is hunched forward, gripped over the steering wheel. It is up to her – if she decides, she can take the angry baton, run with it, hurl the fucking baton out of the stadium.

'I didn't know,' says Luisa quietly. 'Nobody told me.'

She sees Justin look to her, sees his mouth open to speak. Then he looks back at the road. Takes the car down the hill, eases the wheels onto the kerb by the entrance to the hospital multi-storey.

'I don't know if I can work tonight,' Luisa says into her lap. 'I'm not sick. But I am tired. Really tired. I'm just – not sure. Not even sure I'm a good midwife.'

'Of course you are,' says Justin. 'I know you are. You're exactly the kind of woman who should be a midwife.'

'Am I?'

'You'll be okay.' Justin puts a hand on her leg. She wonders if he is going to move it, stroke her leg, but he just holds it there, motionless. 'You'll be okay. And you always say the adrenaline gets you going once you start.'

THURSDAY NIGHT: ON DUTY

Luisa walks down the ramp and enters the concrete doorway of the multi-storey, heading for the back entrance to the hospital, past cars and cars and cars, white painted numbers on the wall of each bay counting down her approach to the lifts.

Her phone bleeps, and without slowing her pace she pulls it half out of her bag to examine the screen. The screen shows no calls, no texts or reminders and she stops, stops at bay number 32, pulls the phone in front of her, swipes across and back, but can find no cause for the beep.

Maybe a message from God, she thinks. God's telling me to stop being a fucking midwife. If I believed in God I could take that as a sign. She returns the phone to her bag and hears the beep again. Perhaps just voices in my head. Beeps in my head. Isn't that a sign of madness, voices in your head? Or I have tinnitus.

'I'm at number 36,' Luisa says. What happened after 32? A car horn beeps out on the street.

She continues on through the darkness, through the flappy plastic doors. At the zebra crossing she stops for a car inching into the multi-storey, peers through the window at a pregnant woman in the passenger seat. Soon she'll be asking me questions, expecting me to help. You don't want to be asking me. The woman peers back at her. Perhaps she is not pregnant, perhaps simply fat. Lots of people are fat. One less pregnant woman.

In the lift foyer a short Mediterranean man struggles to push a trolley over a lip of concrete. Luisa wonders if she ought to help, but instead stands and stares up at the illuminated numbers. It is unclear how long she has been waiting, how long she has occupied the same space as this man. The lift beeps and opens.

A cascading wall of water covers the entrance, the spray pouring from the top of the door. Like in *The Shining*. I have twins and this is a lift and now I am hallucinating, like Jack Nicholson, I am seeing lifts flooded with blood. Except this is water. You might have expected blood, since this is a hospital. I cannot work if I am seeing lifts filled with blood. Or water. I need to tell the co-ordinator, tell them I cannot work if I am seeing water.

Luisa steps forward into the lift, and the water soaks her hair and the shoulders of her coat, runs down her arm and into her bag. This is a very real hallucination. I've gone beyond, gone somewhere else.

'You can't use this lift, miss,' says the Mediterranean man from the lobby. 'You can't use it. The water.'

'You can see the water?'

The man looks confused, as though his English has failed him.

'La cortina de agua? Es aqui?' Where did Spanish come from? I'm a savant, I've moved into savant territory.

The man beams. 'Yes, miss. A room is flooded upstairs.' He enunciates each word, but Luisa is not sure whether to demonstrate his grasp of English or just talking to her like a child.

'Oh. That's good.'

'But you cannot use this lift.'

Luisa steps out, the water soaking her again.

'You take the fire lift,' says the Mediterranean man.

*

'Is it raining?' says Vicky, as Luisa enters the delivery suite office.

'A little,' says Luisa. She sees Katie stood by the board. Tell Katie you're too tired to work. She plays the words in her head, and instead steps over to the pigeon holes, her eyes moving to the K's.

'Strange,' says Vicky. 'Wasn't when I came in.'

'I heard about your hypo in the lift last night, Luisa.' Katie comes over. 'Are you all okay now?'

'I'm not sure.' Luisa turns to Katie to tell her everything. Katie will understand, Katie is kind. 'I'm – I'm not diabetic.'

'That's good.'

'I'm here now.'

'Good. There might be some shifting around tonight. There's a couple of people called in sick.'

Katie is turning away.

'I haven't slept,' blurts Luisa. 'Not really for thirty, seventy-two hours. Three days. I went to Jenny's wedding, and there was a life-coaching class in my house which woke me up, so I went out to get some liver but I fainted on the bus. Actually the wedding was after the bus.'

Katie looks at a sheet on a clipboard. 'Why don't you have a chat with tonight's co-ordinator?' she says.

'You're not the co-ordinator?' Luisa wants to grab her by the shoulders, to shake her until she changes her mind. If Katie isn't coordinator I can't stay, I have to walk out, I have to go. I'm endangering people by working tonight. Although if I go, I'm also endangering people. Is a midwife deranged from fatigue better than no midwife?

'Isn't it you?' Katie is back on the other side of the office, talking to Vicky, and Luisa says this instead to the woman coming through the doorway, a woman wearing a sunhat and floral dress, pulling behind her a large suitcase on wheels. Luisa moves to block any further advance into the sanctity of the office.

'Yes?' Luisa wants to say yes can I help you, but compresses it all into the single word.

'I know,' says the floral woman. 'Do you like my hat?'

'It's very nice.' The floral woman has somehow gained the upper hand. 'Which room are you in?' says Luisa.

'I managed to get a last minute upgrade, and we've got a porthole. Above sea level.' The woman crouches and pushes her suitcase under the desk next to the door.

'You can't keep that there,' says Luisa. 'This is the maternity office.'

'Oh, it's okay overnight.' The woman takes off her sun hat and stashes it on top of the suitcase. 'There's no management here until morning. I'll be taking it straight to Portsmouth when this shift's over. Karl's meeting me there to save time.'

It is Jenny, Jenny in a sun hat. Jenny not in a sun hat. 'I'm so sorry,' says Luisa. 'I didn't recognise you.'

'Face blindness? Prosopagnosia – I listened to a radio programme about it,' says Jenny.

'Not,' says Luisa. Jenny's presence disorientates her again. 'I'm hallucinating. I thought it was you but it isn't.'

'I think you'll find it is me.'

'And I thought I saw a waterfall in the lift.'

'Actually there was a waterfall in the lift, Jenny,' says Katie at Luisa's side. 'I'll explain everything at handover.'

'So you're tonight's coordinator?' Luisa wants confirmation, needs to hear it spoken out loud.

'Yes indeedy,' says Jenny.

'I didn't know it was you.'

'Well I am looking a bit special.' Jenny stands on one foot, lifting her other leg and holding the floral dress out to one side. 'But it's been a special day for us all round, hasn't it?'

Nikki enters the room followed by Gina. Both glance at Jenny.

'Jenny, I'm. I can't,' says Luisa. 'I can't even. I thought you were.'

'Use your words,' says Jenny.

'I don't think I can work.'

'You mean you're ill?'

'You're two down, Alice and Debbie called in sick,' Katie tells Jenny.

'Not ill. But I haven't slept,' says Luisa. 'In ages. About three days.'

'So you're telling me you're tired?' laughs Jenny.

'I am. I am so tired. And I didn't sleep today. When I was at your wedding. When I was bridesmaid. Witness.'

'I was at the wedding as well if you remember,' says Jenny. 'And I'm here.'

'I almost fell asleep at the wheel on *my* way in today,' says Nikki. 'Thought I was going to give this old man at a zebra crossing a heart attack. Though I suppose if I had, at least I could have just popped him in the back and brought him in with me.'

'I'm not sure it's safe,' says Luisa. 'I'm not – I don't feel responsible. Capable of doing my job properly.'

'Of course you're responsible,' says Jenny. 'You were witness at my wedding, weren't you?'

Jenny dips her knees ever so slightly as though executing a ski turn and emits a small fart. She takes a ring binder from under a plate of biscuits on the desk and flips it open.

'Is that true you collapsed in the lift last night?' Gina asks Luisa.

'I didn't collapse.' Luisa watches Jenny run a finger down a sheet in the ring binder.

'I heard they put out an MET call for you.'

'Did they?'

'Numbers are right down tonight,' says Jenny. 'And Molly has been rota-ed again. I've been telling them for months she's off with malaria.'

'Mmm, that makes us what, down to nine?' says Nikki.

'I'm supposed to be working with Debbie,' Vicky tells Jenny. 'But I don't think she's here yet.'

'Debbie's off sick,' says Katie. 'Someone took a message. Said she had to go to hospital.'

'We all have to go to hospital,' says Gina. 'In case she hadn't noticed.'

'Maybe this time she's actually had an accident,' says Annie.

'*Eight* then?' Nikki eyes are wide, alight.

A pungent smell hits Luisa nostrils. Vicky holds a hand to her nose, Gina and Nikki step away.

'We'll cope,' says Jenny. 'We always cope. Luisa, perhaps you can mentor Vicky tonight. She'll keep you lively.'

'Eight's not enough,' says Annie. 'If there's not enough we need to close the unit. If there's only eight we ought to send new women to the Queen Mary.'

'No one's closing the unit,' says Jenny. 'Not after the shitstorm legal kicked up last time.'

'I – I think I'm hallucinating smells now,' says Luisa.

'No, that's me.' Jenny squeezes her lips together and the sulphurous smell intensifies. 'Karl and I had our wedding breakfast at Arkwrights, and I'm not sure the mushy peas agreed with me.'

'Can we start?' says Katie. 'Is this everyone?'

'I'll bar the door,' says Gina.

That's it, thinks Luisa. I'm in now. Hatches sealed, submerging. She lifts her eyes, swivels her head on its heavy ball-socket. Who will drag me out of no-man's-land when I step on a mine? Katie? No, Katie's done. Nikki? Gina? Gina will. Gina's got the hands for it.

'We've got Bridget Downtry in Joy Horner.' Katie points to the bottom right on the handover board, taps the box labelled Bridget Downtry with a marker pen. 'Primip, thirty-seven weeks, induced for pre-eclampsia, type 1, insulin-controlled.'

I can't, thinks Luisa. I can't do anything like that. Pre-eclampsia, so much to go wrong. I need someone who hardly knows I'm there. A nineteenth-century birth. She scans the boxes on the board, moves past those filled with three-letter acronyms, from which pen lines spiral outwards, listing further complications.

'Matilda Smith,' says Luisa. On the bottom left of the board is a box with only a couple of lines of neat writing, one of which says 'multip, 18:00. 6cm'. I want her. I need Matilda Smith.

'Do you know her?' says Jenny.

'Sort of?' Everyone has turned to look at her.

'Well perhaps I'll give her you. As my bridesmaid,' says Jenny, and moves in front of the board to take over from Katie. 'I take it everyone knows about the pool room?' says Jenny. 'About Sarah Marchant? The medical claims lawyer. She's now in the pool room.'

'I thought the pool room was leaking,' says Gina. 'Isn't that why there's water in the lifts?'

'The pipes are leaking,' says Katie. 'Still are leaking, in fact. But we have to keep the pool topped up. Sarah Marchant is in the pool.'

'And that's where she's staying if that's where she wants to be,' says Jenny.

'Isn't the leaking water filling up the lifts?' says Nikki.

'A maintenance problem,' says Jenny. 'Our problem is Sarah Marchant. She gets whatever she wants.'

'Actually maintenance are trying to fix it,' says Katie. 'But they said they can't do anything unless we switch the water off.'

'Water stays on if Sarah Marchant wants it on,' says Jenny. 'So, who's taking Sarah Marchant?'

'She's for me,' Nikki shoots up her hand. 'She sounds brutal.'

Luisa watches Jenny write Nikki's name on the board below Sarah Marchant's, and move to Matilda Smith's box where she inscribes Luisa's name, then adds '+ Vicky' to the right of Luisa's.

'So I think we're all sorted,' says Jenny.

The midwives move out of the room.

'Did you tell him?' says Gina at Luisa's side.

'Tell who?'

'Your partner. The choice,' says Gina.

'I haven't talked to him,' says Luisa. 'I've been to a wedding. To Jenny's wedding.'

'Don't let me down, Luisa. Let any of us down.'

'I have to get to Carol Decker. With Vicky,' says Luisa.

'You'll be all right with her.' Gina envelops Luisa in a crushing hug and spring releases her as though afraid someone might see. 'She's so competent. Still needs the fear, if she wants to be safe. But so competent.'

'And don't forget message of the week!' cries Jenny. 'Priority is infection control, we don't want another incident with an overdone placenta. Check it, Bag it, Sluice it!'

Vicky is already in Carol Decker when Luisa arrives, but she and Karen, the day-shift midwife, are secondary characters in the room. The entire room is filled with the presence Matilda Smith, who blows another noisy breath through her small round mouth, and makes a turn at the wall to pace back across the room. Standing at the opposite wall is a bald man with a neat beard who is even less noticeable – he belongs with the items of furniture.

'So I'll be finishing now, Matilda,' says Karen.

'You've been so good,' puffs Matilda. 'Can't you – stay longer? Not long now. Really not long.'

'Luisa will look after you now. And Vicky here.'

'Hi there, Matilda. I'm Luisa,' sings Luisa. Vicky, Vicky will look after you. You don't want me looking after you.

'So everything's perfectly normal.' Karen hands over to Luisa, works through Matilda's notes: a simple, low risk birth. Vicky is writing notes on her pad, thinks Luisa, Vicky is noting how normal everything is. Except everything isn't normal, is it? How can a birth be normal? This is life and death, new life and the unspoken terror of death, this isn't web design or gardening or building a bridge. Perhaps it is life and death when you build a bridge badly. Though at least people only die some time later, when you're no longer constructing the bridge. But someone might die here, quite soon, if I, we, don't do our jobs well. How can any human being cope with that?

Karen has gone. Matilda ends her pacing at the yoga mat on the floor next to the bed, and drops onto her knees, on all fours, her nightshirt riding up so only the top third of her body is clothed. The room is hers, her domain. No one is going to die. No one is going to die because I will do my job. Matilda is almost there. A couple of hours, a couple of hours of terror and we're done.

'So I'll be very much in the background today,' says Luisa. 'Vicky here, she's one of our senior students.'

'Hi Matilda, I'm Vicky,' sings Vicky.

'I'll be here, at all times. But Vicky's in control.'

Matilda emits another pressurised snort, louder and deeper.

Vicky's in control until she's no longer in control and then I'm in control.

'You're in transition now,' Vicky lays a hand on Matilda's back. 'Just as you should be.'

'Why don't I look after Matilda's notes?' Luisa says to Vicky.

'James,' croaks Matilda. 'James.'

The bearded man jumps forward, kneels down next to Matilda, his face almost touching the floor. 'I'm here, honey,' says James. Matilda's face presses into the mat. She scrabbles around for his hand in order to grip hold.

'It *hurts*,' says Matilda.

'I know,' says James. 'What about the epidural?' James's eyes stare over Matilda's back at Vicky, at Luisa, and back down again. 'You said you didn't want the epidural. Should she have an epidural? Do you think so?' He looks at Luisa.

'No epidural,' croaks Matilda.

'You're doing so well,' says Vicky. 'You've done so well sticking to the birth plan so far. We're getting to fully dilated now. You can do this.' Vicky looks across at Luisa, and Luisa smiles. Don't look to me for reassurance. I'm dangerous, I'm not the one.

A caveman bark sounds from Matilda, and she rotates her buttocks in time with the contraction.

'That's it!' says Vicky. 'You're doing really well.'

Why would these people, these adult human beings, who presumably have enough judgement to allow them to hold down jobs, to keep themselves alive, why do they think it's sensible to put the life of their child, to put Matilda's own life, in my hands? They don't even know me, they know nothing about me. Of how long I have been awake. Dedication to my work means nothing. All midwives here are dedicated to their work, all do their utmost to ensure every woman is safe. That they are willing to do their utmost means they come to work under any circumstances, to ensure as many people as possible are doing their utmost. Everyone cares, except for Debbie, and the fact she does not care and calls in sick means the midwives who do care are here more often. Luisa cares, she cares deeply that no one is going to die. But that does not mean no one will die.

'We wanted to use the pool,' says James. 'Matilda wanted to use it. But it was full.'

'Right,' says Luisa. Matilda has somehow disappeared, is no longer on the mat.

'The pool is very popular,' says Vicky.

Where has she gone? thinks Luisa. The toilet flushes and Matilda emerges, presents them with a sanitary pad covered in a translucent gloop and several dark red globules of blood.

'A bloody show,' says Vicky, 'and with a mucus plug. That's excellent.'

A lot of blood. Should be some blood but that's a lot of blood. 'That's great,' says Luisa.

Matilda is back on her knees, producing long, arching moans, Vicky is telling her to follow her instincts. Vicky holds the probe of the foetal doppler against Matilda's belly, and Luisa listens to the blips of the baby's heart. Is that slow? They sound fine. Vicky has said they're fine. She and Justin still haven't talked about her running out on him, on staying out the night. She steps over to the trolley, to be closer to the monitor. Justin might be the son of Fidel Castro.

'Now I'm going to make up a warm perineum pad whilst Luisa keeps an eye on the baby's heart rate,' says Vicky.

Luisa crouches behind Matilda's buttocks and reaches the foetal heart doppler between her legs. The heart rate is slow – perhaps she has Matilda's heart rate by mistake. Luisa moves the doppler, cannot find the heartbeat.

'So, Luisa is finding the heartbeat again,' says Vicky.

Luisa looks over Matilda's buttocks at the door, at the emergency buzzer left of the door. Press the buzzer, just press the buzzer. Everyone will come running. The seconds tick by, but Luisa cannot tell how many.

'What should we do?' whispers Vicky.

And there is the heartbeat again, faster. The baby's heartbeat. Vicky crouches down again behind Matilda's legs and Luisa stands, backs away, back to the safety of writing the notes.

Everything is fine. Everything is as it should be, Matilda grunting her way through another contraction.

'There we go!' says Vicky. A matt of hair forces open the slit of Matilda's vulva. 'I can see vertex!' Luisa writes the head's appearance in the notes, and the time. 20:33.

'Is this the bit where I pant?' cries Matilda.

'Not yet, we need the head a little lower,' says Vicky. She's excited, shuffling around on her knees. 'Keep following your body's urges. Follow that urge to push.'

Luisa watches as the sliver of hair becomes inconceivably wider. A thin stool squeezes from Matilda's dilated anus.

'Oo – actually it's coming now, quite quick. Pant pant pant pant pant, start panting.' Vicky starts panting. Matilda copies her, though less enthusiastically.

The baby's head emerges from between Matilda's legs. James crawls down to her feet. 'I can see him! Or her! I can't tell.' James smiles up at Luisa.

The hair is matted with vernix, the head stony-grey, dormant. James is scampering now, back and forth on his knees from one end of Matilda to the other.

'Waiting for the next contraction now,' says Vicky.

How long has the head been that way? Luisa looks at the notes, at 20.33.

The time when the head came out, or when vertex visible? She cannot remember. She flips her fob watch up from her trouser pocket. 20.37.

Luisa looks at Vicky, positioned close to the head, ready to catch the baby. This might not be one of your forty births. How long has the head been out? Perhaps the shoulders are stuck. The shoulders are stuck?

'Do you think we should get on?' Luisa says to Vicky.

'I think – only two minutes since the last contraction,' Vicky looks at Luisa. Is she asking for reassurance? I have none to give. If it goes on much longer, I have to press the emergency buzzer. Vicky looks back down. Now, thinks Luisa, now I have to take charge. I have to act. Act now.

Matilda cries out again.

'It's almost – ' says Luisa, and the baby pops out in one movement, slips into Vicky's hands. 'Oh my god,' says James. 'Oh my god. It's a little girl!' He crawls back to Matilda's head. 'It's a girl, honey, a girl!'

A grown man crying, on his knees, thinks Luisa. She looks at the baby girl, at Vicky as she wraps her in a towel, the baby all purple, motionless and purple.

'You did it,' says Vicky. 'Oh, she's beautiful.'

'Is she all okay?' says Matilda, her head twisted to peer back around her leg. 'I want to see her, can I see her?'

Vicky makes no move to pass the baby to Matilda, but instead rubs her vigorously with a towel.

'Come on baby,' coos Vicky. 'Oh, she's *very* relaxed.' Her rubbing intensifies to a level only necessary if the baby was covered in biro stain.

Vicky looks up at Luisa, her lips parted, eyes blinking.

Luisa estimates perhaps thirty seconds have passed since the birth. But who am I to judge the subjective nature of time?

'Is she okay?' James kneels beside Vicky.

How long now? How long can I ask how long until it is too long? Luisa watches Vicky bring the baby closer to her chest, almost to the limit of the umbilical cord.

'It's less than a minute,' says Vicky. 'That's okay. Come on, baby.'

Luisa turns, her sight line taking in Matilda, the baby, Vicky, James, towards the door, to the emergency button to the left of the door. James follows the movement of her eyes.

The baby wriggles from stone into life and lets out a howl.

'Oh baby!' cries James, he's back down on his knees, helps Vicky feed her through Matilda's legs. Matilda pushes herself up off her forearms, back onto her haunches, and takes the tiny girl in her arms. Commotion and movement replace the silence.

Everything is okay – that was good. What was I worrying about? Everything. Keeping the fear. But that went well.

'She's beautiful,' says James. He stands and hugs Vicky, then Luisa. 'Thank you,' says James. 'Thank you for everything. You're all so *calm*. So professional.'

'Oh, it was all Matilda's doing,' says Vicky, her eyebrows high, face wide with delight. James is back down on the floor again, pulling out towels, wrenching off his shirt and cradling the baby to his chest. 'She was so in *control*.'

Luisa watches Vicky put clamps on the umbilical cord and hand scissors to James. The baby nuzzles on Matilda's chest.

'Okay, so we're going for physiological third stage.' Vicky stands and whispers to Luisa. 'Bleeding seems minimal, so my plan is to leave them bonding for a while. That keeps the oxytocin up, doesn't it? For the placenta? Are you okay, Luisa?'

Luisa snaps up her head. Everything is okay. A completely normal birth. Everything worked.

'Oh yes. Thanks. Thank you.'

'You must be all a bit shaken, after yesterday.'

'Yesterday?'

Vicky gathers more towels for Matilda, was not expecting the conversation to continue. 'In the lift. Didn't you get stuck for ages in the lift?'

'Yes. In the lift. But the lift wasn't flooded,' says Luisa. 'I'm fine.'

'Once the placenta is out, I'll make toast for everyone,' says Vicky. 'You need to eat something too. I'll make some toast for us all in a minute,' she repeats to Matilda and James.

'Oh thank you,' says Matilda. 'I'm starving.'

'I'll fetch more towels,' says Luisa. 'We're getting through the towels.

You're okay here for now, Vicky? Just keep an eye on the bleeding.'

Luisa heads to the toilets, straight to a basin, head down to avoid seeing herself in the mirror. She runs the warm tap into her cupped hands, pulls water down her face, over and over. Tears run from her eyes, but merge with the water and are hidden from view, hidden from herself. Her sobs bubble through the water.

She looks up to see Annie at the next basin.

'I'm sorry,' says Luisa.

'Sorry for what?' says Annie, and bursts into tears.

'What is it? What's up?'

Annie frowns, confused.

'Why are you crying?' says Luisa.

'Oh, I'm always crying. I rarely go a whole shift without a good blub.' Annie sounds insulted at the question. She pulls a sheet from the towel dispenser. 'I'm surprised this is the first time we've had a cry together.'

'Oh. Sorry.'

Annie shrugs.

'I'm crying because I'm worried,' answers Luisa, though Annie hasn't asked. 'That I might do something terrible. I'm so tired. Someone might die.'

'Babies hardly ever die any more.' Annie looks in the mirror and combs her hair with her fingers. 'Birth and maternal deaths are both way down. Even since *I* started.'

She knows what Annie says to be true – she learnt this in training. *UK neonatal deaths down 50% between 1984 and 2010.* She wrote it in her dissertation. Did they teach us that to stop us worrying? No, they taught us that because it's true.

'So why are you crying?' says Luisa.

But Annie has gone.

'Luisa.' Out in the corridor Jenny approaches Luisa at speed, then powers past, straight through reception towards the office. 'Get me a sick bowl. I need a sick bowl, right now.'

Jenny continues her trajectory through the office doorway. I have to get back to Vicky, to Matilda, she thinks, as she ducks into the sluice room and grabs a cardboard sick bowl.

'Where should I take it?' asks Luisa. In the office Jenny is on her knees in front of a bewildered Annie, one hand gripped to the desk to hold her body weight. Jenny tears the bowl from Luisa and releases her gripping hand as the force of her vomiting propels her to the floor, where she fills the cardboard bowl with a pale green sludge.

Luisa fetches Jenny a glass of water, helps her up into a chair. She fetches more cardboard bowls, sets them next to Jenny's head, places a reel of paper towels on top.

'Are you going to be all right?' The words sound alien, not a phrase one says to Jenny.

'Oh my dearie,' says Annie. 'Giddy me.'

'Must have been those mushy peas.' Jenny stares at the vomit streak down her arm. 'I knew they were bad as they were going down,' she croaks. 'I said nothing at the time. I didn't want to spoil it for Karl.'

'You'll be all right,' says Luisa. 'You just need to rest for a few minutes.'

'Don't know about that,' says Jenny. 'It'll be the same the other end in a minute.'

'Do you want – ?' Luisa picks up the reel of paper towels.

'I need to get to the toilet.'

'It's that way,' Luisa points.

'And if so someone will have to be co-ordinator.'

'I can't, I have to get back to Vicky,' says Luisa. 'The placenta's not out and I need to check her perineum. Annie, it'll have to be you.' Luisa looks to Annie, and Annie makes a minute shiver of the head.

Jenny is off the chair and onto her knees again. She reaches for another bowl, lurches forward to fill it with watery vomit.

'I'm done for,' says Jenny. 'That's me, out for the count.'

'No, no you're not,' says Luisa, but with no supporting evidence to offer.

'I need to hand over. To one of you. Who's it going to be?'

Jenny crawls towards the doorway. Luisa moves in front of her, barring her way out.

'Hand over to Annie,' says Luisa. 'I'm almost new, remember. Remember how you have to keep checking up on me? Hand over to Annie.'

'Not me,' says Annie. 'It can't be me. Remember, Jenny? Remember what happened before?'

'Not Annie.' Jenny stares up at Luisa, and Luisa moves out of her way.

'Gina can do it,' says Luisa. Jenny crawls out into the corridor. 'Gina is more experienced. And I, I haven't – '

'Fine.' Jenny's head lurches forward, propelled by a force inside of her. 'But I need to hand over now, and Gina isn't here. I'll tell you and you can tell Gina.' Jenny fixes her eyes on Luisa. 'You need to listen now. Listen carefully. Can you do that?'

No, thinks Luisa. No, I can't. 'I'm listening. Let me get a pen. A pad.'

'Now.' Jenny reaches up to grip Luisa's wrist, so tight it hurts. 'I'm on the knife edge of a double-ender, a D and V. Walk with me. Bring that bowl.' Jenny scutters on her knees to the end of reception, looks up and down the corridor and, seeing only Nikola the cleaner, crawls to her right. Nikola sweeps a mop back and forth ahead of Jenny's path. A memory of late-night televised curling at the Winter Olympics pops into Luisa's head.

'Walk with me!' Jenny commands again.

Luisa steps beside her, carrying the full sick bowl. 'I haven't been co-ordinator before,' she says. 'I don't know what I'm doing.'

'It's quite simple. You're just in charge of everything on delivery suite.' Jenny's head is low, her chin almost on her chest, and in order to hear Luisa needs to lean down into a painful semi-crouch as she walks. She waddles alongside, but cannot travel fast enough without slopping vomit over the side of the bowl, so drops to her knees and crawls, pushing the sick bowl ahead of her along the lino.

'I can only say this once.' Jenny reaches a hand behind to press between her buttocks. 'You need to do the quality control checks on the blood sugar monitors, they're overdue. If you don't do them every twenty-four hours, they stop working.'

'Right. I'll tell Gina. Don't worry.' Luisa's knees are cold and wet.

'I'm not sure we have any caesarean packs left.' Jenny's upper body is almost touching her forearms, but she still has forward motion, and Luisa does not want to touch her, to touch Jenny.

'If there's any more caesareans you must talk to main theatre to see if they have any,' says Jenny.

'How do I call main theatre?' Luisa splays her left hand on the glistening floor. Little finger: blood sugar monitors. Ring finger: caesarean packs.

A pregnant woman turns the corner carrying a paper cup. She steers around the two crawling midwives.

'I can't believe I've dropped my contact lens *again*,' shouts Jenny. 'I'm such an idiot.'

Luisa scrabbles her hand around the floor, searching. The pregnant woman continues on, hands resting on her belly.

They arrive at the changing room. 'If you get a chance,' whispers Jenny, 'remember that all babies are meant to have their oxygen-sats checked four hours after birth. Some stupid new protocol, you don't need to do it, but if you don't, make sure you write on all the notes why you haven't.'

'I've forgotten my little finger,' says Luisa. Jenny pushes open the changing room door with a combination of hand and head. Halfway inside she stops, and the door springs against her side. She reaches behind her, holding something out to Luisa.

'Take the bleep. Take the bleep, bridesmaid.' Jenny pushes the pager into Luisa's hand. 'And if it really comes to it, you can always ring the supervisor at home. If you don't feel safe.'

'Perhaps we need to close the unit, Jenny, Luisa says, her words clipped, as though she is in charge. She is in charge. 'Without you, we're down to seven. We can't run the ward with seven.'

'No closing! Not unless you want the paperwork to incite me to violence,' says Jenny. 'Call Diane. Get Diane down here.'

'But Diane's not on tonight.'

'You can always call Diane.' Jenny breathes in staggered gasps. 'Stand outside the supplies room in postnatal and call her name.' Jenny waves a dismissive hand. 'And don't worry, bridesmaid, I'm not going anywhere. Not whilst Sarah Marchant is still on the ward.' Jenny is through the door and the rest of her words are a muffled shout. 'Look, you can forget almost everything I've said. It's just your job to make sure all deliveries are going to plan. Any major screw-ups and you're in court too, remember!'

Luisa stands, stares at the bleep in her palm. She runs her thumb across her index finger, trying to squeeze out a memory of the instructions.

'And get one of these women who's delivered up to postnatal!' Jenny's voice echoes from the changing room, the commandment of a deity from a parallel world. 'There's only one delivery room left! You don't want to be full, bridesmaid! That's when the real trouble begins.' There is the sound of heaving, and a watery splash.

Luisa holds out her thumb to splay her whole hand. Where is Gina, in which room is Gina? Look in the office, on the board. But first check on Vicky.

A call buzzer sounds.

Luisa takes the sick bowl into the sluice room, flips the lid of the macerator and throws it inside. One task done, that's one finger. But that wasn't one of my fingers, she thinks, as the macerator grinds away. She heads out the door and towards Carol Decker, and bumps into Nikki coming out of the pool room.

'Do you know which room Gina's in?' says Luisa.

'No idea. All a bit hectic tonight, isn't it?' giggles Nikki. 'I'm after Jenny. Have you seen Jenny?'

'Jenny's in the toilet,' says Luisa.

'Sarah Marchant, she's been pushing an hour and a half. Not sure whether I should call the Reg. In the changing room?'

'Don't go in there. Jenny's sick.'

'Sick?' For the first time Nikki's grin disappears. 'So who's in charge?'

'Gina. Gina is coordinator.'

'Well where's Gina?'

'That's what I was asking you,' says Luisa.

'Gina's in with me,' says a voice behind them. It is Nadine, one of the student midwives. 'In Mary Cronk. Sorry, but Gina needs the coordinator. She sent me to get Jenny. She needs the coordinator, to deal with – to help with the SHO.'

'What do you mean, deal with?' says Luisa.

'I don't – know,' says Nadine.

'I'm coming to speak to Gina,' says Luisa. 'I need to hand over to her. She needs to be coordinator, to take the bleep.' Luisa displays the bleep for them.

'So you've got the bleep,' says Nikki. 'You're the co-ordinator.'

'I'm giving it to Gina,' says Luisa.

'But you have it now?' Nikki looks at her.

Luisa closes her hand around the bleep.

'Well, just tell me what you think,' says Nikki. 'About Sarah Marchant. She's tonight's princess.'

'I'm – '

'Technically she's only been pushing just over an hour. Perhaps I'll get her to change position and go to the loo, then check again. What do you think?'

'Yes. Okay.' To what is she saying yes? Don't say yes – what if no is better? She runs through Nikki's words again.

'You think that's okay?' Nikki frowns at her, seeking an answer.

'It sounds like a good plan.' Luisa's eyes refuse to fix on Nikki's face, only resting on safe areas such as the floor.

'Okay.'

'She's still feeling good baby movements?' says Luisa. 'Foetal heart is okay?'

'Foetal heart is fine.' Nikki disappears back into the pool room.

'Will you come and see Gina?' says Nadine. 'She said she needs the co-ordinator.'

'I will definitely come and see Gina.' Luisa holds up fingers to Nadine. 'Two minutes, I'll be there in two minutes.'

Erin strides from the office into reception, as though with a message from the commander of the entire army.

'I have Clarissa on the phone again from postnatal.' Erin reads from a notepad. 'She's asking for Jenny.' Erin eyeballs Luisa. 'She needs the SHO in postnatal, to review a woman's blood pressure. Apparently he's not answering his bleep.'

'The SHO is in our room,' says Nadine. 'In with Gina. I think you should get him from Gina.'

'I will get to the SHO,' says Luisa. 'as soon as I've checked in on Vicky.'

'Sorry. I'm not telling you what to do,' says Nadine.

Luisa glances at Nadine as she heads down the corridor, knows that a word of consolation is needed, is what she herself always needs and rarely receives. The words are there, wilting somewhere at the base of her brain, not clear enough to be spoken, translated to a foreign language by the list of outstanding tasks.

In Carol Decker, Matilda is in bed, the baby on her chest, her and James munching slices of toast. Vicky steps in front of her.

'I got her up and onto the toilet,' says Vicky. She whispers, but cannot contain her excitement. 'I unclamped the cord, got her to empty her bladder, and the placenta came straight out. EBL of 300 mils, maternal obs all normal.'

'Great stuff.' Luisa gives Vicky an enormous grin which pains her cheeks. 'Sorry I've been so long. There're problems I had to take care of. With the coordinator.'

'Well we're all good here.' Vicky announces to the whole room.

'Thank you,' says Matilda.

'Thank you both,' says James.

'I never made you that toast.' Vicky's hand flies to her mouth. 'I made it for everyone else and not for you. I'll do it right now.'

'Don't worry about toast.' Everything is okay in here, she can leave. 'You'll be okay?'

Vicky nods. 'Which do you prefer: brown or white?'

Luisa splays her right hand, counts off on her fingers. Need to add: go see Gina. Send the SHO down to Clarissa. She stretches her fingers wider as though this will assist recall.

Luisa rotates towards the door.

'Brown or white?' says Vicky.

'Brown,' says Luisa as she leaves.

She knocks on the door of Mary Cronk, pushes open the door.

'Stay behind the curtain!' calls Gina. 'Not a sound.'

'Gina, I need to have a word,' murmurs Luisa. 'It's Luisa.'

'I must apologise for yet another interruption, Paula,' says Gina. 'This is most inappropriate. Follow your body. Allow the urges. Nadine, the notes are yours.'

'Is he okay? I mean there was quite a lot of blood.' Paula ends her words with a deep exhale and begins a rising grunt.

'It's of no concern to you Paula, then or now. You must focus on you. Nadine!'

Gina punches through the divide in the curtain, pulls it back together behind her.

'Luisa.'

'I'm sorry, Gina. But Jenny is sick, she might have to go home, she wants you to be coordinator.' Luisa holds out the bleep.

Paula's contraction concludes with a shrill gasp.

'Well done. You're doing really well,' says Nadine behind the curtain.

'We've got vertex advancing, Luisa. Now is not the time,' says Gina.

'Jenny needs to hand over to you now,' says Luisa. 'I'll take over here. I can take over Paula.'

'I suppose he did keep trying to give his opinion, didn't he?' calls Paula.

'Focus on *you*, Paula!' says Gina.

'Yes, Gina,' says Paula.

Gina takes Luisa's arm and pushes her towards the door.

'No, you cannot take over my woman,' says Gina outside the room when the door is closed. 'Totally inappropriate at this stage.'

'Jenny is in the loo. She's got D at the same time as V.' Luisa can feel her eyes filling with tears, and she blinks them away. 'She handed over to me and said I was to hand over to you,' she says fiercely. 'Postnatal have rung, they need the SHO up there. Where's the SHO? I thought he was in with you?'

'He's not here now.'

'But where did he go?'

'He's gone to A and E,' says Gina.

'Let me tell you what you need to do,' pleads Luisa. She displays her fingers. 'The oxygen-sats, they have to be checked, actually they don't have to be, but you have to say why not – '

Gina holds up her hand and Luisa falls silent.

'I'm not going to be coordinator now, Luisa. Paula needs continuity of care, and I will do that for her. She's already had her flow interrupted by one unnecessary intervention.'

'I don't know what I'm doing,' says Luisa.

'It's not hard.' Gina's voice softens. 'The co-ordinator doesn't really do anything. You're simply responsible for everything that happens on the ward. Once Paula has birthed, I'll take over.'

'How long will you be?'

'You know that's one thing I'm not in control of,' laughs Gina. 'Mother nature has no clocks.' She goes back inside Mary Cronk and closes the door.

The corridor is quiet, empty. Luisa stands motionless, her back to the door. She closes her eyes.

'I heard Jenny was ill,' says Rebecca, when Luisa opens her eyes. 'So who's coordinator?'

'I am,' says Luisa.

'Right!' laughs Rebecca.

If I stay here that's still coordinating, isn't it? I only have to ensure everything is okay. Perhaps everything is okay. Luisa closes her eyes again. Her head swims, and she steadies herself with her hands against the door. I have to answer questions. Do my fingers.

'Are you still Jenny? Or is Gina Jenny?'

Luisa opens her eyes to see Annie. What if I refuse to answer? 'I'm still Jenny,' says Luisa.

'Jenny was meant to be checking on my lady,' says Annie. 'The baby's heart is a little off.'

'I'm sure you know as well as me,' says Luisa.

'I need a co-ordinator. A co-ordinator's opinion.'

'I need to find the SHO,' Luisa remembers. 'How about I come after that?'

'Oh that's right, leave me til last,' says Annie. 'I'm sure the massive decelerations with a high risk woman will sort themselves out on their own.'

Luisa follows Annie down the corridor.

'Hi-i,' Luisa addresses the two women in Michel Odent room. One lies with her tattooed upper arms on an inflatable ball, the other with her arms under the tattooed woman's waist and her head on her back, as though about to perform a Heimlich manoeuvre.

'Luisa, this is Bella, and her lady friend Serena. Bella, this is Luisa,' says Annie. 'Luisa is in charge of the ward. See.' Annie's eyebrows direct Luisa's attention to the monitor screen. 'See the little dips.'

Those are deep decelerations, thinks Luisa. Call the doctor. I can call the doctor. The SHO's in A and E. Call the Reg. Clarissa needs a doctor in postnatal.

'Well, we've got nice variability. But maybe the doctor should take a look,' coos Luisa. 'To be sure.'

'Is it okay?' Bella nods at the monitor. 'I mean this is obviously not fucking okay, but is all of that okay?' Serena runs her fingers through Bella's long hair. Bella pulls her hair away from the hand in irritation.

'There's nothing for you and baby to worry about, Bella,' says Annie, as lovingly as a favourite aunt. 'But to be certain we like a second opinion.'

'Uuuggh.' Bella rolls forwards and back again on the ball. 'Jesus fuck.'

'Baby doll,' says Serena.

'Fuck off,' says Bella. 'It's not your cunt he's coming out of, is it?'

'It's only a precaution,' Luisa heads for the door. 'I'll have the Registrar come in and check on you.'

'Thank you,' says Serena. 'Thank you so much.'

If there's no problem why call the doctor? Am I calling the doctor? I told them I was calling the doctor.

Annie stands in the doorway, barring her exit.

'I can't listen to it. They keep saying that.' Annie whispers fiercely to Luisa. 'She keeps calling her that word for whoopsie. And to doodle off. Why do they have to say such things?'

'Not now, Annie.' Luisa steps forward, her face only a foot from Annie's. A discussion on the feminist reclamation of the word cunt is really low on my to-do list right now. I'm going to change to silent mode. Only minimal speech.

To her surprise Annie moves out of the way.

Back in the office Luisa dials the number to bleep the Reg. The phone rings back immediately. 'I'll be there,' says the Registrar when Luisa has explained the call. 'Get the SHO to come as well.'

'He's in A and E.'

'Well get him up from A and E.'

Luisa dials the Senior House Officer's bleep number. The phone rings back again. 'He can't come right now,' says a nurse in A and E. 'He's got a nasal fracture.'

'Why's he dealing with a nasal fracture?' asks Luisa. 'He's on maternity.'

'Are you in midwifery? Who is this?'

'This is Luisa. I'm a midwife. I'm – co-ordinator, right now.'

'Well, perhaps it's not obvious in midwifery,' says the nurse angrily, 'but when you punch someone on the nose it does quite often break? Or don't you learn about anything except vaginas?'

'Who punched him on the nose?'

The nurse has gone.

'Where's Jenny?' Sue enters the office.

'We don't have the SHO any more,' says Luisa. 'He's in A and E.'

'I need to speak to Jenny,' says Sue. 'Antenatal have called again, the 5cm woman really needs to come down here.'

'Jenny's sick,' says Luisa.

'Is that her making those noises in the toilet?' Sue exaggerates the shaking of her head, as though trying to vibrate it loose from her neck. 'She can't be. If Jenny's sick we're down to, what, seven? We can't operate with seven. So who's in charge?'

Sue doesn't know. Does she have to know? 'I'm in charge,' says Luisa.

'But you haven't been in charge before, have you? Do you feel safe?'

'Can you be co-ordinator?' Luisa holds out the bleep to her.

Sue steps away from the bleep, kryptonite to her superman. 'You should call the supervisor. If you don't feel safe, you need to call the supervisor. How can we work with only seven midwives? It's ridiculous.'

'Jenny said we can call Diane.'

'Oh right. Diane, Diane, Diane!' Sue waves her arms at Luisa.

Luisa reaches for the phone, but it rings before she can touch it.

'Don't answer it,' says Luisa, but Sue has already picked up the receiver. 'I need to call the supervisor,' says Luisa.

Sue puts her hand over the receiver. 'It's Clarissa in postnatal. She wants to know how long until the SHO arrives.'

'He's in A and E. A and E.' Luisa sits in a chair. I have completed none of Jenny's instructions. Not one.

'What shall I tell Clarissa?' says Sue.

Two men enter the office. In the bright lights of maternity their black shirts and trousers are alien, dreamlike. It would be so lovely if you were a dream, thinks Luisa.

'Where's Gina McAndle? I'm Ravi, this is Frank. From security.' The man puts a palm to his orange hi vis. He is young, Indian, with a neat beard.

'Luisa's in charge here.' Sue points down at Luisa. 'We'll get back to you,' she says in to the phone, replaces the receiver and steps out into reception.

'Oooh,' says Diane. 'Are you?'

'What are you doing here?' asks Luisa.

'Someone called me,' says Diane.

'We're here for Gina McAndle,' says Ravi.

'But why did Gina call you?' says Luisa.

'No one called us, we were sent here,' says the taller, bald man. 'To take Gina McAndle down for questioning. There's been an assault.'

Luisa rises from her chair. 'You can't take Gina away. She's working.'

'Zero tolerance to violence against staff here,' says Ravi. 'Dr Jake James made a disclosure, that Gina McAndle assaulted him at,' he consults his pad, '21:07. We take such matters very seriously. Where she is, please?'

'Gina? Gina's in Mary Cronk,' says Erin in the doorway.

'Who?' says Ravi, and Erin points down the corridor.

What if I punch one of these guards? thinks Luisa. I can't go round punching guards. Gina can't go around punching doctors – that's why they're taking her away. But if I punch someone they'll take me away. I could punch Gina. I wouldn't dare punch Gina.

Luisa pursues the security guards, down the corridor and into the open door of Mary Cronk.

'No!' she shouts into the room. Everyone in Mary Cronk turns to face Luisa through the open curtain. Ravi has a hand cupped on Gina's elbow. Luisa feels her cheeks reddening.

'Not yet?' says Paula. 'Stop pushing?' Paula is up on her elbows in bed, Nadine behind her. A bald man stands by the window – the wall prevents him moving even further.

'You're not taking anyone!' Luisa strides into the room. 'Not without my say so. I'm the coordinator here, and you're endangering patient safety by interfering with Gina's work.'

Gina shrugs her arm from the Ravi's grasp, and pushes the guards back out beyond the curtain, with little resistance.

'What the hell do you mean by this kind of disturbance?' cries Gina. It is not clear whether she is talking to Luisa or the guards. 'Not here. Not where birth is taking place.'

Paula begins a deep inhalation.

'You broke a doctor's nose,' calls Frank.

'I don't know about breaking his nose,' says Gina. 'But that SHO may have caused serious iatrogenic harm to a woman during birth. Mighten he Paula?'

'Might he?' strains Paula.

Gina sweeps the curtain shut, enveloping the bed.

'You can't take one of my midwives away now,' Luisa tells the guards. Her voice is calm, reasonable – she watches herself speak in amazement. 'I'm in charge of this ward, and the women here are my responsibility. You'll wait until Gina has delivered this baby, and we can proceed from there. No one's taking anyone away at the moment.'

'Thank you, Luisa.' Gina calls from inside the curtain.

The guards look at each other. 'We have our orders,' says Ravi.

'And you can follow them after the birth,' says Luisa. 'Gina is staying right here until she has completed intrapartum care.'

'We're going to need to know where she is at all times,' says Frank. 'We can't have a flight risk.' He takes a seat by the door.

'You can't be in the room,' calls Gina. 'This is a mother's place.'

'I don't mind, honestly,' calls Paula.

'You can take those chairs outside,' says Luisa. 'She's not going anywhere.'

Ravi and Frank take a chair each and leave the room.

'How long will you take her for?' Luisa follows them out. 'I can't be another midwife down for long.'

'That's for a judge to decide,' Ravi sits, legs stretched out.

'After the birth means placenta as well.' Luisa's voice hits shrill again. 'Plus repair of any damage to the perineum.'

Ravi and Frank both drop eye contact.

Luisa turns down the corridor to see Sue and Erin hurrying away from her.

'You were amazing,' whispers Sue when they are all back at reception. 'That showed them who's in charge.'

'Who is in charge?' asks Diane.

Me, thinks Luisa. It's me.

'Diane,' says Luisa, 'can you please go up to antenatal, there's a 5cm woman there, bring her down here.'

'Righty-ho. I'll be able to fit her in my pocket,' says Diane.

'Nikola,' Luisa rotates further, round to the cleaner, 'can you go with Diane please? Clean the space in antenatal ready for a woman here to come up. Sue – if anyone else calls, put them off coming in. Once Diane's woman is down, we've no more beds until I can get someone out.'

'What shall I tell people who call?' says Sue.

'Tell them anything.'

'Got it.'

Luisa is alone in reception. I sent them off, thinks Luisa. To do as I say.

Vicky emerges at speed from Carol Decker.

'Vicky!' Luisa shouts from reception. 'Is everything okay?'

'Oh god, Luisa, I'm so sorry,' Vicky looks stricken.

Luisa skids out of the reception entrance, blocking Vicky's path. 'What's happening? Is she haemorrhaging? Tell me.'

'Matilda's fine. Not much EBL. But what about you?'

'I'm fine. I'm the co-ordinator.'

'I didn't bring you your toast.' Vicky has tears in her eyes. 'I'll make it right now. Do you like butter?'

'What?'

'On your toast,' says Vicky. 'Do you like it buttered? Or something else? Some people don't like butter.'

'I don't – mind,' says Luisa. Vicky's mouth stretches in fear. 'With butter. Thanks. And I'll be in soon, we can check the perineum together.'

'Oh, yes!' says Vicky, a five-year-old told she is off to the seaside.

'Sarah Marchant has delivered. SVD at 22:34.' Nikki enters reception via the office. 'Jenny said tell you straight away.'

'Jenny was in with Sarah Marchant?'

'No, Jenny's still in the toilet. Infection control and all that. She grabbed me by the ankle through the doorway.'

'How soon can you get Sarah Marchant upstairs?' says Luisa.

'She doesn't really seem keen to go anywhere for a while,' says Nikki. 'At the moment I'm getting the kitchen to rustle her and her husband up a meal.

Do you reckon they can do anything gluten-free?'

'Where's the coordinator?' The Registrar appears.

'Not me. It's her.' Nikki points at Luisa.

'We need to go review this CTG,' says the Reg.

'So let's do it.' Luisa strides out of the office and through reception.

Annie stands outside Michel Odent, looking in through a crack in the open door. 'I had to step outside for a second,' she tells them.

Inside Bella leans on the ball, her head on her arms. 'Why am I the one doing this again?' Tears run down her face and onto the ball. 'It should have been your fucking turn.' Serena strokes her hair, shushing her. Bella increases the strength of her grip on Serena's wrist.

'I offered.' Serena looks up at Luisa and the Registrar. 'She loves it really. She insisted on being pregnant again.'

'Lying bitch.' Bella rolls forward on the ball again.

'Come on sweetie. Not the B word.'

'Well we're doing okay for the moment.' The Registrar studies the monitor screen. 'Let's increase fluids and move onto the left lateral for a while. 'We're monitoring this way because of your caesarean scar,' she says to Bella.

'Rip it open now,' moans Bella. 'Cut me, I'm yours.'

'She doesn't mean it,' says Serena. 'Let's stick to your plan, yes?' She places a wet flannel on Bella's forehead.

There is a knock at the door. 'Clarissa is on the phone again,' says Erin when Annie answers. 'She's asking again when the SHO will be up.'

'The SHO is in A and E,' says Luisa.

'Haven't you bleeped him?'

'When you're done here,' says Luisa to the Registrar around the door, 'I need you to cover for the SHO. There's a woman in postnatal whose blood pressure needs reviewing.'

'What happened to the SHO?' says the Registrar.

'He's in A and E.'

'Have you bleeped him?'

'He's in A and E because someone punched him. He's got a broken nose.'

'Are you going to rip this thing out of me?' moans Bella from the floor.

'Bleep him again. He might be all right by now.' The Registrar looks at the monitor again. 'And we'll need him if there are any caesareans.' She nods down at Bella, sobbing on Serena's shoulder.

'I don't think he is all right.' Luisa follows the Registrar from the room and into the office. 'Would you be able to go down to postnatal?'

'If you lose those shoulders on the decelerations, you must call me.' On the handover board the Registrar draws the axes of a graph in Bella's box, and a line in the shape of a seagull's wing. 'We might have to consider sectioning. If this slope drops, call me.'

'Caesarean packs!' says Luisa. The Registrar shrinks away from her, alarmed. 'I need to check we have some caesarean packs,' she mumbles.

'Distractions are really good.' Luisa hears Sue say, on the phone in reception. 'Do you enjoy baking?'

'You'll go to postnatal?' says Luisa.

'If that's where you want me,' says the Registrar.

'That's where I want you.'

'I'm going there right now.'

'Well do you have any twenty-four-hour supermarkets nearby?' says Sue. 'A walk is always good, walking brings on the contractions. It doesn't sound like time yet. You'll only come in and go home again.'

Luisa puts up the palms of both hands to Sue.

Sue gives her the thumbs up. 'Well, your partner could hold an umbrella for you.'

The delivery suite doors open, and Diane enters, pushing a wheelchair piled high with suitcases and holdalls. A heavily pregnant woman and a man with a baby car seat follow behind.

'So here we are,' says Diane. 'This is Shirley. Where do you want me?'

'Hello there, Shirley,' Luisa smiles. 'Diane, if you want to take Shirley into Sheila Kitzinger.' That's the last room, she wants to tell Shirley, look grateful at least.

Diane pushes a suitcase back onto the wheelchair to prevent it from sliding off. 'We saw Gary Lineker in the lift,' says Diane.

'I really don't think it was Gary Lineker,' says Shirley. She leans her hands high on the column to the right of reception and exhales a deep breath.

'I heard him on the radio this morning.'

'I wasn't Gary Lineker, was it?' says Shirley to the man with the baby car seat. The man shakes his head.

'If you could take Shirley to Sheila Kitzinger, please Diane,' says Luisa.

'I do like Gary Lineker.' Diane pushes the wheelchair around the corner.

Luisa knocks on the door to Carol Decker and Vicky opens it immediately.

'I'm about to do the toast,' says Vicky. 'I'm so sorry. Matilda needed help with feeding.'

In the bed Matilda has her baby in her arms, the baby's head obscuring her chest.

'We really need Matilda upstairs rather soon,' Luisa says to Vicky at the door. Her default speaking volume has increased a couple of notches – it is an effort to speak quietly.

'I'll really do it as soon as I can,' says Vicky. 'But they have just started the feed? We don't want to interrupt the first feed, do we? How about I do the computing to save time?'

'You're going to need the baby's weight before you can do the computing.'

'Right. I forgot that,' says Vicky, looking upset. 'Well I can at least go make your toast.'

'Why don't we check the perineum whilst we're here?' Luisa steps into the room, over to the trolley, around to the bed and back to the trolley. She settles on the sink, washes her hands and puts on sterile gloves. Matilda and James watch nervously.

'Everything's fine,' she says to them. 'We're going to – move things on a little.' She uses her perky air hostess voice. 'We have to check if you need any stitches.'

'Shall I finish feeding first?' says Matilda.

'We can do both. Take your mind off what we're doing down here.'

Luisa stands between Matilda's legs with Vicky hovering behind her. She pulls apart Matilda's labia, can see no tear. 'That looks good. Just a tiny graze. Might sting a bit when you wee.'

'Oh yes. I remember that. Is that all you need to do?' Matilda looks down, over the baby.

'I'm afraid protocol says I also have to do a PR.'

'I don't know what that is.'

'What I mean is, I've got to stick my finger up your bum.'

'Oh. O-kay,' says Matilda.

Luisa inserts a finger, checks for hidden fissures in the rectum.

There's a knock at the door, and it opens immediately.

'Luisa, are you free?' says Sue.

'Not at the moment.'

'I need a word.'

'How does it look?' says Matilda.

'I'm right there Sue. You're fine,' Luisa waves to Matilda. She rips off her gloves, kicks the pedal of the bin and dumps, them, scoots over to the door and pulls it closed behind her.

'I've got one woman stalled at home making fairy cakes,' says Sue. 'Primip on two in ten. I can hold her for now. But there's a multip Punjabi woman, she's into knitting – I thought I could hold her for a few more rows. But she wouldn't listen, she's on her way in. How long before we have a room?"

'How can this many women give birth on the same night?' cries Luisa. 'It's not natural.'

Luisa re-enters Carol Decker at speed, catches her thigh against the corner of the trolley. Vicky and Matilda turn at the sound, Vicky is taking the baby from Matilda, taking the baby or pulling the baby away from her, Luisa cannot tell.

'So I'm going to check the placenta whilst I'm here,' says Luisa. She stretches her body upwards, to reduce the intense pain in her thigh.

'I can do that,' says Vicky.

'Are you okay?' says Matilda.

'Keep breathing through the pain,' says Vicky.

'Vicky, you get on with the weighing,' says Luisa. 'I'll do the placenta for you.'

'I know how do placentas,' says Vicky.

'We need to move on a bit. I'll be back in a couple of minutes.'

'Thanks Luisa. Thank you,' says Vicky.

On the trolley the placenta sits in its kidney bowl, bathed in deep red blood. Luisa wraps the blue polyester cloth from the birth pack around the bowl and carries it from the room without another word.

'We're leaving in the morning. We're leaving in the morning and heard you were working tonight,' says a voice behind her. It is Eric, dressed in a fresh blue checked shirt, his hair neat, his only unkempt feature some extra-day beard growth.

He steps in front of her, blocking her path down the corridor. 'We wanted to come say thank you.'.

Luisa stares at him.

'So thank you.' Eric takes an envelope from a Sainsburys bag and holds it out to her. Luisa has the blue placenta package in both hands, and she lifts first one row of fingers and the other, as though attempting to take the offering from him.

'I'm sorry about the blanket,' says Eric.

'The what?' says Luisa.

'When I couldn't find the blanket.'

'Oh, that's,' smiles Luisa. She can't think what that is. She dodges to the right, a feint to go around him, but Eric mirrors her movement.

'We wanted to give you this.' Eric proffers the envelope again. Now Luisa makes a jigging motion to show her hands are full, trying not to spill placenta blood.

'Shall I open it for you?' Eric raises his eyebrows at her.

Luisa nods, and Eric pulls the thick card from the envelope. On the front are two fabric owls on a branch – it looks homemade. He opens it up to display the inside: beneath an enormous scrawled THANK YOU! are Cheryl and Eric's names, each in their own handwriting, and, underneath, 'Elijah'. Next to Elijah's name is a paw print illustration with a big X scratched through it.

'Sorry about the paw,' says Eric. 'Got a bit confused. Haven't really had much sleep.'

Eric puts the card back in the envelope and into the Sainsburys bag, looks around for a place to put it, until he settles on balancing it on the blue placenta cloth.

'Not there,' says Luisa. A card on the placenta looks wrong. Is wrong. Perhaps if it had been Eric's placenta. His wife's placenta. Luisa cannot remember her name. 'Cheryl,' she says.

Eric retrieves the plastic bag.

'I mean that's very kind of you. It's just – infection control.'

'Right,' says Eric. He looks her up and down for a moment, tucks the plastic bag into the pocket of Luisa's trousers.

The delivery suite door buzzer makes its long sawing whine.

'Thank you,' says Luisa. 'That's very kind of you.'

Diane rounds the corner of reception.

'Apparently it wasn't Gary Lineker,' says Diane. 'He had a photo on his iPad, he showed me, Dan, Shirley's husband. He looked nothing like Gary Lineker. The man in the lift, not Dan.'

Luisa carries the placenta down the corridor.

Behind her someone coughs, and Luisa turns to see Donal, his clothes crumpled, slept in.

'We wanted to give you this.' Donal looks at the wall. 'Seema really wanted to give you this. A card. To say thank you for all your help.'

He opens the card – there is only Donal's name scrawled inside.

'Go back to your wife,' whispers Luisa fiercely. 'Go be with your wife and baby.'

'Yes.' Donal looks shocked. 'Of course. That's what I'll do. Sorry.' Donal is gone, the lobby space next to the entry doors empty, as though he was never there. Perhaps he wasn't there. She is still cradling the blue-wrapped placenta in her hands. An offering to the gods. The gods of what?

Ravi and Frank emerge from Mary Cronk.

'You can't take Gina,' Luisa runs up the corridor to them. 'We need her here. You can't take Gina.'

'We're not taking her yet,' says Ravi. 'Gina needed someone to hold a lamp and called us in. Paula had a second degree tear, and Gina was explaining how to do the repair. I thought I'd be sick. But I did well, didn't I Frank?'

'Gina said you did really well,' says Frank.

'What have you been doing?'

'The husband was a bit squeamish about it all,' grins Frank. 'It's all very interesting.'

'Ravi! Frank!' calls Gina from inside Mary Cronk. 'We're weighing the baby now!'

The guards disappear back into the room.

'Sarah Marchant has a second degree. I'm going to suture,' says Nikki, exiting the pool room.'

'And can we then get her up to postnatal?' says Luisa.

'She really doesn't seem keen to go anywhere at the moment.'

'Then leave her where she is!' cries a small voice. Luisa looks across the corridor and sees, in the doorway to the changing room, four fingers curled around the edge of the door, preventing it from closing. In the dark vertical strip of the doorway she sees one eye above another. Luisa pictures how Jenny is lying behind the door for her eyes to be positioned like this. 'Luisa!' hisses Jenny. 'In here!'

Jenny's eyes disappear from the crack in the door, and Luisa hears a slithering across the floor, and a crashing open of what must be the toilet door inside. Luisa pushes opens the door with her bottom, carries the placenta into the changing room.

'Tell Gina I said to leave Sarah Marchant where she is!' Jenny's voice, and a heave, echo from the toilet cubicle.

'Gina isn't co-ordinator. Gina had to go.'

'Go where?'

'She's been arrested.'

'So you're co-ordinator? Okay – Luisa, I'm ordering you, leave Sarah Marchant where she is.'

Luisa feels liquid dripping onto her trouser leg – she looks down to see blood seeping from the corner of the blue cloth. She balances the placenta in one hand, pulls Eric's Sainsburys bag from her pocket and shoves the placenta inside. The toilet flushes. The Sainsburys bag rests there on both her hands, a placenta-shaped offering, an infection-control indictment. Luisa pulls open her rucksack that leans against the lockers, shoves the bag inside as Jenny's head appears in the toilet doorway.

'I'll leave Sarah Marchant where she is,' says Luisa.

'Make sure she's pristinely happy,' Jenny pulls her whole body from the cubicle, using the uprights of the door frame to propel her across the floor. 'I'm not having another inquiry because some litigious mother thinks their imperfect birth is in some way our fault. That bitch in legal terrifies me.'

As Luisa exits the changing room, she almost crashes into the Senior House Officer. White bandages cover the centre of his face.

'Is that midwife who assaulted me still here?' says the Senior House Officer.

'It's okay,' says Luisa. 'Gina has security keeping an eye on her now.'

'Is that really practical?' says the SHO. 'Hardly economic to have two guards whenever she's on shift.'

The Registrar appears next to the Senior House Officer.

'I can't do an FBS at 4cm,' says the Registrar. 'And that trace is getting worse. The woman in Michel Odent will need a caesarean.'

'Now?'

'We need to get her to theatre.'

'Theatre is ready,' says Luisa, though she doesn't sound certain.

'It's not a panic. A cat 2.' The Registrar's tone is more sympathetic, and Luisa feels absurdly grateful. 'There's no immediate danger. So theatre is ready?'

'Theatre is ready,' repeats Luisa.

'There might be no caesarean packs left,' whispers Jenny at Luisa's feet.

'I need to check our levels of caesarean packs,' says Luisa.

'You need to bleep the anaesthetist and the ODP,' says the Registrar.

'And I'll bleep the anaesthetist and the ODP.'

'And you need an extra midwife to scrub,' whispers Jenny.

Someone wrenches the door to Mary Cronk open from the inside, and out strides Gina. Ravi and Frank follow behind her. Gina stops and makes chicken wings with her arms, and the guards take one crooked elbow each. Their hi vis jackets are covered in blood.

'Is everything okay in there?' says Luisa.

'Sorry,' says Frank. 'Bit clumsy. I was trying to dispose of an inco pad and it got a bit all over the place.'

Gina strides down the corridor, a proud queen off to exile, not looking at the Senior House Officer, who stands back against the wall.

'But when are you bringing her back?' calls Luisa.

'Oh, I don't think she'll be coming back,' says Ravi.

'Luisa!' calls Gina over her shoulder. 'Remember – my sofa bed is yours when you need it.'

The delivery suite door buzzer sounds. The Registrar and Senior House Officer head towards theatre at the far end of the corridor, and into reception comes a heavily pregnant woman wearing a hijab. With her are a man, another woman, a grandmother, and three children dressed in animal onesies. The man wears a bright green jumper emblazoned with Christmas trees.

Luisa slides in behind reception, to head them off at the pass.

'I finished my scarf,' says the woman in the hijab. 'Naz Hakim. I called in earlier. I finished my scarf, and it felt like time.' A child giraffe pulls a lion's tail, preventing the lion from hugging his mother's leg.

'If you can bear with me one minute,' says Luisa. She goes through into the office and stands over Sue on the phone.

'No, it's exactly the same,' says Sue. 'One teaspoon of baking powder for one hundred grams of flour. That makes it exactly the same as self-raising. And breathe. Breathe through, like the last one. Don't worry about quantities for now. I can wait.' Sue puts a hand over the receiver.

'There's a Naz Hakim in reception. Is she your Punjabi knitter?' Luisa speaks quietly but fails to keep an accusing tone from her voice. 'She's here now. We need to deal with her. I need you to deal with her please, Sue.'

Sue points at the phone receiver, removes her hand from the mouthpiece. 'Remember to keep breathing through, and to pre-heat the oven. No, no. Call again before you come in. Bye for now. Bye.' She replaces the receiver.

'Have we got a room for her? Does she look like she's actually doing something?' says Sue.

'I don't know. She isn't grunting. There isn't a room for her. We have no rooms.'

'What should I do with her?'

I don't know what to do with her, thinks Luisa. I asked you so I wouldn't have to know. 'Just look after her, please.'

'Right. Okay.' Sue heads out into reception, avoiding Luisa's gaze.

'And I need you to scrub for a caesarean,' Luisa calls.

She is unsure if Sue has heard. But now is alone. She sits in the office chair, spins in one slow full circle. The ODP bleep number, the anaesthetist bleep number, where are they? Her eyes rotate around the sheets of A4 paper pinned to the wall, rotate around without resting on any of them. An eight-by-ten photograph is pinned in the centre of the sheets: Jenny in her green lacy hat, standing with Karl outside the town hall. Karl smiles broadly.

This is quicker on the computer. She rotates the chair round to the screen, lifting both feet off the ground, then swivels round to the wall again. She cannot deal with the computer now. There must be a sheet here somewhere. Supervisor, she reads. The supervisor's number!

'Have you bleeped the ODP and anaesthetist yet?' says Annie behind her.

'I'm doing it right now.' Luisa reads the number of the supervisor, looks for a pen to write it down.

'*Are* you doing it?' says Annie.

'First I'm going to ring the supervisor,' snaps Luisa. 'And I need Matilda upstairs to make a room free. I have to do those as well.'

'Would you like me to do it for you?' says Annie.

'Yes. Please. That would be very helpful. Thank you, Annie.' She looks up at her, at Annie's greyness, her hair, her whole life. Don't shout at Annie. 'Do you know the supervisor's number?'

'I have them on my pad. And we can look at the board together if you like. To see how to make another room?'

'Thank you. Yes, thank you, Annie.'

This is what a coordinator does: delegate. Except that wasn't delegation. I need to delegate because I need to be somewhere else, I can't remember where but I know it is somewhere else.

'Someone's been doodling in my box!' cries Annie, jabbing at the board, at the Registrar's seagull wing illustration. 'Who's doodled in my box?'

A small sheep stands at the office door, watching Annie, alarmed.

'Are you going to bleep them?' says Luisa.

'Why do people have to do that? Look!' Annie digs a finger at the illustration.

Luisa reads the anaesthetist's bleep code digits from Annie's pad and pushes them into the phone.

'There's no respect nowadays,' says Annie, close to tears. 'None.'

'What the hell are all these children doing here at one in the morning?' says Rebecca in the doorway, and the sheep runs away.

'They've come in with a new woman,' says Luisa.

'I thought we had no more rooms free.' Rebecca does not wait discover if this is the case.

The phone rings, but Annie is flailing around the office, blocking Luisa's route to the phone. Erin enters from reception and picks up.

'It's just one more thing,' says Annie. 'Everyone scribbling all over the place. They change the rooms from numbers to names, nobody asked any of us if that's what we wanted. What's wrong with numbers for rooms? And what's Carol Decker got to do with midwifery, anyway?' Annie spits on a tissue and scrubs at the seagull wing on the board.

'If that's the anaesthetist, tell him we're going for a caesarean,' Luisa says to Erin.

'We're going for a caesarean,' says Erin into the phone.

'You try to make things nice, make things tidy, and everyone's cursing and cussing and doodling everywhere! Why isn't anybody doing anything to stop this?'

Luisa puts a hand up to Annie to suggest quiet.

'Oh yes. Talk to the hand because the face isn't listening. Well why isn't the face listening?'

'No,' says Erin into the phone, 'not the caesarean woman. That's a midwife.'

The delivery suite door buzzer sounds. Luisa steps out to reception where Sue is showing Naz and her husband some leaflets. She presses the release button. Please not a pregnant woman. I don't want to see any more pregnant women.

The door stays closed.

Luisa presses the release button again, moves around reception and pulls open the door. The giraffe slides off the back of the lion where he has been piggybacking in order to reach the buzzer.

'Who's buzzing?' says Luisa, her voice neither friendly nor angry.

'Our mum's having a baby,' says the giraffe, and the two of them run through the double doors back to their parents.

Luisa enters theatre at the end of the corridor. The pastel walls are calming – the cool quiet gives her a chance to replay her thoughts, and she looks at her hands, knowing that at one point in the evening her fingers were linked to her thoughts, perhaps connected through her nervous system and up to her brain. She checks the rack of caesarean packs and finds to her relief that there is one left.

'Are we ready?' says the anaesthetist.

'I've prepared the caesarean pack. I'll switch on the resuscitaire to warm the room.' She needs to tell someone to scrub up. Nikki, Nikki can do it.

'The other midwives are on their way,' she says.

The anaesthetist says nothing. She turns around – no one else is in the room, there is no anaesthetist. The theatre bed, the trolleys and the anaesthetist's station are silent in confirmation. A machine says beep-bep-bip, and the sound nauseates her, she wants to be out of theatre, out of the delivery suite, out of the hospital. The devices in this room are only used to save lives – all of humanity has been cleansed in favour of industrial hygiene. This isn't her, she isn't this room. She isn't this job, then? Birth isn't this room, birth is like Gina says, messy and unpredictable. And therefore uncontrollable. She is momentarily ecstatic at this revelation. Gina is right. Gina is in control. Gina is in custody.

Luisa reaches for the door handle but the door opens towards her pushed by the anaesthetist, who is followed by Serena dressed in scrubs, wheeling a trolley.

'It's almost over, baby doll,' says Serena, but not to Luisa, she is talking to Bella, crouched on all fours on the trolley.

'I need this little fucker out of me no-ow,' moans Bella. Annie, pushing the trolley from the rear, screws up her face.

'I need to go. I need to tell a midwife to scrub up,' says Luisa, but no one is listening.

Sue emerges from the theatre scrubbing station in mask and visor, arms up as for a T-Rex impression.

'Can you?' she asks, and turns the untied straps behind her to Luisa.

Sue has scrubbed up! I asked Sue to scrub up earlier!

'Everything's ready!' Luisa announces to the Registrar and Senior House Officer, holding the door open for them.

'Great. Thanks, Luisa,' says the Registrar.

Luisa waves goodbye, backing out of the doorway.

'I'm sorry,' says Vicky back at the computer in reception. 'It won't let me do the birth notification, Luisa. I'm sorry. It won't let me submit.' She taps repeatedly at the return key.

Something moves under the reception desk and for an icy moment Luisa imagines a rat, but it is a small boy, the lion, tucked up into the cupboard space. His eyes are huge. The lion puts his finger to his lips.

'You can't play in here.' Luisa does not know whether she can remove him, either ethically or physically.

'Oh, have they found you already,' says Diane behind her.

'The lady found me,' the boy climbs out, keeps low to the floor on all fours.

'I didn't realise Luisa was playing,' says Diane.

'I don't think we should encourage children to play in here, Diane,' says Luisa.

'He was nicely out the way under there, I thought.'

Diane waggles her finger and eyebrows at the lion boy to indicate an escape route through the office. Vicky taps the return key a couple more times.

'Is it true they only noticed you in the lift last night because a dog was howling outside?' says Diane.

'What dog?' says Luisa.

'The basement dog. The one that can sniff for cancer.'

'Let me see.' Luisa turns back to Vicky, sweeps the cursor around the screen until it rests back again on the Submit button, and taps repeatedly at the return key.

'Did you put the birth weight in?' says Luisa.

'I've done birth weight, I selected the feeding method, I've entered the ethnicity details. And the time. It won't let me press the button.'

Luisa presses the return key again.

'Have you checked your grammar?' says Diane.

'I don't think grammar matters here, Diane' says Luisa.

'That machine hates grammar. Let me have a little look.'

Diane leans very close to the screen, so close that Luisa can see light on every side of her head. 'You've got a full stop in there. You need the two dots for times.'

Diane takes the mouse and replaces the full stop with a colon. The cursor changes to a revolving hour glass, and a pop-up window appears in the centre of the screen displaying an NHS number.

'Brilliant, brilliant,' says Vicky. 'Thank you, Diane.'

'Yes, thank you, Diane. Write the NHS number down now.' Luisa makes a barrier with her arm so Vicky cannot reach the mouse. 'Don't X the box whatever you do or it's impossible to get the number back.'

'Oh, it's all go around here,' says Diane.

'And the baby's fed, I've changed the bed and cleaned the equipment. Mum's done a wee.' Vicky presses her lips together in satisfaction.

'Excellent,' says Luisa. 'So we can get Matilda upstairs?'

'Oh!' says Vicky.

'What?'

'I never made you toast! You must be so hungry.'

'Don't worry about me.' The mention of hunger makes Luisa dizzy. She is hungry, so hungry. She tries to remember when she last ate. 'You fetch a wheelchair for Matilda and get her up to postnatal as quick as you can. I'll get Nikola to clean the room.'

'I'll need a couple more minutes.' Any satisfaction has disappeared from Vicky's face. 'Matilda's in the bath. She said she wanted a bath.'

'See if you can get her out the bath. We have no rooms, Vicky. I'll finish your paperwork.'

Luisa sends Vicky away. She is alone again, alone in her own thoughts, and so it is a chance for the machinery to make itself known again, the buzzing of the strip lights. She wonders the time, how far they are through the night, and then does not want to know, is desperate not to know. She angles her head away from the computer screen, from the time in the top right corner. How can I do paperwork without seeing the computer screen? Her gaze lands on the phone. The supervisor.

'Hi. This is Luisa Keane,' she says when the supervisor answers. 'I'm working in delivery suite tonight. I don't feel safe?'

'Okay,' the supervisor says sleepily. 'What do you mean by that?'

'Sorry. I was told to phone the supervisor if I didn't feel safe.' Saying the words out loud makes Luisa feel safer. 'Well actually I feel a bit safer now. But

I didn't feel safe earlier. And that's when I first meant to ring you.'

'You'll have to tell me a bit more.'

'I've had to become coordinator. I'm not the coordinator. Jenny's sick.'

'Jenny's gone home?'

'No, she's in the toilet. Over the toilet. But the pool room flooded into the lift, and one of my midwives has been arrested.' She likes the my, it adds authority, a seriousness, not that it is needed, this is already very serious. 'And I have no rooms free, we've had so many women come in tonight, I've got a woman almost in labour waiting by reception who's going to need a room any minute. And I don't feel safe. Actually that's right, I still don't feel safe.'

There is silence on the phone.

'Hello?' says Luisa.

'Hi there,' the man in the Christmas jumper calls through the door from reception. The giraffe and sheep stand next to him at the counter.

'I'll get some clothes on and I'll be in,' says the supervisor, and the phone goes dead.

'Could someone check my wife, please?' says the Christmas jumper man.

Luisa steps out into reception – Sue is nowhere to be seen.

'Saleem.' The man extends a hand across the desk.

'Luisa. Very nice to meet you.' Luisa shakes.

'I think perhaps it's time?' says Saleem. 'For my wife?'

Naz sits on a chair across the corridor, the sister and grandmother both talking to her at the same time.

'Well, let's not jump to any conclusions,' smiles Luisa. Did Sue check her before she scrubbed up? I asked, didn't I ask Sue? I'm sure I asked Sue.

'She didn't really want to knit a whole scarf,' says Saleem. 'Naz doesn't get cold.' He pats his jumpered chest with both hands.

'Sue checked on your wife a little while ago,' says Luisa. 'Didn't she check?' A call buzzer sounds.

'Could someone just be there with her?' Saleem has a list of lines he needs to say and wants to get them all out. 'Last time it was almost me delivering. When Rima was born.' Saleem rubs the sheep's head and laughs. 'I don't want that to happen this time,' he laughs again, but there is no humour in his words.

Diane holds a plate of biscuits over the counter. The giraffe shovels a stack onto one hand.

'We should save some of those for the women, Diane.' Why is Diane always in reception? I really have to check on Diane's woman, thinks Luisa.

'Oh they need to feed up overnight,' says Diane. 'It is Ramadan, after all.'

'Is it?'

'I almost married a Muslim once. But I couldn't do the fasting. Hats off to you,' she says to Saleem.

The call buzzer sounds again, loud, dipping quiet, loud again.

'Oh, we don't really do Ramadan,' says Saleem. 'So you'll check Naz for me?'

Diane thrusts the biscuit plate into Saleem's arms, sets off at a run behind reception, pushes both hands down on the counter. Then she is up, legs swinging underneath her, vaults the desk in an arc, both feet planted together as she lands on the other side. Luisa intercepts her at the corner of the corridor, overtakes Diane on the inside. She is pleased at being more match fit – but Diane must be in her sixties. Perhaps Diane is not in her sixties at all.

Luisa looks down at her own legs, one thrust forward and then the other. Why am I running? Now she recognises the sound of the emergency bell, alternating between its high and low octaves. She can see the red light flashing in the corridor ceiling, it's in Mary Cronk, Gina's room. Gina isn't in Mary Cronk. Gina is with security.

Luisa does not slow her pace sufficiently, and bursts through the door. Nadine turns, a baby in her arms. She looks terrified.

'What is it?' says Luisa.

Paula's head is angled toward her on the pillow, her neck stretched. 'I feel a little faint,' says Paula. 'I must be tired out.'

'She's bleeding,' says Nadine, rocking the baby too quickly back and forth. 'Victor, I'd like you to take the baby, please.' She pushes the baby into the arms of the bald man by the perspex cot in the corner of the room.

Luisa steps forward and sees that blood saturates the triangle marked off by Paula's legs, blood that is pooling where the sheets have rucked up and form a hollow. Victor is speaking but Luisa does not know what he is saying. An obstetric emergency. This is an obstetric emergency.

Nadine moves next to her, looks up at Luisa.

'I need help,' says Luisa, and Nadine looks away, back at Paula. Luisa grabs Nadine's arm. 'We need help,' she says. 'We need to ensure help is coming.'

'The emergency button,' says Nadine. But they have already rung the emergency buzzer, that option is now closed.

I am the help, thinks Luisa. Someone moans, maybe Paula but possibly Victor. Victor steps backwards until he reaches the wall.

Fuck. Shit. What do we need?

Victor sinks into a chair, the baby clasped to his chest.

Diane comes through the door, wheezing. 'I didn't pace myself,' says Diane. 'What do we need?'

Luisa sees Paula's chest rise and fall, and in her neck, the carotid artery flutters, a butterfly under the skin. Luisa looks to Diane. Will Diane suggest something, tell her what to do? Blood seeps from Paula's vagina, a busted garden tap.

'Put out an obstetric emergency bleep,' says Luisa. 'A fast bleep.'

'Got it,' says Diane.

Diane is gone. Nadine steps to Paula and back, turns to look at Luisa again.

Luisa looks again at the leaking blood. Airway, Breathing, Circulation. The ABCs. Paula's talking, mumbling at least – that's airways and breathing! Circulation.

'We've checked airways and breathing,' says Luisa. 'Nadine, please can you fetch a blood pressure monitor. Then monitor Paula's circulation.' A haemorrhage, this is a haemorrhage.

'What's going on?' asks Paula, her cheek pressed into the pillow.

'Blood pressure monitor. Right.' Nadine rushes from the room, and Luisa is alone. Where is everyone? She puts a hand on Paula's stomach. Why have I done that?

'Is everything okay?' says Paula.

To rub up a contraction. Rub up a contraction to stop the blood flow. She looks down between Paula's legs.

The door opens and Rebecca forces in an emergency trolley, with Vicky close behind.

'Diane said there's been a haemorrhage,' says Rebecca. 'Said you've got a PPH.' She looks at the bloodied bed and stops. She glances at Luisa then turns the trolley, concentrates, with too much effort, on parking at a ninety-degree angle. 'Are the doctors coming?'

Rebecca moves past Luisa and pulls the catches that lower the head of the bed. Flatten the bed to reduce blood flow, that's right, thinks Luisa. She's pressing on the uterus, and it squishes under her hand. Should be hard, not squishy. Hard and contracted.

'Emergency bleep, done,' says Diane, Diane is back. Diane is *back in the room*, Luisa announces to herself. They're back in the room, Luisa, Diane, Rebecca, Nadine, now Vicky as well. This is an emergency. Nadine straps the blood pressure monitor around Paula's upper arm. The electronic voice of the coordinator's bleep in Luisa's pocket confirms: 'Obstetric emergency, delivery suite Level 6. Mary Cronk room.'

Luisa rubs up a contraction. If I carry on doing this one thing, perhaps I don't have to do anything else?

Vicky waves jazz hands over the emergency trolley.

'I'll make up 40 units of synto,' says Rebecca. 'Is that okay? You're okay?' she says to Luisa.

I'm not okay, oh miss Rebecca, I'm not okay. Rebecca pulls out the drawers of the emergency trolley. Don't die. Please don't die, Paula. You didn't come in here today thinking you might die, did you? You came here to have a baby. And you have a baby. But dying is not a choice they have asked Paula to make, it's one choice they haven't entrusted to new mothers. Paula has left that decision with me. I don't want it.

'No synto,' says Luisa. 'Not yet. We need intravenous access first. Can you cannulate, please, Rebecca?'

'Cannulate, right.' Rebecca leaves the tiny glass vials and pulls a cannula packet and tourniquet from a trolley drawer.

'Diane, can you make up the syntocinon, please? Nadine, give us blood pressure readings at five-minute intervals,' says Luisa. People are moving, moving under her instruction. Luisa presses down on Paula's uterus.

The door opens and Nikki bursts in.

'Sorry,' says Nikki. A lump on her forehead is bleeding. 'Got here as quick as I could.'

'My goodness,' whispers Paula. 'Are you okay?'

Luisa sees a droplet of blood detach from Nikki's chin and fall onto the front of her scrubs. She looks again between Paula's legs. Has the bleeding slowed? It has, I think it has.

'Where are the doctors?' says Luisa. 'Vicky, find out where the doctors are.'

'I don't need a doctor. It's only a graze,' says Nikki. She presses a sanitary towel to her forehead. 'Tripped over a sheep in the corridor.'

'Rubbing up a contraction,' says Luisa. 'Bleeding is settling.'

'Blood pressure eighty-five over forty,' says Nadine.

'Thank goodness,' says Victor, and he stands again.

'Victor? Where are you, Victor?' Paula shifts her body on the bed, trying to move her head to see Victor. The sodden sheet under her legs moves and a rivulet of blood runs out of a gulley in the rucked bedding and onto the floor.

Too much bleeding altogether. How much is too much? Over five hundred mils is too much. She looks at the sheets, the bloodied white towels, the used sanitary towels on the floor. How much is that? Tissue, Trauma.

'Have we checked the perineum?' she asks Nadine. 'For trauma.'

'I didn't see.' Nadine opens her mouth to continue, and says nothing. 'But they said it was fine,' she adds. 'Ravi and Frank, they said it was fine. When they checked with Gina.'

Tissue, Trauma. Thrombis, Tone. The uterus, not toned. Boggy, this is boggy. The bladder is too full. Empty the bladder.

'Diane, take over from me, please,' says Luisa. 'Keep rubbing up contractions. I'll catheterise. No, Nikki, could you catheterise please? Get a catheter bag ready.'

'Got it.' Nikki rummages through the drawers of the emergency trolley. 'None here. I'll fetch one.' Nikki runs out of the room again.

'I'm here, love. I'm here. I've got the baby,' says Victor, and shows Paula, as though the child has appeared in his arms out of nowhere. Victor steps towards the bed, then back again, another step forward and back again. He sits back in the chair.

'Come and talk to Paula,' says Nadine. Luisa can hear the fear in her voice. What has she got to worry about? But that's good, keep control of him, keep him out of the way.

'I'll put the baby down,' says Victor. 'I should put him down. Can I put him in the cot? In the corner?'

'No one puts baby in the corner!' cries Luisa, and everyone turns to look at her.

She points to the cot. She is grinning. There will never, ever be another scenario where that line is so damn perfect. No one is laughing, no one is applauding. Which is absolutely the correct reaction. 'Bring the baby nearer. Let's have the baby near Mum.'

'The Reg and SHO are tied up in theatre. And the anaesthetist.' Vicky runs back into the room.'

'Tell them the SVD in Mary Cronk is having a PPH. EBL a thousand mils and not settled. I need a verbal order to start syntocinon.' Luisa opens her eyes wide at Vicky. 'Go. Go!'

'SVD, PPH, EBL a thousand. Got it.' Vicky runs out the room again, almost crashing into Nikki as she comes back in.

'I've got IV access.' says Rebecca. 'Shall I start the synto?' She looks to Luisa, looks to her and waits for an answer.

'Get it set up and we'll start on the doctor's say so.' Luisa turns a half circle in one smooth movement. 'What's blood pressure?' she points at Nadine.

'Eighty over fifty.'

Luisa swings back round. 'Okay, let's start the fluids,' she says to Rebecca. 'Hold off on the drugs.' This language, my words, this is working, as though understood speaking French for the first time. I can speak midwife. 'So, fluids are starting, waiting for syntocinon,' Luisa says to Paula. 'Diane, bleeding stabilising?'

'The doctors are in the middle of sewing up, the Reg said they have a haemorrhage of their own. But they said start synto,' says Vicky, coming back into the room. 'They'll be here as soon as they can, said you should call the consultant.'

'We need the doctors.' Rebecca is smaller, has retreated into the walls of the room. It is unclear if she is informing Luisa or pleading.

'The consultant's at home,' says Luisa. 'They can't get here that quickly. We're going to start synto,' says Luisa. 'Rebecca, can you?' Luisa wants all the activity to involve her hands somehow, and strokes Paula's forehead. 'The doctor's are on their way,' she says to her. 'They like to check everything is in hand. Keep your eyes on the baby, Paula, looking at the baby keeps the oxytocin going, helps with the contractions. My god it's hot in here. Nadine, perhaps you can find a fan. Now we've got things under control.'

No one is talking. No one is saying anything, and it sounds like death.

'Of course, in the eighteenth century,' says Luisa, 'it wouldn't have been like this at all.' Because we should celebrate modern medicine, shouldn't we? Remember how many women used to die in childbirth? Remember, and celebrate. But not right now. 'In the eighteenth century we had the Napoleonic wars, though,' she says.

'Napoleon was the nineteenth century,' says Diane.

'Seventy-six over forty-two.' Nadine's expression clarifies that the descending blood pressure is her own fault.

'I don't know that rubbing up contractions is working,' murmurs Diane. 'Blood flow is still quite heavy.'

Victor collapses backwards away from the bed and Vicky jumps forward, pulling the baby into her arms, leaving Victor to fall to the floor.

'I'm squeezing all I can.' Rebecca compresses the IV bag between the heel of either hand.

No one else is bothering to make small talk, Luisa thinks. No one is pretending this is okay. Perhaps because this isn't okay.

Luisa repositions herself over the bed. Blood continues to pump from between Paula's legs. 'Still got heavy blood loss, we've checked tone, checked trauma, synto is running,' says Luisa. She needs a straight man for her motor mouth, someone to bounce off, but no one is stepping up. 'The doctors may be a few more minutes. Oh.'

Everyone looks at her.

'Do we have to – bi-manual compression?' Luisa says.

'You have to,' Diane says, pointing at her.

'We need to do bi-manual compression.' Luisa looks at her hands, at the blood covering the blue surgical gloves, at the red streaks that have crept down her forearm. There is too much mess, carnage – how can this turn out well with so much blood? Blood should be on the inside.

'Nikki, are you sterile?' says Luisa.

'I've never done bi-manual compression before,' says Nikki, and Luisa sees Nikki is not a midwife, but an everyday woman with a minor head injury. They are all everyday women. Paula is an everyday woman. Paula is bleeding to death.

'I don't think anyone here has done it before,' says Luisa, and her voice is light, almost carefree. 'You can do it, Nikki. I'll remind you. Hand in, like you're searching for a Pringle.' The training session is clear in her mind – they actually used Pringle tubes.

Nikki climbs up onto the bed, her knees sinking into the pool of blood to one side of Paula's legs.

'I'll get another inco pad,' says Vicky.

'Don't bother.' Nikki makes a cone of her fingers and slides her hand through the seeping blood into Paula's vagina.

'A fist, you make a fist,' says Luisa, bunching her own fingers. 'Make a fist and push against it with your other hand, on top of the uterus.'

'Oh. It's working!' says Nikki. 'The blood's almost completely stopped.'

There is a quiet murmur of appreciative surprise from the circle of midwives.

That worked. Why am I so surprised? 'Keep checking blood pressure,' she says to Nadine. 'Paula, how are you feeling? Are you okay?'

'You want me to get up now?' Paula pushes herself to her elbows. Luisa pushes her back to the pillow.

The Registrar enters the room. 'So, how are things in here?' she says.

Luisa looks at the bloodied midwife with one arm inside Paula. 'She had an SVD at,' when was it? Half-twelve? 'Zero thirty-six. She's lost approximately fourteen hundred mils of blood, we've got fluids running, forty units of synto up. Blood flow was still heavy so Nikki had to do bi-manual compression.'

'Okay,' says the Registrar. 'Good. That pretty much covers it. What about him?' She nods at Victor, on his back on the floor, his head in a khaki holdall.

'Oh – he's fine. He was woozy from the blood. Definitely breathing.'

'Let's get her down to main theatre, since theatre's still in use up here,' says the Registrar.

And they go, they all go, Nadine pushing the bed, Paula and Nikki on the bed, the Registrar following the bed. Diane and Rebecca go back to their women, to other women. There are actually other people giving birth on this ward. Surely no other woman will go through with a birth now, not if it might end like this? What kind of woman risks their life so just to have a child? I did. And now I have Eleanor and Elsie. She remembers the pasties at dinner.

'I'd better get back to Matilda,' says Vicky. They look at the baby in Vicky's arms – this baby who not only nearly caused his own mother's death but also selfishly slept through the entire event.

'Give yourself a second,' says Luisa. 'Let's get our heads together.'

Vicky breathes in deeply and out again. Luisa puts a hand on her arm. I should talk to her. Debrief. They stand in silence, both staring at the baby. Vicky appears content to allow Luisa to use her arm as a resting bar.

Victor pulls himself to his feet. 'I'm sorry,' he says. 'What's – where?'

'Everything's fine,' says Luisa. 'We stemmed the blood loss and Paula is in theatre. Everything's under control.' That doesn't quite cover it though, does it? Something more happened here – the reply she wants to give Victor involves whooping and fist-punching the air. Instead she strokes the baby's hand.

Victor looks from Luisa to Vicky to his son. Vicky passes him the baby without a word.

'That was terrifying,' says Victor. 'Thank you. That was – terrifying. I felt like I was in Casualty.'

More like ER, thinks Luisa. I was definitely George Clooney.

Victor looks awkward. Luisa realises she has said this out loud.

'I should debrief you,' she says to Victor. She giggles, puts her hand on Victor's arm. 'I don't mean it like that. This isn't a Carry On hospital.' I've embarrassed him, she thinks, and giggles again. But I'm not embarrassed at all. 'Sorry everything happened so quickly. Some women haemorrhage when their uterus doesn't contract fast enough. But it's quite normal, nothing to worry about.' Nothing to worry about now, now that your wife's not dead. Luisa is giggling again, but this time to herself, she is moving around the room, collecting towels, sweeping her body around Victor's, close but not touching, a contemporary dance move.

Luisa stops, towels cradled in her arms. 'You must be hungry,' she accuses Victor. I'm *starving*.'

'I'm making toast,' says Vicky. 'I'll make toast for everyone.'

A screeching noise is coming from outside – the volume increases as Vicky opens the door to leave. A voice shouts something, and though Luisa cannot make out the words, this tells her that the screech was a human screech. Here comes another one. She runs from the room, narrowly avoiding a lion running in the other direction. I'm there. Bring it on.

Down near reception, in the corridor's alcove next to Carol Decker stand Saleem and Naz, Naz at right angles to her husband, leaning all her weight on him. She shuffles her feet backwards and further apart, pushing her face deeper into the knitted trees on Saleem's shoulder.

A man with a beard that almost reaches the logo on his porter overalls watches from the delivery suit doors, shielding himself behind a polystyrene cooler box.

'You wait, wait, someone is coming,' Nikola says to Naz, brandishing her mop in front of her.

'Here I am. I am coming.' Luisa puts an arm around Naz's shoulder. 'That's it. Naz, yes? Deep breaths. Nikola, we need a room. Can you please clean the room down there, Mary Cronk, it's a bit messy? Quick as you can now.'

'It takes time,' says Nikola and adds another word, probably Russian, certainly rude. It doesn't matter, thinks Luisa. Nikola heads off and the grandmother shuffles past, uttering a continuous low stream of Punjabi, followed by the sister who offers curt replies.

'Sorry – someone bleeped me for this blood,' says the bearded porter.

'Not needed now,' says Luisa. 'She's gone downstairs. We're getting a room ready. But wait.' She holds up a hand to the porter, dipping her head to show respect for his job, that she is not one to abuse her obvious authority. I have tasks to perform here, and I will perform them in the relevant order.

'Do you not have a room?' says Saleem. He waves his free hand at the closed door of Carol Decker.

Naz sounds a vomiting heave, turns from Saleem to face the alcove wall, drops to her knees and onto all fours. She lets forth her own stream of

Punjabi, that sounds less a complaint about her pain than a lament for the desperate immoral state of the modern world.

'The baby is coming,' the sister translates for Luisa. The sister turns her back on the grandmother who is still talking, though her tone is now more conciliatory, her unseen accuser relenting on certain points of order. She ends with a climactic condemnation, sits herself in the only chair in reception, and falls silent.

'So the baby is coming,' repeats Luisa.

Vicky appears beside her, holding a plate of toast.

'It isn't tea time in Kansas any more!' says Luisa in a witchy croak, and Vicky looks confused, perhaps scared. That's not the correct quote, thinks Luisa, and her mind's voice is amused, is chuckling. That's not even the right character. Though it has the desired effect, for Vicky puts the plate of toast on the reception desk.

'Can we get her to a room?' says Vicky, looking to Luisa.

'I can't move,' moans Naz. She looks over her shoulder at Luisa. I am her saviour, thinks Luisa. I am the only one who can help, truly help. She knows this.

'Then we're not moving anywhere.' Luisa drops to her knees, as if in emergency prayer. 'Vicky? I'm going to need your help.' Vicky skips over, her eyebrows buzzing in anticipation, though helping is what Vicky is there for, is her actual job.

'And yours.' Luisa swivels round to the porter. 'Never mind the blood now. There's a screen, at the end of the corridor. Could you fetch it for me, please?' She holds the porter's gaze without expression, until he nods in acknowledgement and leaves. 'Vicky, I need synto, syringes, towels, gloves, a delivery pack.'

'Got it,' says Vicky, and is gone.

'And a mat if you can manage,' Luisa calls after her.

'Let me,' says the sister. 'Get me to do things. I'm not doing anything.'

'Mat's in that room.' Luisa points down the corridor towards Mary Cronk, the image of a mat leaning against the wall vivid in her mind. 'Third door down.' She stands and banks in an arc round to the stand by the corridor wall, plucks up a foetal doppler, turns back and performs a perfect landing down to Naz. 'What we're doing is making a safe space right here,' she says.

The porter returns wheeling a screen, the lion and giraffe helping push from the back.

'This is for our mother,' the lion informs the porter.

The porter and Luisa unfold the screen and enclose Naz and Saleem in the right angle of the corridor wall and the door to Carol Decker. The screen wobbles, won't stay upright because of a broken wheel at one end.

'I'll find another one,' says the porter.

'No time. Baby's coming. You hold,' says Luisa, noting the efficiency of her word count. Naz bellows another groan to confirm Luisa's analysis. The porter grips the screen frame like a sentry, half in, half out of the enclosure. Saleem looks up at him. 'Turn outwards, look outwards,' Luisa says to the porter. 'On guard.'

The sister returns, carrying a green plastic mat and they slide the mat inside before closing off Naz from public view.

'Did you know a man is in that room?' says the sister. She slips behind the screen. 'A nice man, he wanted to help with the mat. But he said he wasn't allowed to put the baby down.'

They shuffle the mat down onto the floor next to Naz, who exhales at it.

'Naz, I want you to move onto the mat, you'll be much more comfortable,' says Luisa.

Someone pulls the screen from the porter's grasp and in comes the grandmother, dragging her chair and muttering. She positions the chair off to one side, sits and falls silent again.

'We'll need to take your bottom things off.' Luisa looks up at the porter, who closes the gap in the screen and turns away.

'You do it,' grunts Naz into the mat.

Luisa peels Naz's green cotton trousers and knickers down to her knees in one motion, removes them completely as Naz lifts one knee then the other. The grandmother has started up again, firing accusations at Saleem with an even greater vengeance than before. To Luisa's surprise Saleem shouts back at her, his anger at odds with his jumper. He leans down into the corner and speaks to Naz. He is calm, calm and soothing. A body thumps into the screen, knocking the canvas onto Luisa's back.

'There're animals, animals everywhere!' Nikola shouts from away down the corridor.

Luisa's hand takes the foetal doppler, reaches forward and holds the probe against Naz's belly. Heartbeat fine. Not even going to count. I'm past counting. The next contraction comes, and as it plateaus, she sees the hair of the baby's head, and watches it disappear again. The grandmother issues another three word retort at Saleem. Tension and stress. Not what's needed. Not for my baby. Naz's baby. Luisa turns to look at the sister.

'I'm sorry,' the sister says to Luisa. 'Mummy thought Saleem would take care of the children. That he would not be here. But he wanted to be here.' She lowers her voice to a whisper. 'I must be here. She said she really needs me here.'

A flood of straw-coloured liquid runs from Naz's vagina and down her left leg.

'No more! No more biscuits!' cries Nikola.

Vicky comes inside the screen carrying a blue birth pack, a pile of towels on top. The giraffe slips in behind her.

'Mum, I want hot chocolate,' says the giraffe, tapping Naz's naked thigh. 'Can I have hot chocolate?' The grandmother grabs the boy's arm, pulls him towards her.

'Right!' Luisa's voice drops to an intense whisper, addresses the entire gathering. 'We're not going to have anyone running around. And there'll be no shouting.' She looks up at the grandmother who sits back in her chair, pulls her handbag to her lap. 'We'll be calm. This will be calm. And beautiful. This is going to be beautiful. Let the other two in. Bring them in,' she says to the porter.

'The children?' says the porter.

'The children,' says Luisa.

The porter opens a gap and shepherds the lion and sheep around the inside of the screen. Luisa ushers them in front of the door to Carol Decker, next to Naz's head. Saleem lies on Naz's other side, whispering to her.

Luisa crouches in front of the children. 'Now,' she says, 'the baby – your brother or sister – can't be born unless we're all really quiet. Do you see?' The children nod, keen to understand.

The door to Carol Decker opens and Matilda stands there cradling her baby, dressed and ready to go. She opens her mouth to speak, then closes the door again.

'Synto drawn up please, Vicky.' Luisa kneels back down behind Naz and pulls on a pair of sterile gloves.

'You're a six and a half for gloves, yes?' says Vicky.

'Thank you, yes,' Luisa smiles.

With the next contraction Luisa can see a full five centimetre width of hair.

'Aiiiieeee,' bellows Naz.

The sheep's eyes widen.

'Just panting now,' says Luisa.

The baby's head emerges, the dead face angled up towards Naz's buttocks. The children lean forward in surprise. Everyone always looks surprised, thinks Luisa. But it's still a surprise to me. She laughs. So big. How can a baby's head be so big?

Vicky, I should let Vicky catch the baby. No, this is my baby. I am the saviour. The baby squelches out onto Luisa's towel, and the cord slithers out behind. She holds the child in the towel with one hand and cleans with the other, removing vernix from her tiny limbs.

'It's a girl,' pronounces Luisa. 'A baby girl.'

The newborn opens her eyes, and arches her mouth for the first breath. Her howl echoes down the corridor, the only sound.

'Let me see,' says Naz. 'Let me have her.'

Luisa passes the baby through Naz's legs, and Naz sinks down onto her hip, turns with the child on her lap. The grandmother leans, reaches a hand forward and takes it back again, hums a low sound, her anger abated, her face settled to one appropriate for her age and wisdom.

Luisa looks from the grandmother to the sister, to the giraffe, and the lion and sheep lying on the floor, the three animals motionless, awed at the sight of their baby sibling cradled at their mother's breast. Saleem is up on his knees, his head bowed towards the baby. Vicky's hair reflects the light from the ceiling above, a blonde glow of angelic youth, and the bearded porter, Luisa sees, has watched the entire scene, his hand gripped to the crook of the screen.

'Behold the child,' says Saleem. Or is he asking to hold her, to hold his child? No one says behold, thinks Luisa. No one has said behold for two thousand years.

'You are amazing,' says the sister. 'So calm.'

'Oh, I did nothing. Naz did the work, *she* was amazing. Anyone can catch a baby, catching a baby is easy. Especially when someone is as amazing as Naz. It's not always that easy, but when a mother is that amazing it's a joy to be part of a birth like that. I did nothing.' Luisa sees everyone looking at her. 'Well, I don't know about anyone else, but I'm starving.' She looks down at her gloved hands, covered in the white of the vernix.

'Wait,' says Vicky and disappears out from the enclosure.

The lion hunches down next to Naz, strokes the baby's head, and his brother and sister follow suit. Naz smiles, and breaks into a sob.

'Here.' Vicky holds the plate of toast before Luisa. 'I toasted one of them a bit more than the other. I don't know which you like best?'

Luisa looks up at her. Vicky raises her eyebrows in encouragement. The sister watches, waiting for Luisa's answer.

'Less – toasted,' says Luisa. She raises her soiled hands. 'But I can't – '

Vicky holds up the slice to Luisa's mouth. Luisa takes a bite, then another, larger one. She shakes her head for enough.

'Where is everyone?' says a voice outside the screen, in another world. 'Who's in charge here?'

'I'm going to leave you all for a moment,' Luisa announces. 'Vicky is going to take over.'

Back out in the light of the corridor the supervisor stands by the reception desk.

'I'm the co-ordinator,' Luisa tells the supervisor. 'I spoke to you earlier. But everything is under control now.' She narrates the story of the evening, the flooding, the caesarean, Gina's punching of the SHO. But she relates the events in the wrong order, and the co-ordinator is first confused and then barely listening. 'Though I never found a new stock of caesarean packs,' says Luisa in conclusion, to ground the story in something real. 'And I didn't have time to write on the notes about not doing the oxygen-sats.'

'Oh, don't worry about those,' says the supervisor, paying attention again. 'It sounds like you had a lot on.'

'I haven't done a wee all night,' says Luisa, and the supervisor laughs.

'So basically we've got a woman with a PPH in main theatres, a caesarean in recovery, three postnates to get rid of and two low-risk women in labour,' says the supervisor. 'Well – let's start with some breaks!'

*

Luisa strides the corridor, swinging herself into each room, rotating off one hand on the door frame, one swing in, one swing out. Gather the minimal amount of information necessary, she thinks. Info necessary. Mary Cronk, empty, check. Michel Odent, empty, check. Sheila Kitzinger, no Shirley, Diane playing games with Shirley's husband on an iPad, check. Luisa grabs a pen from a trolley without slowing her pace, walks and draws, sketches a rectangle on her hand. Portable room plan, much more sensible than one fixed to the wall. Who designed this board fixed to a wall? Luisa scrawls 'board' in trembly letters on the back of her right hand. Tell Jenny, no tell the supervisor at the end of shift, at the end of handover, mobile board, everyone needs one. Electronic, we could have them on tablets. On phones! Mobile Board app. Too boring a name. Medical Records app? She adds 'MedRec app?' under 'board' to her hand. Why has no one thought this before? Because there must be a first, someone must be first with an idea.

My hands, they're all dirty.

She turns a sharp hundred and eighty degrees, swings back into Mary Cronk, washes her hands in the bathroom sink.

Back out in the corridor she finds Shirley, leant up against the wall.

'Big breaths now,' she says, and lays a hand on Shirley's back. Shirley looks round at her, murder in her eyes.

'You can tell me to fuck off if you like,' laughs Luisa, and skips away again. She'll appreciate it later, even thank me. I wonder how many cards I'll get tonight. My legs, it's like they're on autopilot. Perhaps my body has taken control of itself, taken control so that I've left my brain ready for the important decisions – the life-threatening decisions. Perhaps I have acceded to a higher plane. Is acceded the right word? The correct word.

Luisa sits in the office, holding her phone. The icons on the screen, so bright. She examines the square of Justin's face. She strokes the hat with the pad of her finger, and presses down hard on his face.

Everything is going to be okay. My job, it is more than okay. And I am good at it. I should never have told Justin I considered quitting. Did I say to Justin I would quit? She tries to remember, from the car, driving to work. How long ago? I didn't mean it, anyway. This is my job. I can tell him, tell him now. The digits on the phone screen show 03:15. She stabs at the phone to cancel the call.

'Everything is going to be okay,' says Luisa. Nadine looks up from where she is writing notes at the desk, smiles nervously.

The office door opens and Jenny strides in, her face the colour of a show-home hallway.

'You're here,' says Luisa.

'Don't mind me,' says Jenny.

'You should be at home. You shouldn't be here.'

'Pretty much emptied both ends, not much point leaving now.' Jenny wheels her suitcase out from under the work surface. 'Besides, I've got a cruise to catch.'

'So you're feeling better?' Jenny standing, Jenny walking, that's not what I need now. She prefers Jenny lying, Jenny lying immobile on the floor. The floor of the toilets. 'You should – if you're ill. You do what you need to. We've got it covered here.'

'We?' says Jenny.

'I've got it. I'm coordinating.'

'So I've heard. The supervisor was telling me.' Jenny levels the suitcase to the floor and pops the catches. The lid springs upwards and pastel-coloured clothes spill over the sides. Luisa sees a streak of vomit on Jenny's upper arm. She points, then withdraws her hand.

'PPH is down in theatre,' says Luisa.

'Is she doing okay?' says Nadine.

'I'm fine,' says Luisa. 'Honestly I am. Earlier I thought I was having a breakdown but now I'm okay.'

'What I meant was – is Paula okay?' says Nadine. 'But are you, are you okay Luisa?'

'I'm dandy,' says Luisa. She has almost forgotten about Paula – Paula no longer feels real.

'And another woman gave birth in the corridor, very quick,' Luisa continues to Jenny. 'We organised screens because there were no rooms. She's comfortable, we've put her in Carol Decker now. Everyone's dealt with.' She recounts more events of the night, tapping the work surface with a pencil. She hasn't mentioned Gina. Is Gina her responsibility? Everything is her responsibility. Don't have to mention Gina.

'You've done a great job tonight, Luisa,' says Jenny, 'but you're not the co-ordinator any more. It's time to stand down.'

Luisa watches Jenny pull down her floral dress and squirl it into a ball.

'I liked it. Tonight. It was,' Luisa wants to say exciting, ' – challenging. I liked – the responsibility.'

'Watch yourself there,' laughs Jenny. Luisa does not understand what she means, but laughs anyway. 'Well. There are always more opportunities for responsibility. If you want them, bridesmaid.'

'I'm always up for a challenge,' says Luisa. Perhaps promotion. That's the next logical step, promotion. But aren't there times when I don't want a challenge? Most of the week, in fact. But this was a challenge, and I came through it. Perhaps I *am* up for a challenge. Bring those challenges on. This is me. I always wanted to do important work – this is important work.

'There's a lot of research and audits that need doing, you know. You'd be good at them. In fact I'm overseeing one next month. On baby labelling. Important work.' Jenny pulls on a bright yellow dress decorated with butterflies, and bundles the remaining clothes back into the suitcase.

'I can do that.' Work your way up.

'We can talk about it when I'm back from my cru-uise,' says Jenny, crooning the last word. 'Now, what about Sarah Marchant? Has anyone dealt with her?'

'Yep,' says Luisa.

But Jenny is speaking to Nikki, who Luisa has not noticed enter the office behind her.

'She's still in the pool room,' says Nikki. 'Said she wanted a six-hour discharge. So that's what I'm sorting out.'

'But is she happy?' says Jenny. 'The main thing is that she had a good experience. We're not going to end up in court?'

'Yeah. But you know what's funny?' says Nikki. 'She isn't a Medical Claims lawyer after all.'

'What?'

'She mentioned something about her work that didn't make sense. And when I asked why she told you she was a lawyer, she said she'd read some advice on Mumsnet, that said you get a much better birth experience if you say you're a Medical Claims lawyer. Turns out she works in marketing.'

Luisa sees colour return to Jenny's face.

There is a scuffling noise in reception, a woman struggling to force a wheelchair through the double doors. Luisa crosses reception to help, holds the door open.

The woman is Debbie – one of her legs is in plaster.

'Ralph brought me up,' says Debbie, and it is the bearded porter pushing her wheelchair.

'Hello again,' says Ralph with a wave.

'I thought I should come and let you all know,' says Debbie.

'But what happened to you?' says Luisa.

'Oh, it was crazy.' Debbie wheels herself forward to the centre of reception. She looks around her. 'No one else here? Where's Jenny?'

'We've been right down on numbers,' says Luisa. 'It's been pretty crazy.'

'So Ralph told me. He said he hasn't felt that intense since Burning Man. But anyway,' says Debbie. 'So I was driving in to work last night, and I'm coming down the hill behind the hospital.' The story is polished – Debbie has already recounted this more than once. 'And I push the brakes, and – nothing! Like the brake cable wasn't even there, had snapped or something! All I could do was turn the wheel and plow into the back of another car. And whump – completely smashed up my leg. Broken in three places. I'm going to be off for *ages*,' Debbie grins. 'This is better than going on maternity,' she whispers. 'And now I don't have to bring up a kid.'

Luisa steps from the wheelchair over to reception and back again.

'So what was all the commotion here?' says Debbie. 'Sorry I missed it all.'

'It has been a bit full-on here,' says Luisa. 'I mean first of all Jenny had some kind of food poisoning, she was throwing up in the toilets, something she ate at her wedding, and she had to hand over coordinating to Gina. But Gina couldn't do it because she punched a doctor and security came to take her away. So I had to take over, and it ended up being for hours, and yes there was this emergency, not the one he said about,' she nods at Ralph, 'but another one, Paula, had a PPH, was bleeding everywhere, Nikki had to do bi-manual compression, was wheeled down to theatre on the same trolley.'

'Jesus Christ,' says Debbie.

'But it was all okay.'

'I can't believe they left you to be co-ordinator for all that,' Debbie says.

'It was – fine, really,' says Luisa. 'I mean – we all have to step up at some point.'

Debbie stares at her, and spots Annie standing motionless in the corridor.

'Hey, Annie. Look at all this, eh?' says Debbie, indicating her leg. She turns back to Luisa. "Didn't they call the supervisor? I tell you, this bloody place.'

'She came later. But we didn't really need her.'

'This place gets worse and worse.' Debbie wheels herself forward and back again, causing Ralph to stumble. 'You know, it's this kind of shit that makes me feel this accident was something of of a godsend. I feel like I'm actually glad this happened. Be away from here for a while. How fucked up is that idea?'

Annie sweeps past them into the office.

'You must be in shock still, from everything that happened,' says Luisa. She has an urge to take the wheelchair handles from Ralph and push Debbie out of the ward.

'Probably not as much as you.'

'Well, you know.' Luisa can feel her cheeks inflaming.

'I couldn't have handled that. I'd've gone mad.'

'Perhaps it's not really your thing.'

'Right at this minute midwifery is exactly my thing,' laughs Debbie. 'Right now midwifery couldn't be better. A minimum of twelve weeks paid to sit on my arse!'

'You know Debbie.' It sounds strange to use her name, as though Luisa has never spoken it before. 'Perhaps your problem is you've never really given enough of yourself. To discover what midwifery is really about.'

Debbie screws her face inward. 'Sure. Whatever.'

I would never say whatever, thinks Luisa. Actually I say it all the time. But I can, because Debbie didn't organise a bi-manual compression.

'Well I don't suppose there's much point in my hanging around,' says Debbie. 'Are you okay to take me back down again now?' Debbie smiles at Ralph. As Ralph rotates the wheelchair, she turns back to Luisa. 'I just wanted to let Jenny know. The leg? Can you tell her for me?'

'Sure,' Luisa says, and watches Debbie roll out of the door, on her way home.

'I want to show you something,' says Annie, and tugs at Luisa's sleeve, pulling her along the corridor and into the sluice room. 'I have something that will help. Something to get you through.'

Annie closes the door behind them. In one hand she has a stack of greetings cards, which she separates into two equal piles and places on the macerator, either side of the circular inlet. Luisa notes the symmetry, the edge of the card parallel to the edge of the machine.

'Help with what?' says Luisa, but her question no longer makes sense.

'One for me and one for you,' says Annie. 'You mustn't do too many at once or it clogs the machine. I've experimented and found that four is about the maximum load. I'll start us off with a couple.' She flips the lid of the macerator and tosses two cards inside. 'Want to push it?' She closes the lid and points at the big green button on the front of the machine.

'You do it,' says Luisa. Annie pushes the button, and the macerator begins its grinding cycle.

Luisa takes a card from the top of her pile – on the front a teddy bear holds up a banner saying THANK YOU. *To Debbie*, it says inside. *We couldn't have done it without you. We'll never forget the help you gave the three of us.* She examines the next: *Not only did you help me become a mother, but a real woman.*

'These are all Debbie's cards?' says Luisa.

'Why are they her cards? Because her name is in them?' snaps Annie. 'If you're going to spend that long with each woman, whilst everyone else is running around like blue-bottomed flies, doing all the work you should be doing, these cards belong to everyone. To the team. We are a team, aren't we?' The macerator whirrs to a halt. 'Come on. Your turn.' Annie flips the lid again.

Luisa holds the cards in her hand. 'You can do them if you like,' she says. 'I don't mind.'

'No, no. It doesn't work that way.' Annie grabs Luisa's wrist and guides her hand towards the open inlet. The previous cards have gone, a few threads of cardboard on the glistening surface. 'You have to do it yourself. To get it all out. This is something that Harry taught me. He said it was the only thing that kept him sane in the Falklands. Not with thank you cards. Harry was a soldier, in the Royal Engineers. He used to say he'd have been up a pooey river with PTSD if it hadn't been for the penguins.'

'Penguins?'

'That's what the soldiers did, to relieve stress. Put a General Galtieri mask on a penguin and lob grenades at it from behind the lines. Harry said it was the only way he could cope.'

'Like this?' says Luisa. She lays the teddy bear card in the macerator, closes the lid and presses the button. The grinding action is pleasantly organic, satisfying. 'So Harry is – your husband?' Annie has never talked about a husband. What kind of husband would Annie have?

'Ex-husband,' says Annie. 'We got married in Port Stanley. I was a nurse there. But it didn't last. He wasn't the husband I thought he was.'

'Was it the penguins?'

'Not that,' says Annie. She flips the lid and Luisa sees a strand showing the bear's eye. Annie throws in a couple more – she is proficient at this, her action mechanical. 'I mean that was a bit cruel but understandable in the circumstances. In a time of war. No, but Harry turned out to be – a pervert.' She whispers the last two words.

Luisa takes her turn with a card. How quickly this has become another work task: macerating Debbie's cards.

She presses the button. 'Good noise!' she says. Annie has moved closer to her, is smiling. Luisa worries she might be about to hug her. She cannot imagine Annie hugging anyone.

'I had to leave him. In the end,' says Annie. 'When he wanted it – continental.'

Luisa quivers her head in confusion.

'In the bedroom.' Annie face is glistening, her cheeks bright red. She holds a fist in front of her face, forms a wide O with her lips and bobs her head up and down above the fist. She puts the hand to her mouth, embarrassed. 'Sorry,' she says, seeing Luisa's reaction. 'Sorry to have to involve you. I mean, disgusting as it is, it is actually legal. I checked at the Citizens' Advice Bureau. It's probably something to do with the EU. But rather than call the police I packed my things and left there and then.'

Luisa can feel the features of her face rising, falling, circling around, trying to settle on some appropriate expression.

'Harry wasn't all bad,' says Annie. 'I never heard him utter a cuss word in his life. And he taught me a lot. About stamps. About how to fix cars, all kinds of vehicles. I can still give my Volvo a full service without the help of any mechanic.'

Annie is crying now. Luisa puts a hand on her and threads an arm across Annie's shoulder.

'I know I can mess things up sometimes,' sobs Annie. 'I do my best. But I really thought fraying that woman's brake cable would bring her down a peg or two. I thought I'd done it like Harry showed me. I never thought she'd end up coming out of it smelling like roses. Turning it all to her advantage once again!'

'Debbie's brake cables?'

'Harry would have helped me plan it better!' cries Annie. 'I miss him. Why can't Harry come back and doodle me again!'

*

Luisa pulls open the trolley drawer and grabs a bundle of syringes, drops to her knees and spreads the dozen packets in a line on the floor. How long since anyone has organised this? She examines the use-by dates on the packets, holds them up to the light to see the faded numbers. All in date, she thinks with relief. But not in used by date order, not using the oldest ones first.

She rearranges the line, oldest to newest.

She blows one long breath outwards, a contraction breath, and the lights appear brighter. Brighter because of her breathing? No. Don't gasp for air – even breaths. But don't think about breathing – to think about breathing means not breathing. She remembers a training day where the instructor told them that to check a patient's respiration rate you don't ask them to breathe normally – as soon as you ask someone to breathe normally they fluster and breath faster. She gasps for air again.

'Don't breathe normally,' she tells herself.

'How else do you breathe?' says Diane. But Diane is not there.

Need to order 5mm syringes. Keep thoughts brief, use fewer words. Fewer words, less remembering. Fewer words means less air.

'Luisa,' says Jenny. 'Do you want to go on break now?'

Is that really Jenny? Luisa turns to check. Yes, Jenny's there, butterfly dress.

'Hello Jenny. Not right now,' Luisa continues to order the syringes on the floor: size, then date. 'Not til I've gone through these drawers and checked they all contain a good amount of different-sized syringes. We can't be prepared if we can't trust our equipment. I mean there weren't any two millimetre syringes in here. And I found a Terumo syringe and we don't even stock Terumo syringes any more, do we?'

'When I asked if you wanted to,' says Jenny. 'What I meant was: Luisa, go on a break now.'

'Almost done.' The next syringe fits into her new system: first row, second column.

It surprises Luisa to find Jenny's hand under her armpit, pulling her to her feet. As she stands Luisa sees a man behind Jenny – it is Karl. He wears a pink polo shirt and chinos, but uncomfortably, as though someone else has forced them onto his body.

'Hello there husband,' says Jenny, and releases her grip on Luisa to kiss Karl on the cheek.

'So, we'll be off now, yes?' says Karl. 'You're ready to go?'

'Oh no,' says Jenny. 'I can't leave yet. I must be here til the end of the shift. You remember Luisa? Our bridesmaid,' she smiles.

'Well when's that? Soon?' says Karl.

'Luisa's going on break now,' says Jenny. 'So, Luisa, break's starting. Please leave the delivery suite. Now. It's – ' Jenny lifts her watch fob from her tunic pocket, ' – ten past six. I don't want to see you for an hour.'

'But I need to date order the syringes,' says Luisa.

'When?' says Karl.

Why does he care? thinks Luisa.

'I'll be done by eight, darling,' says Jenny. 'Starting the holiday countdown.'

'But we're supposed to be there at eight! The ship boards at eight, you told me.'

'Boarding's not til ten. I said eight to ensure you were on time. Why don't you get a coffee and rest yourself?' Jenny is off, down the corridor. 'Luisa!' she calls over her shoulder, indicting to Luisa with a hand motion that could cuff a Victorian boy's ear.

Luisa looks at the syringes on the floor, then up at Karl.

'That's exciting,' she says to Karl. 'Your cruise.'

'If you call getting up at half-four to take the children to my mother's exciting, I suppose.' Karl throws himself onto a seat by the corridor wall.

Luisa quickly puts the syringes back in the drawer, trying to keep them in order.

'I didn't see them,' says Luisa. 'Your children. At the wedding?'

'Well. We didn't want to share out all that joy with anyone else,' says Karl. 'Just between us lovebirds, wasn't it?'

'Jenny's been a bit ill, this evening.' Why is she defending Jenny? 'Something she ate. At your wedding – reception.'

'No chance of it being fatal?'

'Food poisoning, maybe.'

'Not botulism?'

'I don't think so.'

'Oh good. That's good.'

'Well.' Luisa closes the drawers of the trolley, pushes it back against the wall. 'I'm glad you had a lovely day.'

*

Up in postnatal the overhead strip lights are off, the only visibility from the dim night lights in the rooms, that show through the open doors. Jenny told me to leave the delivery suite, she never specified where exactly to take my break. So I'm going to take it on postnatal, thank you Jenny.

Luisa sways as she walks, unable to balance normally. She can hear the blood in her ears, hear it draining down her ear canals and into her neck. Do you even have blood in your ears? She enters the nearest room, peers around each of the curtains, sees Matilda in one bed.

I'll check if she's awake, thinks Luisa. If she's sleeping, I'll go.

Luisa steps within a foot of the bed and Matilda opens her eyes.

'Just checking you're getting some sleep,' whispers Luisa.

'Oh yes,' says Matilda. 'Thank you.'

'Good. You get back to sleeping.'

Outside in the corridor she bumps into Clarissa.

'Seeing if there was any help needed down here,' says Luisa. 'A lot of these women were mine downstairs.'

'Jenny said you might be down.' Clarissa takes a step back. 'No. We're fine.'

'Sure? I could do – the morning drug round?'

'Diane's doing the drug round.' Clarissa nods towards the equipment storeroom.

She looks suspicious, thinks Luisa. Or worried. Embarrassed?

'Do I have pen on my face?' Luisa wipes her cheek with her palm.

A call buzzer sounds. 'I have to go,' says Clarissa.

But Diane's not here, thinks Luisa. If Diane's not here, who'll do the drug round?

She looks at the door of the equipment storeroom, pushes it ajar.

'Diane?' calls Luisa. 'Diane?'

'Here I am,' says a voice in the storeroom.

Luisa pushes open the door and turns left down the narrow corridor. A shaft of intense light hits her eyes, blinds her. She staggers forward into the central aisle of the store room, trips and fall to her knees by a shelf of incontinence pads.

Perhaps this is actual death. The end. She is angry with herself for letting things go this far. This fatigue, it has been fatal, my last moments were a heart attack as I entered the cupboard, I'm now lying, not kneeling, my head resting on incontinence pads, or a cheek on the cold lino. Another midwife will find me, and now I'll never be co-ordinator again. These are my final moments. Though I did well tonight, went out on a high. Elsie and Eleanor will grow up without a mother.

The light dims, and she sees Diane on a mattress in the corner, a book in one hand held up to shield Luisa from the glare. The vivid blue light blasts from the fluorescent tubes of multiple phototherapy lights, lined along the middle row of two sets of shelves at right angles to each other, marking off the corner where Diane sits on a mattress.

'Sorry, Diane. I – needed some pads.' She is not dead after all. 'Are you on a break?'

'Oh no. Am I needed?'

Besides Diane are two Morrisons bags filled with groceries. An empty plate dusted with breadcrumbs sits on top of one bag.

'But what are you doing here?'

'They got all funny about my sleeping in the staff room. Ever since they found that homeless man in A and E, the one who'd been wandering round in scrubs for weeks. That's what started the fuss, anyway. So I ended up here. But I'm much happier in here.'

'You – come in here? On breaks?'

'You can always find me if you need me.' Diane looks offended. 'You can just call me.'

'All these lights aren't good for your eyes.'

'Well it's not like you really need your eyes much to do a vaginal exam now, do you?' giggles Diane, and holds up a hand to waggle her fingers. 'And it's good for your skin. One doctor said I needed more Vitamin D. If it's good enough for jaundiced babies, it's good enough for me. And I use this for eyes.' Diane taps the head torch on her forehead, which, despite all the additional lighting, she has left switched on.

Diane returns to reading her book.

Luisa examines Diane, her round reading glasses, her grey bob, her equally grey skin.

'How old are you, Diane? Is that a rude question?'

'Don't mind me.' Diane continues reading.

'So, how old are you?'

'Thirty-three.'

'Really?'

'No! How could you think that?' cackles Diane. 'How could I have my children if I was thirty-three? The sums wouldn't add up.'

'You have children?'

'Oh yes.' Diane puts the book down again. 'Must be almost teenagers, now. If you ask me, they can take care of themselves. Though Douglas said not yet. Soon, but not yet.'

'So Douglas – he takes care of the childcare?' Luisa tries to picture Diane at home, with a partner, leading an everyday life, but it is impossible.

'I don't really get involved,' says Diane. 'It's easier letting Douglas take care of all of that.'

The deep shadows cast by the phototherapy lights make Diane's edges indistinct – she has become part of the mattress. Part of the room. A piece of equipment.

'So you're not together any more,' says Luisa.

'Oh we're still married. We thought it best, for the sake of the children. But being together didn't work out, with my being here so often. I mean I suppose if I upped sticks and went home now perhaps we'd just carry on as normal. But it's never the right time. You stay late one night, grab a bit of sleep somewhere, and the next night you find out they're short-staffed again, and before you know it a whole week has gone by. And after a while it doesn't seem worth going home.'

'You live in here?'

'Shh. We mustn't call it that.'

'But what about – your children?'

'Yes. That can be a shame. But keeping in contact became so much easier once they invented Facebook.'

'But where are your children?'

'Cornwall, perhaps,' says Diane. 'Possibly Spain. Douglas said something in one email about Spain. I saw a palm tree in the background of one photo.

But they have palm trees in Cornwall, don't they?'

Luisa's attention on Diane is fading, switching over to another sound, a physical switching, voice off, buzzer on. Call buzzer.

'I'm there.' Diane throws down her book and is on her feet. 'I'm coming.'

I'm there too, thinks Luisa. She follows Diane out into the ward.

*

'You're so good. You've all been so good to me. I can't tell you.'

Sarah Marchant sits in delivery suite reception in a wheelchair, cradling her new baby in her lap.

'So good,' echoes her husband.

'And you didn't have to call a taxi for me. We're going to need to get used to doing a few things for ourselves, now aren't we Peter?' she laughs.

'Not a problem,' says Jenny. 'All part of the service.'

'Bye,' says Luisa.

'It was a pleasure,' says Nikki.

'Bye,' says Sarah Marchant. 'Thanks again, to all of you,' she says, this time to Karl.

'Bye,' says Karl.

Peter pushes the wheelchair out through the double doors.

'I'm back,' Luisa tells Jenny.

'So I see. Now, wave,' says Jenny.

Luisa raises a hand in imitation of Jenny as Sarah and Peter Marchant exit the double doors.

'See you for number two!' calls Nikki.

'Not too enthusiastic,' whispers Jenny. 'I don't want them to get suspicious.'

'No one's ever found out before,' says Nikki.

'Found out what?' says Luisa.

'I thought our Sarah Marchant deserved a Jenny special,' says Jenny.

'All women deserve our best care,' says Luisa.

'No woman gets the best care in this ward through pretending to be a Medical Claims lawyer,' says Jenny. 'Not without suffering the consequences.

They get a taxi driven by my brother-in-law Alfie. Alfie was once in prison for armed robbery. He's always keen for extra money on the side.

'He's going to – kill them?' says Luisa.

'No!' laughs Jenny. 'I would never go that far. He'll drive them to a field on the edge of town and dump them there.' Jenny sniffs her hand.

'That's not a bit – dangerous?' says Luisa.

'I specified no violence.'

'I mean for a new baby.'

'Oh all the fussing over new babies! They're hardy little things, once they're out. She's got a wheelchair, hasn't she? What about the fuss and danger she caused by pretending to be a lawyer? I did it for all of us, bridesmaid. It's only fair.'

'I guess so,' says Luisa.

'Well worth the three hundred quid. Though I'm sorry, darling,' Jenny moves over to Karl and gives him a hug. 'It means we're going to have a bit less to spend when we get to Marrakesh.'

FRIDAY DAY: OFF DUTY

Luisa emerges from the hospital entrance and daylight surges through her, quickens her pace, saturates her colours. She strides up the road towards Blackdown Hill.

At a junction a bearded man stands with a pushchair, just one more object in the scrolling background screen of Luisa's existence. The child in the pushchair is hysterical, her face red raw, stretched with the exertion of crying. As Luisa passes, the man leans down to speak to the girl, then straightens and says nothing.

'She's fine,' he smiles at Luisa. 'It's okay.'

Luisa slows down, stops.

'I forgot to say goodbye,' says the man.

'But you're still with her,' says Luisa. 'There's still time to say goodbye.'

'I mean back there. I forgot to say goodbye, and she wants to go back.' The explanation is a relief, that there is someone to listen. 'I can't, it's miles back. There's no time.'

'The parrot-eagle!' screams the girl. 'You didn't say goodbye to the parrot-eagle!'

'What's a parrot-eagle?' says Luisa, keen to know.

'It looks like a parrot,' sighs the father. 'As well as an eagle. It's a statue. On a house.' He takes a step backwards, releases his grip on the pushchair. 'It's too far to go back. I have to get her to nursery.'

'I can take her if you like,' says Luisa. 'She's going where – Bluebell nursery, I'm guessing? Let me do it.'

'Um. Yes, Bluebell. Really?'

'It's not a problem,' says Luisa, delighted with her powers of deduction.

'Do you work there?'

'No.' Luisa wonders if she should have lied. Better to be honest. Though no one would charge you with kidnapping for taking a child to nursery on time, would you? For masquerading as a nursery worker? Perhaps you would.

'I have two girls myself, they used to go there,' she says. 'It's on my way home.'

The girl draws breath then starts a new howl.

'What bout the doggy?' Luisa drops onto all fours, crawls up to the girl, pants at her, tongue hanging out. The girl stops mid-cry, stares at her. Luisa nuzzles the girl's arm with her nose and takes a lick of the ice pop in the child's hand. The girl frowns.

'It's okay,' says Luisa to the bearded man. 'I'm a midwife.'

'Are you?' says the father.

Luisa crouches, on her hind legs, and pulls on the retractable reel at her waist to show him her hospital swipe card.

'I have to go to work,' says the father, 'I'm so late,' he apologises – to himself, or perhaps to his daughter's mother – apologises that he is about to allow this woman he has only known for a few moments, who is crawling on all fours around his pushchair, to take his daughter to nursery.

'I've just come from work,' says Luisa. 'At the hospital. A crazy night, one woman gave birth in the corridor. But I kind of liked it. And it's okay, I work with children, tiny ones, at least. She's all right with me. What's her name?'

'Robyn.' The father is almost in tears. He hands her a blue and yellow satchel. 'That's her bag, you leave that one with her at the nursery. This one's mine.' He lifts the strap of a laptop bag from the handles of the pushchair, nestles it under his arm. Luisa jumps up from all fours, steers the pushchair in a circle, heads back down the hill. Robyn peers round the edge of the pushchair back at her father, holds up a hand to wave goodbye. Luisa also waves, and the father stands there for a moment, then turns and runs in the opposite direction.

He stops and turns around. 'What's your name?' he calls.

'Luisa,' Luisa shouts back. 'I'm a midwife.' She pulls her bag from her shoulders to hang on the handles. There's my lunch I didn't eat at work. And the full bottle of water I haven't drunk. It doesn't matter. I don't need sustenance any longer.

At the nursery she does not recognise any staff from the twins' time there. And is glad, because the events of the story she rehearses in her head do not make a story, include apologies, and apologising aligns too closely with abduction. Why is she here again?

'I've brought Robyn,' she says to a girl in a blue t-shirt. 'This is Robyn.'

'Hello, Robyn!' sing-songs the girl, but her eyes are not singing.

'Her dad asked me to bring her,' says Luisa. She unclips the pushchair buckles and Robyn climbs out, and without looking back goes to sit at a low round table covered in pens and paper.

'Juice?' says Robyn.

'Robyn, you want juice?' says the blue t-shirt girl, and brings a large juice carton and white plastic cups to the table.

'I'm going now,' says Luisa, but no one wants to know.

Luisa can see blue t-shirt girl hasn't opened the juice carton properly, and as she pours its flow is erratic and spills onto the table. Chaotic flow, not enough air.

'Let me.' Luisa takes the juice carton, and both the girl and Robyn defer to her without protest. Luisa grasps a pencil and plunges it through the carton lid. She pours a cupful for Robyn: the flow is smooth.

'Thanks,' says the blue t-shirt girl, and means it. 'Are you a parent?'

'No. Midwife.'

Luisa turns with the pushchair and heads out. She doesn't want the pushchair. Though if she kept it who would know? She looks around for a suitable storage place. Then releases her grip, leaves it in the middle of the room and walks out.

*

Luisa lets herself in the front door, hits her head on the action man suspended from the light shade. Her opening of the door is no longer blocked by sofa cushions, but otherwise the hallway is as chaotic as the night before: chairs, sheets, tins of food, torn strips of crepe paper, cutlery.

In the lounge Elsie and Eleanor sit in armchairs at opposite ends of the room, their faces both lit by an iPad screen. On the carpet is a circle of multi-coloured sand, its neat shape smudged with footprints. Elsie wears what looks like a white priest's gown several sizes too large for her.

'Hey, lovely girls,' says Luisa. 'Mummy's home.' Neither of the girls looks up. She kisses both on the head, trying not to make more of a mess of the sand. 'And morning to you too,' she says.

'I've almost done the frog's genome,' says Eleanor.

'No you haven't,' says Elsie. 'Look at him. You didn't grow his leg properly so he can't run and my sabre-toothed sheep is going to catch and eat him.'

'What are you doing?' says Luisa.

'Don't look,' says Elsie, holding the screen of the iPad against her chest. 'I don't want Ellie to know. Boom!'

'I've got a mammoth coming next,' says Eleanor.

'Where's Daddy?' asks Luisa.

Luisa lugs her bag into the kitchen, but Justin is not in there, only pans and trays and duvets and unwashed plates. She pulls her uneaten lunch from her bag, pushes the plastic bags into the bottom shelf of the fridge.

Upstairs she opens the door of the bathroom. Justin has his foot up on the basin. Foam covers half his scrotum, and the other half is shaved and hairless.

'I got out of work early,' says Luisa. All those shaved women's pubes I've seen, she thinks, and these are my first shaved testicles. She looks up at Justin's face and back down at his genitals. 'I actually ran the ward for a while last night. It was crazy, but kind of – I've told you this already? They sent me home early because it wasn't so busy. I know I'm not actually home any earlier, but I met Robyn and her dad and had to take her to nursery. Robyn's a girl. I had to deliver her to Bluebell, where the girls went.'

Justin holds the razor in mid-air, undecided whether to continue.

'Though I had to leave in case they started that fucking Hop Little Rabbits song,' says Luisa. 'What are you doing?'

'Back, crack and sack?' says Justin.

Luisa tries to form the supplementary question, but silence seems to work as well.

'I thought you might like it?' he says.

'How will you do your back?'

'I might stop at the sack.' Justin goes back to shaving.

'This means – you want me to shave too?'

'Not at all.' says Justin. 'No, I don't want you to. I wasn't even sure myself, anyway. It's all prompted by the porn industry, shaving, isn't it? Are you going to bed? Going to sleep?'

'I don't have to sleep yet.' Luisa smiles at him.

'The girls are downstairs.'

'We could send them out.'

'I need to make them breakfast.'

'I'll help with breakfast. I'm starving.'

Luisa bounds down the stairs.

'You know how they discovered the genome in the first place?' she says to the girls, back in the lounge. 'A man called Mendelssohn and his experiments with peas.' Mendelssohn, is that right? Right enough. 'He was a monk. And he kept growing different types of pea and observing how they changed when he grew one pea with another one, he sort of mixed them together. Splicing, I think it's called. Anyway, he spliced peas for many years, actually perhaps only months, peas don't take long. What are you doing now?' She looks at Eleanor's screen, where a crude wheeled vehicle traverses a rocky terrain.

'We're not playing that any more,' says Eleanor. 'We're on Rugged Rover. I'm seeing how far my space vehicle can go on Mars.'

Luisa wakes, slumped in a corner of the sofa, a cushion pushing into her back. The girls are gone, as is the sand circle. The whole room is immaculate and smells of air freshener. Did I do this? she thinks. Tidying in my sleep would be an excellent new skill.

The hallway is cleansed, everything extraneous removed bar the action man and his noose.

'You didn't have to tidy it all,' says Luisa in the kitchen.

'Perhaps I did,' says Justin.

The kitchen surfaces are not only empty but shiny – she barely recognises this as the house where she lives. Her presence is making the room untidy. Eleanor and Elsie sit at the table with Justin, eating cereal. Luisa watches for a stray rice pop to fall from spoon to table, but no: everything remains in place.

'We didn't want to wake you.' Justin moves to kiss her, a dustpan in his hand. Amongst the dust and crumbs in the pan are two small doll's heads: *across the forehead of one is the word ABRUPT, on the other, SORROW.* 'Breakfast is up if you want it.' He tips the lid of the bin and slides the rubbish inside.

'How long have I been asleep? Hello lovelies.' Luisa kisses both girls on the top of their heads.

'You already said that before,' says Elsie without looking up from her cereal. The girls are dressed in identical dungarees and green t-shirts.

'I cooked some of your liver,' says Justin.

'I'm not eating liver,' says Eleanor. 'Thank you Daddy.'

'Okay,' says Luisa. 'For breakfast?'

'Good for your iron levels,' says Justin. 'Like black pudding?'

'Pudding!' says Elsie in a deep voice, a drag queen aping Vincent Price.

Justin puts the plate of cooked breakfast in front of her, and Luisa remembers that all she has eaten since a pastry-filled pasty the night before is the double-munch of Vicky's toast. She digs at the liver with a fork, giddy at the idea of vegetarian transgression, adds baked beans on top as an afterthought and shoves it all into her mouth.

'I might make some other changes.,' says Justin, 'Along with work. And I might go paleolithic. Fifty-eight percent of mental health issues are linked to overconsumption of carbohydrates. I'm going to cut the carbs more. Not completely. Semi-paleo.'

Justin is talking too much, or perhaps Luisa is listening too much. 'I'm only eating bread,' she says. Meaning that's what she's eating now, though it sounds like she's adopted a bread-only diet out of spite.

Justin appears unperturbed, continues eating. 'It's strange,' he says, 'this organic liver. More bobbly than I remember. Where did you get it?'

'What kind of other changes?' says Luisa.

'Can't question their customer service, anyhow,' says Justin. 'They even put a thank-you card inside.' He stands and clears the table, even though Luisa is still eating. 'We need to be going. I'm taking the girls to my mum's. You should go to bed,' he says to Luisa. 'You'll need to get some sleep if you're working tonight.'

'I'll be in bed,' smiles Luisa. 'So you're coming back. When you've taken the girls?' She reaches across the table, takes his hand in hers. Elsie reaches forwards, places her hand on top. Eleanor copies her.

Nobody speak, thinks Luisa. Let's stay like this.

'We're going to grandma's,' says Elsie. 'Grandma's going to tell us about Grandad Cuba and his guns. You should come, Daddy.'

'I've got some grown-up things to do,' says Justin, looking at Luisa as he says this.

Justin and the girls leave Luisa sat at the table. They move around the house, gathering, and Luisa goes to sit on the stairs to watch them. The front door closes and they are gone.

Luisa remains on the stairs for a minute, and for an additional unit of time she cannot gauge. She wonders if she can stay there, there on the stairs, until Justin returns, until they are alone in the house, until he can help her upstairs to bed, can climb in with her. Can fuck her asleep. Not actually asleep. To fuck her *to* sleep.

Wait. I didn't buy liver.

*

Luisa lies in the bath, her mind replaying the image of Justin's bald testicle. She asks herself if this is a turn-on, wants the answer to be yes, wants to ignore the easy answer that if asking the question then the answer is no. But how does she know before she tries? At least he is performing experiments. Here I am, ready and waiting, an experimental subject. And if he's prepared to give shaving a go, so am I.

That's how we operate, isn't it – we argue against our subconscious urges but sometimes we need to give in to subconscious urges, need to allow our biology to come to the forefront of decision making, for our mental health. This is how I operate as a midwife on little sleep. Not operate, I'm not a surgeon. But I could learn to be a surgeon, given time. I'm more than capable of performing operations on as little sleep as the doctors. Not listening to the mind, but letting the body's instincts kick in. We intellectualise solutions, when we ought really to listen to our bodies.

Luisa tries to remember an example of one of these times, but a moment later she cannot remember what it is she is trying to remember. Shaving. She pushes up her hips so that her pubic hair rises above the water line. What a particularly uninhabitable island. She squeezes a blue sphere of shaving gel onto the island and swirls it around with Justin's shaving brush, dipping her hips back into the water to create lapping waves with which she foams up a lather. She looks for a razor on the bath edges, but there is none in sight.

Luisa pushes herself to her feet and the room sways beneath her, she has to lean against the wall to stay upright. Many seconds pass before she can step out of the bath and open the bathroom cabinet.

She takes out an almost new packet of disposable razors. There is a leaflet stuck to the packet. Hurst Clinic, the leaflet says in bold type across the top. Your Vasectomy: What *You* Need To Do.

'What the hell are you doing?' cries Luisa into her phone. She is downstairs in the hallway, naked save for an Eve-like modesty-cover of foam. 'Don't do it. You can't do this without asking me. You're meant to be coming home, coming home to have sex with me!'

This is the second message she has left on Justin's answerphone, the first an angry build up of steam quiet enough to be indistinguishable from no message at all.

'Hi, er, Justin, it's me,' she says on the third attempt. 'I'm hoping I haven't got the wrong end of the stick. But if you are having a vasectomy, we should have discussed it first! And if you're not, don't worry, everything's fine,' she adds as an afterthought.

'I need a cab,' says Luisa. She is dressed and standing on the driveway outside. 'I need to call a cab.'

'Luisa?' She turns to see Claudette, and the sight prompts her to touch the paint-splattered Peugeot, to stroke the roof with her hand.

'You want me to call for a taxi?' says Claudette. 'I know the number.'

'Where did you come from?' says Luisa.

'I live next door, do you not remember?'

'I need to get to Hurst Clinic.' Luisa stares down the road, as though the clinic might squint into view.

'Is that for an emergency – shall I tell them it's a medical emergency?' says Claudette. 'Maybe they'll come quicker. For a medical professional?'

'Has André had a vasectomy?' Luisa spins round to Claudette.

'No. No. But I don't think he wants one. Thank you for asking.' Claudette looks worried.

'How would you feel if he did?'

'Is this for research?' Now Claudette is excited, moves closer to Luisa. 'Am I part of a survey?'

'I just need a taxi.'

'If it is for a survey, I am against it,' says Claudette. 'If the children and I were all killed, André and I agree that he should marry a new, younger wife and start again for more children. We have picked out his new wife together. We are against all forms of sterilisation. Both of us are. Do you want to include André in your survey as well?'

'Maybe,' says Luisa.

'But why don't you take your car? Instead of a cab?'

Luisa looks at the paint all over the Peugeot's roof. 'Should I?'

'You dislike the car now?' says Claudette? 'But after all your work?'

'Sure. I'll take the car.' Luisa runs back inside and grabs her bag from the hallway, then straight back out, digging her hand into the bag and coming up with the keys first time.

Luisa climbs in and winds down the remains of the broken window, the glass shards dispersing themselves between the inside of the car and outside on the driveway.

'In France we do not have emergency vasectomies,' says Claudette. 'Do you have a blue light for the car?'

The car's ignition barrel hangs down loose and rests on her knee, and Luisa has to hold it in one hand to insert the key. The engine starts first time. She pulls her elbow away from where it rests on the broken window glass and looks to Claudette. 'You and André □ you must come to ours for dinner sometime.'

'Thank you. That would be nice. Your midwifery, it is so exciting!' calls Claudette as Luisa screeches out of the driveway.

*

The clinic is only ten minutes away, and rush hour is over, her phone tells her that traffic is clear. We didn't discuss this properly, she rehearses. We can come back for another appointment, she says to the surgeon, watching herself in front of him, explaining the situation as one medical professional to another. We need to discuss the implications further, we haven't had time to consider the consequences. The surgeon is nodding, is indicating to Justin that he should dress, ready himself to leave.

'At the next junction, turn right,' says the phone from her lap. The female voice is too genteel, should bark instructions at her, as to a soldier or junior investment banker or assistant chef. As she slows up at a T-junction, she punches on the stereo, turns up a woman talking about the brazil nut industry to full volume, presses the arrows to change station. Now it is The Rolling Stones at full volume. To her left she sees a car, still at some distance, heading in her direction and pulls out. A horn sounds an extended bass note behind her.

Luisa checks the rearview mirror for how close the car is behind, but can see nothing. Where is the mirror? She looks to her wing mirror but there she sees only two wires straggling out of the car body, and remembers Justin and the scooter, the karate chop. Is there another mirror, a backup mirror? She looks back to the rearview, and the mirror *is* there, is there but displays nothing but coloured darkness, dark because the back screen is covered in paint, is covered in the paint she herself threw onto it some number of nights ago. She looks down at her phone for help, but all Google can tell her is that she has 0.6 miles to the next roundabout.

Am I safe? I don't feel safe.

If you don't feel safe, you should call the supervisor. Call for support. She presses the emergency button – the horn. The car behind sounds their horn louder. Luisa pulls the steering wheel to the left, drives across the cycle lane and onto the verge, slides over the grass, tips forward into the drainage ditch.

She leans on the steering wheel, gravity forcing her down, looks up and across as the car behind goes past. In the driver's seat is a white-haired old woman hunched over the wheel, her forehead almost on the windscreen, who doesn't even glance at her.

Luisa looks up and down the road. There are no other cars in sight. She listens to her heart in her chest. I'm awake, she thinks, fully awake now, now I am ready for this emergency. But be safe, call for support. Call a taxi. She grabs her bag and phone, pushes open the door and jumps out of the car, stomps along the verge without looking back, along to where the grass turns into pavement, dialling a taxi as she moves. Keep onward, forward motion.

*

At the clinic the taxi leaves her by the glass double doors. Luisa pulls at the handles but they are locked. The receptionist circles from the desk, stands behind but does not open the door. She points to a buzzer panel.

'I'm here for my husband,' cries Luisa through the door. The receptionist points again at the panel. Luisa pushes the buzzer. 'I'm here for my husband,' she says to the speaker.

The receptionist is only just back at her desk. She points once more at the panel, and nods.

'My husband is here,' says Luisa into the speaker. 'Justin Singyard.'

'Is everything okay?' The receptionist's tinny voice asks from the speaker.

'I'm sorry,' says Luisa. 'I've worked a night shift. I promised to be here, here to help him, but my shift overran and I'm late. But now I'm here.'

The receptionist ushers her through to the waiting room. 'He won't be long,' she says. 'It's only a short procedure.'

'Where's the toilet?' Luisa says. 'I need the toilet.'

The receptionist points down a corridor. Before she reaches the entrance, Luisa sees another door half-open to a changing room, nips inside and grabs a bunched up pair of scrubs from a chair. This is my domain, she thinks – respond in the moment, trust my instincts in order to anticipate. She slides into the toilet, closes the cubicle, pulls the scrubs on over her clothes whilst thumbing her phone with the other. Justin does not answer.

She prowls further down the corridor, opens a door and strides in. Five men, all holding mugs, stare at her from recliner chairs on two sides of the room. None of them are Justin.

'I was looking for theatre,' she says to the nurse behind the desk. 'I'm from the agency.'

'Back out, to the right, two doors down,' smiles the nurse.

Luisa smiles at all the men, and they look worried, as though it is Luisa who will perform their vasectomies.

Down the corridor she peers through the small square window of theatre. The surgeon stands upright from a leaning position over the theatre table, and she knows it is too late, she has failed, she has done her best, followed all the procedures, but to no avail.

Luisa pushes open the door and stands in the open doorway, not moving into the room. Justin lies on the bed, his legs splayed in a V, naked from the waist down. She sees the hole in his scrotum, a livid, unnatural opening.

A nurse looks up at her from where he squats by a cupboard. The surgeon, his hands clad in plastic in front of him, frowns at Luisa.

Justin is the first to speak. 'It's okay,' he says. 'She's a midwife.'

'He hasn't signed the forms,' says Luisa. 'He hasn't had proper consent for this operation.'

'I've already made the incisions,' says the surgeon. 'I saw them, I saw the forms.'

'I have signed the forms,' Justin tells the surgeon. 'This is Luisa, she's – '

'I'm his wife and no one consulted me,' Luisa moves into the room. 'I'm a midwife, I know you need proper consultation. You need to decided in tandem.'

'There aren't any sutures here,' the nurse says to the surgeon. He glances at Luisa. 'Shall I fetch some from the stockroom?'

The surgeon nods at the nurse. 'You didn't talk about this with your wife?' he asks Justin.

'She's not actually my wife,' says Justin.

'Well who the hell is she?' The surgeon is exasperated, what with infection and patient care and intruder identification to deal with all at once.

'I mean we're not married. We talked about this, Lu,' Justin pleads with her. 'You agreed it was a good idea.'

'That was years ago! I was breastfeeding two babies at the same time! Why didn't you tell me this morning?'

'Is everything okay in here?' asks the receptionist, coming into the room.

'We're fine,' sighs the surgeon. 'She's a midwife.'

'I thought she was here for her husband,' says the receptionist, leaving again.

'It's for the best, Lu,' says Justin. 'You agreed it was for the best.'

'How could you do this without telling me?'

'My Body My Choice?' Justin nods towards a poster on the theatre wall, of an anxious woman looking down at her distended belly.

'That's not the same thing!'

'But you don't want any more children, do you?'

'No!'

'And now it doesn't matter.'

'What doesn't matter?'

'How much – sex we have.' Justin looks to the surgeon. The surgeon lifts his eyebrows, as if to say, you've gone this far, say what you like, don't mind me. He moves away from them, back to the cupboards.

'It seems to matter to you,' says Luisa.

'You need to leave so I can finish this procedure,' says the surgeon. 'You need to leave or I'll have to call security.'

'But now it won't,' says Justin. 'Now it won't matter at all. Now there won't be more children.' He nods down at his scrotum.

'Is that why you think I want sex more than usual?' cries Luisa. 'Because I want another child?'

'Isn't it?' says Justin.

'No! Why would you think that!'

'Well, I mean, it's your body's last chance to reproduce. Isn't it? Maybe you don't even know it yourself? And what about the liver? And feeling sick.'

'The liver?'

'Your liver cravings. You're vegetarian.'

'You get cravings and feel sick if you *are* pregnant! Not if you want to get pregnant! It wasn't even liver.'

'But what about you being, you know? Over keen. That means something, doesn't it?' Justin looks to the surgeon again, but he has subtracted himself from the situation.

'Don't you try to belittle my libido!' cries Luisa. 'You're scared of it, of a woman who likes a lot of sex. I don't want another fucking baby!'

'You haven't slept,' says Justin. 'You're all – you don't think straight when you haven't slept. Perhaps that's the reason for all this. That you don't sleep properly.'

'I slept this morning! And I can think fine without sleep, thank you!'

'I've pressed the button,' says the surgeon.

'But it's done now.' Justin sits up on the bed, wincing.

'Careful there,' calls the surgeon.

'It's only an explanation,' Justin lies back down again. 'It's evolutionary psychology.'

'I don't give a shit about my reasons for wanting sex!' shouts Luisa. 'I don't need to justify it. And I'm not having you explaining it to me! Or you,' she directs at the surgeon.

'Perhaps we can all calm down a little,' says the surgeon.

'Or you telling me to be calm!'

'Lu – '

'Now you won't be able to have sex for ages!'

'It won't be that long,' says Justin, looking to the surgeon.

'Absolutely,' says the surgeon. 'You'll be fine. It's fine after only, what, forty-eight hours? We always say forty-eight hours as the minimum.'

'You were going to come home and have sex with me this morning!' says Luisa.

The door to the room bursts open. A man in a black shirt with an eagle pocket logo flies into the room. He grabs Justin's arm, pulls him off the bed and forces him face down on the floor. He drags Justin's trousers with him, keys and coins emptying all over the floor.

'Not him,' cries the surgeon. 'Her, the midwife. She's the one. Put him back.'

The security guard drops Justin to the floor and seizes Luisa's arm.

'Please take her out of here.' The surgeon looks to Justin, waggles his useless latexed hands.

'Can't we help him up first?' says Luisa. 'Let me help him back on the theatre table.'

Between them Luisa and the security guard pick Justin off the floor and back onto the plastic mattress. Justin's screws his eyes in pain. To avoid looking at him Luisa sweeps around the floor, collecting coins and keys and trousers.

'I'm very sorry sir,' says the security guard, 'I thought it was abortion day. Sorry,' he looks at Luisa, 'I mean termination day.'

'But I've got no pants on,' says Justin.

The security guard shrugs. 'It's not always easy to tell. Right,' he pulls Luisa towards the door. 'We're leaving.'

Luisa allows the security guard to drag her from the room. The deep hum has returned to her day. The nurse almost knocks into them as they leave the room.

'Found them,' he cries, a stack of plastic packets in his hand.

The receptionist follows the guard and Luisa to the door.

'She's the wife,' explains the guard. 'She was trying to stop proceedings.'

'It's more complicated than that.' Luisa remembers Gina and pulls her shoulders back as the guard escorts her outside. Getting dragged from buildings by a security guard – that's what proper midwives do. The door lock buzzes shut behind her.

'I still have his trousers,' shouts Luisa through the door. The guard looks from Luisa to the receptionist, cups his hand to his ear. Luisa holds up the trousers like a trophy. The receptionist returns to the door, stabs a finger at the intercom.

'I have my boyfriend's trousers,' says Luisa into the intercom.

The receptionist holds up a finger, returns to the desk, points at the intercom again.

'I have Justin's trousers!' shouts Luisa.

'There's no need to shout,' says the receptionist via the intercom. 'Those will be our scrubs you're wearing. Kindly give them back.'

'And you have my bag,' Luisa calls back. 'My bag is in your changing room.'

Luisa pulls off the scrubs with extravagant movements, to show her lack of care at undressing in the car park of an abortion clinic. She exchanges these and the trousers for her bag, through the small crack the guard has allowed in the door.

'You get yourself home now,' says the guard. 'I don't want to have to call the police.'

'Call who you like.'

As she walks away across the car park Luisa realises she still has keys in her hand. Justin's keys. I've added a power, she thinks: sleight of hand. As if to demonstrate she holds the key fob high in the air, presses the button and is delighted by the beep and indicator flash that direct her to the courtesy car. I don't need Justin. Why am I in a relationship with someone who thinks this energy some kind of procreating urge? This is a creating urge. I'm creating. it's just me and the girls now, we can go. Go to Spain. Buy that caravan, the one with the green roof. With that wood-burning stove. Won't need a wood-burning stove, not in Spain, hot enough without. I'm saving money already.

This train of thought takes her all the way, at courtesy car cruising speed, to the estate where Bea lives, where the twenty-mile-an-hour limit and speed bumps bring her back to the present. The car controls are unfamiliar – she pushes the brake pedal for the clutch which causes her to panic and screech to a halt. She sets off again at ten miles an hour, along Bea's road, but there is nowhere to park. The idea of parking and the manoeuvres required make her nauseous. She turns at the junction and circles the block, all the way back round to Bea's, then once more. How can she move to Spain if she cannot find anywhere to park? A parking space is the first step to Spain, and she cannot manage the first step.

A car pulls out a few houses ahead of her, and she parks the car at the first attempt.

'Oh!' Bea smiles as she opens the door. 'Well we weren't expecting you! I thought Justin was collecting the girls later. Are you here for them now?'

'Um. I don't know. Yes.' She doesn't want to go to Spain, or buy a caravan. She cannot afford a caravan. How much money does she have in her bank account? Does this mean she is leaving Justin? When did that happen, who decided? She doesn't want to leave Justin.

'Ah, well. That's fine! Come in, come in.'

'Mummy!' Eleanor flies along the hallway and thumps against Luisa's leg. 'We're learning all about Grandad Cuba.'

'I'm not sure what I'm doing,' Luisa says to Bea.

'What a wonderful opportunity.' Bea closes the door. 'I always say to my clients, the ones who tell me they aren't sure what they are doing, that they are the luckiest people. All that opportunity ahead of them, no avenues closed off, all that life potential.'

'Really?'

'Of course, most of them aren't lucky at all. They wouldn't be seeing a life coach if they were, would they?' Bea laughs – a sleazy, guttural noise. 'But that's what I tell them, anyhoo.'

In the lounge the carpet is covered with old photographs, newspaper clippings, a blue-and-white striped flag with a starred red triangle, and endless medals, ribbons and berets.

'So you've been playing?' says Luisa to Eleanor at her leg.

'Know Where You Came From, Know Where You Are, Know Where You're Going.' Elsie is examining a photograph, her nose almost touching. She wears a camouflage jacket, and hugs Luisa without affection, as ritual.

'Look.' Eleanor holds a rifle, gripped diagonally across her chest in a pose obviously practised earlier.

'Don't worry,' says Bea. 'It's not loaded. We learnt that first off.'

'All this is – yours? From Cuba?'

'Oh, not the rifle. Too recent a model. You wouldn't get something like that through customs nowadays, even as an air hostess. They're far too strict.' Bea picks up a handgun from a table. '*This* one was from Cuba. What do we know about this, girls?'

'M1911 point 45,' says Elsie. 'American made.'

'And?'

'We're not allowed to touch it,' says Elsie.

'That's right,' says Bea.

'Why are you here?' Elsie looks up. 'Daddy said he was picking us up.'

'I'm here because I wanted to spend the day with you.' Even though she has invented this reason, she does, she wants to spend the day with the girls. Some of the day at least. They don't have to travel to Spain to spend the day together.

'But Daddy said today was a sleeping day,' says Eleanor.

'Mummy doesn't need sleep any more,' says Luisa.

'And Daddy needs a rest,' says Bea. 'Daddy's been working very hard.'

'Is that what he said?' says Luisa.

'Oh no. Justin never says anything. He just looked exhausted. He thinks I don't know. But I'm his mother.'

'He's having a rest right now.'

'He's okay, then? As far as you know?'

'Justin's fine.'

'And you? Are you okay?' Bea puts a hand on Luisa's arm, and her gaze locks on to Luisa's. The silence is crushing – Luisa swivels her eyes in their sockets to rotate her line of sight away. Still Bea stares. Is this a life-coaching thing?

'Mummy. Your phone is ringing,' says Eleanor. Did she say this to break the silence, thinks Luisa. How does she know to do that? Luisa takes her phone from her bag, the trill louder that usual.

Justin's face is on the screen, Justin's stupid face. A telephone icon with a number 3 next to it indicates this is not the first time he has called. She thumbs the End Call button.

'We need a digital holiday.' Luisa strides over to Bea, stabbing the phone at her for emphasis.

'We're going on holiday?' says Elsie. 'Where?'

'Did you read that story, that article, about digital holidays?' Luisa continues to Bea. This is her again. Taking control. Step two: divert Justin's attempts at communication. 'How we need to spend at least part of our day with our phones switched off. With our phones off and not worrying about who might call us. For our own sanity. They did it with baboons and looked at their brains and found the baboons with less phone use were much healthier. I'm turning mine off now.'

'How do they look at a baboon's brain?' says Bea. 'Fascinating.'

'Phones are like crack. We need times of no contact. To wean us off them.'

'I can't say I'm in the know about crack these days,' says Bea. 'But what about my clients? They need to contact me if something arises.'

'These are the excuses we make to ourselves. Always some reason we cannot switch off, disconnect from the grid.' Luisa can feel adrenaline coursing through her again, the tiredness slipping away. 'Your clients will understand. You can explain to them –you can teach them about digital holidays. Teach them about the mental benefits.'

'So that's why you came,' nods Bea with satisfaction. 'To teach us about digital holidays.'

'Turn it off, Bea.' Luisa is commanding again. Coordinating. This is her, her role – a co-ordinator. A co-ordinator of life.

'I want to go on holiday,' says Elsie. 'Somewhere good though. Not France.'

'This isn't that kind of holiday, sweetie.' Luisa watches Bea hold down the side of her phone and the screen go black.

Elsie is on the verge of tears, and this is so unusual that Luisa's heart dips, a painful lurch downwards. She crouches in front of her. 'But we can have an adventure, lovely. We can all have an adventure now, this afternoon.'

'It's a delight to be on the business end of coaching for once,' says Bea.

'Where are we going?' says Elsie. 'Can I choose?'

*

'Red off, take it around the tree, red on again,' calls Bea from below them on the steps. 'That's what the young man said. Blue on at all times, unless you get to the end.'

'I've got that. Got that.' Luisa holds the ribena, the carabiner, whatever the fuck it's called, in her hand. This is the red one, it's covered in red tape, and Luisa needs to unclip, to unclip and clip on again.

'What is it, Mummy?' says Eleanor.

The girls stand close to her on the wooden platform, so close that Luisa knows that to clip and unclip she must move them backwards, backwards towards the edge of the platform, towards the drop to the ground, the ground far, far below. She looks again at the girls, checks again – yes, they are attached to the cable.

'I'm going over the safety checks,' says Luisa. 'Making sure we're doing everything the man told us in training.' She knows when she unclips the red thing she will be unable to turn, to turn and face the cable bridging the chasm from the tree to the other side of the valley. So there is no point unclipping the red thing. I'm going to stay like this, motionless. I'm fine if I stay here, looking at the girls.

'There's a queue coming up behind,' Bea yells from down the steps. 'Is everyone okay?'

Elsie looks up at Luisa, stares right into her eyes, with what Luisa is certain is an expression of contempt.

'*Are* we okay?' says Elsie.

Is she asking me because she thinks I know the answer? thinks Luisa. Or mocking me because she knows I don't?

'I don't know,' says Luisa. 'Are we?' Luisa snatches a quick look to the side, to the drop, and closes her eyes as her head spins.

'I don't think I want to do it, Mummy,' says Eleanor. 'And I'm not eight. I'm six.'

'It's okay, sweetie.' Luisa grasps the cable tighter.

'Why did grandma say we were eight?'

'Grandma said that?'

'Shall I go first?' Bea swings herself around the tree and steps onto the small section of empty wooden board built around the tree.

Luisa sees a man, the instructor, waving his hands at them from below. Bea waves back.

'I think he's saying there's too many of us up here,' says Luisa.

'I want to go down,' says Eleanor.

'Come on now, says Bea. 'Watch grandma.'

Bea unclips both red and blue carabiners, and steps along the edge of the platform, hand-over-hand, the cable her only attachment. She clips back on ahead of Luisa, sits herself in the canvas strip of the harness, and pushes off.

'Wheeeeee!' The sound descends as Bea disappears into the foliage opposite.

The girls both look to Luisa.

'We don't have to zip wire,' says Luisa. 'No one has to zip wire if they don't want to.' Her voice has upped an octave now, and tears flow down her cheeks. 'I'm sorry,' she says. 'I'm just – I'm scared. I'm a bit scared too.'

'Come on, Ellie.' Elsie takes Eleanor's hand and leads her back around the tree, Eleanor following without question. Luisa watches through blurry eyes as Elsie helps her sister back down the steps, calls ahead to the queue of adults waiting halfway up, explains to them that her and her sister are coming back down. The queue obeys Elsie's demands and descends, the shaven-headed teenage boy at the front smiling as they pass, a caring smile, no sneer. Luisa is still standing on the platform, facing the opposite direction to travel, as her daughters reach the ground, as Elsie points Eleanor toward the wooden cafe. Elsie stops, turns to look up and waves. Luisa waves back, and heads down the steps after her girls.

*

'Sometimes I don't have a head for heights,' Luisa says to Bea later. She knows she could have used the girls as an explanation for her failure to follow Bea along the zip wire, but she is in the grip of an honest streak, clings to the idea that through brazen honesty all these problems might resolve. She has been honest to Justin. Even if she has stolen his car. He hasn't asked if she stole the car. She has made a start by being honest about her feelings. What are her feelings?

She watches the girls in a sandpit, on the other side of the wooden fence from the cafe where she sits with Bea.

'Well, I've done this before,' says Bea. 'Rather different circumstances. It's surprising how it comes back to you, after all those years.'

Luisa vibrates her head, as though shivering with cold.

'Is there anything else? Apart from heights?' For once Bea does not stare into Luisa's eyes as she speaks, and instead at her spoon as she stirs her tea. 'It's not best practice, of course. With family. Too much baggage. Martin never wanted me to coach him. Not that we used to call it coaching. Back then it was just talking. Which he wasn't that keen on, either. But I'm here, now, as life-coach. If that's what's needed.'

Bea is part of my family, thinks Luisa in astonishment. This woman shares the genetic code of my children.

Bea ends her stirring and folds her hands across her stomach, lowers her eyes to her hands and sits completely still. Five, ten seconds pass. Luisa looks at the sandpit again, focuses on the cries of young children, but is drawn back to this grey-haired woman, who still sits without movement. Luisa stares ahead herself, at the untouched coffee in front of her, but cannot hold motionless. The concrete ballast in her limbs forces her down into the chair. She pulls herself up straight, snatches a glance at Bea again.

'I'm tired,' says Luisa. 'With work, this week. Last night – it was crazy. Exciting, but crazy exciting. And what with, with half-term, you know? And shifts, night shifts.' Are any of these answers to Bea's question? Did Bea even ask a question? 'And yes, Justin is tired too. He's finding it – ' She wants to say difficult. How difficult is it for Justin? He has never explained in a way that makes sense.

'And sex?' says Bea.

'What?'

'That's what you mean by tired? That sex is a problem? That sex isn't happening,' says Bea, now animated. 'Usually when my clients say they're tired, they mean they are not having sex. They always admit it in the end. And how does your partner feel about sex?'

'Justin?' I'm not talking to you about sex, thinks Luisa. Not about sex with your son. An image of naked Justin slides into her head, Justin standing by their bed ready to pull himself under the sheet, and Bea is watching, sitting on the purple chair in the bedroom's corner. Unembarrassed. Now the real Bea is motionless again, but her head turned, her eyes fixed on Luisa, an interrogating mannequin. Luisa looks down. Bea rests her hand on Luisa's wrist. She shivers again.

'Justin had a vasectomy,' says Luisa. 'He never asked me. Never told me.'

'Possibly a religious thing,' says Bea. 'Catholic men can have a sense of shame about such matters.'

'But Justin's not Catholic.'

'He is kind of. By bloodline. Perhaps only latently.'

'But if he was Catholic he wouldn't want a vasectomy, would he?'

'Sometimes they're acting out. Rebelling. Against their religious upbringing.'

'But you're not Catholic either.'

'His father was a big Catholic. His biological father. And religion is at least partly passed down through the genes, isn't it? Or so I'm told. I'm only throwing out ideas, here. The cornucopia principle. Throw enough food in the pot and some has to stick. Perhaps it's a self-harm thing. I must stop using the word thing.'

'Justin hasn't harmed himself – '

'Not the teenage variety. The more adult, informed consent type. Which isn't something I would have guessed about him. Although there are many initiation ceremonies that involve what we might term self-harm, I've read them in the literature.' Now Bea is animated again, in her element. 'Perhaps Justin's reason for having a vasectomy is that he feels he hasn't truly become a man. Hasn't entered adulthood. I must take my share of the blame for that, of course. But it might explain the comics, don't you think? And the computer games? I wish I'd known earlier. I'd have recommended a less brutal, more shamanic ritual. Malcolm's a superb shaman. Delicate with a razor. Modern vasectomy is so final, such a brutal cut-off. How can anyone be certain they want no more children? I've often wondered if I might want more myself.'

Bea uses Luisa's wrist to pull herself closer in, close enough to smell her. A flowery, youthful smell. 'Do you think perhaps that's what you want, Luisa?'

'I don't want any more children,' says Luisa. 'And I'm completely sure about that.' She looks over at the girls in the sandpit – Elsie is barring the way of a smaller boy so that Eleanor can climb the slide first.

'Sometimes it's difficult to read even our own bodies.'

'Neither my mind nor my body wants another baby,' says Luisa. 'What my body wants is more sex than it's getting. I want sex, that's all! Why does everyone think I want another baby?'

'Oh, I remember my forties,' says Bea. 'Vividly. So deliciously sleazy in many ways. There's a real forceful energy going on in a woman's body. I often think of those times, like when I'm waiting for a train. Or for the bread to rise. Don't do yourself down for wanting physical fulfilment, Luisa. I've seen that over and over with my clients.'

Is that who I am, now? Am I your client? Am I going to crawl into a duvet in the middle of my kitchen? In the middle of someone else's kitchen?

'If you'll forgive me for relating my personal experience,' says Bea. Oh god, thinks Luisa. 'When I was the age you are now – '

'What?' says Eleanor. 'You mean, when you were a little girl. Tell me.'

Luisa grabs Eleanor around the waist, pulls her onto her lap and holds her tight.

'Not a little girl,' says Bea. 'A big girl. As big as your mum. Bigger. I was saying how when I was in my forties I had so much love inside of me. So much love there was too much just for Grandad Martin.'

'Is that why you had to love Grandad Cuba as well?'

'Oh not Grandad Cuba. He was too busy. It wasn't just grandads.' Bea looks at Luisa, nodding as if giving advice rather than a confession.

'Look,' says Luisa in Eleanor's ear. 'Elsie has a new friend over there.'

Eleanor jumps from her lap and runs off.

'It's perfectly normal, Luisa.' Bea's hand is on her wrist again. Why Bea's hand, why Bea? Why is she not having this conversation with one of her friends? Because she never gets to see her friends. Doesn't really have any friends, not close friends, not any more. Because she is always working. 'Perfectly normal to find men, young men even, attractive.'

'What young men?'

'Young men are very attractive,' says Bea, which is enough of an answer for them both.

'I don't want to sleep with young men,' says Luisa. 'With other men.'

'Everyone needs excitement in their life. At whatever age. I find it exciting, going to Goa, with Ian.'

'You and Ian? Your client Ian?'

'At Christmas. It's become something of a ritual.'

'And you – share a room?'

'Oh yes. You save a lot of money that way.'

'And what about – ' What question will she ask here? Details? Will that *help* her? 'What about, the coach-client relationship?'

'Oh, no one is bothered about that,' laughs Bea. 'It's not like there's a governing body or anything. It's complex, the relationship between clients and their coach.' Bea is more serious now. 'You need a delicate line between professionalism and intimacy. I mean Ian calls me every day but I insist it's always at 4pm. And I'm happy to wrap him in my arms as he cries, but only on a timer. I use the chicken timer from the kitchen, it's more homely.'

'I don't want an affair.' Or to have to plead this to my boyfriend's mother.

'It doesn't have to be sex,' says Bea. 'Just finding that thrill that works for you.'

'I get my excitement from work,' says Luisa. 'It's exciting. Last night's shift – it was thrilling. In its own way.'

'It must be so rewarding, being a midwife.'

'But not only rewarding. Also exciting, in a life-saving way.' Luisa demonstrates with her hands, attaching invisible IV lines. 'It's scary as hell. You might – cause someone to die. You make decisions, decisions that save people's lives, save their babies. Last night, I co-ordinated a bi-manual compression.' She is losing Bea, she can see. 'I was in charge of another midwife compressing a mother's uterus from inside her vagina. Anyway.'

'So you've found an outlet for your feminine powers?'

'Yes. I have.'

Bea is searching in her bag. She pulls out her phone and squeezes the side. 'It's after four – I must check on Ian. Back from holidays.'

'It's a very feminist role,' says Luisa.

Bea's phone trills. 'Oh look. There's Justin now.' She puts the phone to her ear. 'Hello darling. I must be quick. I have a client who – . Oh yes. Of course! She's here with me now.' Bea holds out the phone to Luisa.

Luisa puts the phone to her ear and hears only silence. Perhaps he has gone, cut off. She can say someone cut them off and Bea's phone went dead. There is more silence.

'Hello?' says Luisa.

'It's me,' says Justin.

'Yes.' This is the correct procedure. Re-establish the world one item at a time.

'Are you – okay?'

'I'm.' How to describe her current state of mind? 'It's not clear.'

'I'm fine, by the way.'

His resentment kicks her straight back to her earlier mindset: the wronged wife, the wronged not-wife who's not-husband had a clandestine vasectomy. I'm not a fucking baby machine, she wants to cry out, but she does not, she is sad, sad also because they can be tender to each other, thought they were back to being tender to each other, sad because she stole Justin's car, because the security guard threw Justin and his bloodied genitals to the floor, the genitals that were the origins of their girls. She does not cry out because she is sitting in a cafe in a children's adventure playground.

'Where are you?' She jumps from her chair and heads towards the fence at the back of the cafe.

'At home. And I'm sorry. Sorry that you felt so angry about it. About the vasectomy. I wanted it – over and done with. We talked about it, didn't we? A few years ago?'

'I'm – sorry too. The security guard, he – shouldn't have done that. And he only did because, because I was there. I'm sorry.' Luisa sticks her head between the two wooden struts of the fence, intending to climb through, to stand in the bushes beyond. She tries to fit her leg through the gap at the same time as her head, but it is difficult to manoeuvre, in particular because one of her hands holds a phone. She pulls her leg out again, watched by a young mother and her scottie dog, who is angling to offer his help.

'I don't think the guard throwing me to the floor actually made the pain any worse,' says Justin. 'And the main thing is – it's all done with now, isn't it?' He falls silent.

Is that it? she thinks. A wave of relief sweeps across her, that they have made up, resolved their differences, but the relief wave is too fast, sweeps straight past, off and over the cafe roof, their differences not resolved at all. She is not relieved – only exhausted. She leans over the fence for support.

'You're with the girls, then?' says Justin.

'Yes. With Bea. We're at Treetop Rooftops. I wanted to see the girls.'

'How did you get there? You took the car?'

'No.' She cannot admit to the car, not now. 'Bea drove,' she says, truthfully. She can tell him later. Since it wasn't stealing. You can't steal your own car, a car you are insured to drive. Any policeman would confirm that. She remembers the Peugeot, abandoned in the ditch. Maybe he is talking about the Peugeot? Joyriders took the Peugeot, like before.

'You can't drive our car,' she says. 'Joyriders vandalised our car, remember? No one can drive it.' This feels so clever, so cunning a turn around of his question she needs to suppress a giggle, until she remembers that it wasn't actually joyriders who vandalised their car, but her. Her and Justin. That was fun. Was that the last occasion they had fun?

'Someone's stolen the courtesy car,' says Justin. 'From the clinic car park.'

He sounds so sad. She tries to think of something to console him, but the obvious words of comfort are *I took both of the cars, and abandoned one on a busy roadside where it is probably causing an accident as we speak*.

'So you didn't take it?' says Justin. 'I can't find the keys.'

'I can't drive after a night shift,' says Luisa. 'I'm too tired.'

'I'll have to call the police again. I must have dropped the keys.'

'Or this time it *was* joyriders,' says Luisa. Maybe joyriders are a catch-all excuse for all any middle-aged misdemeanours. Maybe joyriders don't even exist.

'It doesn't matter,' says Justin. 'It's only a car. Cars. So long as we're all okay. The vasectomy's done with and we're all okay with it. Aren't we?'

She remembers the clinic, her anger.

'But are you okay?' says Justin.

'You did believe me when I said I didn't want more children?' says Luisa. 'You know I don't want any more, don't you?' She turns to look at the woman with the scottie and decides she doesn't care what she or the dog think. 'My libido. Wanting more sex. Why do you think this is me wanting to be pregnant again?'

'It was only a – '

'Don't you remember? I wasn't exactly keen on being pregnant with the girls. I mean, god, I love the girls, and now I – couldn't imagine. But I'm not one of those crazed maternal people.' The woman with the dog is on her feet now, walking back over towards the tables closer to the cafe. Fuck you, thinks Luisa, and raises her voice. 'It was you who was more keen on having them, remember? Don't you remember? We even – I mean I don't want to even think about it now, but you know? I got the phone number.'

'I was pleased!' cries Justin. 'I mean I don't want any more children now. But I was so pleased when you got pregnant. I don't think I've said that before. But – you know, I love you Luisa – and back then, before you were pregnant, it felt – like we were drifting. Drifting apart, doing different things. And I hated that. You were, you know, you were doing midwife training, and I was out, clubbing all the time. But it wasn't what I wanted. I wanted to spend time with you. But you were, you were always on shifts, or tired from shifts, or doing coursework. So when you got pregnant I was really pleased.

And we spent more time together again. It was about us again.'

The wealth of additional information has overfilled her brain. Luisa sits down with her back against the fence.

'So you mean – you mean having children was good for you because it meant we would spend more time together?'

'Yes. I – '

'Because it meant I wouldn't be working? As a midwife?'

'Yes. Well I mean, partly. Having children was something we did together. You didn't work as much and I stopped going out.'

'I didn't work at all.'

'No. Well you couldn't.'

'So my having the twins meant I was stuck at home where you could spend time with me when you wanted. With the bonus feature of my being some kind of drugs minder stroke nanny because you weren't adult enough to know when to stop.'

Justin emits a noise like a small poodle pushing a very heavy weight.

'That's not – fair,' he says.

'In what way?' Luisa is up on her feet, her mind clear, her words lucid. She is ready – ready to perform an emergency caesarean. 'You've always hated midwifery. You told me so only a couple of nights ago. You couldn't handle my being a woman with an empowering job? Is it because you can't be part of it? Because it's something I can do that you can't? It's pathetic. I didn't realise you thought that way. Is that you?'

Justin is silent for so long Luisa checks her phone to see he is still on the call.

'What the fuck do you want from me?' cries Justin, and his loss of temper, not the violence of the reaction, but the rarity of his anger reminds her that the threads that hold the world, her world together are tenuous, and she almost says down the phone, *don't, let's stop*. Night has fallen without her noticing, except it hasn't, she's standing in the muddy shade of the woods on the other side of the fence.

'It's not like just any job, is it?' says Justin, only a little quieter. 'You work nights, and weekends, and sometimes they tell you which nights and weekends only a couple of weeks before, and what does that mean for the rest of us? For me and the girls? How can we plan fucking anything? Are we supposed to wait around doing nothing, in case your shifts change – in case the hospital decide that it's more important for you to be there, instead? Even when you're here, at home, you're not really here, you're thinking about being there, at the fucking hospital, resting up beforehand, or recovering or whatever. And I, sometimes when I've been working all week, maybe I'd like to hang out with my family, my whole family, including Madam Midwife. At the weekend, and not sit in a fucking playground on my own the whole time! Otherwise what does that make us – equal business partners in a twenty-four-hour child-minding service?'

'I'm a midwife! Someone has to be! Don't you know it's an important job? And I'm good at it!' The decibel level of Luisa's voice catches her by surprise. 'What do you think will happen otherwise, women will give birth on their own? Someone has to do the work.'

'I just wish it wasn't my girlfriend,' says Justin.

'And what if every midwife's partner felt the same?'

'They still have partners?'

'Many of them do!'

'Perhaps it's a job for single people.'

'So now you're socially engineering the lives of – '

'I don't know! I don't have an answer!' cries Justin. 'But it's like your work is organised by Salvador Dali, a really drunk Dali. I don't want to be part of it. I didn't choose to be part of it.'

'I've only been back eight weeks! When have you given it a chance?'

'What's going to change? How's it ever going to change?'

There is a silence – she expects him to continue speaking, he thinks it her turn.

'You think I'm selfish, then,' says Luisa.

'I never thought you were selfish. Never. You're the least selfish person I know.'

'Do you know how jealous I was of you at work when the girls were small?' she launches back into wanton rage, with immediate regret, but there is no pulling back. 'That you got to leave the house? That you got paid, paid for having a shit at work? My god.'

'But why this work? Why the least child-friendly job ever?' To her relief he is shouting too. 'What kind of person continues in a job that expects so much of them? That treats all of us so unreasonably?'

'Stop telling me what I should and shouldn't do! Maybe I don't like you telling me what's good for me or not!'

Now a bona fide silence falls, and the thunder inside her head subsides, washes down her body and out, leaves her ravaged. She sits heavily on a tree stump.

'Luisa,' says Justin, and though she can hear the tears in his voice she finger-punches the screen and leans forward, head on her knees.

*

'Always good to bring it out in the open,' says Bea as Luisa sits back at the table.

'Can we go home?' says Luisa. 'Actually I was wondering if you'd mind taking us home. Instead of me. Instead of Justin. Justin asked it you wouldn't mind. If you would mind.'

'So what am I doing again?'

'Taking us home. Please. Take us somewhere else.' She needs to be somewhere else, where Justin is, she needs to rage, rage at Justin.

'Anywhere?' says Bea.

'Not anywhere.' Mustn't say things like that to Bea. 'Take us home, please, Bea.'

'Justin isn't picking them up?'

Luisa looks over at the girls, at Elsie explaining some point of order regarding sandcastles to a small boy in red shorts. I should be with the girls, she thinks, and remembers the tree, her fear. She wants to tell Elsie how well she did leading Eleanor down the tree, out of danger. Away from danger, because she, Luisa is danger.

'He doesn't have a car,' she tells Bea. He doesn't have a car because I stole it.

'Perhaps he's not able to drive. Too much wrenching of the lower body after the brutalising.'

'He can drive. He's just lost all the cars.'

'Then I can do. Not a problem.'

'I have to go to work,' lies Luisa. She cannot go home, not now. Even the image of the house in her mind defeats her, is the stage for an argument with Justin she cannot win, does not want to win, is not an argument that has a winner. She needs to be somewhere else. Needs to be someone else. 'In fact would it be okay if you dropped me in town? The town centre. I'm going into town first.'

Bea drives back to town as though ferrying a consignment of medical supplies to the city centre's bombed out field hospital. With one hand out the open window, she waves back pedestrians who risk zebra crossings, and creates an additional outside lane at traffic lights where the road planners have clearly advised one was plenty.

'I don't need to be at the hospital right away,' says Luisa.

'Got it,' says Bea. 'City centre drop off, yes?'

'Yes. Thank you.' Why has she chosen the city centre as her destination? What will happen now, with the rest of her life? Tina, she remembers. I'm supposed to go out with Tina! Luisa is suddenly delighted. I'm *meant* to be going out with Tina. Wasn't Tina going to call me, to let me know the arrangements? She pulls out her phone to see if she has any missed messages.

Still up for tonight? she texts to Tina.

Did Tina even take my number? She might read the text but not know the sender.

It's Luisa by the way. In case you don't have my number in your phone.

She'll think I mean meet later, if we're going clubbing she won't want to meet until much later. What will I do until then?

Had a slight change of plan, she swipes, then deletes the first two words and sends. More punchy, more spontaneous. **Can we hook up a bit earlier?** she adds.

That still doesn't mean now, does it, she thinks as she taps send. That's still leaving me in town.

Can we meet up for a chat beforehand?

She inserts the word 'girly' before 'chat', deletes it, swipes it in again, presses send. Looks at the green rectangles stacked on top of one another.

That's five texts. Five beeps. Don't send more texts. Tina won't reply to that, will she? Would I reply to that? But I'm not Tina.

Luisa looks over her shoulder at the girls in the back seat. Neither appear at all perturbed as their grandmother takes a corner that makes Luisa feel weightless. She winds down her window and leans out her head. The rush of air pushes her hair behind her.

Bea pulls up in the bus stop by the clock tower and Luisa jumps out, actually jumps out with both feet on the pavement together, and slams the door.

'I'll see you later,' she calls to the girls. But they cannot hear her through the glass, and Luisa pulls open the sliding door as Bea slams into first.

'Wait a second, Bea! You going to be okay, lovelies?' Luisa climbs on her knees into the back, gripping the corner of the fabric between their seats for support.

'Will we see you in the morning?' says Elsie. They both look at her with the same frown, as though they have discussed this interrogation beforehand, and decided it should fall to Elsie to ask.

'Of course.' If they plead with me, she thinks, if it's really heart-rending I'll tell them I won't go to work, that I'm going home with them. I don't have to go out. I have no one to go out with, anyway. She clambers further into the van, hugs and kisses Eleanor, then Elsie.

'Love you,' she says, as evenly as she can manage.

Elsie giggles.

'What?' says Luisa.

'Your hair's gone crazy.'

The people carrier is gone, and Luisa is alone by the clock tower. A backpacker on the first leg of their travels, feeling homesick. With insufficient luggage. She checks her phone.

It hasn't been long, she thinks. Give her time to consider options. Time to finish a shower, end a phone call, make some food. She tries to picture Tina doing these tasks, watches her movements, analysing the time they take, time before she will be able to look at her phone, but the mental images are fuzzy, with someone else playing the role of Tina.

Luisa crosses at the lights to the cafés opposite the shopping centre, pushes on the door of the one nearest. A man through the glass holds his palms up to her and smiles apologetically. She checks her phone: 18:15. Still no message. She hurries down the line of shops, all the cafés are closed or closing, except at the end: Starbucks: 9am–8pm. Thank god for multinational companies gunning to corner the market.

'What can I get you?' asks the barista. No queue, she thinks. I could have used a queue. Should I drink coffee? If I'm going out, if Tina calls and we're going out, we're going out out, coffee is a great idea. But if she doesn't? Then I want to sleep, then I can sleep. I'll book a room at the Premier Inn. I'll do that now! I can walk to the Premier Inn, ask for a room, and lie on a Premier Inn bed. No one would know. Turn off my phone, turn it off because I'm at work. Will Justin know I've been to a Premier Inn? Who cares?.

'What would you like?' says the barista in an identical tone. He is sharp, professional, even though only a teenager.

'I ought to go home,' says Luisa.

'So a quick coffee to go?' The barista moves a cardboard cup to the centre of the counter in readiness.

'I don't think I want coffee.' What Justin said about wanting to spend more time with me when I was pregnant, wasn't that rather sweet? In a disturbing, patriarchal way? Maybe I'm an undercover feminist. Didn't I read about that somewhere? That was an economist. An undercover feminist, do they surprise people with unexpected feminist remarks? Or are they expressing their feminism in the background, in secret, with no one knowing? Is that different from not being a feminist? Like Justin, the undercover patriarch. Fuck Justin.

'Perhaps something else?' The barista's corporate facade is showing signs of wear, his training inadequate for this level of customer interaction. He looks over Luisa's shoulder. 'Perhaps you want to decide whilst I serve someone else.'

Luisa turns – there is no one behind her.

'A tea?' he says.

'I don't think I want anything.'

'Okay.' He grabs hold of a cloth, rubs at a corner of the coffee machine's casing.

'I'll have a coffee.' Tina and I, we made a plan. She checks the screen of her phone again. Why would Tina have changed her mind? As far as Tina is concerned we've always been going out tonight. We needed to firm up the arrangements. 'But I need to receive a message, a text, first.' She holds up her phone to the barista. 'To know if I want a coffee.'

Luisa wants to sit down, but that feels rude, rude to sit down before she has bought a drink. Why the hell shouldn't I sit down? I didn't ask this company to fill our high street with their massive coffee chain? I'll sit where I like. She moves to a booth by the window, sits on the edge of the red cushioned horseshoe, her phone held out before her to demonstrate that this is only a temporary sit, that soon the phone will tell her whether coffee drinking is a necessary part of her night. The booth seat is comfortable, so comfortable. She tilts herself over, until first her calves touch the seat edge, and lowers herself onto her back. She is hidden, almost, most of her body between the upright of the booth seat and the table. I wonder if anyone can see me, she thinks, and places her cheek down on the seat.

'Madam,' says the barista, and Luisa starts. She opens her eyes to see him standing by her legs, looking side-to-side. 'Madam, you can't go to sleep there.'

'No.' Luisa jerks upright, brushes her legs without knowing why, and stands. She pulls her phone up – no message. 'I really can't go to sleep. I don't – I will have that coffee. I think I've decided I will. A latte.'

'I'm afraid I'll have to ask you to leave.'

'Really? Oh. Okay. That's fine. I'm sorry.' She strides to the door, the barista close behind. 'I've got it.'

'Madam?' The barista hands her her bag.

Luisa is on the pavement, on the street. 'I'm sorry,' she says again to the barista. 'I'm sorry about that. I work nights. Night shifts.'

'And you're – going to work now?'

'Yes. I am. I'm a midwife.'

'Aw. That must be such a rewarding job!' The barista sighs. 'I can still make you a coffee, if you wanted,' he says. 'You could – wait here? I'll bring it out to you?'

'I don't need coffee.'

Luisa strides east, moving quickly, takes the crossings on red, judging the traffic, timing her runs. Still striding, she pulls her phone from her pocket again. No message. I'm not going out with Tina. I've pinned my hopes on her, pinned my hopes on someone who, if the few interactions at school are anything to go by, would not only win the award for flakiest parent, but display the certificate at home.

This is a trigger point. A singularity, is that what they're called? Where all the forces align, to form a point, or a curve? Where all the events, all the fucked-up elements of my life intersect, time slows down, and each important moment occurs at the same instant. Or something. It doesn't matter what a singularity is, except that this feels like one.

She realises she is walking in the direction of the hospital, but even with this realisation it makes no difference to her direction or the speed of her pace. I'm going somewhere to be of help, where they know I can help, she thinks. And before long there she is under the covered walkway of the multistorey car park, the familiar dark eeriness.

'Hey Luisa,' says a voice behind her. It is Carmen, one of the newly qualified midwives. 'Where are you tonight? Labour? Postnatal?'

'I'm not really sure,' says Luisa.

'They haven't told you?'

'I'm not on duty. But I thought I'd play it safe. Be here in case. They couldn't call me. Because I'm on a digital holiday. No phones.'

'Do I have to do that?' Carmen moves her own phone from her palm back into her bag.

'It's healthier,' says Luisa. 'Not always being on call. Not available. I'm not available. I'm seeing – how far I can take it,' continues Luisa. 'Besides, if you phone you can never get hold of anyone. Why should I put myself out? That's part of it. And I was passing. After last night – ' Luisa describes all the events of the previous night, follows Carmen as she moves into the lift lobby. The story is filling her again, filling her with its energy. She strides ahead of Carmen to thump the button for the lift.

'That sounds – well, most of it sounds terrible. Not terrible. But scary,' says Carmen as they wait for the lift.

'It is. It was terrible. And it's not right, is it, that we do terrible things?'

cries Luisa. 'I mean we help with terrible things, that we help people when terrible things happen to them. That we help them but it has terrible consequences for us. We can't even have sex, there's no time for sex.' The force of her words has edged Carmen into the corner of the lobby. 'I mean do you have time to have sex? Plus I want to go out and have fun.'

Carmen is crying, and Luisa wants to apologise, but understands that Carmen's tears are, in fact, some kind of answer in themselves. 'Sometimes this place is so, so stressful,' says Carmen, not to Luisa, but to the opening lift door. Carmen steps in, and Luisa follows.

'Sometimes I can't even bear to look in the off-duty to check when I'm working,' sobs Carmen. 'It makes me actually feel sick.'

'Why is it even called the off-duty?' says Luisa. 'Off-duty is when you're not working! We shouldn't allow this place to tell us when we're not working! Sorry. What I mean is – I don't know what I mean.'

Luisa takes a tissue from her bag, hands it to Carmen. The noise of Carmen sobbing and gulping sounds in rhythm with the lift cables as they ascend through each floor, both noises shut off by the ding of arrival.

'Maybe it's not for you,' says Luisa. 'Being a midwife.'

'Of course it's for me!' cries Carmen. 'What would I do with myself if I wasn't a midwife?'

Carmen steps out, turns to look back. Luisa shakes her head, presses the button for the ground floor, and watches Carmen disappear in the narrowing gap.

FRIDAY NIGHT: OFF OFF DUTY

Luisa stomps back down the hill, along the main road towards town. She passes a bus stop, turns and comes back to the empty shelter, where she sits for a few moments, examining the display. The next bus is due in three minutes.

That's my bus, she thinks. I don't need to carry on walking. Why am I walking? The decision made, she relaxes into the seat, only for all her muscles to tense again.

Take the bus to where? To the end of the line? Where will I go, sit on a bus until it stops? She pulls out her phone to check the time. To see how much time until morning?

Hey babe, says the text from Tina. **Sounds like a plan.**

Luisa hits the call button, and the phone is answered after a single ring.

'Hey, Tina!' says Luisa.

'Well hello you,' says Tina.

Don't sound boring. 'God it's been a really shit-fucking crazy day. You wouldn't believe it.' She decides not to risk any kind of silence and plunges on. 'I nearly got assaulted by a security guard. At an abortion clinic. And this afternoon I found myself forty-foot up a tree. And now I can't go home, don't want to go home. I told Justin, told him a bit of a lie, that I'm working, popping babies out tonight.' Pathetic, or interesting? Eccentric, maybe too much. Bring it down. 'Just want to get that first glass of wine in me. Wondered if you'd be up for it. Before we go out later.'

'Sure, babe. Come on round.'

'Cool. See you soon. So – what's your address?' Luisa changes tone to a little pixie voice.

'14 Station Terr-ace,' Tina sings back in a matching voice. Is that joining in or taking the piss?

'Ok, see you!' Luisa says into a dead phone.

*

Half an hour later Luisa follows Tina down the stairs into the basement of her house, clutching a bottle of prosecco to her chest. The walk into town has sapped the energy she had saved for conversation – to say any string of words now requires several seconds of pre-analysis for sense and interest. She wonders if she is the only person Tina has invited, and which answer she prefers. Tina's long, wrap-around skirt, with multi-coloured curves of sequins spiralling down from her waist, suggests to Luisa that a party has been in progress for some days downstairs, that she is one in a rotating stream of international partygoers.

The basement kitchen is empty, both of people and furnishings: an enormous, almost entirely bare cavern with lights embedded all across the ceiling.

'Lots of lights,' says Luisa. 'Lots of light, I mean.' She runs her hand down the exposed brick wall next to the stairs, and crumbs of mortar rub off on her fingers. Perhaps it's not meant to be exposed. She pulls her hand back to the comfort of the wine bottle.

'Boris has this thing about Vitamin D,' says Tina. 'He claims he never gets to see sunlight. Which if you ask me is his own fucking fault for becoming obsessed with the Tokyo stock market. He keeps banging on about getting multiple sclerosis. Hence, all these special bulbs which costs a fortune and come from Oslo or somewhere ridiculous.' She holds a hand to the lights like a compere introducing the next act.

Luisa can't decide where to move, where to position herself. There's so much room in the room. She puts her bag down on a sofa by the crumbly wall, moves to the brightly lit work surface in the centre, which feels too far away from her bag. She hugs the prosecco.

'So what's this about a security guard?' Tina is at the fridge, has her own bottle of prosecco out, and two glasses held in her other hand. Luisa can see food inside the fridge, back lit and inviting. When did she last eat a proper meal?

'The abortion clinic?' says Tina. 'One of yours?'

Perhaps I should say yes. 'No,' says Luisa. 'Justin. It was Justin.'

'Ergh. So he knocked someone up? What, and it turned a bit nasty?'

'No.' Luisa wonders at the story Tina has concocted. 'No, they do – vasectomies there as well. He was – he was there for a vasectomy.'

'Oh.' Tina does not say *boring*, but might as well have done. She has opened her prosecco without Luisa noticing and is vaping with one hand whilst pouring into two champagne flutes on the counter. Tina pushes a full glass in front of Luisa. Sip, don't drink it all, she thinks. Luisa looks at her drink, at each of the walls, and takes a gulp of wine.

'It's not a big deal,' says Luisa to fill the silence. The story of her day has lost its sheen of amusing gossip. 'It's not like I want any more kids, anyway.'

'Amen to that.'

'But enough about me.' Luisa's laugh disappears into the corner shadows.

'You sure?'

'I didn't come round to pour out all my woes on you like some lovelorn teenager.' Is that what she's doing? Is lovelorn what she is?

'Get it out there if you like.'

'Sorry?'

'Spit it all out. Isn't that what we do, us women? Spill the beans, show our vulnerabilities? Showing your vulnerabilities is what allows intimacy.'

This is so obviously a line Tina has read somewhere that Luisa looks around for the source book.

'What's on your mind, babe?' Tina puts a hand on top of Luisa's.

Tears well in Luisa's eyes. 'That's not why I'm here. To tell you all my stuff.'

'Why not?'

The story flows out of Luisa, edited for style: fewer child anxieties and near-death midwifery, more car vandalism and failed bondage and bawling out a vasectomy surgeon.

'And so why is it you're together?' says Tina.

'With Justin?'

'There must be a reason to stay. Or you want someone to tell you to go?'

'I – don't want to go.'

'You need to find your commonalities.' Tina steps from her stool and pulls Luisa into a hug which is so unexpected Luisa almost tips over in her own seat. 'You know what we do? Me and Boris? We make certain to continue the shared pleasures we once had. B.I. Before Isobel.'

'I want that. That's what I want.'

'Because before, it was about me and Boris, we were everything. And Isobel comes along, and there's three, and our little triad is everything. But it's not everything. You must also maintain the dyad, the adult dyad, and remember what there was before, before all this – shit.' Tina throws up her arms, as if to indicate the kitchen, the house, perhaps the whole country. 'And because, you know, everyone's different, I totally accept that, I totally accept other people have a different point of view' – she totally doesn't, thinks Luisa – 'but for us, the commonalities, our commonalities – they're all about getting wasted. We've been there together, through all those times getting wasted. I mean there are so many *stories*.'

'We used to,' says Luisa. 'We did that. We used to have fun. That's what I want Justin and I to do again. When I was, when he, when I got pregnant, he got on this completely clean kick, he didn't want to, you know, do stuff any more. We've done nothing more exciting than drink wine since before the girls.'

'Don't think it's all sweetness and light with me and Boris.'

'Oh, I didn't mean that – '

'Everyone has their problems. You deal with it the way you know how. You know what I do when I'm really pissed off with him? I go out and fuck a couple of guys.'

'A – couple?' She tries to imagine Tina seducing two attractive young men at once, and it is all too easy, tableau after tableau popping into her mind. Perhaps Tina is some kind of radical, the kind for whom normal rules of sex or parenting hold no sway.

'One can be a bit hurtful,' says Tina. 'Two's not such a biggie because it's unsustainable. It you do two they know there's nothing emotional in it.'

Is that two together, thinks Luisa? Or consecutively?

'Hungry?' says Tina.

'Little, yeah.' She is starving.

Onto the counter Tina places two bowls of Monster Munch, and an open box stuffed to the brim with half-eaten cakes. The side of the box says 'Claridges' in a delicate font.

'I can't stand waste,' says Tina. 'A mate and I helped the editor of *Men's Health* with his plumbing, and he took us there for tea to say thanks. Everyone leaves so much. I'm not letting all that go to waste. What would the hotel do with it? Feed it to the Filipino waiters?'

This contains so many clues to Tina, but there is no time to sift them, since a half-eaten bowl of ravioli has arrived on the counter.

Tina adds a long rectangular platter of white stringy vegetable to the collection of food.

'Sauerkraut and olives. I can't get enough at the moment.'

Tina digs in with a fork, without offering one to Luisa. Luisa pulls the ravioli bowl towards her, feeds the squares into her mouth with her fingers. Casual, she thinks, pleasantly casual, none of that nonsense of etiquette. She pinches a handful of sauerkraut off the platter whilst Tina is still forking her own. Cold ravioli and sauerkraut is delicious.

'How can you be down here with no music?' Boris has entered the room without Luisa noticing. He is short and completely bald, wearing a black t-shirt with tresor.berlin stamped in white across the front, and goes straight to a black speaker stack in one of the room's alcoves. The music he chooses has a clean, crisp bass and he turns the volume to just below the level at which it would be impossible to hear each other speak.

'So you're the famous twins' mum?' cries Boris, coming over to the counter.

'That's me.' Luisa turns to him and he kisses her on the cheek. His smile contains the remnants of a snarl, an expression Luisa imagines he has fixed in position while on the phone to investment bankers in Tokyo.

'Hi. Boris.' Boris shakes her hand as well, turns to Tina and brushes her lips with his own. 'Hey, babe. So. We're making a night of it?' he says, back at Luisa.

'Think so.' She is pleased by his presence, somehow.

'Always good to hook up with some other parents. I don't do the school run so much, with work and all. Some of those mums, they're a bit scary.

Don't think they really want to talk to me.'

'There's a quite a few guys there, nowadays.'

'And of course their teacher Mr Brosnan is a man. Unusual in a primary school,' says Boris, as though he's recently published a survey of the current gender split in education. 'And with him also being gay.' Boris pulls up a stool next to Luisa, pours himself half a glass of prosecco. 'And I love the way the kids are all completely cool with it. All excited about him getting married.'

'Oh god, tell me about it,' says Tina. 'Isobel was up all one night crying because she wanted to be his bridesmaid.'

'But still very cool,' says Boris.

This is cool, thinks Luisa. A glass of wine with new friends, talking about modern gender politics, all as a polite precursor to going out dancing. Proper dancing.

Boris moves to a leather-topped desk in one corner, and Luisa watches him take a large bunch of keys from his pocket, unlock the top drawer and bring a blue cash box back over to the counter. He finds a different key and unlocks the box.

Luisa smells the sweet odour of grass. But that's too big a box for just grass, she thinks. There has to be more inside.

'I mean god, people were so homophobic where I grew up.' Boris takes a baggie of white powder from one of the coin compartments in the removable top layer.

'No coke,' says Tina. 'You promised.'

That's right, no coke, thinks Luisa. I'm not taking coke with Tina and Boris. She sways to one side, dizzy. But I'm so tired.

'Let's stick with some nice MDMA. Don't you think, Boris?' The way Tina uses his name makes Luisa wonder if this is one of their own particular brand of domestic issues. Perhaps an objection to coke is another of Tina's moral issues, in solidarity with oppressed Bolivian coca growers and their exploitation by cartels. Luisa is still thinking about this when she is distracted by the huge pile of crushed crystals that Boris tips onto the counter from a different bag.

You used to like this, thinks Luisa. Dancing, MDMA and dancing – where has that gone? All gone the way of good character? What the fuck is good character? I'm so tired.

'I mean,' says Boris, 'hands up, I was too.' Boris holds his thick hands up in the air. 'The guys I hung around with back then, we were essentially skinheads. We were happy to go about gay-bashing. Mainly verbal, but you know. And look at me now.'

Luisa does look at Boris, scrutinizes his face, and sees a man who still looks capable of small-scale violence, if ten years younger and not spooning sauerkraut from Cath Kitson tableware. Is that a large drug collection? If police were to burst into the kitchen right now, would they arrest me as an accessory, would I get a record? If I don't get a record how would the National Midwifery Council ever know? She tries to count all the bags in the cash tray. No, that's an okay amount. So long as the main compartment isn't also full of bags. Though maybe I should go home now. That's okay. I can say I'm tired and I need to go home. I *am* tired and I do need to go home. I'm not going home though, am I?

'You never worry about, you know, Isobel coming in?' says Luisa.

'Nope, all sorted. She's at my mum's. In London.' Boris grins, the snarl catching the edge of his mouth again. 'Uh huh huh,' he Elvis-es.

That shows responsibility, doesn't it? thinks Luisa. 'So we're going out?' she says. 'Out out? To Cable?'

'We're proper adults, aren't we?' says Tina. 'We can do whatever we like.'

'I might wait,' says Luisa. 'I always come up really quickly. With MDMA. I want to be good for the club. You know, for dancing.'

'Oh, don't worry, we always start with a little,' says Tina. 'These days I need a little earlier on. To ensure I stay awake til the clubs actually open.' She laughs. 'What will we be like in our fifties?'

Luisa laughs along with her, with Tina. Perhaps she means in our fifties we'll need a lot *more* drugs in order to actually go out. Luisa looks again at the three piles Boris is crafting with a credit card.

'When I think of some of the things *I* used to say about gay people,' says Tina. 'Makes me cringe. But I mean everything's changed. *I've* changed. If anyone's asking me, I subscribe to the Gore Vidal view of homosexuality: no such thing as gay people, simply gay acts.'

'Some *very* gay acts,' laughs Boris. 'But amen to that.'

'Ever kissed a girl, Luisa?' says Tina.

'Guests first,' says Boris, and offers up the three piles.

I'm not working, am I? thinks Luisa. What fucking business does the hospital have, saying what I can and can't do when I'm not working? She wets her index finger on her tongue and dabs at the smallest pile of crystals. Instantly Tina and Boris sweep away the remaining two.

'Bleaaargh!' cry Tina and Boris in unison, and now the powder is in her mouth Luisa recalls the disgusting taste, the chemical violence.

'Get it down quick!' cries Boris, and it has become a game, a childhood game of giggling at bodily functions.

Luisa takes a swig of prosecco and dabs up the remains of the pile into her mouth, washes it down with another swig.

'To us, tonight!' Tina raises her glass, and they all clink.

'And to the end of homophobia,' says Boris.

*

What *is* dancing? thinks Luisa. She faces the crumbly basement wall and moves her feet so that with each repetition the edging of her trainer aligns with the border of the curved aura of a ceiling light. She looks down at her arms, it isn't clear they are her arms. One foot left, back again right, palms depressing pistons to either side of her, all her limbs moving without thought, without her having to tell them where to go. So natural, so fluid.

'Yeah!' shouts Boris, from a distant hollow on the other side of the room, separated from her by the thunderous beats emitting from the speakers. Luisa turns, circling round, utilising the same foot patterns, widening the reach of her feet each time to take her closer to Boris and Tina. Boris' eyes look up to the ceiling, upwards but squeezed tight shut, Tina alternates pointy hands towards his body, conducting his movements as he gyrates one way and back again. In unison they turn to Luisa: and grin, wide, welcoming grins, that cause her to pick up her movements, her legs higher, shoulders in motion, wiggling her way over to them with looser movements attached to each bass thump. This is dancing, she thinks. The dance switch is flicked.

The music dips down to only bass, and a new track begins, a tune Luisa recognises, recognises so well but for which she has no word labels. I love this, she says to Tina, but Tina doesn't notice her speak, or perhaps Luisa has not actually spoken, or perhaps she has spoken but no words have come out of her mouth, or perhaps she has spoken and words have come out of her mouth but they are inaudible, inaudible because Boris is skipping back from the amp where he has cranked the music even louder. Now they are locked in a triangle, each of them ensuring they fulfil their dance floor position, micro adjustments of their feet keeping the triangle intact.

'Here,' says Boris, 'it's coming.' He grabs first Tina's hand, then Luisa's, pulls them towards him. This isn't it, thinks Luisa, I don't think this is it. I know this tune. The music drops to, what is that, a conga drum? She knows the word conga but can't remember if it's a drum. Isn't conga a line dance? I'm really rather hot, she thinks. Tina grins at her, a genuine, friendly smile, an expression Luisa has never seen on her before.

A chorus of female voices: 'Cuh-uh-um. To-oo-ge-ther as wuh-uh-un!' Luisa sees Tina and Boris' mouths make the shape of the words, they sing to each other, turn and repeat the line to Luisa, Boris lifting their hands into the air for the second repetition, Boris and Tina sounding as though they are not just singing along, but actually are this angelic choir of voices. Who are, who were these women? Do they realise what incredible art they have made, art that will last through all time, that will last as a high point of human creative achievement?

Boris has disappeared, Tina has an arm around Luisa's shoulder, their faces raised to the ceiling. This is it, thinks Luisa. All I need, right here, right now. That's a great song title. Perhaps that is a song title. Yes, it is. She repeats the chorus line again with Tina. Why don't I sing more often? And without warning the song reduces to silence, and Luisa feels awkward all over again, awkward at rest. She looks about her for an explanation – why would anyone want to switch the music off now? Has Boris switched the music off?

'Just what is it that we want to do?' cry the speakers without warning.

'We want to get loaded!' Boris stabs a finger at her, a van driver indicating her appalling piece of parking. He has been over at the counter, but now he is back, Luisa is glad he is back, pleased at the reformation of their triangle. To her relief the bass line begins, and she can return her limbs to a comfortable, natural state, that of moving in time to music. Tina has an arm around her waist and leans her head on Luisa's shoulder.

'I am *so* glad you're here,' Tina says, very close to Luisa's ear. 'So good to meet other people, other parents who like to do something. Something other than talk about their child's fucking food intolerance.'

Luisa puts an arm around Tina and hugs her. 'Me too. Me too.' They release their grip on each other, open up to Boris.

'Thigh toot?' Boris says to Tina.

'Go on then.' Tina moves to the dark red sofa at the side of the room, sweeping her glass from the counter en route, and Boris follows, right behind her. She sits at an end of the sofa, brings one leg up to lie along the sofa cushions, and divides the split in her skirt so it fully exposes the skin of her other leg.

Luisa laughs, though is unsure why, and she takes up dancing again, straight back to effortless movement, rotating around, angling herself away from a view of the sofa. What are they doing? But she is more concerned they have gone, that she has lost her dancing gang.

'What the hell is a thigh toot?' shouts Luisa.

'Watch,' grins Boris, and Luisa dances over to the sofa. She is gyrating in a holding pattern as Boris kneels between Tina's legs, and taps the side of the bag of MDMA over the horizontal plane of Tina's thigh. More drugs, thinks Luisa, they're doing more drugs. I don't need more drugs, and she turns away, but not before she sees Boris' enormous protruding tongue, moving up Tina's thigh, lapping up the crystals.

'Tickly!' laughs Tina, and as she wriggles her glass sloshes prosecco onto the floor. Luisa laughs, and laughs and dances and laughs.

'Over to you,' says Boris. He stands arms open wide, one hand indicating to Luisa a new pile of crystals on Tina's thigh. For her? Luisa imagines the wry grins she and Tina will show each other in the playground on Monday. On Monday?

'I shouldn't do any more,' says Luisa.

'What!' cries Boris, a priest whose favourite parishioner has refused communion.

'All ready and waiting,' sing-songs Tina, and jiggles her thigh.

This is a test, thinks Luisa. 'I think I'm good. I'm really – I'm really out of it.'

'Long night ahead of us, babe,' says Tina, and grabs hold of Luisa's hand. Boris is across the room, pumping his arms down from the shoulder. Tina pulls Luisa to sit down beside her, and Luisa falls heavily on the edge of the cushion.

'Careful there,' grins Tina, shifting her bare leg.

'Sorry.' Luisa slips off the sofa cushion, down to the wooden floor, onto her knees. I should do a bit more, she thinks, I've got to stay up for god knows how many more hours. I haven't slept properly for – forever. I don't want to be rude.

She leans in towards Tina's leg, towards her black knickers. I have my face close to women's vaginas all the time, don't I? Though this is unusually close. Don't look up. How long have I been down here? With one sweeping motion she licks all the crystals onto her tongue.

'Bleearrgghh!' Luisa pulls up her head. 'The taste, it's that taste!' She wafts her hand in front of her mouth.

'Here.' Tina takes a big gulp of her prosecco, leans down, and with one hand behind her head, clamps her mouth onto Luisa's.

There are bubbles of prosecco on Luisa's lips, trying to find their way into her mouth, and she parts her lips to avoid the liquid flooding down her chin. This really isn't an efficient method by which to pass liquid between human mouths, she thinks. Now Tina's tongue is in her mouth, and something solid is in there as well, a small metal ball. A tongue stud, a tongue stud on Luisa's own tongue because Tina's tongue is in her mouth.

Why is Tina's tongue in my mouth?

Luisa pulls away.

'You said you'd never kissed a girl,' says Tina.

'I don't think I said.' Luisa turns her head, trying to see where Boris is, and her head almost brushes his jeans.

'Don't mind me.' Boris takes a seat on the sofa next to Tina. He takes his phone from his pocket and thumbs up the screen.

'Bit more comfy up here.' Tina shifts over to the sofa's corner, covering up her bare leg with her skirt as she does so. She pats the empty middle cushion.

Boris lays an arm across the sofa back, his hand on Tina's shoulder. 'Glad you're up for this,' he says, as though Luisa has agreed to join them on holiday the following summer in their French villa. He leans over and delicately kisses Tina on the lips. 'We weren't, you know, sure. That it was your kind of thing.' He points at his phone. 'Sorry, do you mind? You know, videoing? We like to, you know.'

'Aren't we – going to a club?' Luisa can still taste the last of the bitterness in her throat, but the taste of MDMA and Tina's thigh are now sunk in the depths of long-term memory. The super-heating of her body has taken on a late night shiver. 'We're – going out, dancing?'

'This is good, isn't it?' Tina looks up at Boris, reaches down and brushes Luisa's nipple through her top.

'We can go dancing. Can't we just go dancing?' Luisa twists to one side so her breast is out of Tina's grasp, in a way that could have been accidental. 'I really want to go dancing.'

'I don't think we want to do much more dancing,' says Boris.

'But what did you think?' Luisa pushes herself to her feet. 'What about dancing?'

'You seemed so up for it,' says Tina.

'I need – the toilet. Some water. Where's the toilet?' Luisa pinballs diagonally across the room, bounces with a hand off a wall and propels herself towards the stairs. She scoops her bag from the chair and climbs the steps two at a time.

But I'm not up for it, she wails to herself. When did I say I was up for it? I was – I didn't know I was kissing Tina. I should go back, go back and tell them, tell them I'm not up for it, they've made a mistake, it's not their fault, I've misled them and I'm not up for it. But I haven't misled them! When did they, when did they ask, ask for consent? When has licking drugs from someone's thigh ever been taken as consent? Maybe loads of times. But I couldn't say no. How could I refuse the hospitality?

Luisa pauses in the hallway. She has left the doorway to the basement open, but can hear no sound from downstairs, no voices. In her current state the sight of exposed floorboards and a photo collage of differently aged Isobels unnerves her. She wrenches open the front door and runs down the steps.

The night air clamps an invisible mist around her bare arms, even into her armpits, but though she can see the goose pimples, rigid, there is no sensation of cold. She walks away, but less a walk, more a power-charge directed at the post box on the corner of the road.

Luisa exits the end of the Tina's road, and she has upped her pace, upped her pace so that each step matches one beat of her heart. She pictures herself opening the front door of her house, quieter than on weekend mornings when returning from the hospital, clicking the latch behind her amid the silent balm of her sleeping family. Justin will be asleep, won't he? She pulls her phone from her bag, it is not a phone, but a bottle of water, chugs almost half down, now exchanges the bottle for her phone. The numbers onscreen echo away from her, reflected three, four times to a perspective point somewhere down in the darkness. 22.45. Justin won't be asleep. If he's not asleep, he'll be awake, he'll be in bed, almost in bed. He'll be warm. Warm and cuddly.

Sorry to wake you, sweetie, she pictures herself saying to Justin-in-bed, in a tone that contains a cavernous sorrow for their arguments that day. Work sent me home early, she is saying.

Don't worry, says Justin. I only just nodded off.

She knows this is not true, that he has not been asleep.

I'm glad you're awake. I wanted to – .

I was worried, interrupts Justin. About what happened earlier. Worried you're really mad at me.

Not mad. Luisa kneels on the bed, kisses him.

Can I explain what I meant? says Justin. Because – perhaps you misunderstood me?

I think I understood exactly what you meant, she cries. I understood exactly what you meant, she repeats, with a smile this time and Justin appears not to have heard the first delivery. But let's not talk about it, she says. Kiss me.

Justin pulls his t-shirt over his head. He is better built, better built and even more hairy than she remembers. A really hairy ballet dancer. He threads a hand into her hair, pulls her mouth to his, his tongue. He has a stud, a stud in his tongue, no, no, he doesn't have a stud in his tongue.

Why did they send you home from work early? says Justin.

They rota-ed too many people. That never happens. They did the rota wrong.

Oh for god's sake. Justin throws his t-shirt to the floor, it lands with a crash. But I'm home now.

So they'll pay you for tonight? Or you have to work another shift to make it up? What if we've already arranged childcare?

What if *we* have arranged! she cries. Who's we?

I can't do it, can I? He is calm, calm and once again wearing his t-shirt. How can I rearrange childcare when I never know which days you're working?

Everyone else seems to manage it!

Well everyone else is fucking mad! Justin is by the window, has opened the bedroom window, is screaming, screaming *Everyone else is fucking mad!* out the window, late on a Friday night, car alarms blaring, people coming out of their houses, no, no one is coming out of their houses, everyone stays in their houses, they're stewing, silent, doing nothing in their houses. They *are* fucking mad.

Now I've thought this through I can't go home I can't go home, she thinks as she passes the cinema. Not until he's asleep. I can walk instead, it's warm, no it's cold but I'm warm, I'll walk. I'll take a walk, what's stopping me walking? I like walking. Walking and seeing all these people. Walking is a bit like dancing. Luisa rotates her hips a little with each stride, John Travolta with a paint tin. Dancing is even more like dancing.

'Excuse me?' Luisa has stopped, she is outside a pub, outside with the smokers. 'Excuse me,' she says to the nearest man, a man in a long khaki jacket that has not seen active military service. 'Do you know where Cable is? The club?'

'Cable?' The man looks to his companions, a man and a woman. Luisa watches his calculation: what is the fastest way to be rid of this woman? He pulls his phone from his pocket.

'Oh yes,' laughs Luisa. 'I could have done that myself, really.' She pulls her own phone from her bag to demonstrate, but again the numbers peel away from her, peel away towards the glow of the man's cigarette.

'Do you mind? If I have one of those?' Luisa traces her finger along the perspective line ending at his roll-up.

The man makes another calculation and hands her a tobacco pouch.

Luisa tries to remember her last cigarette, perhaps eight, ten years ago.

'Here,' says the woman. She smiles, takes the tobacco pouch from Luisa.

'Haven't had that phone long,' says Luisa. 'Still haven't really worked it out. My children know more about it than me. They're all right though, at home. I've left them at home with their father. My boyfriend. Justin.'

'Here you go,' Khaki jacket man holds his screen up to her, and Luisa recoils from its brightness. 'Turn right at the end of this block, two more roads on your left.' The woman presses a roll-up into her hand, alms for the poor beggar.

'Thanks!' calls Luisa, and she is already a distance down the street. She puts the cigarette in her mouth, inhales. It is unlit. She continues walking, chanting *right, then two left* to herself. Who might have a light? She turns the corner and hears it, hears the bass, low, deep. There's an illuminated sign, letters constructed from what look like chunky computer leads, the letters spelling CABLE.

In a fenced off area to the front and side of the entrance there are people smoking. She is smoking too, will be smoking when she can find someone with a light. She wants to ask through the fence, but although everyone is smoking they are also talking, talking to their friends and she is there on her own. But isn't clubbing just as fun alone? How many nights did I end up losing all my friends, making new friends, really friendly friends? It doesn't matter that I'm on my own. I'm forty-three.

Through the fence she sees the doors to the smoking area open to let someone out, and Luisa glimpses the club's inside: fractal wall hangings, dayglo upside-down marquees full of holes on the ceiling. I know that, she thinks. Are these nights still the same, everything as I remember?

'You can't bring that in,' says the bouncer.

Luisa looks down at her bag, all around her body, cannot work out what he means. The bouncer nods at her, right at her face.

'It's not lit,' she says.

'Well can you take it out your mouth? Put it away, please.'

Luisa pulls the cigarette from her lips. 'Sorry. Didn't realise.'

'Show your ID before paying.'

'I'm over eighteen.'

'I know that. New regulations.'

He could have made a joke, she thinks. Could at least have smiled. The bouncer's lack of interest in dialogue, in her reasons, along with the plain wooden structure of the entrance doors, peeling and chipped at the edges, is draining her confidence. He fishes through her bag and points up at a screen fixed near the ceiling. She sees her face moving on the screen and the picture freezes, her mouth half open.

'Can you take that again?' says Luisa.

'No. All done,' says the bouncer, and now he smiles. 'Pay the man and in you go.'

The double doors open into the bar area, and the music is louder, much louder than outside. There are six, maybe seven people, with pints in plastic glasses, and almost the same number of bar staff, leaning on the bar or chatting. She strides in, across the room and onto the dance floor, separated from the bar area by two thick columns.

There are three people on the dance floor. A young guy trying to move limbs without spilling his pint, and a couple who must be in their fifties. The wall hangings camouflage their outfits.

The DJ looks up at Luisa. She heads back to the bar.

Let's have a drink. No, not drinking, I'm here to dance, use this feeling to dance. Can't dance with a bag. Can I dance to this music? I like this music. But can't dance with a bag. Get rid of bag. In cloakroom, now I'm forty-three I can afford the cloakroom! She leans against a wall, pulls her purse from her bag.

Money out of purse, money into pocket. Keys into bag, don't need keys. To remove her keys from her pocket Luisa has to take the money back out. Holding the two scrunched tenners in her hand makes her feel conspicuous.

Phone, keep my phone. In case of emergency. This is already something of an emergency. She slides the phone into her back pocket.

Downstairs in the cloakroom she hands her bag to the attendant, a middle-aged black woman. You probably have kids as well. You're doing this and you have to look after your kids tomorrow. She wants to say she understands a life where you work all night and mind your kids the next day.

'I'm a midwife,' says Luisa, and the woman nods, says nothing.

Back on the dance floor two more people have joined the original three, and Luisa sets off dancing again, recalling her movements from earlier that evening, recalling the precise order of limb motions. She moves her legs wider and suddenly she is there, snaps back into the feeling again, circles from near the wall out towards the middle of the floor. Her eyes flash past the woman in her fifties, and the woman smiles. Luisa smiles back.

Her legs, her legs are so heavy. So very heavy. Is it her jeans, because she is wearing jeans? I always wear jeans. They hurt, her legs, hurt-heavily hurt.

In a back alcove the long, L-shaped sofa is old but comfortable, the cushions relieve the weight of her legs. There are more people on the dance floor now, she can see more coming in through the entrance. If I stay, I can sit here, no one will mind.

A young woman throws herself onto the adjacent cushion, leans back and exhales at the ceiling. She wears flimsy cotton trousers, stamped with flower patterns by a blind, infuriated screen printer, with a neon orange crop top, and in her hair a purple scarf ribbed with beads. If laid on a bed under consideration as an outfit, these clothes are a disaster – but on her they are wondrous. And besides, the clothing scarcely matters compared to the golden limbs on which they hang. The skin of her arms glows with an unblemished, supernatural radiance. Luisa bites back her bottom lip, closes her eyes in frustration at not being able to touch, to stroke the girl's arm, then reaches over and strokes the girl's arm.

'You don't have gum, do you?' smiles headscarf girl.

Luisa shakes her head, looks away and back again.

'Do you have any chewing gum?' The girl half stands and taps the arm of an older guy in jeans and a white t-shirt. The man and his two young male friends turn to face them, and Luisa remembers the power of a young woman, an attractive young woman under the gaze of men.

But I stroked her arm, she thinks.

'Here,' says the girl, and hands her a small pillow of gum. Luisa puts it in her mouth. She sees that the older man has neon orange dots all over his face, a rash of rave measles.

'Karl?' says Luisa.

'Why, hello bridesmaid,' grins Karl. 'Fancy seeing you here.'

'I thought you – you and Jenny were on a cruise.'

'Well *I* certainly am.' Karl leers in the direction of the two young men, who have moved off closer to the dance floor.

'But what about – your honeymoon?'

'I'm on my honeymoon,' says Karl. 'Because I travelled with my wife to Portsmouth as arranged, but it appears she hadn't put my passport in the suitcase as she promised she had.' His enunciation of 'my wife' utilises the full capabilities of his mouth muscles.

'That's – a shame.'

'Not for her. I'm sure she's having a lovely time.'

'Jenny went on her own?'

'Wouldn't be the first time.

Luisa looks away towards the two young men, and notices how similar they are, in fact almost identical.

'Portuguese,' says Karl, as if this explains everything. 'Twins. Remember: no blame culture.' He wags a finger at Luisa, and trips over to join them.

'That was pretty weird,' says the headscarf girl. 'There are – two of them, yeah?'

'Twins,' says Luisa. 'Portuguese, apparently.'

'Right.'

'He's my boss' husband,' says Luisa.

'And do you think he knows about – ?' The girl smiles in the twins' direction.

'She actually. No I doubt it. They only got married yesterday. But she's had loads of affairs so it's only fair. I'm not really friends with them, anyway. But I fell asleep on a bus, I was only going to buy some liver, and ended up at their wedding.'

'You like liver?'

'Not really. I'm vegetarian.'

'That's probably why you fell asleep. Our bodies have their own way of knowing such things.'

'I'm not sure what's going on with my body at the moment,' says Luisa. 'My legs feel so heavy.' Though now that she thinks about them, she cannot feel her legs at all. 'I've been up for four days.'

'Cool,' says the girl.

*

'Here,' says Molly. 'You need some of this.'

Molly is a friend of headscarf girl, and small even compared to Luisa. Molly stands on tiptoe in order to touch temples with Luisa, and twists her body in time to the music even as she rubs against Luisa's head in a circular motion. Is this a new greeting? thinks Luisa. Perhaps they've adapted it, from Maori culture or somewhere. Have I remembered correctly, is that how Maoris greet each other? She touches her temple – it is gritty, and she sees Molly has silver glitter in sci-fi arrows to the sides of her eyes.

'Now you're looking it,' says Molly, and she has to lean in again to make herself heard above the pounding bass. The rest of the packed dance floor surrounds them, as Luisa curves herself to either side. Whichever way she turns there is another gyrating body, someone grinning, experimenting with their own method of composing their body to the music.

Molly throws her arms around Luisa's neck. 'So you're a friend of Sophie's?' she says into her ear. 'Or do you work with Danny?'

'No,' says Luisa. 'I'm a friend of Karl's. The man with the Portuguese twins.'

'Right!'

'Who's Sophie?'

'This is Delphin!' Molly grabs the arm of a young guy dancing nearby and draws him into their circle. Luisa shakes his hand.

'So you don't know Sophie?' Molly opens the circle again and the headscarf girl swirls in towards them. 'Sophie, have you met – ?'

'Bridesmaid!' Sophie throws her arms around Luisa. 'I know bridesmaid. *She's* the one who's boss is having gay revenge sex on his honeymoon.'

'Woah! cries Delphin in delight and pulls the four of them in for a big hug.

*

'My dad actually lives in Varkala, in India,' says Delphin, and he looks sad. Or perhaps tired, thinks Luisa. I should ask him, sad or tired?

She sits on the floor with Delphin at the back of the dance floor, their backs against the wall, the bass edging them forward a few millimetres with each thump, the crowded dance floor forming a writhing wall around them.

'I mean I've got two Indian half-brothers,' says Delphin. 'God I really love them, but I never see them. It's hard to see how I can.'

So pretty, even in the dark. Not even handsome. Pretty. A beam of light rotates down to their floor level, and for a moment Delphin's face is lit up in purple.

'What about your Mum?' says Luisa. 'Tell me about your mother,' she adds with a deep Russian accent and a giggle. To her delight Delphin giggles as well.

'Oh, my Mum's still in Essex.' Delphin stares up at the ceiling. Luisa stares at his Adam's apple. 'It's actually really beautiful there. My Mum's a complete hippy. Hence my stupid name.'

'It's not stupid. Unusual. I like it.'

'You get a bit sick of people making dolphin noises after a while.'

Luisa tries to remember what noise dolphins make, is about to try out a few different possibilities when she realises this is a poor idea if she wants this man to – to what? A woman dances close to the far side of Delphin, and he shifts nearer to Luisa.

'The commune was great, and all. That's where my mum still lives, on a commune. There was so much freedom, and always someone to look after you. But my friends now, they have, you know, proper mothers to go home to. And only the one. One who won't be in the middle of a ten-day silent meditation.'

'Well. What is a proper mother, anyway?' Luisa stares up at the sweaty backs of the dancers, feels her own sweat lining the elastic of her underwear. 'I mean I never even see my mother.'

'Hey. I'm sorry.'

He lays a hand on her upper arm, and she looks down at his fingertips close to the outer edge of her breast.

'Oh. Well, no. It's fine. She's on a ship. Not working, just on a ship. All the time. With my dad actually.' She sees with relief that Delphin isn't really listening.

'It's so nice, sitting here, talking to you,' says Delphin. 'Sometimes – '

Well that's a line. Isn't that a line? That's a line and his fingers are almost on my breast. Oh. He's taken them off.

'God, I really need to dance now. Come on, let's dance!' Delphin jumps to his feet, his face beaming, and disappears into the crowd.

*

'So how the hell do you know this place, Karl?' Luisa makes for Karl, who is standing against the bar, leaning back on his elbows. Karl's funny, she thinks. Angry, but funny. I could be friends with Karl, I could make Karl my dancing buddy. Though I don't think I've actually seen him dancing.

Justin should be my dancing buddy. Luisa takes a great gulp from a plastic glass of water. In a little while, when I've come down a bit I can go home and climb into bed next to Justin, cuddle up next to Justin. Her whole body aches, to stand by the bar is an effort. But it is also easy to imagine that her body belongs to someone else, that the pain belongs to someone else. She remembers a night out dancing long ago, not long after meeting Justin, when in the dawn light Justin had guided her and her aching body to the door step of the house where she lived in Primrose Hill, the house where she was the nanny for an actor and his family, and the doorstep where the family found her, crying, about to begin the day looking after their two-year-old. If Justin was here, he'd look after me now.

'Oh, you know,' says Karl, but Luisa doesn't. 'You're one of the midwives, aren't you?', he says, as though this confirms some suspicion of his.

'Uh-huh,' says Luisa, and wonders why this sounds reluctant.

'That must be so-ooo rewarding,' says Karl, and dissolves into a cackle more suited to a sitcom ghost.

Luisa laughs, a genuine laugh.

'I didn't want to come here.' Karl takes a sip of his pint. 'I mean the Guinness here is completely shit. We're only here because the boys wanted to.'

Luisa follows Karl's gaze over to the twins, to where they are standing by a fruit machine. One twin turns left and right in a robotic mime, jerks his forearms up and down and slams a fist down on the flashing button. The other twin stares motionless at the screen as the barrels spin, they stop and he rotates his fists back and forth in front of his eyes.

'Portuguese, you say?' says Luisa.

'It takes a village to raise a child,' says Karl.

'Nudge volunteer!' cries the robot twin, so loud it can be heard over the music. The twins turn as one and each grab a wrist of a short, dreadlocked man in billowy cotton trousers. Between them they punch down both his hands on the button, holding onto him tight as the barrels roll again. The machine's lights all flash and coins chunk down into the trough. The twins high-five the dreadlocked man and everyone looks delighted.

'They're quite – striking, aren't they?' says Luisa.

'Not to mention easy,' says Karl. 'Watch this.'

Karl strides over to the nearest twin, puts a hand on both his cheeks and kisses him full on the lips. He pulls away and presses something into the twin's palm.

'Whay!' whoops the twin and pushes the coin into the slot of the fruit machine.

Karl comes back over to Luisa. 'Do you want a go?' he says. He takes a handful of change from his pocket and hands her a pound coin.

'I'm fine, thanks,' she says.

*

'Think I will make a move,' says Luisa, surprising herself with the news.

'Nooo!' says Molly, gyrating her body in front of Luisa.

Luisa sits on a cushioned bench in the downstairs room, right next to the speaker. The music no longer registers at the surface level of her thoughts, instead somewhere deep inside her belly, and is only apparent if she focuses her attention there.

To her left Sophie drinks chai from a cardboard cup which she has more than once pushed into Luisa's mouth without asking.

'Coming down too much now,' says Luisa quietly, to herself. I've been up for four days, you know.

'Yeah, I'm getting that,' says Delphin on her other side. 'You should come back to ours.'

'Time for your wedding breakfast, bridesmaid,' says Sophie. 'After party back at the ranch.'

'I think I need to sleep. I've been up for four days.'

'A few more hours won't make much difference,' says Delphin.

'Last French dab, darling?' says Molly.

Luisa watches Molly lean down over Delphin, her face close to his mouth – her tongue in his mouth. Oh. Okay. She looks away from them. Okay, Delphin and Molly, I never realised. Never realised what? What difference does that make?

'I really have to go,' says Luisa.

Molly pushes away and up from Delphin.

'Danny,' says Delphin. 'Your turn.'

She watches Delphin dip a finger in the plastic baggie on the seat to his side and touch a disc of white dust onto his own tongue. Now Danny leans over Delphin, his tongue in Delphin's mouth. Delphin's head is angled away from Luisa, she can see Danny's fingers lightly rested on the neat hairline ending in pale smooth skin. The neck of a swan, a grown adult swan.

'Luisa?' says Delphin.

She looks away.

'Your turn.'

'Wait,' says Luisa. She should call Justin – this will be okay if she calls Justin, tells him that there is nothing going on here, that it's the way people take drugs nowadays. And Justin being Justin – he would understand. If he was with her now, dancing that tight little dance of his – he dances like Molly really, that quivering shake of arms and legs – if he was watching her he'd laugh at her confused state. And continue to laugh that she thinks it appropriate to ask if she can have this young man put his tongue down her throat. Not down her throat, don't be lewd. No one puts tongues down throats, it's physiologically impossible. Phys-i-o-log-i-call-y. That rolls over the tongue. Is it a word? But Justin wouldn't mind, because he and I, we're – we're what? Justin isn't here. I can't ring Justin, it's two o'clock in the morning. 'Okay,' Luisa tells Delphin.

Delphin turns to face her, she angles her head over his, and he is kissing her – not kissing her, there is no lip pressing, he just threads his tongue into her mouth. Oh but now with the lips, yes their lips are touching, they are touching each other. The bitterness of the MDMA hits her, again. That's why this is okay, this is okay because this is actually quite disgusting. The disgusting thing lasts until the disgust is all gone.

'Okay?' says Delphin.

'Bleeuugh,' says Luisa.

'Bleeuugh,' repeats Delphin, keeping his eyes on her.

They are out the front of the club, and it's gorgeous outside – the street lined with Victorian street lamps, and quiet, so quiet once the doors shut behind them. I should be outside more at night, thinks Luisa. I can go for walks in my break when I'm on night shift. It's so – serene. There's a cab by the kerbside, they are standing by the cab, her and Delphin and Danny, Delphin smoking, Luisa taking a drag on his cigarette, Sophie leaning on the taxi driver's window, and the taxi driver is shaking his head, and now Molly is leaning down as well, and now the driver is nodding his head. Okay, we're in, in the cab, and she's sitting in the back by the window, sitting next to Delphin, Molly is on Sophie's lap on the other side, Molly talking to the driver, talking all the time.

It is boiling in the cab. Luisa winds down the window.

'Hello Mr Brosnan,' Luisa shouts out of the window, and there is Eleanor and Elsie's teacher, standing on the pavement, also waiting for a cab. Mr Brosnan turns to see who is shouting, but does not recognise her. That's okay, I'll mention it to him next week. She winds the window and the cab pulls away.

*

'It's just the idea, really,' says Danny, 'according to this guy I saw, anyway – it's the idea that while you're brushing your teeth, you know, when you're first up and awake, and you're looking in the bathroom mirror – it's the idea that you point at yourself and say, *I love you*. Not narcissisticly, not at all. To see if you can, if it feels sincere. And if you can do that, if you can look yourself in the eye and say, *I love you*, to yourself – well, you're okay. You're doing okay.'

In the lounge of their shared house the only illumination comes from a long strip of fairy lights strung around three walls, flashing on and off in a pattern that Luisa cannot fathom. To her left on the sofa Delphin rolls a joint in his lap, and she is loath to move for fear of causing a cushion dip that will up-end his construction.

I can say that, can't I? she thinks, and imagines her face in the bathroom mirror. My face has none of the beautiful youth of these people. But I can say *I love you* to my face, can't I? But right now I don't really want to. Here is much better. On the sofa, sunk in the sofa.

On a screen a polar bear pads down the side of a snowy mountain. Danny stands behind a pair of decks, eyes fixed on the bear, wearing a pair of headphones on one ear. He adjusts something on the decks and a low techno rumble takes place of the polar bear soundtrack.

'Who said that?' says Delphin.

'Can't remember,' says Danny. 'Doesn't matter, really. There's a truth there, somewhere.'

'So can you?' says Delphin.

'Not right now. If I looked at myself in the mirror now, I'd probably throw up.'

Sophie enters the room carrying a silver tea tray of tiny porcelain cups. 'Shall I be mother?' she says.

That should really be me, thinks Luisa. 'Not for me, thanks all the same,' she says. No caffeine, not at this late hour. What *is* the time? She puts a hand to her pocket, remembers the perspective shift of the screen. Takes her hand back again.

'You've turned down David,' says Sophie. 'Why have you turned down David?'

'Only because of the music,' says Danny. 'The music they use, it's so manipulative. I love Attenborough as much as anyone, but you can't watch it with that music they use. It's so overdone. Much better to provide your own soundtrack.'

'But what's the point without David?' Sophie sets down the tea tray on the floor and steps over Molly's prostrate body to harass the screen with a remote control and takes some time to realise this has no effect. 'Bring David back,' she pleads with Danny.

'But it really gets me, the music! It's so cruel.' Danny's voice skips an octave under strain. 'You can't anthropomorphise like that, it's not fair. Don't go all Disney on us again.'

Sophie steps over and hugs him. 'Okay, okay. But how about for the bear cubs? Let us have David back for that.'

'Of course,' says Danny. 'Of course for the cubs.'

A thin young man with long curly hair enters the room, brandishing a screwdriver. 'Has anyone borrowed our micro Phillips set?' he asks. 'It's no problem, but we really need it back right now. They're in a red box with a clear lid. Anyone?'

Everyone shakes their head, including Luisa, and the thin man leaves without a word.

'Does he live here too?' Luisa asks Delphin. She moves her eyes from his profile down to the almost-completed joint. That will help me sleep, she thinks. A few tokes, and I'll ask for a blanket, I can curl up anywhere.

'Nate and Simon rent the front room between them.' Delphin looks to her, and returns her smile with a beam of his own. 'They've got some server they're building in there, underneath their beds. We don't see them much during the day.' He lights up the joint, exhales a long stream of smoke, and lies his head back on the sofa. 'They don't really do much else.'

I can look in the mirror, thinks Luisa, I can look myself in the mirror because I've done something tonight. I've put myself out there, haven't I? It's possible to enjoy an evening with these people, these lovely, these young people, I can do that, I can enjoy an evening and still be me. I can go home, home tomorrow, today, this morning and feel – what? Sated?

'*I* can't!' Molly bursts into tears, sits up and leans her head on her hands, sobbing. 'I can never do that. Why would I tell myself I love you, why would anyone say I love you to me! That won't work for me, will it? How can I love me when my life is so fucked up?'

'Hey, hey.' Sophie crouches down and envelops Molly in a hug, rocks her back and forth. Delphin hands the joint to Luisa, crouches and wraps the two of them in his arms. Danny pulls off his headphones and joins the circle. 'Your life is fine,' murmurs Sophie from inside the circle. 'It's fine. You've got friends, you've got work to support yourself. That's more than me, right now. And I'm fine, and you're fine.'

'I can't feel it,' sobs Molly. 'It feels all – too fragile.'

'And so it goes,' says Delphin.

Should I join them? thinks Luisa. Is it rude *not* to join them? She sits forward on the edge of the sofa and instead looks at the joint.

'You don't want to worry. Honestly,' says Luisa. She has no notion of has upset Molly. One of her parents could have died for all she knows. She presses on, regardless. 'I remember, throughout my twenties, everything always felt fucked up. Feeling clueless and fucked up about life, that's fine, it's the, the true mode of being in your twenties. If you're not feeling like that, you're not – thinking. You're – '

'You're an automaton,' says Danny. 'Right.'

'There,' says Sophie. 'Listen to bridesmaid.'

All the young people look in her direction. Are expecting more. She recognises the underside of being a young lion – barely out of childhood, really. The neediness.

'And it doesn't matter, about screwing things up, so long as you feel okay about it, about the way you are.' Is this, in fact, proof I have not screwed up – that I have the authority to say what is and what is not screwed up? 'I mean look at me now. My life still feels pretty fucked up, my job is out of control, I'm not sure I have any real idea of the best way to look after or bring up my children, to give them what they need in order that they don't feel fucked up. But I feel – I feel okay about it.' I really like saying fucked up, she thinks, really like saying it over and over. 'Because although I'm fucked up I'm also pretty much happy with my choices. I think. Because I think I've made them with – good intentions? And that's enough, really.' This is true, she thinks. This *is* true. Though I haven't mentioned Justin. Is that bad? Should I mention Justin, for completeness' sake, as full disclosure?

The room is silent, save for Danny's low drum track. The polar bear stands on an ice flow.

'Well I'm going to have to go to bed,' says Delphin. He gives Molly an individual hug, stands and steps past Luisa to the door.

'I've got to be up early,' he nods back to Luisa.

'Oh yes! You've got work,' says Luisa.

'Actually it's not work.' Delphin looks sheepish and runs a hand up through his hair. 'My mum is coming. She's taking me out, for lunch. For a picnic, rather. Do you want to stay? Do you need somewhere to stay?'

'Sure,' says Luisa. For a moment she thought he was inviting her to a picnic with his mum. She hands the joint to Sophie and follows Delphin from the room.

'Do you want a shower?' Delphin says in the hallway. 'Must be pretty sweaty. I know I am.'

'Oh. I – well, I am a bit sweaty.' So now, is this the move? He only asked if I was sweaty, didn't he?

'I'm going to have one anyway,' he says, and climbs the stairs two at a time before she can answer.

'Okay.' Luisa follows behind him. Showering, that's normal hygiene.

Upstairs Delphin emerges from a doorway, hands her a towel and pushes open the door of the bathroom.

Oh. He means together. When he follows me into the bathroom – that's when to say. Tell him politely but firmly. That I just want to sleep. The hallway is silent but also buzzing with a metallic sound she cannot identify, a sound that has encased her body and made it much less primed for sleep.

She takes the towel and goes into the bathroom. She turns and sees he has gone back into his bedroom. He's nice, he's a modern young man. I'm of the late twentieth century, whether or not I like it. Nowadays we can co-exist like this, a man and woman.

Luisa closes the door behind her, and Delphin pushes it open again.

'Let me go first,' he says. 'The temperature on this bath system, it's really tricky.' His tone is technical, as though he has studied plumbing in a formal sense. He turns on the taps, puts his hand under the mixer as a test. 'You'd better jump in straight away after,' he says. 'So we don't have to turn off the water.'

So sweet, calling us 'we', like I live here or something. She catches sight of her face in the bathroom mirror, she points at herself. *I love you*, she thinks, but the voice in her head is less serene hippy, more drunken vagrant.

Delphin is naked. Naked but with his back to her, his buttocks sculpted and smooth, unlike any buttocks she has seen for years. Perhaps the water is still not the right temperature, she wonders, perhaps he'll need to test it again. But Delphin has climbed behind the shower curtain. But not a move, not really, not from behind a shower curtain, naked or not, still nothing at which to make a definitive response. This isn't Victorian England. She removes her clothes, the sweat in her garments making them more difficult to pull against her skin, and wraps the towel around her.

'Are you still there?' says Delphin.

'Is it my turn?' says Luisa.

'Sure.'

Does he mean with him? Perhaps it's my turn but in there with him? Why does everything require so much thought? Fuck it, she thinks, and drops the towel, steps over the edge of the bath, and bumps into Delphin as he is coming out. They bump into each other, both go to her left, then to her right, and the awkwardness offsets any acknowledgement of their mutual nakedness. Luisa is in the shower – she is in the shower and Delphin is not.

'You know where my room is, yeah?' he says.

That's it – there's the line. 'No,' says Luisa, but this could answer any number of questions. She does know where his room is, she saw him go into it, but he has closed the bathroom door, closed it behind him, now he cannot hear her. The nakedness is too confusing. This is a household where it is acceptable to administer drugs via the tongue. Young people are *nice*, she thinks again, and the thought, and its consequent confusion, brings tears to her eyes. She turns off the taps and the shower falls silent.

Delphin comes back in, she hears him lift the toilet seat to an upright position, and the sound of him urinating.

'Delphin – ' says Luisa and puts her head round the shower curtain.

Danny turns, and twists into himself as he tries to zip up his trousers. 'Sorry!' he says. 'I was really desperate. I thought – don't mind me.' And he is gone again.

Luisa dresses in her sweaty vest top and knickers, and wraps the towel around her, over the clothes. She stands motionless on another towel that serves as a bathmat. The bathroom, the lack of a unifying aesthetic – the discarded empty shampoo bottles, the torn carpet, the life-size voodoo doll torso with six baby teats for nipples – these are a source of comfort.

Luisa pushes open Delphin's bedroom door. He is wearing a t-shirt and boxer shorts. She steps in and shuts the door, holding onto the door handle behind her back.

'Do you need a fresh t-shirt?' says Delphin, and hands her a plain white one before she can answer. He sits on the double bed and thumbs through his phone.

Luisa turns to face the wall, drops the towel and swaps her vest top for the t-shirt. He has already seen me naked, she thinks, and the word naked sends a cold thrill through her. The clean t-shirt feels delicious against her freshly laundered skin, and she rubs at the material that covers her upper arm. She picks up the towel, in order to wrap it around her again, then drops it back to the floor.

'Sophie's put photos up already,' says Delphin. He turns the phone screen towards her, and she sits on the bed, takes the phone from him. The photograph shows her face squeezed up against Molly and Delphin's, expressions of wide-mouthed glee on all three on them. She has no memory of the picture being taken.

'I look okay, don't I?' she says in surprise, and puts a hand to her mouth for her crassness.

'You look great,' says Delphin.

She is sitting right next to him. His legs are hairless. Do men shave nowadays, she wonders, shave their legs? What do hairless male legs feel like? I don't know. I will not find out. When he, if he, when he makes a move on me now, I can say, I can still say I didn't realise. Then I'll have to go home. I'll have to leave.

'So you want to do anything?' He stares at her, completely unembarrassed.

'Any – thing?' How can he not be embarrassed? Delphin holds her gaze – she is forced to look away.

'Because if you just want to sleep – that's what I'm going to do,' he says. 'So how about it?'

It? It? her mind screams.

He raises his eyebrows.

'I'm – sort of seeing someone?' says Luisa.

'Is that a question?' he grins. 'Are you asking *me*?'

'I am seeing someone. Live with someone.' Luisa looks down at the floor. 'Nothing is – going to happen. I'm forty-three.'

Delphin shrugs his shoulders. 'And?'

'Oh. But nothing is going to happen,' she mumbles.

'Absolutely. If that's what you want. Sleeping it is.'

She can see his erection pushing against the material of his boxer shorts. He jumps onto the other side of the bed, climbs under the duvet.

'You're okay,' he says. 'There's loads of room. It's a big bed.'

'It *is* a big bed, isn't it?' she says.

Luisa lies on her back in the dark. A woman meets a man, at night, both are eager, desperate even, for affection, for love. If sex is love. How can we ever convince ourselves this is the right way to act, a genuine event? But not now. Now it's a never event. Too much else to pile in on a fleeting good feeling, too much to keep it pure. Luisa weeps quiet, stupid tears.

The silence is complete, broken only by an occasional thrum of distant traffic. She cannot even hear Delphin breathing. The chemical residues have encased her brain with a ribbon, a band that constricts and loosens in a rhythmic pattern that could be pleasant if it matched the pattern of her heartbeat, which it doesn't. The space she occupies between the edge of the bed and Delphin's looming physical presence feels constricting, claustrophobic, but she cannot judge the reality of this. She creeps a hand in Delphin's direction, pulls it back before it touches anything other than duvet. This is no good, she thinks, no good in too many ways. She listens again for Delphin's breathing.

'Luisa-aa,' Delphin's voice suddenly chimes in the dark. 'Are you awake?'

'Yes,' she says, as though answering the school register.

'Would you mind,' says Delphin, 'and you can say no, I so understand – but I just wondered if you'd mind if I quietly had a quick wank?'

'Oh. No. Of course.'

'I can go the bathroom that's better.'

'No. I don't want you to. It's your room. It's fine.'

Luisa hears a rustling of bed sheets and lies still, not daring to move. Her hand is down between her legs. She sits up with a start.

'I can't sleep, anyway. I'm going to – get up for a while. Smoke a joint or something. Make myself sleepy.' She clambers out of bed, takes a dressing gown from the back of the door.

'Okay,' says Delphin. 'Sorry.'

'No – ' says Luisa and slips from the room.

In the lounge only Sophie remains. She sits cross-legged, right up close to the screen where the same polar bear and her cubs scrabble along the same snowy mountain slope. Luisa sits down next to her, and they watch together.

'This steep slope is not the easiest place to take your first steps,' says David Attenborough.

'My grandad is nothing like David Attenborough,' says Sophie. 'All he's obsessed about is cats shitting in his garden. He's got this complicated hose defence system he uses against them. Sometimes my Mum gets caught in it and he says it's her fault. And his voice is all high-pitched and croaky. It's not fair.' She looks at Luisa, and at the dressing gown she is wearing.

'I couldn't sleep,' says Luisa. 'Would you mind if I smoked a joint?'

Sophie drags the rolling paraphernalia from the table, pushes it over towards her.

'I can't really handle this recent series,' says Sophie. 'They're too much of a reminder about mortality. *His* mortality.'

They both stare at the cubs sliding down the ice flow.

'I'm so glad I met you tonight, Luisa,' Sophie says.

'I'm glad I met you too. All of you.' The cigarette papers Luisa has stuck together have come apart.

'Shall I?' says Sophie. Luisa nods.

Sophie takes the papers from Luisa. 'Because it's made me decide something. I can't cope any more, with reaching the end of each summer and all the festival work ending. All that struggling through the winter. And what are most festivals now, anyway? I want to do something meaningful. So I've decided, I'm going to train as a midwife. Like you.'

'Right.' Luisa is listening, but only as an accompaniment to watching Sophie's rolling of the joint.

'I'll apply by Christmas – it starts in September, the training, doesn't it, like school? I was looking it up. I was always quite good at biology. And I already know where my own cervix is, I learnt how to find it on this feminist retreat last year. Should I put that on the application form?'

'Don't rush into anything,' says Luisa. 'It's something you need to think about.'

'I want to stop messing around. Do something fulfilling, I suppose.'

'But is it, though?' says Luisa. 'Perhaps it's not everything it seems.'

'It's life though, isn't it? It's actually life.'

'But it's not only life. It's not really life at all.' Luisa points a finger at Sophie. 'This week, this week I've been, I mean yes, I've seen two new lives. I've perhaps saved a life. Helped to save a mother's life. Though she would probably have been fine without me. But I can't sleep, in the day. I've got two six-year-olds I've hardly seen, who seem to have joined some kind of life-coaching cult with their grandmother. And whenever I work, I shit myself that my whole career might be over, because you never know if a baby, a new life, will emerge all wrong and someone might blame you. Even if it wasn't really your fault. I don't eat, or wee for a whole twelve-hour shift, I forget to drink. Once I was humiliated in triage by an astrophysicist.' Luisa pauses, out of breath. 'I mean being a midwife means I haven't slept for about four days. And god knows the last time I had sex.'

'But it must be so rewarding,' says Sophie.

Luisa leans in closer, so close that she loses her balance and tips forward on top of Sophie, knocking her backwards. Sophie's knee knocks the joint and tobacco flies onto the carpet. Luisa takes advantage of their bodies' arrangement to push her hands on Sophie's shoulders and pin her to the floor.

'Promise me,' says Luisa. 'Promise me you won't become a midwife.'

*

Luisa wakes with an unfamiliar sensation: her mind empty, her thoughts somewhere outside, not yet processed. Good empty, rather than drunken-amnesiac empty, ready to deal with the oncoming day.

A pale blue duvet covers her head. She can see colour, so knows it is past dawn, but knows no more. This is all she wants to know for now. Sunrise. If it's dawn, I must have been asleep for at least a few hours. It's a kind of victory, although she is not sure over whom.

She pulls back the edge of the duvet – the room is bright, it's not dawn, but proper morning. Perhaps more sleep, perhaps five hours! The mattress next to her squeaks with the weight of another body. She remembers, and she is okay. Nothing happened. No bad things. It is morning and nothing happened.

She checks and yes, he, Delphin, is still the same man from the night before. The same boy, but a boy with whom she did not have sex. A boy she declined to have sex with. Because he wanted to, didn't he? she smiles to herself. She turns to look again, at his creased face, his mouth open on the pillow. His eyelids flicker at their exposure to the light.

Luisa explodes with dynamic, intense action, leaping out of bed and sweeping all obvious clothes of hers up and out of the door in one fluid movement. She stands on the silent landing in her knickers. Her knickers that she has worn all night. What about trousers? There were no trousers on the floor, she is certain. She listens at the door for a moment, and pushes it open, causing the door to creak and her to run and shut herself in the bathroom.

And there are her jeans, lying next to the bath. She pulls her phone from the pocket: 08:45. 08:45? She ought to be – home, home from work. Justin thinks she has been working. But she did nothing wrong, did she? Except go to a club and dance and take drugs with some lovely young people. Nothing wrong.

She swipes a text into the phone: **Work overran, home in.** She pauses, then adds: **45 mins,** finger-punches to send. *Why do you always let the hospital take advantage of you?* she moans, channelling Justin, but it is a comforting, familiar moan. Please let Justin moan at me this morning. Get outside, call a cab. Drop me a couple of roads away. She remembers the taxi driver from a couple of mornings before and makes a mental note to avoid jogging.

Her phone beeps, loud, too loud, and she smothers it with a nearby towel. **No problem. Me and girls up and all good. Waiting for you.**

Luisa is outside, out on the pavement, and the bright sunny day welcomes her with a beating across the eyes. Waiting for her for what? She holds up an arm which she finds difficult to rub in the cold air. Her coat – she has left her coat inside. She looks back at the Victorian house – what an enormous shared house! – but the door is shut, she will not ring the bell, no way. But she didn't have her coat, didn't bring her coat, did she? Where is her coat, did she leave it at the club? At Tina's, her coat is at Tina's. But her bag, where is her bag? She cannot recall the last sighting of her bag and her together, scans the mental snapshots of the night before and none of them feature her with her bag, not in this house. The club: her bag is at the club. In the cloakroom at the club. Her bag containing her purse is at the club.

Her phone beeps. She wants it to be Justin again. Justin saying something nice. He's waiting for you – waiting to talk. To discuss, to inform me that – this cannot continue. Did he say that already? He did say that. Because otherwise I would never have. But I didn't, did I?

The text is from Helena. She ignores Helena, cursing her for not being Justin.

In the map app on her phone she types: **home** – she is *Wizard of Oz*'s Dorothy looks down at her trainers and when she sees they are in fact not red her eyes fill with tears, and with more tears when the phone informs her she is 4.72 miles from home.

She sets off, obeying the instruction of her phone's blue arrow, but her legs ache, and at this speed Google's estimated journey time of 1 hour 27 minutes seems optimistic.

Luisa stops again, finds the taxi number from the day before. 'Can I have a cab please? From Lansdale Avenue, number 72.' She takes a small jolt of pleasure at reading these from the road sign on the corner and the nearest house. 'But I have no money on me,' she says, in the voice usually reserved for spelling her email address to public service employees.

'You want the driver to stop at a cashpoint?' The man sounds bored.

'Yes. No. I have no cards. Not on me. But if you take me home I can get some money, from – from my boyfriend?'

'Right. Well, we're quite busy at the moment.'

'I can get money from my boyfriend. I have a boyfriend.'

'Won't have anything for at least an hour.'

'Don't worry. Don't worry about it. I don't need a cab.'

She ends the call and notices the text from Helena again:

Still good for swimming this morning? See you in there at 10.30?

Not good for swimming. Not good for anything. Not good. Luisa sets off walking again, crosses the road and continues down the long leafy avenue towards town. She presses Helena's number.

Helena answers after one ring.

'I'm so sorry,' says Luisa. 'I'm really sorry but I won't be able to make it this morning.'

'That's okay. That's okay,' says Helena, shouldering the burden of Luisa's apology, as though it was her fault for suggesting it.

'I had to work last night. I'm on my way home now.'

'Oh you poor thing. Don't worry, don't you worry!'

'I should have called earlier. I was at a home birth in Selsdey and it overran. I got a bit stuck and now I'm walking home. That's why I only just saw your text.'

'I'm sure whoever you were with, I bet they were pleased to have you there. Don't mention it at all. Was it a boy or a girl?'

'Boy,' says Luisa. 'I'm sorry. It'll take me some time to get home.'

'Justin can't pick you up?'

'Justin's not around.'

'Why don't I come and pick you up? I can do that. Now we're not swimming I've got plenty of time.'

'I can't – ask you to do that.' Luisa looks down at her clothes, feels the heaviness of the sweat contained within them. Orange glitter covers one knee of her jeans.

'Yes you can. I'll get Leonard to take the girls swimming while I come and fetch you, everyone's happy. You're in Selsdey?'

Luisa can hear Helena moving about the house, readying herself for her mission. 'Well that's very kind. I'm heading into town. Along the Oxford Road.'

'Give me ten minutes.'

*

Luisa climbs into Helena's car, and the warmth and comfort almost overwhelm her.

'I almost missed you, you know,' says Helena. 'I was looking out for your midwifery uniform.'

'We're not allowed them,' says Luisa. 'Not at home births. Too authoritarian.'

'It must be very complicated,' laughs Helena. 'All these rules you have to remember.'

'And bags.' Luisa looks down at the phone she grips in her hand. 'We can't take bags to home births either. For security reasons.'

'And coats as well, I suppose?'

'Yes. That's infection control.'

'But how will you get home?'

'They won't pay for taxis.'

'Well that's hardly fair, is it,' says Helena. 'I mean you've been up all night, and it's a very physical job. If you're not allowed a coat, they could at least pay for a taxi.'

'Well, you know, what with the cuts.' Now she's back on safer ground. Almost anything can be blamed on cuts if you think hard.

'I've a good mind to write to the local paper about it.' Helena nods questioningly at Luisa, seeking executive approval.

'Don't do that. There are confidentiality issues.'

'I understand. I'm glad I could help, anyway. I can always help, pick you up, you know. Rebecca and William like a drive.'

'Thanks,' says Luisa. 'Thanks so much for this. I'm very grateful, by the way.' Helena will never shove her tongue down my throat, will she? 'If ever I can help you with something.'

Helena smiles. 'That's kind. Thank you.'

In silence they pass by people going about their regular Saturday mornings: the young parents, the joggers, the shoppers at the bus stop glaring as the joggers dodge around them.

'There is something actually,' says Helena. 'Rebecca is struggling a bit with maths.'

'Of course.'

'Would it be okay if I took some photos of you? Of you taking apart Leonard's lawn mower? To show, you know, that women do such things?'

'Sure. Okay.'

'And if you could do the photos dressed in Dutch national costume. You know, clogs and the pinafore thing? Would that be okay?'

'Okay. Would that – help with maths?'

'That's the plan,' says Helena. 'It's all about role models. And contrasts.'

'And the – Dutch national costume?'

'Don't know,' giggles Helena. 'I just like the idea.'

They turn into Arcadia Close, and Helena pulls up outside Luisa's house.

'How about next weekend?' says Helena, as Luisa climbs out of the car. 'For the photos? Bring the girls, and Justin?'

'Sure. That sounds great.' Luisa leans down into the open door. Helena smiles.

'And thanks so much again,' says Luisa.

She hurries up the driveway, goes to put the key in the front door. But it is her phone in her hand – she has no key. She stands before the door.

I was at a home birth and left all my clothes at the hospital. It really wasn't cold when I left the hospital at three in the morning, I was fine in a vest top. The woman giving birth was from a family of clowns, and hence all the glitter.

The door suddenly opens. 'Mum's home!' cries Elsie, informing someone further back. 'Mum's home,' repeats Eleanor from inside.

'Hello lovelies.' Luisa steps inside to hug them, closes the door behind her.

'Can we go now, Dad?'

Elsie and Eleanor are wearing coats. 'Where are you two going?' says Luisa, enthusiastic for the plan to go out, as though she has simply forgotten some of the details.

'We're off to to buy ice cream,' says Eleanor.

'Oh. Does Dad know?'

'It was Dad's idea,' says Elsie.

'Bye!' Elsie reaches up to open the door, and they step past her and out. She watches them leave the driveway and head up the close. Now they are out of sight.

'So how was work?'

Luisa turns to see Justin leaning on the doorframe to the lounge. I've already taken off my coat, she thinks, if he asks. Why would he ask? She pats the nearest coat on the rack, one of Justin's.

This is my house, she thinks. My coat rack. I want this to be my coat rack.

'Fine. Good,' she says. 'Where are the girls going?'

'They're off out,' says Justin. 'To give us some time.'

'I don't know if I can talk right now.' That can't be fair, what to discuss living arrangements, custody? I'm delirious, with fatigue, with – coming down from a night of MDMA. And I can't tell him, if I tell him he'll get full custody. Any solicitor would say so. But he has a bag of grass? 'Where are the girls going?'

'I thought they could get some practice in navigating their environment,' says Justin. 'We did a practise run last night, I tracked them at a distance with binoculars. They were fine. Leave the two of us alone.'

'I know we need to talk – '

'Not now. I thought we could smoke this instead.' Justin pulls a huge joint from his pocket. 'Smoke this and go back to bed.' Justin wraps both arms around her.

'Oh. Okay, I – yes,' In absence of a proper response Luisa squeezes him tight. 'All right.'

'I thought you were keen,' says Justin.

'I am. Yes I am,' says Luisa, an unconvincing politician. So this is what, the last fuck? He's not sure how long until the next one and is happy to risk genital tearing? 'But what about?' She nods down below his waist.

'All tied up and ready to go.'

'But the girls, won't they be back soon?'

'They'll be a while.' Justin takes her hand and leads her up the stairs, each step slow, one at a time. 'They're off to that new gelato place they keep mentioning. I gave them enough money for two each.'

'Right. Good. Good plan.' Luisa stops on the stairs, causes Justin to release her hand. Why has she stopped? Sex is waiting upstairs. There is Justin – go to Justin. Should six-year-olds be buying ice cream on their own? Yes. She moves up a step.

'Are you okay?' Justin frowns down at her. 'You – '

'I'm good.' She stops and sits on a stair. 'But what – you don't want to talk? About us?'

'No,' says Justin.

'Are we – splitting up?'

Justin looks horrified. 'What? No. Is that what you want?'

'No,' she mumbles.

Justin sits on the stair above her.

Luisa looks at him, at his greying temples, the lone hairs growing at strange angles from his ears. When she was younger she used to look at middle-aged men and think, why would anyone love them, want to sleep with them? Now she knows.

'So we're – all okay?' she says.

'We are. Come on,' smiles Justin. He pulls her up another stair.

'Because I've been thinking, I had a lot of time thinking last night, it wasn't so busy, and I feel like, despite everything – '

Luisa stops on the stairs again, stretching their arms between them, and Justin comes back down a step. He nods, minutely but rapidly, and widens his eyes. Go on. Go on go on go on.

'I was thinking,' she goes on, 'last night, last evening, that – ' What was I thinking? It was real, it was true. But what was it?

She sits down again. 'When we in London, before the girls – there was a sense I was waiting for something. That we weren't really doing anything, anything good. Not for longer than one night, a weekend. I didn't want that to be my whole life.'

'I didn't want that to be my whole life, either,' says Justin.

Luisa nods, agreeing with herself rather than Justin. 'But now when I look at the girls, and I'm stressed and I feel like shouting, and I do shout, or I don't, but I think here's something I've done, something good. And you. You.'

She sees him watching her eyes. She cannot remember the last time he did that.

'I'm sorry,' she says. 'Was I saying something?'

'I like it,' says Justin. 'Say more.'

'I don't think I can,' she says.

'Shall we?' Justin holds out his hand.

*

'I really don't think we should carry on any longer,' says Luisa.

'I can do this.' Justin's voice is an octave higher than usual.

'I'm not actually – '

'Keep going. Slowly. And – try to avoid sitting as heavily as before.'

'I'm sorry.'

'And is it okay if you stop talking? I need to focus.'

'Justin, please. You don't have to. I think we should stop. I'm going to stop.'

Luisa eases herself off his penis, which Justin is careful to catch before it falls anywhere with any amount of force. She lays down beside him, puts an arm across his chest.

'I might have a bit of this.' Justin holds up the joint which they have forgotten to smoke. 'Ibuprofen's not really doing it for me at the moment.'

'Thanks for trying,' says Luisa, which is insufficient in the circumstances. She rolls over to her bedside table and takes a lighter from the drawer. No other man I've known would have risked their genitals for me in that way, she thinks. As she rolls back to hand the lighter to Justin, she risks another look downwards at his blackened testicles.

'My job,' she says. 'The hospital. I know it's often – not good. Completely shit, in fact.'

'Not always,' says Justin.

'But sometimes it is terrible. And exploitative. It's okay if you say you hate it. Sometimes. Sometimes I hate it.'

'I don't hate it now,' says Justin.

'Maybe if you could not hate it when I've had a great shift?'

'How would I know?' he says. 'You could text me.' Luisa starts at the sarcasm, until she realises he is not being sarcastic, in fact he is trying to help. Texting could work. They could make it part of their schedule.

'Because when it is great, I get off on it a little. The excitement,' says Luisa. 'The other night a woman almost bled to death and I sorted it out.' Is that bad – the thrill of a woman almost dying? Partially. Maybe less than fifty percent. 'And that's when I like the job, when it's rewarding. Midwifery. You get that, don't you? That's okay, isn't it?'

'To get off on women almost bleeding to death, I guess so,' he smiles. 'There's probably a whole female porn genre devoted to it.'

'Is there?'

'I don't think I'd know about it if there was.'

'Well, that's good.' Luisa wonders what it might be called.

'So last night was one of those nights?' says Justin.

Luisa stares at the ceiling. The room, the house, the road is entirely silent, the world waiting for her answer.

'Not last night,' she says. 'I wasn't at the hospital last night. I went – out.'

Justin takes two lungfuls of the joint, grins at her. 'Cool,' he says, and chokes on the smoke.

'You don't mind?'

'Out where?'

'Dancing. We went out dancing. I meant to go out with Tina and Boris but went on my own.'

'Who's Boris?' he says.

'But Tina and Boris turned out to be swingers, so I ran away. But I went dancing, because I took, well Tina and Boris made me take, no actually I wanted to, to take some MDMA. And I ended up in this club. It was so *good*, I've wanted to go dancing for ages. Dancing like we used to.'

She looks over at him. Justin leans his head on his hand to hear the story.

'And I wanted you to be there,' she continues, 'but you weren't and I met this lovely group of students, not students, but almost, they were lovely, so nice, all of them, the girls and the boys, and they seemed to – like me. Well enough to invite me back to their house. That's where I was. So I didn't go to work.'

'Back to mine's?' Justin grins.

'And I got – a bit stoned watching David Attenborough with this girl Sophie. I think Elsie will be like her. I hope Elsie is like her.'

'That sounds – lovely.'

'I'm really sorry. That I lied about it.' Luisa takes hold of his hand, holds it up to her chest.

'Do you think we can go out with them again?' says Justin.

'I didn't – I don't think so. I didn't get their numbers. I didn't know you'd want to.'

'Post-club getting stoned with a young woman called Sophie? I want to already.'

'Perhaps Sophie won't want to though.' says Luisa.

'I don't mean in a sleazy way.'

'I wasn't sleazy. But I could have been. Not sleazy. But one guy there – he did come on to me.' Not actually on to me, thank god.

'And?'

'And nothing.'

Justin pulls her into a hug. He is smiling, he is smiling and so Luisa is smiling. They are lying in bed, together, and she can say anything she feels like saying, there is no need to pass it by the censors beforehand.

Justin looks at the joint billowing out smoke. 'I can't smoke this,' he says. 'Let's have it later.' He stubs it in a mug on the bedside table, and after a considerable time it appears to have gone out.

'I think perhaps I went a bit crazy,' says Luisa. 'You said I was crazy.'

'I like you crazy,' says Justin. 'Going out crazy.'

'But at work. They made me co-ordinator. On Thursday.' She thinks about relating the rest of the events of the Thursday emergency, but they are less clear to her now. Less important, less part of this world right here, the world she lives in. 'I don't think I want to be co-ordinator again. Not really. Maybe I shouldn't be a midwife any more. How can we go dancing if I'm a midwife?'

'I don't want you to stop being a midwife.'

'I don't want to become Jenny,' says Luisa. 'Or Diane. But you don't have a job. How would we live?'

'I'm going to work freelance. And we'll live cheaper. There are other ways to be a midwife. Let's not get a new car. Let's keep the insurance money.'

'I got rid of the Peugeot. The evidence,' says Luisa. 'I left it in a ditch.'

'Nice,' says Justin. 'That'll really confuse the insurance people.'

Children's voices float up to their bedroom from the road outside. Luisa jumps out of bed. It is two other children with a bored-looking father, no one she recognises.

'The girls,' says Luisa. 'They'll be okay, won't they?'

'Of course. I gave them my phone in case.'

'Not only with ice cream. I mean in general.'

'They will,' says Justin. 'They're good, aren't they, the girls?'

'They are. They are.'

Everything they say feels sensibly, simply human: no more and no less than the same problems behind the eyes of each grey stranger on the street. She herself is a grey stranger to grey strangers. But not to Justin. She looks at him. Justin, Eleanor, Elsie. Those times when, on waking, the thoughts crowd in: I want this, I want that. I want to be a film director, I want to start a fruit tea company, I want to live in San Paolo. I don't want to want things any more. At least not if it means giving up this. Justin absorbs, obliterates those thoughts, through – through being there. The girls obliterate thoughts through – being demanding. Is that what it comes down to? This is better than being alone with my thoughts?

'I know something else that's rewarding,' says Justin as Luisa climbs back into bed. He threads his hand down below her stomach.

Luisa smiles, kisses him.

'Tell me something really wrong,' she says.

a request from the authors

Thank you for reading all the way to the end. If you enjoyed the book, it would be very helpful if you could leave a review for us. That's the way other people find out about books nowadays! We're particularly intrigued to discover if the story chimes with the experiences of other midwives . . .

If you're interested in the real-life stories that served as inspiration for the midwifery scenes in this book, see Talia's blog posts at The Secret Midwife:
www.thesecretmidwife.co.uk.

acknowledgements

Ethan & Talia: A huge thanks to Lucie, Juliette and Di as early readers of the book.

Ethan: the biggest acknowledgement I have to make is that despite the painful few years documented in this book, Talia is still the greatest person I could have spent my life with.

Talia: I would particularly like to thank all the amazing midwives with whom I've worked – although I do worry that all of us midwives are doomed to end up like Diane. And to all the lovely women I've looked after – you are nothing like the characters in our story. (Well only a tiny bit. You are in labour after all.)

I'd like to thank Ethan for turning his pain into something creative rather than leaving me . . . so far.

Also, for all midwives reading, please blame any errors in obstetric protocol on Ethan – this is a result of my losing the argument of medical accuracy versus storytelling.

Lastly – another thanks to Ethan for letting me take up all of the acknowledgements.

Printed in Great Britain
by Amazon

83297243R00190